MARCIA'S DEAD

A gripping psychological domestic suspense murder mystery set in a beach house in beautiful New Zealand

Tannis Laidlaw

Forth Estate Books

For permission requests, write to the author, addressed "Attention: Permissions Coordinator," at the email address below:

Forth Estate Books :
tannislaidlaw@gmail.com

Also by Tannis Laidlaw

The Madeleine Brooks Mystery series:
Book 1: Death at Cherry Tree Manor
Book 2: Death at Valley View Cottage
Book 3: Death in Lachmore Wood
Book 4: Death at the Olde Woodley Grange
*Prequel: Death in Cold Waters (*ebook and paperback*)*

Domestic suspense mysteries:
Bye Baby Bunting (ebook and paperback)
The Pumpkin Eater's Wife
Half Truths and Whole Lies
Thursday's Child

Non-fiction:
*Full Stop: Eat until you're full and stop gaining weight (*ebook and paperback*)*

Contents

Chapter One

HER HAIR FANS OUT in a hazy cloud which undulates in concert with the kelp below. Her arms hang gracefully in the salty sea, floating loose, curved as if ready to embrace a lover; her bare feet point down, her sandals lost hours before. Her eyes, open, disturbingly flat, conceal secrets as effectively as they had when alive.

She drifts just under the surface in an uneasy balance between sinking and floating, her body suspended by a cord wrapped tightly around her neck and attached to a lifejacket. Its upper surface, tomato red against the blue of the sea, sends a mute signal to the empty sky.

The tide has turned and now, in slow motion, she is coming home.

Chapter Two

"WHAT?" TED GRIPPED THE telephone tighter. "Marcia's dead? How?"

"An accident. Drowned. This afternoon." Jonathan's voice seemed to be coming from a long way away. "I'm sorry, Ted. But I can't get hold of Holly. I have to... she's got to be..."

"That's terrible. I'm sorry too. Very sorry. Don't worry. I'll call Holly. That's fine. Better to hear from her father, anyway." Ted swallowed. "Drowned? Where are you? Up at the bay?"

"Yes, yes, of course." Jonathan's voice was tremulous. "Sorry, Ted. I'm not functioning too well. Maybe you could ask Holly...? Maybe she'll want to come up."

"Leave it to me. I'll be in touch."

Ted put the phone down and held his head in his hands. Marcia, dead? Vibrant if impossible Marcia? Hard to believe. He picked up the phone again and speed-dialled Holly's Dunedin landline. Voice-mail. He left a message to call him at home. He rang her mobile and left the same message, glancing at the time on the edge of the computer screen. Late. For him maybe, but not for students like Holly. Probably out with some boyfriend or other. He turned off the desk lamp. It was dark outside and still; a typical Auckland late summer's evening. A waft of Queen of the Night drifted in the open window. He closed his laptop then sat a moment, eyes unfocused.

Dead.

Marcia.

He shook his head as if so doing would clear the thought. Not that he hadn't wanted her out of his life many a time, both before and after she had left him and married Jonathan. But dead? No. He had just wanted the impossible: for Marcia to change.

The phone. He fumbled for it, squinting at the display. Holly.

"Am I too late?" she asked. "You did say to ring and it didn't matter when."

"No, no, it's fine." Ted sat up in bed and fumbled for the light. Damn, he should have practiced what to say to her. "Holly, darling, I've some bad news. About your mother."

"Mum?" Her voice was sharp.

"She's had an accident." He took a deep breath. "Up north. Jonathan rang. She died, Holly darling. Your mother has died."

There was emptiness at the other end of the line matching the blackness of the night. Ted wanted to be doing anything other than telling his daughter her mother had died. Anything. Finally, some breathing noises.

"Holly?" His voice was strangled.

"Yes, Dad. I heard you," Holly said, her voice so soft he struggled to hear. "I just... it's unbelievable. You're sure? You talked to Jonathan?"

"He's pretty cut up. Wants to know if you'd be willing to go up to the bay."

"Of course!' Her voice caught. "Accident? What do you mean? In the car?"

"Drowned. I've no other details. What flight?"

Holly gulped audibly, fighting for control. "First plane up to Auckland in the morning?"

"I'll book online and text you the details. I'll meet you at the airport, of course." He searched for something appropriate to say. "I'm so sorry, Holly. It's dreadful. Unexpected. Shocking." This was fresh territory for Ted and he struggled. "But that's a lovely thing for you to do, going to Jonathan. He sounds frantic." Ted paused. "You don't have to, you know, and if you have second thoughts...."

"No. I'm okay. I want to go."

"You can borrow the car, if you want."

"I can't think. Yes. That would be good. I'll need wheels to get up there, won't I. Oh, Dad, this can't be true!' Her voice ended in a wail.

"I feel the same way. Impossible to take in." Crying in the dark, both of them. "I'm so sorry, so very, very sorry."

"Drowned. So unlikely. Mum."

"You'll set your alarm?" He wanted her back in focus.

"Yes," she managed to say through her distress. "See you in the morning."

"You can drop me off at home on the way up north. You'll be there by lunchtime, probably. Should I tell Jonathan, or do you want to?"

"I'll ring him." Her voice had quietened. In command of herself again.

As soon as he'd booked her ticket, Ted burrowed back under the covers and turned out the light. The nights were slightly cooler than they'd been but, for comfort, he still needed to stretch his feet out from under the summer-weight duvet. His mind flipped back to Marcia. Their last lunch? Only a fortnight or so back. Up to her old tricks: flirtatious, dressed to kill, always wanting something. He couldn't remember what it was that time. A printer problem? He'd downloaded another driver for her—no, that had been the time before. This had been something to do with photograph management; again something trivial. He envied men who could make a clean break from their ex-wives. Marcia had not allowed that to happen, and what Marcia wanted, Marcia got.

His last thought before falling asleep was that he would no longer have to deal with her: no more demands on him; no longer would he feel obliged. Relief briefly flooded his being until he refocused on Marcia, the person. Her death was untimely. Poor woman; part of him had always felt sorry for her. She was forever after something and, in spite of potential in spades, never quite achieving it.

Chapter Three

TED TOOK ONE LOOK at his daughter's face as she came into the arrivals section of the domestic terminal and knew he couldn't lend her his car. He hugged her, and she kept her arm tightly around his waist as they made their way out of the building. "I'm taking you up north. You're in no fit state to drive."

Holly got into the passenger seat. "Sorry. Couldn't sleep. Then got all tearful just before getting on the plane. Cried from Dunedin all the way here. I'm a mess."

"Holly, darling, it's natural. Don't worry about it. But I'm still not lending you this car. I'll grab some things from home and we'll go together."

Holly just nodded.

He believed, and she had always accepted, that one of his duties as a father was to take burdens off her shoulders. "Did you eat breakfast?"

"No. Couldn't."

"We'll stop in Wellsford for a bite." He could see Holly's eyes at half-mast and figured she'd nod off as soon as the car started moving, just like she did when a little girl on this same trip north.

True to his prediction, by the time they arrived at his home, Holly was asleep. Ted left her undisturbed, made himself an instant coffee in a travelling mug, grabbed a few clothes, his computer and a car rug to put over his sleeping daughter and set off north. Another three hours and they would get to the bay. He could probably overnight with the neighbour—he and Duncan went way back—and head home the next day. Although he had known Marcia's husband Jonathan since they had worked together years before, they were hardly friends. He yawned, still jet-lagged from his last overseas trip.

Travelling up the familiar route was enjoyable, he had to admit, bringing back past pleasures of holidaying at the bay. Thoughts of Marcia intruded, as could be expected, but nothing could ruin the delight of making the familiar trip north once more. Wellsford came and went, but Holly was sleeping so soundly Ted was loath to waken her. He'd just go hungry.

He reached for his big mug of coffee. Cool now, but drinkable and the caffeine was welcome. He looked over at his daughter. Dark hair with waves, so like Marcia's, a shiny curtain partially covering her face as she slept. She looked younger than her 22 years, curled in the passenger seat, her jeans-covered legs pulled up as if she was still a child.

Holly woke when they started on the journey from the main road out to the coast north of Whangarei on an old coach road, the first land route up to the Bay of Islands in the nineteenth century and, with all its twists and turns, felt like it. Vast valleys fell away from the road and vast tracts of dark New Zealand native bush spread towards glimpses of the sea. The road would swoop down briefly to a valley dotted with cattle or forests of *pinus radiata* before climbing into the hills once more. Tiny Maori settlements appeared out of nowhere; in this part of the country, children still rode horses to visit friends; everyone waved as you passed on the road, and growing marijuana was accepted as an ordinary occupation.

"They've done some major repairs on the hill since we used to come up regularly," Ted commented when he realized Holly was awake and looking out of the window. The hill, a pass over a prominent ridge, crested and sent them down towards the sea again.

Holly stretched her arms above her head and yawned. "Big slips since." Slips. Somehow calling a landslide a 'slip' made it sound innocuous. "Mum and Jonathan had to use the Opua ferry route for ages one winter."

Ted knew that added more than half an hour to the journey. He grunted.

"Mum hated it. I think that was when she started becoming disenchanted with weekending at the Bay House."

Ted glanced at her, his forehead creased. "Disenchanted? I thought she loved it." Marcia had insisted she keep the place when they separated. He'd tried to talk her into taking the Auckland house, money, anything else. It affronted him she wanted the Bay House. Devastated. Gutted. Used every power of persuasion he had. Until the divorce, he had no idea she loved it with such a passion.

"I was always a little suspicious about that," Holly muttered.

"What do you mean?"

"Oh, nothing. Mum just being Mum." At that, her eyes filled. "Doesn't help though."

Ted reached over and placed his hand on her forearm. "She was a complex character." Holly just shook her head.

Finally, some good views over the Pacific Ocean to the horizon that signaled they were only minutes away from their destination. Ted slowed as they reached the gate which opened onto a long drive leading through a green tunnel through the bush up to the house. As always, Holly jumped out, swung the gate open and waved Ted on so she could walk up the winding lane at her own pace. He'd made the same walk many a time; the anticipation of stepping out of the shady woods into sunlight and far horizons was irresistible. The terra cotta house nestled into the hillside, providing foreground against the intense blue of a sea that stretched forever.

Ted parked under the carport roof that spanned the gap between the garage and the house proper and he was too preoccupied to pay attention to the beauty. He jerked back to the reality of the situation when he spotted Jonathan hovering, waiting.

"Ted! Thank you for coming." Jonathan extended his hand as soon as Ted got out of the car. "And our little girl? Holly walking up the drive?"

"Gramps!' Holly cried as soon as she saw her stepfather. She flew into his arms. "Oh, Gramps. I can't believe it. Are you okay?" Ted felt again that twinge of relief that Holly had never called her step-father 'Dad'. 'Gramps' was more appropriate, given that Holly was the age of Jonathan's grandchildren.

"I'm so pleased you've come, my dear. Just your being here ... and you too, Ted. Come on in."

Jonathan set a load of make-your-own sandwich makings in the middle of the table. Typical Bay House lunch. Ted felt a surge of nostalgia.

"Eat first, then I'll tell you what I know. Come on, dig in," Jonathan commanded with something of his former authority.

"Have you eaten?" Ted said as he put the lid on his sandwich, glancing at his host. Today Jonathan looked every day of his 74 years and then some. It could be the cancer he'd been fighting for the past year or so, or it could be losing his beloved wife – most likely a combination. He was a caricature of his former self.

"Not hungry."

"Hey, not fair," Ted said. "You're making us eat and I agreed to that because we need to keep up our strength. But the same applies to you."

Jonathan looked startled, then nodded. "Okay, but really, I won't be able to eat much. My stomach feels...."

"Tuna with mayo. You love tuna. Here, have mine. I'll make another." Holly deftly substituted her plate with the sandwich she'd just completed for his empty one. "Dad's right. We need to keep our collective strengths up. You especially."

Jonathan dutifully took a bite, chewed and swallowed. "Sorry, Holly. It tastes like sawdust."

"Don't care. Just eat it." She busied herself with making a second sandwich.

"We came up the night before last," Jonathan said. "I'd had my check-up at the clinic in the morning. Marcia was a little quiet, but nothing out of the ordinary." He paused as he took a gulp of hot tea. They were sitting in the atrium with the summer blinds pulled down over the glass ceiling. Doors were open at each end and a breeze ruffled the sparse hairs on the top of his head. "In the morning, she told me she'd forgotten to get my prescription filled. That meant a trip to Russell. She seemed out of sorts, headachy, didn't feel like going; went for a walk instead. But I needed the damn pills. Waited for her, but she didn't come back, so I drove into Russell myself." His voice became quiet.

Holly shook her head. "You shouldn't have been driving."

"No, no. It was fine. I wouldn't want to drive the long trip up here, but errands are fine." He was over-hearty. Holly just shook her head. The chemist was over half an hour away, hardly just an errand.

"Anyway, where was I? Oh, yes. Going into town. No problems. Prescription filled right away, then home again. Oh, and I bought a few groceries. Then home." He paused. "And no Marcia." His eyes filled.

Holly moved over so she could hold his wrinkled hand. "Were you worried? I mean, she's always going off to sketch, or calling on Duncan or something."

"No, not at first. Not until time for drinks. Still no Marcia. I looked for her. Went to Duncan's place, but it's his Whangarei afternoon. Looked in her studio, in all her favourite haunts, went down onto the beach. Didn't notice the boat wasn't there."

"Well, you wouldn't. Not relevant. She hated that thing," Ted said. He had been married far longer to Marcia than Jonathan had, and he knew more than he was given credit for.

Jonathan nodded. "Duncan arrived back and thought he saw a life jacket floating out in the bay."

"So he went out to check it out?" Ted knew sharp-eyed Duncan would have been scavenging. He picked up lots of flotsam from passing yachts.

"But when he got his dinghy out, he noticed ours heading for the rocks so hightailed it out there. A bit of a southerly had come up. How he managed to grab the line, I don't know, but then he could turn his attention to the life jacket. Gave himself a fright when he saw a body suspended underneath." His voice cracked. "Sorry. It was ... Marcia. She was drifting. Below the surface. Entangled in the straps of the life-jacket. Hadn't done it up properly, I guess."

"I'm surprised she was even wearing one," Ted murmured, remembering her antipathy at any restraints, whatever they were.

Jonathan shrugged. "Duncan figured she must have come from the beach beyond the rocks. The pebble one." Jonathan took a long, juddering breath, wiping his eyes with his handkerchief. "I owe Duncan. He tried resuscitation, but it was too late. Far too late. She was long gone."

Holly ignored the tears streaming down her face. "Where is she? I want to see her."

"Tomorrow, my dear. The police took her. We can see her tomorrow."

Ted felt his own throat constrict. Marcia, dead. It didn't seem possible. She had been a feature in his life since he was twenty-eight years old.

They sat, the three of them, in that airy atrium with its view of the vast Pacific Ocean, the slow sound of surf pulsating the quiet, each enveloped in their own memories.

"Tomorrow," Ted said, dreading it.

Chapter Four

JONATHAN INSISTED TED STAY overnight. “You can bunk in the studio,” he offered.

Ted nodded, pleased. It was a space fashioned from converted loft space over the garage, made light and bright with skylights and windows facing east and west. Marcia’s space.

After lunch, Jonathan nodded off in his chair and Holly went into her own room to lie down, catching up on needed sleep. Ted collected his bag and climbed up the hill to Marcia’s studio. He found the door unlocked. Inside, he noticed that someone, perhaps Marcia herself, had left open the French windows that led onto the little ‘sniffing’ deck. He dropped his case and stepped outside, leaning on the balcony railing. The house spread below him, its terra-cotta coloured adobe walls blending into the land just as he had envisioned when he first thought of this design: thick walls, solid, built to last three hundred years. He lifted his eyes to the westerly horizon above the ‘moor’, a hillside that contained the last remaining field of grass in the bay. Slowly but inexorably over the dozen years of Ted’s tenure here, he had noticed the grassland decreasing. The bush was reclaiming its own.

He took a deep breath. Tea tree and a hint of iodine from the seashore. Breathing the city out of his lungs. Above the rhythm of the surf on the beach came the distinctive call of a tui. Melody mixed with raucous squawks. Like Marcia. His smile was sad.

Marcia had furnished her studio with a futon couch that transformed into a bed; duvets and pillows were hidden in the eaves space behind and it took Ted only a few minutes to make up the bed. A normal sort of thing to do, somehow, in a matrix of disorientation.

Marcia, dead.

The world had shifted on its axis.

Marcia had set up the studio to suit herself and, as a result, it was a practical room. A kitchenette was fitted in the other eaves space, one large sink for her painting and another small one for tea making. The sloping ceiling and walls were a stark white, but the furniture screamed Marcia's personality: reds and yellows and oranges. The duvet cover picked up the theme. Trust Marcia to have everything coordinated.

Ted put the jug on. Something to do. He needed time to absorb the fact that Marcia really was gone.

Most of the studio was given over to artwork. General painting clutter covered the worktable in contrast to the neatness of the kitchenette and the little sitting area. He could detect a faint smell of acrylic paint, slight in comparison to the stink of the oils she originally used.

He idly flicked through a large batch of paintings in a stack leaning against the wall. Oh, dear. She had not improved. Marcia was no artist. Persistent and enthusiastic, but strictly amateur. She had tried again and again to capture the landscape around the bay.

He got up and paced, shifting a large easel near her worktable to give himself room. The last painting, the one on the easel, was different. A portrait. He hauled it out into better light and caught his breath. Why did she want to paint a portrait of that bastard? Not the greatest likeness, but he had no doubt who it was. She had captured those winged eyebrows right. He roughly put it back on the easel, turning it the wrong way so it was face in and he didn't have to look at it.

The jug clicked off, and he helped himself to a peppermint tea bag. No choice. Typical Marcia—how she loved peppermint. Once upon a time, she demanded he set aside part of his gardens to grow the pesky stuff both at home when in the city and at the Bay for her summer supply.

At least with peppermint, he didn't need milk. While the tea cooled, he took his laptop out of its case. He carefully unplugged Marcia's computer and eased it into the drawer of the desk before putting his on the top surface. At one time she was going to write a novel, but somehow she'd never got beyond the first chapter. Ted suspected she was too impatient. She wanted to tell her stories, but she had to see her audience and feel their reactions.

He pulled out some papers he needed to review for work. Doing so might clear his head. Besides, he might as well earn his living until someone needed him. One good thing about working with software. He might have to travel to see his clients periodically—like the recent week he'd spent in London—but he could work anywhere. Occasionally he set up his traveling office when in hotels in exotic locations like Tokyo, KL, Sydney or wherever, but the majority of the time he worked from the spare bedroom, now office, at home in Auckland. Anywhere meant, of course, he could also work in a location like this with views to die for. He winced at the term but working here had been his dream – to live up in this little slice of paradise and work when he felt like it, at other times swim in the bay or tramp the hills or fish. Instead, all his dreams had shattered with his divorce and it left him with a cramped suburban house for both work and living accommodation.

Now that Holly was finishing her university studies, he promised himself he would do something about his living and working environment. He and Marcia had sold their home to build the Bay House, plus they'd had enough to buy a small Auckland house as a future rental to help fund their dream lifestyle. But New Zealand divorce law divided everything neatly. Somehow he ended up with the little house on the North Shore of Auckland and his business, while Marcia got the Bay House and, of course, custody of their daughter.

Holly interrupted him several hours later.

"I'm so glad you're here, Dad."

"Couldn't let you drive in the state you were in."

"That too, but glad you're back from London. When did you arrive?" She flopped onto one chair and curled her legs up under her.

"On Saturday. I'm still a little whacked from the jet-lag." He reached over and switched the jug back on. "Cuppa?"

"Thanks."

"Only peppermint."

"Fine with me." She watched him find the tea bag. "You should have woken me. I would have driven. Part of the way, at least."

"I was fine. Am fine. How's Jonathan?"

"He's sleeping. I bet he hardly slept last night. Like me." She yawned. "Sorry. Tired still." She stared at the back of the painting on the easel. "What's that one?"

Wordlessly, Ted turned it face out.

"It's not too bad, is it, Dad? Better than most of hers."

"If you like that sort of thing." He passed her the mug of tea and took a swallow of his own and made a face. Too cold. He poured in some freshly boiled water.

"You don't have to like the subject to realize it's one of her better ones. You're just jealous she never painted you."

"She did paint me, don't you remember? It was so awful, no one recognized who it was even when I dressed identically and stood right beside it. One day it was on the wall, the next it was gone. Forever." He grinned. "Thank heavens."

"I wonder why she painted him?"

"She probably did it back then." He picked it up. "No, I'm wrong. Not then. Recently. Look." He held up one finger, now a bright blue. He turned the canvas over. "See? There's a thick bit here that's still wet." He wiped the worst off on the back side of the canvas and easily cleaned up his finger with soap at the sink. Holly's was a good question. Why was Marcia painting him now? It didn't make sense.

Holly stared at the painting. "She must have been touching it up yesterday...." Holly squeezed shut her eyes. "Bloody hell."

"You're allowed. You're her daughter. Cry as much as you like, young lady." A wave of despair washed over him. So difficult knowing what to say, to do. He moved behind her chair and lightly massaged her neck and shoulders. "I've read that crying straight away makes for an easier transition. Much better than bottling it up."

She wiped her eyes. "I've never been much of a bottler."

Ted took the painting off the easel and replaced it with a study of blue-sea-and-sandy-beach from the pile of completed canvases. "Let's find out if Jonathan is still asleep. If he is, I think we should wake him up. He'll be stiff sleeping in that chair."

Holly put her mug into the sink. "You're right. Besides, too much sleep now and he'll have another dreadful night." She linked her arm with her father's and it was Ted who was comforted.

The studio path formed a tunnel through oleanders, their flowers glowing pink in the afternoon summer sunshine. Ted congratulated himself on the recycled brick paving he'd put down years before. Warm and inviting and looking a hundred years old or more. The path gave onto the main track that descended through the terraces—his vegetable plot terraces. Ted had taken on the role of gardener in their marriage, not Marcia. But no vegetables grew now. Jonathan had allowed the area to revert to grass. The place was now all easy-care. No gardener had been living here since Ted had given it over by court order.

Ted and Holly were emerging out of the oleanders when they heard a sports car's low grumble coming through the bush.

"Oscar," Holly breathed when it stopped beside Ted's four wheel drive. "How funny, just after seeing his portrait."

"Who's that with him?" The other figure was bent down, still inside the car.

Holly shrugged. "Maybe his sister? I've heard she's here from England. Or a new girlfriend? He's split with his wife."

Ted glanced at Holly. Oscar had married not long after his father had married Marcia. What did women see in the man?

"He's one of nature's specimens, isn't he," Holly sighed as they watched him grab out bags from the boot, his fair hair gleaming in the sunlight.

"Physically, I suppose."

Holly grinned at him. "You're still jealous. Come on, Dad, it was a fling, nothing more. Get over it. How many years has it been?"

Chapter Five

OSCAR TURNED HIS FACE to Holly still above him on the path. "Look who's here. Hello, little one," he called up, a grin lighting up his face. "I'd hoped you'd come."

"Oscar!' Holly rushed down to her step-brother with open arms. He glanced up at Ted over her shoulder and nodded. "Ted."

A tall and graceful woman was extricating herself from the low-slung sports car. She glanced first at Oscar and Holly, then at Ted. "I'm Vivien, Jonathan's daughter. And you're Ted." Her voice was low-pitched, easy on the ear.

Ted descended down to the drive and held out his hand with a smile. "So you *are* real, Vivien. I've heard lots about you over the years." Her hand was cool in his.

She smiled up at him. "Including why I'm here in EnZed?"

Ted nodded. "Marriage troubles, your father was saying over lunch. I'm sorry to hear it. Jonathan seems to think you might stay?"

"I'm here at the moment, although how long I can stay is in the hands of the gods."

"Oh? Which gods?"

"Those that decide whether I can be gainfully employed or not. I've applied for a work permit, but I haven't heard yet."

"But I understood you were born here."

"No. We immigrated here when I was three. Then Mother and Father separated and he married again. I shuttled back and forth across the world spending more time with Father in New Zealand than Mother in England. But I've never had permanent residency here."

Ted remembered the story. The poor little rich girl having a paid companion when she crossed the world from one parent to the other. He had heard of her when he was not much more than a child himself. That would put her closer to his own than her brother's age.

"Nice to meet you at last," he said. "And I do hope you get the work permit."

"I'm sorry to hear about Marcia. Thank you for being here to support Father. And Holly, of course."

Holly joined them. "Hi Vivien. Long time no see."

The older woman kissed Holly on both cheeks. "Your mother, Holly," she said. "I'm so sorry."

Holly just nodded and looked at her feet. Ted was acutely aware, yet again, how vulnerable his daughter must feel losing her mother so suddenly.

The four made their way inside. Jonathan shook hands with his son and gave his daughter a long hug. Oscar put his arms around both. A pretty picture of a grieving family.

Ted turned away. "Time for drinks, Jonathan?" he asked.

"Not yet, old man," said Oscar. "I want to get settled into the studio. Vivien is taking one of the old caravans. She offered because of my asthma."

"No, Oscar, I've put Ted in the studio," Jonathan said.

"I don't mind," Ted quickly interjected. "I'll have the other caravan. I have very fond memories of those caravans." Jonathan didn't need these shenanigans at this time.

Oscar said, "Thanks, old man. I really can't take the mustiness."

"Musty? Since when?" Ted asked. He knew Duncan religiously changed all bedding even when it was unnecessary. And aired everything a couple of times a week. He took his caretaking duties seriously.

"They're not musty," Jonathan said.

"We should check them out," Ted said to Vivien. "You'd better come with me. Where's your bag and I'll take it up." He couldn't wait to get away from Oscar's smarmy face. Besides, he felt superfluous now that Jonathan's own family was in residence. He would leave in the morning as soon as he could.

Ted grabbed Vivien's suitcase and collected his own bag from the studio along with his computer. He got perverse pleasure that he'd taken Oscar's portrait down from the easel.

The two caravans were perched at the edge of the woods at the top of the hill above the beach house. He arrived at the little porch that connected them and turned to watch Vivien picking her way up the brick path in her high heeled sandals. He waited for her to choose where she wanted to camp.

"Hardly the Ritz," she commented as she looked around. "Is there any other guest accommodation besides where my dear brother is staying?"

"If you want, we can see if our neighbour Duncan will put you up. These caravans are not new, that's for sure," he said, aware of his defensiveness. "We bought them second-hand about ten years before we finished building. We lived here while we built the house. The bigger one for us, the little one for Holly."

"You were married to Marcia a long time."

"Long enough." Suddenly he didn't want to talk to this elegant woman. Memories from happier times crowded out the here and now. He flashed onto a younger Marcia getting splattered with mud as she slammed the wet mixture into adobe formers. Marcia was dead, he told himself yet again. But, in this place, his history with her was alive.

"Amazing."

Ted came back to the conversation with a thud. He'd caught something in her tone. Amazing he'd stayed married to Marcia for a good length of time? Enough. Time to change the subject. He turned towards the larger of the two caravans and tossed his bag inside. "This one is older. You can see if you can tolerate the newer one. Holly's." He picked up her bag and gestured for her to enter the smaller caravan. He knew he was being brusque. "A bit younger even if it's a bit smaller, as you can see but Duncan's place is always there if you don't like it." Without further ceremony, he went into his caravan, his mouth set.

He put Vivien out of mind and became super-efficient, making up the bed as he had in the studio. He opened his case then decided not to unpack anything other than what was necessary. He wouldn't be staying long enough.

He changed into shorts and sandals and headed downhill to the beach. Sunlight filtered through the massive Pohutakawa canopy dappling the wooden boardwalk in a mixture of light and shade. Hardly the path he had built. His had been rustic in the extreme, dependent upon roots to define steps and carpeted in leaves but, he had to admit, only suitable for the young or fit. This new set of ramps and stairs complete with handrail was better for people of Jonathan's age, probably better for all. It was solidly done, in keeping with the Bay House.

Wooden ramps had once been on his 'to-do' list and probably Marcia had badgered Jonathan to complete it once Ted was out of the picture but it slightly rankled. Somehow he always saw the Bay House being kept for Holly and her future family. Pristine as he had built it and any necessary changes would be done by him in the style he'd always envisioned. The walkway connected seamlessly to the older boardwalk he had constructed high above the road. It brought the walker down to a safe place to cross over the road to the wide path down onto the beach. So far, he approved of almost everything Jonathan had done. Maybe not the grassing over of his veggie plots.

The beach was deserted, as it often was late in the afternoon. He kicked off his sandals to better feel the sand and headed to the waterline. He found himself doing what had once been his routine when first arriving back at the bay: a brisk walk to one end of the beach where black volcanic rocks stretched out to sea. He'd always touch the rocks then turn and power walk the 300 metres to the other end of the beach and touch those rocks, too.

Today, the bay was almost calm, typical for March. The small excuse for surf periodically curled up to his feet and away again, as he paced the gentle curve to the southern set of volcanic intrusions. The exercise cleared his head and soothed his restlessness.

Marcia. Dead. Still very hard to believe.

It wasn't that he was in love with her. Probably, to be honest, he hadn't been in love with her for some years before they'd separated. So why did he react to Oscar so badly? He kicked the surf and white foam skittered across the wet sand. Because Oscar was the means. Simple. Just a male thing of being bested.

And Oscar was a good looking bastard. God's gift. And years younger than he was. Years younger than Marcia as well.

Odd though: he'd often wondered why Marcia had thrown over the good-looking son to marry the rather frail looking father with nothing much to recommend him except wealth. Could money have become so important to her? She liked it, for sure – who didn't? – but she liked lots of things that had nothing to do with money. She'd been a bright spark, both in personality and intelligence and she certainly had a business-like mind. Ted figured with that mix of devil-may-care attitude and the craftiness she had possessed, she could have made pots of money herself if she had put her mind to it.

He spotted the dinghy pulled high above the tideline and roped to the Pohutakawa tree roots as always. He glanced up to Duncan's front garden where they always hid the oars. Hidden from nobody but strangers, of course. He ran his hand along the gunwale. Still in good nick. He knew that Jonathan used to take the dinghy out regularly for his early morning fishing expeditions, coming back if he hadn't had a strike in an hour or so. He knew where to fish, though. His Maori friend Cushla had pointed out the best spots. What had always amazed Ted was that none of the younger Maori fellows ever intruded, as if they acknowledged the right of the elderly to the best and easiest fishing spots. That main one certainly was a goodie.

Ted wondered what Cushla was doing these days. She was a wise old kuia. Not that she ever had much time for Marcia.

He grabbed his sandals and put them on while leaning against the back of the little boat. He took a deep and cleansing breath. This bay was his idea of perfection. The rocks protected the bay from high seas and gave the beach a pleasing symmetry while providing food and shelter for fish. It was as if he'd had the property on loan for more than a dozen years and for that he was grateful. Not that he didn't resent Marcia taking it. He did. Deeply.

Time to move on, especially now. He turned and slowly climbed back up the hill.

Vivien opened her case in the little caravan. Once she saw the place didn't smell and appeared to have the requisite creature comforts even though all walls and ceiling of the little caravan was painted pink, her irritation vanished. She realized having an external source for her anger had helped. She collapsed onto the bed by her case, her head in her hands. Bloody Gerald. The bugger. She never used 'bugger' out loud. But inside her head, 'Gerald' and 'bugger' were intrinsically linked.

Everything she did was filtered through Gerald's expectations. Everything. She glanced at the neat pile of t-shirts in the bag. She angrily shoved it into an untidy heap.

Yes, that felt better.

She stood and looked into the little mirror on the wardrobe door. She pushed her hands through the tidy cap of hair and messed it.

Yes!

She pulled off the grey suit and flung it into the corner.

Double yes!

She scrabbled though the mess in the suitcase to pick out a t-shirt. White and ironed of course, but that was okay. She took a deep and shuddering breath and pulled on the t-shirt and stepped into her khaki shorts. She folded her other clothes none too carefully onto a shelf in the closet.

Holly, not much younger than her daughter Steph, had been a teenager hiding under a fringe of hair that covered her eyes when Vivien first met her but she had no trouble picturing her as a little girl up here in her own private pink world.

She missed Stephanie and Liam. Her daughter, an organized personality, called weekly; Liam whenever he felt like it. The downside of the move to New Zealand would mean giving up seeing them except periodically. What were they doing right this minute? She glanced at her watch. Half way around the world – at that moment they were asleep in their own beds. Presumably. Vivien smiled wryly. Stephanie had a new young man.

Not hearing from Gerald was another thing completely, the silent treatment yet again. Fine. Just fine. She'd survived this type of behaviour before. No way would she heal the breech this time, crawling for forgiveness about nothing. As far as she was concerned, the silent treatment could go on indefinitely.

She reached into the corner where she'd tossed her grey suit, shook it out and hung it in the miniscule closet. Suitable to wear for the job interview she'd had earlier in Auckland but totally out of place here at the bay.

Now what? She had a choice of places to read, either the bed, at the miniscule table or in the covered porch that joined the two caravans.

Vivien collected her book and descended the two steps into the porch with its see-through roof.

Cool. Lovely.

The caravan site overlooked a sunlit scene. She could see over the adobe house and through wide-spaced pohutakawa trees to a cerulean sea. No wonder Marcia had wanted to keep this place. What it must have cost Ted to give it up, though, especially when he was the injured party.

A low table was placed between two old rattan chairs. She sat, pulling her feet up onto the cushion and opened her book. Time to get her head in a suitable place so she could cope with the intensity of her father's grief once more.

Not long afterwards, she caught sight of Ted slowly making his way up through the terraces towards their caravan eyrie. He was a tall man with a craggy face, his movements lithe. Not that she was looking. She'd sworn off men. Gerald in particular, of course, but all men shared similar characteristics and once bitten .... except they could be useful. Occasionally.

"Hi, Ted. Can I ask you a question?" she asked sweetly when he was close enough. "Do you know where the bedding is?"

He came up the steps onto the front deck and entered the porch. "In the cupboard at the left of the bed. Lift the top and you'll find duvets and pillows. Look, I'll show you." He crossed the floor of the little porch and climbed into the smaller caravan.

"Do you find it musty?" he asked while disentangling the duvets. He pulled them out with such force, Vivien was almost sent flying. She quelled a fresh dose of irritation. This was not a caravan for more than one person.

"Not in the least. Funny that." She took a long sniff, her nose buried in the bedding. "Fresh as."

"Your father pays good money to our neighbour in the green cottage. Duncan airs everything every week, besides keeping the grass down and seeing that nothing is amiss."

"The one who could have put me up?"

Ted just nodded and changed the subject. "Yikes, ages ago I suggested drinks, and instead I've been off exploring the beach. Should we go down?"

"Fine with me. I've a few questions to ask my little brother. Asthma? Since when?"

Chapter Six

Vivien and Holly disappeared into the kitchen, and Ted set the table. Oscar and his father were in the office and once or twice Ted could hear raised voices. They had been at loggerheads forever, both before Jonathan had taken Oscar into the business and after. Ted remembered wondering aloud to Marcia about why, when they obviously didn't get along, Jonathan wanted his son in the business. She said it was natural. Blood is thicker, etc.

Once Oscar seated himself at the dining room table, Vivien finally had a chance to speak to him. "What is all this nonsense about you having asthma?"

"Oops. Caught." He smiled, glancing at Ted across the table. "Sorry, old man. I hate those caravans and you put them there; kept them there—you must positively adore them. Couldn't bear to be in one, so made it all up." Oscar had a charming smile, which only irritated Ted further.

Ted shook his head. "Doesn't matter to me, 'old man', but it doesn't do to lie to one's sister."

Oscar laughed and put his arm around Vivien. "She practically brought me up. I can do no wrong, can I, Sis?"

"I love you dearly, brother dear, but I have trouble catching you doing anything right. So mind your manners."

Oscar lifted an eyebrow to Ted as if to say, "See?"

The viewing of Marcia's body was to take place in the morning. Holly's eyes filled when Jonathan brought up the subject after breakfast.

"I really don't know….'

"Do you want me to be with you, darling girl?" Ted asked, giving up his idea of leaving for Auckland early.

"Oh, yes, please," she said, touching his hand.

"I'll stay. For as long as I can be of use. Plenty of time to drive down to Auckland whenever."

Oscar offered to take Holly in his racy car to Kerikeri; Ted drove the others in his four-wheel drive. The little sports car roared ahead and Ted sedately followed, with Jonathan in the seat beside him and Vivien in the back. Jonathan was ashen and visibly trembling. Vivien sat quietly, occasionally leaning forward and placing her hand on her father's shoulder.

"What's the itinerary?" she asked when they neared the town.

Jonathan cleared his throat. "First to the funeral home. Then to the police station. You can all have a cup of coffee till I'm finished with them."

"If that suits you, Jonathan." Ted gave him an encouraging smile. This was terribly difficult for someone in his mid-seventies and Ted felt for him.

The house that had been turned into funeral rooms was almost as old as a house gets in New Zealand: well over a hundred years, made of kauri, with a large shady veranda across the front. The little group mingled there while Jonathan had his private time with Marcia. When he came out, red-eyed and swaying on his feet, he collapsed onto a well-worn settee placed conveniently close to the door. He looked over at Holly and Ted and nodded.

Ted put his arm around his daughter, and they walked into the hush of the old building. Someone ushered them into the room where the casket held pride of place; soft lighting, softer music coming from somewhere, temple-like. Holly took a deep, shuddering breath and stepped forward, almost dragging her father. Ted couldn't look for a moment, but Holly was handling it and so could he. He allowed his eyes to focus. Marcia almost looked like Marcia. Makeup perfect, not a hair out of place and dressed in a lacy summer dress he had not seen before. He felt only sadness at a life cut short.

"Goodbye, Flower," Ted murmured, the old pet name uttered without thought or intent.

Holly became still, and her arm around Ted's waist dropped. She stood, tears pouring down her face, unmoving, just looking. "See ya, Mum," Holly whispered. It was how they had always parted.

When they re-joined the others on the veranda, Oscar said, "Me. Now me. God, if I can get through it." He walked into the house. Ted was thrown for a moment. He noticed that Jonathan had gone still. Vivien was sitting with him on the settee, holding one hand, the other on his shoulder. She whispered something, and Jonathan nodded.

Ted looked down to see how Holly was coping. Her eyes had followed Oscar into the shadowy corridor. She looked up at Ted and said, "I need the sun." She moved down the wooden steps into the sunshine, rubbing her bare arms as if chilled.

Ted moved over to Jonathan. "Just tell me when I should take you to the police station." He looked at Vivien as he said it.

"Now." Jonathan heaved himself to his feet. "Better to get it over and done with than worry about it."

"I'm going with him," Vivien said softly to Ted. "I don't need to see poor Marcia. I'm here for him." Ted nodded. He had expected as much.

At that moment, Oscar reappeared. "So young!' he said to all. "It's just not fair. She had so much living to do." Ted froze. There was nothing wrong with the words, but.... He moved to his four-wheel drive and opened the door for Jonathan.

"Hey, where are you going?" Oscar called out.

"We're off to the police," Vivien said as she clambered into the back. "You take Holly for coffee, please." Her voice was firm. Ted suppressed a smile. He started the engine and moved away quickly.

Ted and Vivien helped Jonathan into the police station. His trembling hands betrayed his frailty. The desk sergeant invited them into a room where they awaited the inspector. Ted settled Jonathan into a chair at the table with Vivien beside him, then moved to the door.

"Stay, please, Ted. I want your strength," Jonathan said. Ted hesitated, looking at the corridor beyond, part of him wanting to get away, but Jonathan's neediness prevailed. He sat down on a chair in the corner.

The place was unnaturally quiet, an institutional room, but hardly the concrete box of television police procedurals: sunlight streamed through a top window, the walls a soft green. He had half expected to see an unshaded bulb dangling from the ceiling and a concrete floor. Instead, sand coloured tiles covered the floor and he could see recessed lights in the ceiling. He slouched, then straightened before slouching again, trying to fit his lanky frame onto the folding metal chair made for a midget. Of course, he wouldn't be sitting there long; when the inspector arrived, he fully expected to be chucked out.

"Thank you for coming in," a dapper man said from the doorway. "Saves me an hour going out to your place." He extended his hand to Jonathan. "Inspector Grant, Mr Fleet. And this is..." He looked at Vivien.

"My daughter, Vivien. And my... er, my..."

Ted rushed in. "I'm Ted Frazer, Marcia Fleet's ex-husband and Jonathan's friend."

The inspector stared at him. "Ted Frazer? I know the name and I recognize you. Where do I know you from, Mr Frazer?"

"Perhaps you did the IT training last year?"

"Yes, I did." The inspector smiled and pointed his finger at Ted; smiled. "You lectured to us; that's how I know you."

Ted nodded. "Good for you. Yes, I consult with headquarters in Auckland. You attended 'Hackers and Hackers', I believe."

"Yes, sir," the inspector said. "One of the more interesting parts of that course." Ted had a fleeting idea that the inspector was about to rub his hands together. Instead, he sat down opposite Jonathan and asked about the day Marcia died. Slowly and with painstaking detail, Jonathan went through the same story he had told the family.

"What was Mrs Fleet's state of mind that day?"

"She said that she was a bit headachy. That's why she didn't go into town for my meds. Normally, we're together all the time up here. Or, if I'm not well, she does those sorts of chores. Did. She was good that way. That day was the first time I'd driven into town in months." His eyes filled and his voice cracked. Vivien put her arm on the back of his chair and leaned toward him.

"State of mind, other than headachy?" the inspector prompted.

"Do you mean was she depressed? No, not at all. A little jumpy maybe. Yes, a little agitated. She hasn't wanted to come up north so much lately. But she suggested it this time. Oh, I don't know. Not depressed anyway." He dropped his head into his hands. "She just probably didn't fancy doing all the driving. I used to do it when I was well."

"Well? You're not well?" asked the inspector. Jonathan gave him a detailed history of his cancer. The inspector nodded and took a few notes. "Has she ever been suicidal?" he asked.

"Marcia? Heavens no. Not the type." Jonathan's voice was stronger. "Not the day she died, not ever."

"Did she drink?"

Jonathan sat straighter in his chair. "Normal, I suppose. A glass of wine with dinner. Often a sherry or a gin before. Why?"

"Her blood alcohol was reasonably high," the inspector said.

There was a dead silence. "Alcohol?" Jonathan said weakly. "Not Marcia. Not before the sun was over...' His voice cracked.

"Yes, well, the lab reports are clear. She had a blood alcohol level that was measurable." The inspector's voice was solid, brooking no argument.

"You must be mistaken. Not in the middle of the day. Or, only on special occasions. Like a fancy luncheon. Not at the bay, Marcia wouldn't, would never...."

"I'm told to ask you about Sangria or Pimms or something where fruit is added to an alcoholic drink." The inspector looked up from his papers. "Mr Fleet?"

"Loved them. Summer drink. We often had Sangria at Pierre's. You know, in Parnell. Never made it here. Only when we went...." His voice ended in a choke.

Vivien half stood. "Inspector. Please. My father has just come from the funeral director's. He's just seen his wife's body. Can you not postpone this until he's more composed?"

"Of course." The inspector gave a momentary smile. "Could you please take your father out to the car? I would like a quick word with Mr Frazer."

Ted helped Jonathan to his feet and Vivien nodded, indicating she was all right to take over. Ted sat down in the chair Jonathan had left. It was fractionally more comfortable than the folding chair in the corner.

"Now Mr Frazer, forgive me, but we have to get down to the business at hand. Where were you between ten and two on Tuesday?" His voice was flat and Ted felt the room cool.

"I was in Auckland. At my home office. I was working on my current project. Software project, nothing to do with the police. And before you ask, no one lives with me and no one came to the house during that time." He was acutely aware of the change in atmosphere and realized the inspector's kindliness to Jonathan was in respect for the widower's fragile state of mind. Never mind Ted's position with the police in Auckland. Here he was involved, however peripherally, with a death.

"No need to get defensive, Mr Frazer. These are routine questions."

"Not routine for an accident, Inspector Grant. Routine if you have a question mark about how she died. Are you suggesting suicide or...?"

"Not suggesting, Mr Frazer. Merely keeping an open mind." He shuffled some papers. "You must have known Marcia Fleet well, being her ex-husband. Do you think she was capable of suicide?"

Ted took his time. "I would agree with Jonathan and say 'no'. She wasn't a depressive type. Temper? Yes. Not depression. I last saw her two weeks ago, and she seemed her normal self."

"The blood alcohol?"

"Strange. Marcia wasn't a drinker. I can honestly say I've never seen her drunk. She didn't like losing control, even by drinking a bit too much." Ted stopped talking. The inspector let the silence drag. "Another extraordinary thing," Ted said, musing. "She hated that dinghy. Never went in it if she could help it." Belatedly, he realized who he was talking to. Not the time or place to be casually open. He resolved to stay focused.

"Tell me about the dinghy."

They had bought it ten years before. He kept to himself that Holly loved it, anchoring it in the bay so she could use it as a swimming platform, collecting mussels from the far rocks and taking it up or down the coast on still days. For years, it was more Holly's boat than anyone else's. He gathered that lately it had been more Jonathan's. He sat in silence, apparently lost in thought, but inwardly berating himself for opening up the subject.

"Mr Frazer?"

"Sorry, just lost in memories."

"You're perhaps affected by your ex-wife's demise as well?"

"You can't dismiss fifteen years of marriage with the papers of the divorce court."

"No." Grant straightened the already tidy papers again. "I may want to talk to you once more, Mr Frazer. You're staying with the Fleets?"

"Yes. With Jonathan and my daughter. And his two adult children, of course."

"Please stay in the district. Perhaps tomorrow I'll come out your way." He stood up.

"I thought I would travel home to Auckland today," Ted said.

"Put it off, please. We should talk again."

Ted got up. What had he got himself into?

Chapter Seven

On the trip back, Vivien didn't feel like talking and Ted remained silent. She was vaguely aware of the glimpses of secluded bays and islands and distant shores, but the enormity of what was happening had come home to her. This was so far from her usual life in London that she couldn't imagine trying to tell her friends—or even her children—and do justice to the confused mêlée of emotions within herself.

Once back at the Bay House, she and Ted headed up the brick path to change.

"I should fill you in," Ted said, "on what happened at the police station after you and Jonathan left."

"I'll just get out of this gear," Vivien said, flicking her skirt dismissively. "Can you make us a cup of tea in that caravan kitchen of yours, then tell me all?"

"Coming up," Ted said.

They sat on the old rattan chairs overlooking the view of rooftop, trees and a sparkling sea. Sunlight flicked the tops of waves and the crash of the surf on the beach provided a varying background roar. Vivien had tucked herself into the right-hand chair as before. She filled her lungs. Fresh air scented with tea-tree. New Zealand as she remembered it and as it should be.

"Next stop, Chile," Ted said, waving his mug at the horizon.

Vivien closed her book. Obviously, there would be no reading. "I can't imagine a more perfect spot," she said, and meant it. "Father waxed on about it when he first married Marcia and I knew it would be something out of the ordinary. It's not just the site, but the house looks like it grew out of the earth. You've achieved that permanent look. Probably because you built with mud."

"That's what I was trying to achieve, and I used mud from the section. I'm a frustrated architect. Of course, Marcia was a frustrated artist."

"I remember she painted." Painted? Daubed, more like.

"Not very well. What she could realize with her hands could never quite match the visions in her head."

"You didn't have that problem," Vivien said, looking down at the massive walls of the house. "You achieved what you set out to achieve."

"Then lost it in the divorce settlement. I should have built a boring little box, and I'd have it today. This house was too damn desirable."

Vivien heard the bitterness in his voice. She nodded and took a long sip of her tea. She knew Marcia, and she knew he was right. "Drink up, Ted. We need it right now."

"Divorce is much like dying for those going through it," he said. He put his mug down a trifle harder than necessary.

"Unnecessarily cruel." Gerald came to mind along with a brief surge of anger.

"And you? Are you having to give up something so vital that it's like a limb being amputated?"

Her mind flicked past Gerald to Liam and Stephanie, the house in London, her life there. "I'm willing to give up many things. Things that are not important in the long run. But—and this is a big 'but'—I'm having a big problem with my grandchildren, technically my step-grandchildren. That's very hard." It surprised her she was talking to him about it.

"Will time fix that?" Ted asked.

"I've almost lost hope. So it probably doesn't matter whether I stay in the UK or move down here." She took a deep breath. "I practically brought up the two of them. Their mother, my husband's daughter, was—how to put this delicately — somewhat unreliable due to certain substances she liked to put into her body. She couldn't look after the girls and the choice was, either they stayed with us or they were sent to a boarding school. Not much of a decision. No way was I having those two little girls in a boarding school at that age."

"And now the mother has cut off access?" Ted asked.

"Primarily because my dear ex-husband supported her in this. His wonderful daughter, now she's been through rehab, can do no wrong. And second, it turns out she didn't like all sorts of things I did with the girls. Discipline, for instance. The junk food I wouldn't let the children have, as another example. She was always grateful that I took the kids when she was incapable, but now it seems I've ruined them." Vivien's eyes blurred. She reached for a tissue.

"How old are they?"

"Ten and twelve. I got a ring from Annabelle a week or so after I arrived here on my English cell phone, but she had her own phone confiscated because of it. Annabelle is the older one; Juniper the younger."

"Juniper?"

Vivien laughed easily. "I've always imagined my step-daughter was going through a gin phase at the time." She put her mug on the table and tucked her feet under her. "Sorry, we got diverted. You've something to tell me."

Ted repeated the conversation he had at the police station.

"They're questioning how Marcia died?" Vivien realized the implications. "Oh no, poor Father. Ruling out an accident."

"It's not as strong as that. It's just that there are unknowns that raise questions. The blood alcohol, for instance. And her dislike of small boats."

"I hadn't heard that."

"Hated them. Hardly ever went out in that dinghy. I can't imagine why she would have used it that day."

"You told the police that?"

"Stupidly. The inspector glommed right onto it. Then he started on about my whereabouts when Marcia died. He's coming out tomorrow, and he wants me to stay around for more questioning then."

Vivien stared. "You're a suspect?"

"I have qualifications. As does your father. Presumably they start with family, partners, people with connections."

"I wonder if Oscar and I are to stay here too? He wants to go back to Auckland; there's his part of the business to run."

"It surprised me Oscar came here in the first place. It's not that he's close to your father."

Vivien glanced at him sharply. "Yes. Surprised me, in a way, too, but I was grateful for the ride up."

Holly appeared on the path. Vivien waved and Ted walked to the edge of the deck.

"Family conference before dinner. As soon as you can?" Holly called up to them.

Ted yelled back, "Just the family? Not me?"

"You and me, too. Gramps said." She skipped down the steps again into the atrium.

He turned back to Vivien. "Ready?"

She nodded. Into it again. This little aerie was a haven of sorts. She gathered up the two mugs and took them into the larger caravan where the kitchen was still usable. She rinsed them out and left them on the side. The bed was tidy with a pair of shoes tucked underneath; a neat man. Another neat man. She joined Ted, and they set off down the hill.

"Look," Holly said when they entered the glazed atrium that joined the two wings of the house. Everything was open to catch the late afternoon sea breezes. Holly was standing on the deck to the seaward side of the atrium and pointing downward. A large navy-blue van with an oversized trailer attached was in the parking area above the beach. Several men were heaving the dinghy, now totally enclosed in some sort of plastic wrap, onto the trailer. Vivien could see Oscar down there, his arms making staccato jabs into the air. They could hear nothing over the sounds of the crashing surf.

"Your dad was just telling me that the police are not satisfied Marcia's death was an accident," Vivien said to Holly, keeping her voice down. "And this looks like confirming it."

"Gramps knows that. He's had a phone call about tomorrow's visit. But they said nothing about the dinghy." Holly's voice was husky. They stared at the scene below them.

Vivien reached over and put her arm around the younger woman. "We'll get it sorted, Holly. Just take it one day at a time. We're here for you." They watched the van manoeuvre its way back onto the road. "Do you know where Father is right now?"

"In the snug. Nursing a whisky."

"I'll go to him," Vivien said as they watched the van slowly move off and Oscar turn to climb back up to their castle-on-the-hill.

Jonathan had called the 'family meeting' to tell everyone that the police wanted no one to leave so they could be available for police interviews in the morning. Ted looked around the dinner table afterwards. Jonathan was clearly exhausted and hardly ate; Vivien was fussing over him; Oscar was using his fork as a shovel, and Holly kept glancing at his scowling face. Ted couldn't get out of there fast enough.

He headed for the beach. Not the first time he had avoided conflict and a heavy atmosphere by walking on the beach. The evening sun lit up the rocks offshore, leaving the shoreline in shadow. He kicked off his sandals as usual to feel the sand on his bare feet. Warm and dry, soft and primeval. He walked closer to the sea, stepping onto the packed damp sand left behind by the retreating tide. His pace slowed, and he drank in the sea, the air, the horizon.

Something caught his eye coming and going at the edge of the water. Closer, he saw it was a fish, a John Dory, dead of course, flat on its side, already nibbled by other creatures of the sea. He quickly averted his eyes and swallowed hard. He walked back to the dry sand above.

Ted headed for the north-western side of the beach so he could climb the small cliff to a natural bench halfway up the rock. It was still warm from being in the sun all day, and he stretched out his legs in front of him. The horizon was a sharp line where the dark blue sea met the washed out blue of the sky. He noticed the breeze had dropped, and the sea had calmed. The waves against the sand were now whispering rather than crashing. He watched pied shags circling high above the opposite cliff before settling on a large and very dead pohutukawa tree on the other side of the bay. Did they pick the tree because it was dead, or did their guano kill it? Someone in Wikipedia would know.

Slowly, the tension ebbed from his body as the rocks out in the bay became more and more golden. Evening: Ted had always found it the most peaceful part of the day. First the near rocks, then the ones further out, lost the sun till only the end of the peninsula to the north captured its dying rays. Ted sighed. He knew he was conflicted about Marcia, had never really got away from her in spite of their divorce some years in the past. Not that he felt anything positive about her. Maybe not for years before the divorce. But somehow, one way or another, she had continued to mess with his brain. Up to and including the present moment.

Something made him look back at the beach, filling in the curve from one rocky outpost to the other. Holly was running along the shoreline, waving. She would have known where to find him. If he had to be interrupted, she was the only person in the world who had the right.

"I knew you'd be here," she gasped as she plunked herself down beside him. "And I wanted a word without the others."

"No rush, Holly," he said. "Catch your breath. See the shags?" They were silhouetted against the sky, which was now a medley of pinks and purples.

She nodded and took a deep breath. "Yeah. Too much happening and no time to observe nature." The colours deepened and Ted could feel his daughter relaxing.

"Now," he said. "You wanted a word."

"Oscar," she said. "Can I please ask you to cool it?"

Oscar? Why would she want to spoil a perfect moment by mentioning him? Ted turned so he could see her face in the gathering gloom. "Cool it? I thought I was behaving impeccably."

"Oh, Dad, of course you are. Outwardly. It's just that somehow you do things that make it so obvious you can't abide him—obvious to me, anyway. Like tonight. You just got up and left the dinner table when he was in the middle of a story."

"Was he? Did I?"

"You don't even remember, do you? He's of so little consequence, you didn't notice you were being rude."

Ted shook his head. "Sorry. I'll be better, I promise. It's just I can't understand why he's hanging around. He has no right to be here because of Marcia. And I doubt he's here for Jonathan."

"I guess he thought Vivien would be a help and brought her up. She hasn't got a car yet." Her voice petered out. "Maybe."

Ted thought it was a weak excuse. He couldn't imagine Oscar doing anything that didn't suit himself. "We'd better get back." He heaved himself to his feet and offered his hand to Holly. "I'll be more aware. Promise. I'll be leaving after the police have come tomorrow, anyway. What about you?"

"Depends on when Gramps has arranged the funeral. I can go down to Auckland with him. He'll want a driver." They clambered off the rock and walked in companionable silence over the sand towards the path.

"Do you think it wasn't an accident?" she asked him.

"I just can't imagine it being suicide," he said gently, knowing that was at the top of her mind. "If it's not an accident and we can rule out suicide... the alternative is impossible. Who would want her dead? That's crazy. It has to have been an accident."

Holly nodded. "It's just that I keep having these thoughts about when you two split up. She had this aura about her. Sort of suppressed excitement – not as blatant as that, but sort of... I don't know... she was kind of cagey with it. And I noticed something like that the last time I saw her."

"Like she had a secret? That sort of cagey?"

"It's hard to describe. Cagey's as good a description as any, I suppose. She was just different. A bit silly." She grinned up at him. "Sillier than usual, anyway."

Ted thought back to when he and Marcia broke up. Yes, she'd been noticeably over-excited then, something he'd only acknowledged in retrospect. Everyone seemed surprised when she moved out, including him. Which begged the question about how well did Marcia and Jonathan get along? Could anyone outside of a marriage really know?

Chapter Eight

OSCAR ACCOMPANIED TED AND Vivien up the moonlit path and Oscar called out a cheery "Good night" when he split off to the studio. Ted lifted his hand in a perfunctory wave thinking Holly would approve.

"How did Marcia and Jonathan get along? Do you know?" he asked Vivien as they entered their common porch.

Vivien turned on the lights briefly then off again letting the light spilling from the little caravan serve for their conversation. The sky was still light and the sea a silvery blue. She slumped into one of the rattan chairs. "Well enough, I think. Father has a terrible history, but you know that. The longest lasting wife was my mother and that was only nine years. Oscar's mother died, of course, when he was only two. Several girlfriends lasted a few months. There was a two-year marriage – can't remember her name, never met her. And it's been six years with Marcia, hasn't it?"

"Seven. At least since they got together. Five married."

"That means it's still early days for my father. But surely he's getting a bit long in the tooth to be switching to another woman. To say nothing about his cancer."

Ted grabbed two small glasses and waved them in the air. "Scotch? I have some Glendronach."

Vivien nodded. "Glendronach? Lovely. With just a splash of water, please." She frowned. "Why do you ask?"

"Something Holly said. That Marcia was in a silly phase just lately."

"Oh. Marcia. Not my father. That would make more sense. I always found it slightly embarrassing having a step-mother younger than me. But I'm one to talk. I married an older man too, but he's not old enough to be my father."

"I'm sure Marcia's motivations weren't simple. In all the years I've known her, they never were." He handed her the little glass, one of a pair he had found in a second-hand shop in Henley-on-Thames more than ten years ago. One hundred year old Edwardian whisky glasses and he was vaguely annoyed to find they'd been relegated to the caravans. "Did you get along with Marcia?"

"So so," she said waggling her hand. "We had little in common except an interest in art. I think she was a difficult person to get to know. I always thought she had an agenda."

Ted guffawed. "Spot on, Vivien. But it took about five years of marriage for me to work that one out."

Vivien looked at him over her whisky. "But you married her, stayed by her until that unfortunate episode with my brother."

"That's a new way of putting it – an 'unfortunate episode'." Ted finished his whisky with a gulp. He hadn't meant to get into a dissection of his marriage. "I was counting the months until Holly would be off to university."

"Snap."

Ted looked at her sharply. "You?"

She nodded. "I said to myself I'd stay with Gerald until Liam left home." They quietly conversed, exchanging family histories, tales about children and now being alone. When Ted was readying himself for bed in his caravan, he realized he felt comfortable with Vivien. Comfortable. A word he rarely used.

The police arrived just after the breakfast dishes had been cleared away. Everyone gathered in the atrium. Inspector Grant positioned himself with his back to the view. Ted could barely make out his face against the glare of sea and sky. His own would be open to the policeman.

"Mr Fleet." The inspector nodded at Jonathan. "Mr Frazer and Mrs McAvoy." He turned to the others. "You're Mrs Fleet's daughter, Holly?" She nodded. "And you, sir?"

"Oscar Fleet, Jonathan's son." Oscar got out of his chair and extended his hand. The inspector shook it and waited for him to resume his seat. Ted gritted his teeth.

"Thank you, everyone, for being here. I'm afraid there appears to be more to Mrs Fleet's death than was first apparent. There's no question that she was found in the sea and sea water had filled her lungs. It appears she died by drowning but circumstances around her death are still unclear. As I've told several of you, Mrs Fleet had some alcohol in her blood and, according to Mr Fleet, erm, senior, it was early in the day for her to be drinking. We now know she had taken other substances as well and we will be questioning you all about these other aspects of Mrs Fleet's lifestyle today." He shifted his feet to move out of the direct sunlight allowing Ted to see the expressions on his face a bit better. "I've just asked Mr Fleet and would like to ask the rest of you to allow my team access to the household this morning. You're free to be in this room, the kitchen and dining room and the toilet of course, but I would like you all to stay away from the bedrooms, the caravans, the study and the studio. If you want to walk down to the beach, please let me know when you're leaving and when you arrive back. I'll be in the lounge, the room you call the snug. I'll be asking each of you in there for a private conversation. I would prefer that you didn't discuss anything of relevance amongst yourselves until later. Any questions?"

"I was planning on leaving today," Oscar said with a smile. "I've a business to run. I can't be away much longer."

"We can discuss it when we meet, Mr Fleet." He looked down at his clipboard. "Holly Frazer. Would you please come this way?" He gestured to the entrance to the living area of the house and they all watched the little procession of the inspector, Holly and the sergeant make their way across the dining room and into the snug where the door was shut.

"Maybe we need a lawyer," Oscar said. Ted vaguely remembered that Oscar had studied law in university. He now ran the transport section of his father's business.

"Don't be ridiculous," Jonathan said. "Marcia didn't commit suicide and no one could possibly have wanted to murder her. So it's an accident, as we always thought." He looked grimly at his son. "Don't make a drama out of it, please."

"I'm not making a drama out of it." Oscar's voice rose. "Stop criticizing everything I say, Father." He got up and left the atrium. Silence prevailed after the interchange and Ted, for one, was loath to break it. He stood up and went out onto the terrace. The day had clouded over and waves were breaking in successive surges over the far rocks. He could see whitecaps standing out against the dark grey sea. The hills were protecting them from a south-westerly blow. Vivien joined him.

"It's beautiful even in bad weather," she said. "Are we in for a storm?"

"Not a nor-easter anyway. They sock in for three days at a time. This is probably just a front. A day of clouds, then a few showers and it'll be fine again."

"The weather makes an interesting metaphor," she said as she turned away. Before Ted could think that one through, Oscar came in noisily.

"Bloody cops won't let me get my things," he said as he flopped onto the wicker couch. "Just wanted a book to read, fergawdsake." Nobody answered him.

Ted's turn came after Holly's. The inspector started with the same questions as the day before and Ted told the same tale. He had been working alone. He had only come up north because Holly needed him to drive. Yes, he had known Jonathan for decades because he had his first important contract with Jonathan's firm years ago. No, he hadn't introduced Marcia to Jonathan; Oscar had done that. No, he never found out how Marcia met Oscar and no, he had never been curious. Yes, it had broken up their marriage. Yes, he had been surprised when Marcia had married Jonathan not Oscar. No, it didn't affect his relations with Jonathan; acquaintances of long standing only, never close friends. Yes, he continued to see his ex-wife periodically. Yes, they got along fine. Substances? No. Never in all their marriage. No, not even those that are prescribed.

"Thank you, Mr Frazer. We'll need fingerprints from everyone, so please call into the station before you return to Auckland." He got up to indicate the interview was finished. Ted nodded and left, with the inspector close on his heels.

Next, the inspector called for Vivien. Ted gave her an encouraging smile as she passed him. He walked out onto the terrace to take the long way around the house up to the caravans. He thought he'd ask if he could rescue his computer and do some work. He might as well do something useful as sit twiddling his thumbs. A bored looking young policeman said he could work in the porch if he wanted. He wanted. He was sufficiently self-aware that work was his time-honoured way of avoiding having to deal with unpleasantness.

The police didn't release control over the sleeping areas until late. Ted realized it would have to be another night staying over if he didn't want to drive in the dark. He would do the fingerprinting in the morning and leave immediately afterwards.

Dinner that night was a desultory affair. Vivien spoke of the funeral arrangements she and Holly had spent the afternoon finalizing. Marcia was being taken down to Auckland by the funeral director from Kerikeri. The ceremony would be held at the Purewa Cemetery chapel in Auckland on the following Monday. Jonathan pushed the food around his plate and Oscar shovelled great mouthfuls down without contributing to the conversation. Ted wanted the meal over as soon as possible.

Oscar turned to Holly. "Did I ever tell you the one about when the Jew and the Moslem met St Peter?" Holly shook her head, all ears. Ted inwardly groaned. From planning a funeral to jokes about St Peter. Ted had had enough. He gathered the dirty plates and took them to the kitchen, followed by Vivien. They completed the task of loading the dishwasher and tidying up in silence, the only voices those of Oscar and Holly still sitting at the table over the coffees Vivien had made them.

"I'm going up to the caravans again," Ted said. "I've a good book waiting for me."

"I'll check on Father then join you. A quiet read before an early night is what I want too."

Ted made his way slowly up the hill. By then the stars were out in full glory, the Milky Way a broad arch of glowing light stretching from one hillside to the other. He could make out Orion's belt and the Southern Cross, and figured out which bright orb was Jupiter. He had intended buying a decent-sized telescope some day. The city sky was a pale imitation.

Ted had put in roll-down insect screens when he had built the caravans' porch so people staying up there could enjoy the night air without moths and mosquitoes. Experiencing his design again was proving to be a distinct pleasure. Seven years. It had been a long time.

Vivien closed her book and yawned. "I'm off to bed. See you in the morning."

Ted looked up from his book to see her climb the two steps into the little caravan. She had good legs, he found himself noticing. Slim and muscular. Slightly big hips, but she carried it off with her height. An attractive woman. He realized he didn't want their association to end when they went back to Auckland. He had enjoyed her company and she had all the feminine attributes to boot.

He mentally shook his head. She was not quite out of a marriage and a long-standing one at that – not enough time yet. In fact, way too little time. Ted well knew the dangers. It had taken several years before the numbness following his failed marriage had dissipated enough to allow him to feel anything but lust. He had been no monk, but he looked back at that time with faint distaste. Then Linda had come along and all his barriers had melted. She had been just out of a divorce herself, and too late, he realized he was her 'transition man' validating her self-esteem and returning her to her rightful place as a fully functional human again. No, he wouldn't make any move towards Vivien in the short term. If she were still around in a year or so, he might look her up.

The second procession into Kerikeri took place the next day. They would all return to Auckland from there. Oscar drove Vivien and disappeared with a roar; Holly followed, sedately driving Jonathan in his car and Ted brought up the rear. They met up at the police station. Oscar had finished his fingerprinting and Vivien was waiting on the step for the others. She touched Ted's arm.

"Any chance I could come back with you? I'm going to be moving into Father's house but I need to get my gear from where I've been staying first. Would that be an imposition?"

Ted was slightly surprised but agreed immediately. With Holly driving Jonathan, he far preferred to have a companion for the trip than not. When all the fingerprinting had been completed, Vivien told Oscar she was transferring to Ted's vehicle.

"Now that's a first, sister dear." Oscar's mouth laughed. "No female of my acquaintance has ever refused a chance to be in this little beauty." He patted the bonnet of his red Ferrari.

"You drive like a maniac, brother dear. And you never listen to me when I say I'm uncomfortable. You go on ahead. You'll get there ages before us and you'll enjoy your ride much more without me whimpering in the seat beside you."

Ted glanced at Holly. He knew there'd have been no contest if she were in Vivien's shoes.

Chapter Nine

"HOLLY IS A LOVELY young woman," Vivien said as they made their way onto the highway. "The funny thing is, I didn't even know that Marcia had a daughter until Holly was into university."

"Jonathan didn't tell you?"

"Nope. And I know why."

Ted glanced at Vivien. Her mouth was set. "Go on."

"You really want to know? This is ancient history."

Ted nodded. "And we have three hours to explore it, that is, if you want."

"Definitely not. But I'll give a potted version, if you're interested." She stretched her arms in front of her. "Not the best time of my life, I can tell you. I was almost ten when my parents divorced and mother took me back to the UK. I adored my father. Still do, obviously." She smiled. "They put me into an English boarding school and I cried so much the school got concerned. So they decided I could transfer schools back to Auckland but spend every holiday in England with Mother. But having a ten-year-old under foot didn't suit Father either. By that time, he had started a new relationship, which changed things. He changed my status at the school; I was now to be a weekly boarder at a school in Auckland. Silly really, the school was within walking distance of home." Vivien had spoken in a monotone throughout. Ted was aware that this was the bare-bones version.

"You didn't blame your father? I'd have thought you'd have pointed the finger at him. Most kids would have."

"But, you see, he was all I had left. Mother had made it clear I was a nuisance and now father had other things on his mind. I couldn't admit that both were wanting. I should have felt rejected by both, but I decided it was all Mother's fault. And Father and I had a good time on the weekends. That compensated a lot."

Ted knew the story well. The poor little rich girl. His parents had thrown it at him whenever he was arguing with them. Just appreciate you have both parents and a stable home. That sort of thing.

"You must have hated boarding school. Understandable. Marcia put Holly into a boarding school when our marriage broke up. Dear Marcia wouldn't hear of her living with me. That's where your mother at least did you a favour. I would have had Holly like a shot: I worked from home; I could be there for her after school; I wanted her."

Vivien shook her head. "Marcia's decision ... probably to be in control. She didn't want you to have her and I guess she must have wanted her for herself, but at a distance. She and Father did a lot of travelling those first few years of their marriage."

"I remember." And he did. He used that time to take Holly for weekends and holidays whenever Marcia allowed it. Never out of the country, though. Holly didn't own a passport; her name was on her mother's, as had been what happened at one time. "Marcia and Jonathan had a grand time those years. Still, I've always wondered why she married him, with him so much older."

"Money." Vivien said it flatly. "My father is rolling in it."

"I suppose it must be a factor, but I never knew Marcia to be overly concerned about money."

She looked over at him. "Sorry. I'm dragging up all sorts with this conversation."

"No problem, Vivien. I'm not emotional about any of this. I really have thought long and hard about why she picked Jonathan. Obviously, he's a nice guy, but there are plenty of nice guys, rich ones too, and I can't say she ever reacted to them. No, I think it's more basic than that." He sighed. "He was more interesting than me, plain and simple. I'm a quiet bloke, a dull nerd, really. And Jonathan loved partying, excitement and doing interesting things. Travelling the world on cruise ships. Going to Sydney for the opera. Me? I like gardening, having good conversations with friends, the occasional movie and my beloved beach house. No comparison." He couldn't help a little bitterness creeping into his voice.

"I would never describe you as dull," Vivien said. "Most people our age would identify with your choices." Her voice was kind and Ted felt embarrassed. What else could she say?

"We did have one exciting period of our lives," he said as he accelerated up the passing lane beyond a fully laden logging truck. "I used to work for a large multi-national and got transferred to London. We were young and not long married. Marcia found a flat for us in the city and we were out almost every night. Plays, shows, openings, art galleries, museum exhibitions, you name it. People everywhere, so much to do. She revelled in the life but I grew to hate it. Just part of our mismatch." He glanced at his speedometer and slowed a little, remembering Vivien's comments about Oscar's driving. "When she got pregnant with Holly, I used that as an excuse to get us back to Auckland. We bought a house in suburban Pakuranga and put up the picket fence. I settled into a life of interesting work, attractive and lively wife and beautiful daughter at home in a new house with a large garden. My life was complete. A fool's paradise, as it turned out."

"Much the same with me, I guess. I married Gerald for security and got it. What I didn't reckon on was that I would eventually struggle against the constraints of being married to a dominating man. He made all the decisions and he could never tolerate my having opinions different from his. I'm sure that was a factor in choosing a much younger wife. Compliance."

"What was the final straw?"

Vivien laughed. "The last argument we had, if that's what you mean, was over what I was wearing to his office Christmas party. He wanted me in something conservative, and I had just bought a trendy red top with sequins and glitter and a low décolletage. Perfect with my black silk scarf. Worn with my skinny, floor-length black skirt with a slit up to my knees. He told me to change; I refused; he stomped out and went to the party without me. I went onto the internet and bought a ticket to New Zealand."

"And here you are."

"It was almost that simple. I first thought I would give him a scare. Come visit Father and Marcia and various friends for a couple of weeks, then go home. But Gerald played the heavy—from the moment I told him I was off to New Zealand until the taxi came to take me to Heathrow five weeks later. But I'd had a revelation. This was just a microcosm of the entire marriage. So I told him I would decide when I was coming back, IF I was coming back, but not to hold his breath. I said this on the doorstep and he just slammed the door after me."

"Unfinished business."

"Yes, I suppose so." She frowned. "You know, with all that's happening with Marcia's death, I haven't let myself think it through. Of course, for me, bopping back and forth between New Zealand and England was just part of my growing up. No big deal. Something like heading up to Yorkshire or down to Cornwall." She gnawed at one fingernail. "I haven't heard a word from him. Nor have I even thought about contacting him. We haven't communicated for years and years. I don't miss him and I don't care if he's shacked up with his secretary or the cute young waitress at his lunchtime café."

Ted stole a look. She was staring out the side window but he doubted she was taking in the scenery. "Are you going to do something about it?"

Vivien nodded. "I must."

"And?"

"Tell him I'm not coming back except to make the necessary arrangements. Then I'll have to let him cool off before actually going back to do so."

"Frightened of him?"

"Not physically, if that's what you mean. But he shares a characteristic with Father, always wants—maybe needs—to get his own way. He'll be angry. Very angry."

They rode in silence for a while, travelling through a steeply sided valley replete with umbrella-like Ponga tree ferns reminiscent of a Dr Seuss illustration. Except for the road winding along the bottom with its trucks and cars travelling at insane speeds, there was a primeval feel about this part of the country.

"You were saying about Holly?" Ted queried.

"Oh, just that Father knew I wouldn't have approved of Marcia shoving her into boarding school right after the divorce. But Holly seems to have survived fine. That says she must have got along well with her mother in spite of it."

"There were troubled waters for the first few years. She called Jonathan 'Gramps' and it was not a compliment, at least at first. But good old Jonathan just chuckled. He said to me once that he certainly didn't want to be a father to another child, but becoming a grandfather suited him just fine. And their relationship improved steadily. You've seen how they enjoy each other now."

Another silence. Vivien broke it. "I lied to you when you asked me how I got along with Marcia."

"Oh?"

"Couldn't stand her. Sorry. She brought out all the stupid stuff in Father that I had hoped he had got over long since. And she despised me. It was mutual."

"I don't think I've ever heard her talk about you other than saying you all met up whenever she and Jonathan were in England."

"Don't remind me."

"Not good, I guess."

"Awkward. Every time. I had them for dinner when they were on their extended honeymoon. It was a fiasco. Marcia hardly touched anything I had cooked and went on and on about the wonderful food on the ship. Rude. I haven't cooked for Father from that day until coming up to the Bay House just now. Come to think of it, until Marcia was dead." Vivien sighed. "After that, we had restaurant meals any time they came to the UK. Even that met with disdain. I put it down to her being used to grand cuisine, but now I think she had to be dragged to those dinners and she was telling everyone, especially Father, that it did not suit her. She was in a bad mood. Why? Because Marcia did not like me."

"She was a black and white person. Either you were in or out with her, no compromises. If she had decided you were out, that's where you would stay.

Who knows? You may have touched a nerve inadvertently, and she blackballed you from then on."

Ted slowed down as they came into Whangarei. They stopped at a red light and he stretched his arms. His muscles were telling him it was a long drive.

"Then there was Gerald. He couldn't stand her either. But for completely different reasons." She glanced at Ted. "You sure you want to hear all this?"

The light turned green and Ted sped up on the right-hand lane to pass a lumbering two-trailer lorry. "Go ahead," he said. "I want to know. I hate not understanding."

Vivien nodded. "Me too. Okay. Gerald." She took a deep breath. "He started mentioning Marcia in our arguments when he could see I was changing. Not giving into his every little whim. And he thought he had figured it out. It was all about Marcia."

"Sorry?" Ted felt as if the conversation had derailed. "What about Marcia?"

"He saw her leaving you and marrying Jonathan as 'bettering herself'." She made motions with her fingers, putting 'bettering herself' into quotes. "He thought Marcia's success had inspired me."

Ted grunted.

"Look, Ted, it wasn't like that at all. He got a bee in his bonnet about Marcia. And he thought I wanted the same thing—to better myself by ditching him and finding a sugar daddy like Marcia had done. And I had a role model to follow. He thought I wanted more—more money, more prestige, more freedom. He was right about the freedom thing." She smiled.

Ted smiled back, then sobered. "If he believes personal relationships run on money, then it would make sense to him." Ted shook his head. "So, given this theory, Marcia did better herself."

"It just shows how little he knew about me, his own wife," Vivien said. "I've never given a thought about not having enough money. I've always lived within my comfort zone."

"I thought that about Marcia, too," Ted said with a glance at Vivien. "Marcia had more money—a lot more—after marrying Jonathan, so she spent more. No big deal."

"And it was probably true for me too," Vivien said. "If money was scarce, I would have spent less; if more plentiful, I'd have spent more." She laughed. "Maybe if Marcia and I had ever had this conversation, we might have found some common ground." They rode in silence for a couple of minutes.

"You were saying that Gerald kept on about it?" Ted asked.

"Yes. He kept accusing me, whenever we argued, of planning 'a Marcia'."

"Meaning, planning on ditching him and finding someone better?"

"He had no idea how his arguments demeaned him in my eyes." She sighed. "Funny how Marcia and I disliked each other." She suddenly straightened in her seat. "I've just had a thought," she said. "The girls. I had Juniper and Annabelle living with us that first time I met Marcia. They were very little and quite damaged by that mother of theirs. She was going to put her two little girls, one only five years old, into a boarding school. I couldn't bear it, so they were living with us."

"Boarding school! You may have figured it out. Marcia had a very unhappy Holly at boarding school then."

"I probably rubbed her nose in it—saintly me taking the girls to save them from being sent away."

"No wonder you were never told about Holly," Ted said. "I can picture the entire scene. You going on about how you loved having the girls and why. Marcia getting more and more steamed up that her mothering was in question and Jonathan quietly dying a thousand deaths." He inwardly chuckled. Oh, to have been a fly on the wall.

"She made me feel like shit over the years," Vivien said tightly. "She got her own back, plus, plus. And the result was that I lost all respect for her. I hated her for putting Holly into a boarding school, hated Father giving into her every whim, hated what he was turning into." She resolutely kept her face towards the road curving ahead. "Sorry, Ted, but she was not a pleasant woman."

Chapter Ten

After dropping Vivien off, Ted arrived home to find light streaming from every window and he knew why. His heart sank. Pauline. He'd totally forgotten.

"No telephone reception?" Her voice dripped sarcasm.

Ted gazed at Pauline's long and lissome figure in the doorway. Legs that reached forever. "Sorry. Too much going on," he said as he pecked her cheek. Touched the mass of dark curls. "I'm really very sorry. It's Marcia. She's ... she's gone. Died."

"So I've heard," the young woman said, turning away. "Your charming daughter is in her room. Staying the night, she says, and won't tell me how long before she goes back to Dunedin." Pauline and Holly didn't exactly see eye to eye. Never had. Probably embarrassingly too close in age.

"For god's sake, Pauline. She's just lost her mother." He swung his bag over his shoulder and walked towards his bedroom. Holly's door was shut and he could hear music through it. His own bedroom was now exponentially more tidy, bed made and both bedside lamps lit.

He had somehow found himself in the habit of having Pauline over each weekend. Ted wasn't quite sure how it developed. They had worked on a project together some months ago, had a few meals out, and, to his delight, Ted found himself seduced by this young and interesting colleague. Not that he had found her particularly sexy at the time, but somehow he found himself in a weekend routine that most definitely included sex.

She must have followed him down the hallway. "You must be worn out," she said in a far gentler voice. "Go sit down. I'll get you a drink."

He swung his bag off his shoulder and onto the one chair he had in the bedroom, now no longer piled with his gardening clothes but pristine in its tidiness. "Thanks," he muttered. "I'll have it in the lounge."

When she brought him the whisky, he resolved to tell her he needed to be alone with his daughter. How could he have forgotten Pauline would be here?

The truth was, he'd never given her a thought since well before he got that world-shattering phone call from Jonathan.

"Look, Pauline," he said. "Holly is staying until the funeral at the very least and, so far, we don't have a date for it."

"I know," she said, flopping onto the couch and keeping her eyes off his. "It's family time and I'm not family."

"I'm sorry," he said with some relief. This might not be as difficult as he'd thought. "Sorry for saying sorry all the time. But these are awkward and very trying times."

"Come to bed and I'll help you forget all that," she said with a smile, her head tilted to one side. Ted just stared at her, his heart sinking again. Didn't she realize this was nothing to do with her? He'd have to be very direct indeed.

"Pauline, please. Marcia has just died. Holly has just lost her mother. The Fleet family is going crazy and now the police are involved." He stood up. "I'll call you when things settle down."

Silence. Ted waited it out.

"I guess I knew you'd say that," she said, her head down again. "I'll get my things."

"Sorry." He was too tired and too unsettled to do anything but apologize. He'd make it up later.

Not long after he turned out his bedside light, finally his thoughts settled enough to think it through. If Pauline realized she was intruding into family grief, then why didn't she take herself out of the house before he got home? He was too out of sorts to think any further about it.

Ted drove into the cemetery grounds past beds of flowers in yellows and oranges growing along a drive which meandered through a canopy of pohutukawa trees. Attractive, as cemeteries go, perhaps to offset the bleak reality of life's final show. Sir Edmund Hillary's cortege had come this way some years before and Ted had watched it from under these trees, giving a nod to a remarkable life. He'd been there on a whim, but once standing as the procession made its slow way to the funeral chapel, it felt as if he was participating in a piece of history.

This time was different, personal and commensurately more difficult. He had trouble finding a park, as the previous ceremony must have finished not long before, and the mourners still gathered in groups. They behaved as if their goodbyes to each other were irrevocable, and maybe they were. Death changes everything.

He followed a path to the chapel, also nestled in greenery and at the top of a long slope of grave markers in among tall trees. The day was cloudy and fresh. Ted hesitated before going inside, stepping aside as other mourners arrived.

By the time he entered the chapel, few seats were left. The organ music was muted in sympathy with the solemnity of the ceremony and only a minority of people whispered to their neighbours. He was too self-conscious to walk up the aisle to the pew at the front, even though the family expected him to join Holly there. She must have sensed his presence because she turned and caught his eye, giving a half-wave. Perhaps he should have sat in the family pew to support her, but she seemed okay and he was only here because of his daughter. He could see Jonathan's bald head and Vivien's fair one. Then Holly and, like a bad penny, Oscar.

The funeral had its moments. A celebrant who said she had known Marcia for years conducted it, although Ted didn't recognise her. Half way through her address, he realized. She'd probably officiated at Marcia and Jonathan's wedding. That would qualify as years. Five years, in fact. The first eulogist was a New Age high priestess called Stargazer, someone Ted remembered well. He had never known her by any other name, goofy or otherwise, but she was one friend of Marcia's who had lasted. Her voice filled the little chapel—she always had known how to use her voice for dramatic effect—telling little anecdotes about Solstice ceremonies, crystal gazing and the time on a radio show when she and Marcia had been accused of being witches. Ted smiled. All these stories somehow involved Marcia as an acolyte and centred on Stargazer. He remembered Marcia's scepticism about poor Stargazer. But she had been a loyal friend over a long period and he thought it appropriate that Jonathan thought to ask her to speak.

The second person up was Oscar. Ted gritted his teeth. How could Jonathan have allowed it? Ted had an irrational desire to put his fingers in his ears. Instead, he kept his eyes firmly on the back of Holly's head. She was staring fixedly up at Oscar. In the event, he spoke of Marcia's love of art. Nothing controversial.

Afterwards, most of the mourners made their way to Jonathan's latter-day mansion, where caterers provided copious amounts of food and drink. Holly and Vivien were both playing hostess while Jonathan held court from his leather armchair by the fire. Ted felt reasonably comfortable because he knew many of the people. With each, the topic of Marcia and her untimely death would be mentioned briefly before conversation wandered onto more ordinary catch-up topics. By the end, Ted had many promises of invitations to dinner. No specifics, and he knew they would not act on their vague good intentions, yet he didn't mind. To his surprise, the entire experience had been a positive one. Old friends. He hadn't realized how much he missed intelligent and wide-ranging conversation.

Eventually, very few were left. He knew all but one, an odd-looking man in an old-fashioned raincoat who slouched near the door. The man looked awkward, out of place.

"Who's he?" he asked Holly.

She shrugged. "One of Mum's waifs and strays, I bet," she said. "Or a former lover?" She grinned.

"Hardly," her father said. But he appreciated the flash of humour. Marcia would have laughed long and loud at the comment.

As Ted readied himself to make his farewells, Vivien dragged forward a man he didn't know, young, yet comfortable in his dark suit.

"Ted, I'd like you to meet Mr Finnegan, Derek Finnegan, Marcia's solicitor. Apparently, she made a new will years after she and Father had drawn up their mutual wills."

The man was nodding. "Good to meet you, Mr Frazer. You're mentioned in the will, and I'd like to speak with you fairly soon." He handed Ted his card.

"I'll call you, of course," Ted said, recovering from his astonishment. "Is Jonathan not the executor?" He had noticed that Vivien had said 'Marcia's solicitor', not Jonathan's.

"No, your daughter Holly and myself," Vivien said. "Marcia nominated us as the two executors."

Chapter Eleven

TED SETTLED BACK INTO his routine: rise early and dive straight into problem-solving, what he did best. He wrestled with computer software as if it were an internet game and enjoyed it almost as much. Most of the time, anyway. He usually made himself a light breakfast a couple of hours later and in the early afternoon, a bigger late lunch. After that, mostly, the day was his own. He could nap (on rainy days), or get some fresh air and exercise by working in the garden (on fine days). Or he could go for a walk or head for the flicks or puddle around his garage workshop. It didn't occur to him that most of his activities were solitary.

It was late summer and there were things to tidy outside ... he wanted to make a plan for the new rock garden he was working on. A melee of different hued leaves was his aim for continual colour year round. From bright green and brilliant pink to black grasses. The idea was to play with contrasts so they would show up from his back terrace whatever the season. He was sitting at the outdoor table under the big market umbrella, making sketches, when the phone rang.

Vivien.

"The police have been again," she said. "Father is tremendously frightened by it all. In fact...." Her voice broke. "He's curled up in a ball right now and hardly responding. I talked to Holly, and she suggested you. Any chance you could call in?"

"Of course. Just tell me when."

"Late afternoon? Come and have drinks with us. Stay for dinner if you like."

Ted visualised a depressed Jonathan, the conversation going over and over what they knew or didn't know. He didn't mind helping out, but a finite visit would definitely be preferable. "Late afternoon is fine, but 'no' to dinner. About five?"

***

Ted parked his car in the sizeable area of pea-gravel sweeping past the front door and leading towards a four-car garage. The house was imposing, built only a few years before. Marcia had wanted a new home, one designed with her own hand firmly at the helm, planned around her growing art collection. Jonathan's solution was to sell the grand old villa in Epsom to buy a small house on a large section in Remuera. He promptly had the existing house knocked down and Marcia's architectural statement put up instead. To Ted, it looked like a design by a child with a winning way with glass building blocks. The grounds had a distinct South Island High Country look, all grey boulders and arid grasses of various subtleties. Easy care for non-gardeners.

The door was double-sized and made of wood, the only natural material visible. Ted liked wood and he had coveted the Epsom villa which had kauri everywhere. Although he could admire intellectually this glass box, he could never imagine living in such a place.

He knocked, and Vivien opened the door. She was dressed in white trousers and a blue-grey top that matched her eyes. Barefoot.

"Sorry, Ted. Intruding into your life yet again. But I honestly don't know what to do." They walked through the two-story, lofty entrance hall into a smaller and cosier room that Ted had never been into before. Two walls were lined with books and a third contained a fireplace. French doors opened out onto the side garden—a plot of grass ending in a massed display of dark pink Naked Lady nerines set to advantage against the mottled greys of a stone wall. Jonathan hunched in a leather armchair, his size diminished by his posture.

"Father?" Vivien's voice was that bit too loud as happens often when speaking to invalids. "Father, Ted's come. We're having drinks and nibbles. Should we bring them in here, or do you want to come into the sitting room?" She caught Ted's eye as she spoke.

Jonathan straightened. "Ted. Good of you." His voice was weak, his half-hooded eyes focused on Ted's chest rather than his face.

"What's up, Jonathan?" Ted wasn't sure how to play this, but he decided ordinary was best. "You look awful. What's been happening?"

"He's been at..."

Ted motioned Vivien to stop. He kept his eyes on Jonathan. Vivien stopped, nodded and muttered something about bringing everything in here and left. Ted sat in the other chair.

"Come on, Jonathan. What's happened?"

Jonathan straightened his spine and visibly shuddered. "Thanks, Ted. You're trying to help, but no one can do anything."

"About what? Put me in the picture. Please."

Jonathan shaded his eyes as if the light were strong, balancing his head on his other hand. "The police say ... say she was murdered, Ted. Someone murdered her. And...." He took a long and shuddering breath. "And the police now think I must have ... that I was the jealous husband and deliberately drowned her."

Ted bit back the obvious question. Asking Jonathan if he'd killed Marcia would be tantamount to an accusation. But the question remained. Could Jonathan have murdered Marcia?

He didn't articulate the question but Jonathan answered it anyway. "No." Jonathan looked Ted in the eye. "No. I could never do that to her. As exasperating as she could be, I couldn't." His mouth twitched in what could have been a semblance of a smile, gone as quickly as it was expressed.

Ted nodded. Jonathan wouldn't have murdered her and most likely couldn't with his present state of frailty. But a little voice said the opposite. Jonathan would be acting the exact same way if he had murdered her. Curling up into a ball. Coming out with the denial when Ted arrived.

He shook himself. "Yes, she was exasperating, all right," Ted agreed. "Drove me nuts sometimes."

Jonathan sighed. They both knew Marcia very well, and the camaraderie that shared knowledge produced was unspoken but acknowledged. "Me, too. Not enough to drive me to murder, though. Stupid to think so." Jonathan sat up straighter. "It wasn't you, was it Ted? Sorry, shouldn't ask. I'm going crazy."

"No." Ted said it flatly. It felt like an accusation. Bloody Jonathan. Arrogant sod. "Like you, I couldn't kill her, no matter how exasperating."

Vivien backed through the door holding a silver tray containing chips and various dips, followed by a large Polynesian woman who carried a tray of glasses and an ice bucket. Jonathan struggled to his feet and opened a glass cabinet nestled within the wall of books. "You're a whisky man, if I remember correctly. Laphroig? Or I have a nice single malt."

Vivien glanced at Ted from behind Jonathan's back and gave him a thumbs-up. He must have handled something right. And his little voice noticed how quickly Jonathan was coming back to normal once the two offending things were accomplished—the establishment that he couldn't and wouldn't have murdered his wife and the accusation of Ted.

Ted sighed. Jonathan had never been easy.

Over their drinks and fortified with the spread before them, the story came out. Marcia had been up to something. The police were sceptical that anyone else was involved, but they seemed to have been given a new lease on life with the decision they had come to. The little group munched and drank, and the silence grew.

"The worst of it is that my timings don't match," Jonathan blurted out.

"Timings?" Ted asked. He stared at Jonathan.

"I took too much time getting home from Russell."

Vivien frowned. "You drive slowly. You're not well."

Jonathan shook his head. "Nope." He put his whisky glass down, having thrown the last of it down his throat. "They don't know I visited Cushla." He coloured faintly.

"So? Why don't you just tell them?" Ted asked. "There's nothing wrong with stopping to see an old friend."

Jonathan shot a quick glance over to his daughter. "Cushla is ... Cushla has always been... yes. A good friend. Don't want her involved, especially now they think it wasn't an accident."

"Why so protective? Surely if you talk to her," Ted said. He'd known Cushla for years, an older *kuia* who lived up the road from the Bay House. "I'll talk to her, if you like."

"No!' Jonathan's voice was sharp. "No, I've thought it through. I can't see why she has to be involved."

"But, Father, if the police are querying your movements, surely there's no problem? I can't imagine her hesitating if she's an old friend." She sought Ted's approval with her eyes, and he gave the tiniest of nods. "Why don't you?"

"It's a long story. Ted knows the background." He glanced at Ted. "Tell her."

The story was indeed a long one, but there were essential bits that implied the rest.

"Do you remember the 1984 Queen Street riots about the Springbok tour?" Ted asked Vivien.

"Of course." The protests had divided the nation. One faction believed that apartheid was being tacitly bolstered by having sporting links with South Africa, a view opposed by those who could not see that politics should dictate changes to a long-standing sporting event. Many people had experienced their first arrests during the upset. Somehow, it stirred up emotions like few other subjects ever had. There was an added problem that protesters with only marginal association with the two sides to the argument came out in force, taking the opportunity to push their own message.

"Cushla, using her Maori name, Kotuku, was a stroppy and vocal leader of Maori interests." He turned to Jonathan. "Can't for the life of me remember which side she was on."

"Doesn't matter," Jonathan said. "She got arrested. Made a scene and got herself on national television. For all the wrong reasons."

"And you want to protect her from police interest now?" Vivien asked.

"She's an old woman now. Still feisty, don't you worry about that, but she'd get herself in trouble again. And she's not strong enough."

Ted saw his lips thin in quiet determination.

"I'll get through this on my own, thank you. No Cushla. I have right on my side, after all. The police will leave me alone soon." Ted read doubt in Jonathan's face. Talking through his anxiety.

"Honestly, I think you're creating a mountain out of this protection thing. Making far too much of it. Why don't you just ring her and ask?" Vivien couldn't keep exasperation out of her voice.

Suddenly Jonathan looked frightened. "No. I won't. And I want your solemn promise that you will not ask her either. Both of you. Promise." His eyes flashed in a semblance of the old Jonathan, CEO of an international company.

Vivien held her hands up. "Okay, okay. I give up. For god's sake, Father, you go from being a non-talking, non-responsive lump to dictating to us as if we were servants."

Jonathan glared at his daughter and turned to Ted.

"I promise." Ted met his eyes. "Calm down, Jonathan. I don't want to cause any distress for old Cushla. Wouldn't harm her for anything and if you think this will cause trouble, I'll keep my mouth shut."

"Vivien?"

"I promise. I said I gave up. So I won't ask her, even though it's against my better judgment."

When Ted arrived back home, he was filled with disquiet. He rang Holly.

"Do you know Cushla, the Maori lady up at the bay?"

"Of course. Jonathan's friend."

"How did she get along with Marcia?" Ted needed to keep the conversation well away from the hot topic. He was only after background information.

"Couldn't stand her."

"Come on, Holly."

"You know Mum. Knew." Ted could hear Holly take a deep breath. "She had to be *numero uno*. Always. And especially with Jonathan. He and Cushla go way back. Did you know she protested outside his factory? Years ago."

"I did. That's how they met, I gather."

"They had a screaming match! Well, Cushla screamed and Jonathan got haughty, or so she told me."

"That doesn't say why they became friends. The opposite, one would think."

"She invited him onto the marae for a hui. He ended up staying into the wee small ones. Gradually people left until it was just Cushla and him talking."

"And friends ever since?"

"I really don't know why he didn't marry her rather than Mum." Holly gave a little gulp. "Sorry, Dad. Anything sets me off."

"No wonder Marcia didn't like her," Ted said to get things back on track. "How did she cope with Cushla as a neighbour?"

"Ignored her. My suspicion always was that Jonathan used to go visit Cushla on his all-day fishing expeditions. But maybe that was just my nasty mind when I was a teenager."

Ted smiled. Another instance of Marcia treating someone as if they'd ceased to exist. Not a smiling matter, actually. "Well, if you thought Jonathan was having a secret friendship with Cushla, your mother would have thought it too, and worse." He knew his ex. She would go onto hyper alert when one of her 'enemies' came within cooey. Marcia hating old Cushla? Now it made sense.

After the call, Ted headed into the kitchen. He had pigged out with Jonathan and Vivien and his hunger had gone, but he was thirsty for a cup of tea. He turned the conversation over in his mind while leaning against the bench in his kitchen. Why did Jonathan never marry Cushla? Maybe he really saw her as just a good friend and never had the slightest desire to further their relationship. Why, for that matter, did he marry Marcia? Ted rinsed out his mug and left it upside down to dry. He remembered the conversation where Jonathan was saying he couldn't ever have killed her. Given it was the obvious time to say he loved her, Ted had expected him to say it. But he hadn't. Ted had noticed.

As usual, Ted read for a while after going to bed, but his novel couldn't hold his attention. He put it down and turned out the light, his eyes exploring the patterns on his ceiling. The louvers were open at the top and the night-flowering Queen of the Night perfumed the room. Jonathan was crazy about Marcia. Wasn't he? He was certainly upset at her death. No one could fake that. Besides, the question was one not worth bothering about; who could tell why one person married another? Ted tried shutting his eyes.

But once the question had been asked, it hung there like the smell of Rotorua sulfur. And brought to mind the older question too: why did he himself marry Marcia? During his marriage, he had asked himself that question too many times to count. The answer he gave himself back then was the only one that made any sense: because that's what Marcia wanted. He had never asked her to marry him. The topic had never crossed his mind. Yet somehow one sunny day they were into wedding plans and everyone was congratulating him and he was too embarrassed to back out. Naïve. Intimidated. But also excited about this vital step towards being a grown-up. Eons away from Jonathan's circumstances. He wondered if he would ever ask him. Or whether it had any bearing on Marcia's fate.

Chapter Twelve

TED DROPPED INTO AUCKLAND'S central police station the next day.

"Hello, stranger," his police contact, Gary Cardiff, said when Ted entered the office. "Have you finished that report?"

"Decided to bring it in myself," Ted said, placing a heavy file on Cardiff's desk. "What you hear is a sigh of relief. It's been a long one." He patted the folder.

"Two years, near enough," Cardiff said. "I've kept the prosecutors up with the play, but they want your report ASAP. The trial date is coming up fast."

"Will it be enough?"

"Bloody hope so, Frazer. Thanks for this." He got up, taking the report into his hands, flicking it open, reading a paragraph here and there. "He's a clever geezer. And I hate clever crims."

The two men, chatting about the more amazing details of the case, walked out together, parting at the lifts. The fraud was clever indeed and for almost the first year of poking around in the databases, Ted had been unsure any crime had been committed at all.

These consultancies for the police were often long-winded and, for the main part, the people being investigated were neither stupid nor careless, or there would have been no need for the police to hire his expertise. He enjoyed the cases, nonetheless, because of the intricacies in the hunt for evidence. Candy for his brain cells.

Ted had a visit from the Auckland police not long after he returned home. This time an Inspector Johnston, a big man with plenty of Maori blood in his ancestry, invited himself in and overfilled Ted's small front room. A compact policewoman who did not meet his eyes followed him. A sergeant.

"I need to set things straight," Johnston said after introducing the two of them. "You're not a consultant on this case, Mr Frazer. You're involved as a member of the public."

"You can cut out the 'Mr' bit. And do sit down."

"It'll be Mr Frazer. Part of what I need to get plain," Johnston said as he sat. "You're not working for the police on this case; is that crystal clear?"

Ted swallowed his irritation. "Fine. I answer to Mr Frazer as easily as I answer to Ted or plain Frazer. Remember, I want you to find the perp as much as you do."

"You were in contact with your ex-wife, I've been told," Johnston asked, his eyes on Ted's.

"She used to ring. Asked favours. That sort of thing."

"Tell me about the last time you saw her." Johnston glanced at his notebook. "Two weeks ago on the Thursday."

"I've made a full statement up north. If you ask...."

Johnston made an impatient shrug of his shoulders. "Just bear with us, please, Mr Frazer."

Ted drew a deep breath. He had almost finished tweaking a piece of software, but now his train of thought had been thoroughly interrupted. "She rang. That's what always happens. Happened. She invited me to lunch. Ditto. That meant I was going to be asked to do something. But I'd be given an excellent lunch at Pierre's as a sweetener. Marcia could afford it. She married wealth."

Inspector Johnston nodded. "Did you drink Sangria?"

"Sangria? The Spanish summertime drink? No. Why?"

The inspector let the question dangle unanswered.

"I've tasted it a couple of times in Spain," Ted said. "Too sweet for me."

"Never when you were out for lunch with Marcia Fleet?"

"I heard Jonathan say she liked Sangria. Not a custom with me, either when we were married or afterwards. She always drank white wine when having a lunch out." Their lunches were not 'special' enough, probably. Or a tradition she'd developed with Jonathan. He didn't share this observation with the big inspector. He was learning.

"Go on, Mr Frazer."

The sergeant was scribbling on a notepad. An unobtrusive woman who melted into the background.

"That's it, really. She treated me to lunch, then asked me to do ... to do something or other."

"And this was...?"

"Let me think ... what was it this time?" Ted looked up. "I can't remember. They were always inconsequential things. Just to show that she still could ask me to do things, I suppose. And I would do them. Just a small vanity I indulged her in, that's all."

"Think carefully, Mr Frazer. What did she ask you to do?"

Ted's mind focused on that day which had been hellfire hot with little wind. He had overdressed for the temperature in long trousers with shoes and socks in deference to the restaurant's predictable cool temperature and bitterly regretted his excess clothing when he was caught in traffic on the Harbour Bridge in a car with inadequate air conditioning; but inside Pierre's, it was always cool with soft music in the background. He didn't often eat in Parnell, but he was familiar enough with Pierre's because of the Marcia lunches.

He'd walked into the restaurant, his eyes still adjusting after the strong sunlight outside, when he made out a hand fluttering somewhere in the far corner, Marcia's preferred table. He walked towards her, as always, half of him anticipating a decent meal, half wanting to get out of there as soon as possible.

They looked at the menu, in spite of knowing it well. Marcia had her usual one glass of white wine; Ted had water. This lunch interrupted his routine, and he still wanted to get another hour of work done that afternoon. They ordered. She had... what did she have? No, he couldn't recall. But he did now remember that he had eaten Lamb Gnocchi Gratinée — he knew it well—made with Hawke's Bay lamb. Tender as tender with homemade gnocchi. Nevertheless, with those prices, he couldn't see himself eating there now Marcia was gone.

Yes, it was after the plates had been cleared and they were having coffee that she always asked her favour. What did she ask him that day? It was as trivial as always; he did remember that.

Ted glanced up at the inspector. "I think it was something to do with her laptop."

"Take your time, Mr Frazer."

Ted put himself back in that shadowy corner. Marcia would probably have thought she looked better in the gloom than in harsh light. He would ask Vivien next time he saw her, get a woman's viewpoint. He remembered Marcia sitting there, coffee cup cradled in both hands, her head on one side. Whenever she asked for something, she put her head on one side. Her Princess Di look.

"I have it!' Ted said, surprising himself. "She asked me to change the preferred program for her photo manager. She'd bought a new piece of software and it had become the default and she decided she didn't like it." He sat back on his soft couch, across the coffee table from the inspector, satisfaction producing a grin.

"That's all? Did she ask you to do something else?"

"I doubt it. Besides, she would have saved something else for another occasion. She only asked one thing at a time, Inspector. That was Marcia. Never too much, never too little. Always precise."

"So, control over what she did. Why, then, did she go out in that boat?"

Ted shrugged. "All I can guess is that she went out in it because it suited her. She wouldn't have otherwise."

"Or forced, Mr Frazer? By someone else?"

Ted laughed. "You didn't know my ex, Inspector. It was always difficult to force her to do anything she didn't want to do. Impossible, I would say."

"You're saying that she would only have gone in that boat because she decided to do so."

"That's exactly what I'm saying." Ted sat straighter. "Find out why she wanted to be in the rowboat and you've probably got a lead to your murderer. That is, if there is a murderer."

"Oh yes, Mr Frazer. There's a murderer because Mrs Fleet was murdered. No doubt about that. People don't tie straps around their necks after death."

Ted shuddered. No, people didn't tie straps around their necks after death, even Marcia.

Vivien perched on the edge of the chair and picked up her phone, then put it down again. The house was quiet, her father asleep and his maid-of-all-work, the wonderful Lela, somewhere in the kitchen.

Escaping to New Zealand had so many consequences that had nothing to do with leaving Gerald and their marriage. Friends she'd made over the years. Confidantes. Normally, she would be on the phone to Sally or she would run along the road to Bridget. Here she just had her Kiwi friend Gretchen. Not that Gretchen hadn't been marvellous, but she was, Vivien had to admit, more than a tad boring. Her principal topic of conversation other than the gossip from around the office in which she worked, was her health, symptoms, signs, preventive measures (if Vivien heard one more time about Omega-3, she thought she would scream) and what her doctor had said the last time. The only other person she knew well was her brother; this was definitely not a suitable subject for Oscar. Besides, she hadn't yet forgiven him for his behaviour up north. Which brought her back to Ted.

Should she ring him? For a man, he was an okay sort, quintessentially Kiwi with his shorts and thongs on his bare feet, but helpful and decent. It wasn't just an excuse because she was sure he would like to know about the accident, anyway. She leaned back in the chair. Was it just because she was lonely? But, she reminded herself, she was off men. Especially tight-arsed obsessive men. His neat'n'tidy caravan popped into mind and she inwardly winced.

Maybe she could call Steph? She glanced at the time. Nope, not appropriate for calling the UK and besides, she didn't want to worry her sensitive daughter.

She wanted to talk to someone her age. Ted. As long as he didn't misinterpret. And as long as she kept on-subject and got off the telephone quickly. She rang.

"Am I disturbing you?"

Ted reassured her.

"Do you remember what happened to Oscar's mother?" she asked.

"Was she called Terri? No, before my time. Didn't you say the other day that she died?"

"Yes, she drowned," Vivien suddenly felt hesitant about talking about her family. She squared her shoulders and went on. "It was a boating accident. And the police have dug it up. And poor father..."

"Is being questioned about it," he said, finishing her sentence.

"I guess it's obvious why. Losing one wife to a boating accident is...." She stopped and again queried herself if Ted was the right person to be talking to.

"You okay, Vivien?"

"Not really." She took a long breath. "No. I'm not."

"How about going out for a drink?"

She glanced at her watch. Just before eight. "Love to, but I'm not one for late nights, so I think..."

"We agree with that. I wake fresh in the early morning raring to go. That means no late nights. Boring, I know, but my best working hours are early and I don't want to waste them." He paused. "Let's have a quick drink. Get out. How about you and your father get ready and I'll be right over. He might appreciate some alcohol if old memories are being dragged up."

"No, I mean, yes, I mean I'd love a quick drink out somewhere," she said, her voice unsteady. "But not Father. He came home from the police station and knocked himself out with a sleeping pill. I suppose ... okay. I'll tell you all about it when we meet. Where, by the way?"

"I'll pick you up. Just give me time to get into some proper clothes."

Chapter Thirteen

Vivien was quiet in the car, staring fixedly straight ahead, now feeling slightly nervous.

"This place used to have an extensive garden where the noise doesn't blow your eardrums out. Shall we find out?" Ted asked.

Ted guided Vivien back to a shadowy picnic table 'under the stars' as the sign outside the pub had promised and she sat herself down while Ted fetched drinks. Fairy lights were scattered everywhere, woven through the branches of small trees, just enough to brighten the darkness yet allow access to Jupiter and the brighter stars of the Auckland night. The work of an artist, Vivien thought. The evening was warm, and her hands were sweaty but not from the ambient temperature. This means nothing, she reminded herself. Nothing.

The picnic bench had a long history. Someone had carved "WF ♥' into the wood of the old table top where Vivien was sitting. "WF' like her father's initials but she could never imagine him carving up a picnic table. Who this WF loved was a mystery as she couldn't make out the letters of the beloved. She traced her fingers over the carving and stopped, one finger over the first part of the W. "VF', her initials from before she was married. Would her teenaged self have done such a thing? Probably not. She was too much a good girl but had a boyfriend got out his knife, she would have been thrilled, no question. Crude but romantic, something she had never had in her relationship with Gerald. He used to sneer at Valentine's Day, remember her birthday only when she reminded him and give her only those presents she requested, and then with bad grace if he deemed them too expensive. She wrenched her mind away from Gerald.

The beer garden at night was romantic, too. Her eyes sought groups of people around picnic tables, some with oversized umbrellas silhouetted against the lights of the pub, pools of activity scattered over the broad lawns. Waves of amorphous music, like on the beach, were too far away to be recognizable yet provided a background that set the scene. Laughter punctuated the murmur of voices, muted by her seclusion at the back of the garden. And somewhere in the darkness, a night flowering plant discharged pungent perfume. She had taken on the role of an onlooker and that suited her.

Ted brought back their drinks and after that obligatory pause while they tasted them, he asked whether Vivien had been in contact with her husband.

"I've had a lawyer's letter. This morning." Another reason for being in this weird mood. She had forgotten that.

"So things are quite serious. It's over as far as he's concerned? Your marriage?"

Vivien nodded. "Stupidly, I'm having a hard time with it. Part of me rejoices that we're that far along, but another part of me feels rejected that he didn't try to woo me back. Silly, I know."

"Rejection is familiar territory." He massaged his temple as if he had a headache. "I know about the rejoicing bit. I went through it after Marcia left. All I can say is that it does wear off. Both the feeling rejected and the joy settled into a sort of satisfaction that things have played out the way they did."

"Thank you, Ted." She meant it.

Ted met her eyes. "I've done a lot of thinking about those pesky feelings of rejection. I think they're just a hold-over from schooldays when it didn't take much to feel on the outs. Nothing more. We can safely ignore them." His eyes were dark under his brows in the half light. She was hyper-aware of him and dropped her eyes.

"Actually, it's true Gerald didn't try to woo me back with any energy, but he did make what he probably thought was an attempt. The first time I rang home, he said I was forgiven and I could come home." She gave a laugh that was more a snort. "Trying to give the impression that it was he who kicked me out. When I said that I was staying in New Zealand, he became arrogant. That set things in stone. As if I'd leave Father when he needs me." She met Ted's eyes. "Just Gerald being Gerald." She sipped the wine and felt her shoulders settle down a notch. She felt a tremendous relief being able to discuss this with someone who had an ability to understand.

"One of the truisms of life is that personality basics don't change. Sometimes I wonder how I stood Marcia's antics for so long. I actually felt more relief than distress when she went off with...." Ted looked embarrassed. "Sorry. I don't know if you've heard the story."

"Oscar? Yes. Then Father. Pretty distasteful, all in all. I was looking forward to meeting you, Ted. Your behaviour is a model for us all." Vivien kicked herself for being so pedantic. But she meant it. He had behaved impeccably to her father.

He shook his head. "The stunned mullet model? Hardly one to follow."

Vivien smiled. "You're doing all right. You just have to look at Holly. She's one to be proud of, that's for sure."

He nodded. "Holly's great. You have children?"

"Two. Stephanie and Liam. There's a problem, though. I don't know what Gerald is pumping them with—either the fantasy that he asked me to go and has now forgiven me and I'm still not coming back or how I've abandoned him." She paused. "But they're both emailing me to come back to the UK, sort of pleading his case."

"I don't envy you. That was my worst hour, telling Holly. We were both in tears."

"At the very least, my kids are not that young and not at home. Liam's at university in Nottingham; Stephanie is working in Edinburgh. I made the mistake of letting them think I was coming on holiday over here. Now I've been saying that I'm here for their grandfather, but I guess I have to come clean. Dammit, why is life so complex?" She took a gulp of white wine.

"Your kids are adults. Surely you can be straight with them?"

"Liam is twenty; Stephanie is twenty-three—Holly is in between the two of them. Adult in so many ways, yet so young and vulnerable in others."

Ted nodded slowly. "You get along with them?"

"Stephanie and I have always been close, but Liam went through a tough stage a few years back. I always got along better with him than his father did, even at the height of the binge-drinking."

"Over that now?"

"Thank goodness. He's doing well now he's at university. Reading chemistry."

Ted drank deeply. A pint of the best. "That first boating accident. Oscar's mother. What happened?" he said, blotting his lips on the serviette. Vivien noticed.

She gathered her thoughts. "I remember it really well. It was such a dramatic thing to have happened, and I didn't like Terri very much anyway. It's not as though she was my mother, never even pretended to mother me, so I wasn't really affected emotionally. Oscar was too young to understand."

"How old were you?"

"Twelve."

"Too young to really appreciate what was going on but old enough to remember it all?"

Vivien nodded. "I thought it was all very exciting. The police, well, everyone really, was treating me with kid gloves and threatening to send me back to England." She shook her head. "Now I wonder all sorts of things. Terri had left me babysitting that day, as she often did. Oscar was only two. A twelve-year-old babysitting a rambunctious two-year-old while she was off by herself? She was deep in a book where he couldn't bother her. Now I think it inappropriate."

"Where was the boat?"

"We lived in a house right on the upper harbour on the North Shore then, not far from where you live now, come to think of it. We had a little dock of our own that stretched into the entrance of a tidal creek. A rubber dinghy—quite a small one—lived upside down on the shore. Terri liked to float it out from the dock on a long painter. High tide only, of course. She would just lie back and read in the sunshine. It was her escape."

"What happened?"

"It was windy that day. Gusty anyway. We think she had a seizure and toppled out. She had epilepsy that had been well controlled for years. At the time, I didn't have any idea how she fell into the water and I've had no further ideas since. But she wasn't in the boat and the only possibility was that she had a fit and just tipped out. Nobody made any suggestion of foul play or even suicide. She could swim like a fish normally, but her death was due to drowning."

"Where were you?"

"Ted, stop it. You're sounding just like the police did this afternoon."

Ted looked disconcerted. "I'm sorry, I didn't mean to."

She was behaving like a gauche schoolgirl. "No, I'm sorry. I'm overwrought. It's all too much. Poor Father."

Ted reached over and put his hand over hers. "Let's change the subject," he said. She pulled her hand free a long second later.

When they were getting back into Ted's car, Vivien returned to Jonathan's problem. "It does seem incredible that a man could lose two wives to drowning. Both small boat accidents, at that. Uncomfortably coincidental."

When Ted got into bed that night, he had to turn his thoughts deliberately away from Vivien. He had decided to give her space, and he knew that was the right decision. But he had caught a glimpse of her that evening as a sexy and desirable woman, silhouetted against the brighter background of the pub, her long legs stretched out. Ted thought of himself as a 'legs' man and Vivien could fit into all sorts of fantasies. He pulled his thoughts away. She possessed more than sexiness.

Most of the time they'd been easy together, although this evening had its awkward moments. He was tired, and it probably conveyed itself to her. Of course, she might be feeling totally neutral towards him and nothing he did affected her in the least. With that self-deprecatory thought, he pulled up the duvet. What he hoped for was a kinship of souls. With that more classically romantic thought, Ted slipped into sleep.

Ted remembered he had promised to see the lawyer about Marcia's will. He was oddly touched that Marcia had remembered him. He tried to guess what she could have left him. The Edwardian whisky glasses? He had loved them, but they had relegated them to the caravans, thus probably not valued by either Marcia or Jonathan. Some of her paintings? The only appropriate one was the portrait she had painted of him, but that had disappeared, probably destroyed, years ago. One of her bland studies of the beach? That could be awkward. Nothing else occurred to him. He rang Holly, now back at university in Dunedin, and asked her.

"I've no idea, Dad. I didn't even know she had made me executor."

"She said nothing to you? Not even a hint?"

"Nope. No one knew. Not Jonathan and not Oscar. Jonathan was affronted, I think. He kept repeating that they had made wills together years ago. Oscar just laughed. I don't know what was so funny, but anyway, he thought it was."

"Just Oscar being Oscar," Ted said as neutrally as he could.

"As soon as you know something, give me a call, would you? Mr Finnegan said he'd be in touch, but he hasn't yet." She sighed down the line. "I can't get my head around all this."

He made an appointment with Mr Finnegan's secretary for the following day.

Ted put on his suit for the second time that month and made his way to the solicitor's rooms in downtown Auckland. The receptionist ushered him into the office straight away. Mr Finnegan seemed to be a one-man band, with a secretary, of course.

He motioned Ted to sit down on the opposite side of the desk. "I wanted to talk to you as soon as possible because of the nature of the bequest from Mrs Fleet's will."

Ted nodded.

"I gather from talking to your daughter this morning that neither of you knows anything of this?"

"That's right. We're both surprised about the whole thing. My daughter didn't know she was executor and I certainly never thought I would be a beneficiary. Mr Fleet was under the impression that they had wills that differed little from each other. Holly thought that too."

"Mrs Fleet wrote a letter to each of you. When she gave them to me, she said she expected she would collect them again after her husband passed away. Evidently, he had cancer, presumably with a shortened life expectancy." He passed a pink envelope over the desk.

Ted slid his forefinger under the sealed flap of the envelope, strangely worried.

Dear Ted,

I feel a little embarrassed writing this but if you are reading these words, it means I have been killed in a car smash or felled by a heart attack—something like that anyway — even though I fully expect to live my full share of years and then some at this point.

My gift to you is only fair. You are one of the few people in my life who have been constant. Only Stargazer and you. And I appreciate it, even though I treated you so terribly. Every time I ask the impossible, I can see in your eyes that once again you will do your best to keep me happy. Sorry. I wish things had turned out differently. All I could do was try to keep in contact.

Don't do anything sentimental about Jonathan. He has plenty and then some. My last and most important request is for you to respect my wishes in this matter. I am writing separately to Holly, to Oscar and to Jonathan to explain everything.

Actually, I am being true to my nature with all of this. Believe me, this is such fun! You know me – never in my life predictable. But it's only once in your life you can do something on this scale, and I'm anticipating the look on your face when Mr Whatsisname reads out the will.

Enjoy.

Your devoted ex-wife,

Marcia

Ted put the letter down. It was pure Marcia, no doubt about it. "What did she leave me, Mr Finnegan?"

"A house. The Bay House. I understand you built it."

Ted felt himself take a deep breath and hold it as if he were sinking underwater. He closed his eyes. The Bay House? His again? He swallowed and looked at the papers in front of the lawyer. "The will. Would you mind if I read the operative bit for myself?" His voice sounded tinny to his ears.

"Here." Mr Finnegan pushed a paper over the desk and deftly turned it around so Ted could read it.

There it was, in black and white. "To my ex-husband and true friend Edward Frazer, The Bay House, Northland."

Ted swallowed. His mouth was dry. "And my daughter. What did she leave my daughter?"

"I've asked her permission to talk with you about the rest of the will and she has kindly said I may do so. Mrs Fleet has left Holly all her jewellery, a portfolio of investments made in her name and her art collection. It is quite a sizable bequest. She left Mr Fleet her personal paintings, her books and any other effects he wants other than what has been left to her daughter and others in the will. Most of the real estate other than the Bay House was jointly owned with her husband, thus not subject to a will. She left her collection of crystals and dream catchers...' Mr Finnegan looked up from the papers. "I believe they have something to do with American Indians." He looked down and read again, "... 'to Stargazer Mills'. The friend, I believe, who spoke at the funeral. "To Mr Fleet, junior, she has left her spectacles." He shrugged. "That's what it says. Her spectacles."

Ted knew Marcia. Those spectacles would mean something to Oscar, no doubt, and to no one else. A message. Very Marcia.

He stood up. "Thank you, Mr Finnegan. I appreciate your taking the time to tell me about Marcia's will. I'm overwhelmed by her generosity." He felt pompous saying this, but pomposity matched pomposity and he felt the man deserved something. Mr Finnegan would not have a pleasant time with Jonathan, he reckoned. And even worse when Oscar was told he had been left a pair of spectacles.

Ted heard from the police the next day. Could he please call in at the Central Police Station, ten the next morning, to see Inspector Johnston? Of course he could. With pleasure.

That didn't take them long, he noticed, as he replaced the phone in its holder. And why were the police interested in him? Because, unbeknownst to him, he had a motive for killing Marcia and a powerful one to boot. He called Holly, and she was as surprised about the Bay House as Ted himself had been, delighted her mother had come up trumps for once. That was the positive. She made light of his appointment the next day. No one could ever consider he would murder Marcia because she had left him a beach house at her death. Ridiculous. Ted went to bed that night with distrust burning at that deduction, fighting with joy at the bequest.

Marcia. Never one to shy away from creating chaos.

Chapter Fourteen

TED DECIDED HIS SECOND trip into Central Police Station deserved conservative non-formal attire, that is, dressing in something between the casualness of his shorts and the formality of his suit. He settled on tan chinos and an open-necked white short-sleeved shirt. Light coloured socks and loafers. The wearing of socks and shoes was what he resented most.

To his surprise, it was Inspector Grant from up north again. He had made a special trip down to Auckland for this interview. Ted's anxiety, already high, soared further.

"You told Inspector Johnston the last time you saw Marcia Fleet, you agreed to do a fix-up on her computer," Inspector Grant said, and, out of the corner of his eye, Ted saw Johnston give the smallest of nods. He had noticed that the inspector hadn't finished this line of questioning last time.

Ted nodded. He knew enough to wait.

"Please say 'yes' or 'no' for the tape," the inspector requested.

"Yes, I agreed to fix her default picture manager." Ted didn't fool himself that the rest of the interview was going to be this easy.

"And you said that you haven't had any contact with Marcia Fleet since that time?"

"That's right. No contact."

Grant frowned. "So you didn't do what she had requested. I find myself wondering, why is that?"

This question Ted could answer. He was almost enjoying himself. "No. Wrong assumption. The right question would have been, 'When did you do it?'"

The frown deepened. "Answer your own question, Mr Frazer."

"I had no further contact with Marcia because I didn't need to see her again. I had fixed it right then and there."

"Explain yourself, sir."

"Marcia had the laptop with her. I turned it on in the restaurant and fixed her problem. Took me two minutes from opening up to closing down again."

He thought he saw Johnston give a fleeting smile once again. Yes, a bit of a dark horse and one to keep an eye on.

"This was typical? Asking you to do some trivial job and paying you with an expensive lunch?"

"Yes." Ted felt he was learning. Just answer the question. Add nothing. Co-operate, but don't give them anything.

"And why would she do that when she could take the laptop into a shop and get someone to do the same thing at very little cost?"

"Money didn't mean much to her."

"Are you sure?"

"No. I'm not sure. How can anyone know someone else's motivations except by guesswork?"

The frown was there again. "Could you please answer my question about why she didn't go to a shop, Mr Frazer?"

"She didn't take it into a shop because it was an excuse to go out to lunch with me. Is that what you were after?"

"And why was that so difficult to answer?"

Ted reminded himself to stay grounded. These questions were meant to disconcert him. Just take each question, strip any implications from it and provide a clear and unadorned answer. "She was my ex-wife, Inspector Grant. After the shock of the divorce, we stayed...." Ted fought for words. "If not exactly bosom pals, we still had a type of friendship. She liked asking me to do things for her. I indulged her. Her requests were always accompanied by expensive lunches." Ted had stopped enjoying himself. He noticed the inspector's frown had disappeared. He realized he didn't much like being on this side of the desk.

"Now the Bay House." The inspector shuffled papers and the sergeant in the corner turned to a new page.

"The Bay House," Ted repeated.

"You've inherited the Bay House."

"Much to my surprise, I have."

"I'm asking myself, why would an ex-wife leave a valuable house to an ex-husband?"

"Me, too." He glanced at Johnston sitting back with his sergeant. The inspector's eyes were boring into his; she was scribbling. Why, when they were recording the whole thing?

The inspector sighed. "Please Mr Frazer, do I have to pull everything out of you like I was a damn dentist?"

"No, inspector. But I would prefer you just asked straight out. If you had said, 'Why would Marcia leave you the Bay House?' I would have answered, 'No idea. Except that it is my pride and, yes, joy. I designed it; I built it from scratch and I had little chance to live there once I finished it.' Maybe she felt I deserved it more than Jonathan, should she pre-decease him. Maybe it was *noblisse oblige*."

The sergeant was openly grinning now, even though her head was down and she hadn't stopped scribbling. Maybe writing down things kept her from being too bored. Maybe she liked his French.

"Thank you, Mr Frazer. Maybe we're beginning to understand each other." The inspector nodded. "Your pride and joy. It meant a great deal to you. So you must have been angry when you lost it in the divorce settlement."

Angry? Ted had been more than angry. He was furious. Enraged. Yet there was no way out. New Zealand law said that Marcia was entitled to half of their assets even though she was marrying serious wealth. Half can be difficult to gauge when big assets are involved. The obvious division was the Bay House to one and the little house on Auckland's North Shore, plus both halves of the software business to the other. Ted couldn't have both his business and the Bay House. Emotionally, he got screwed; financially, it was more or less fair.

"Distressed. I guess no one wins in a divorce," Ted said.

"Angry enough to want to get your own back sometime?"

Ted felt his heart thump. "I'd accepted it. our divorce was a long time ago."

The inspector carried on as if Ted had not spoken. "Angry enough that you tricked Mrs Fleet into the small boat, a dinghy that used to be yours and in waters you were totally comfortable with, and you pushed her out of the boat knowing everyone would assume she would panic? Drown?"

"No!' Ted couldn't believe what the inspector was saying. He took a deep breath to calm himself. "That's a ridiculous suggestion. We're talking ancient history here. The divorce went through more than five years ago." He willed his voice down, slow.

"We know you were in the boat, Mr Frazer. And there's only one reason you would be in that boat. To murder your ex-wife."

"I didn't murder her; I didn't want her dead. She was.... she was...."

"She was what, Mr Frazer? Irritating? Manipulative? Driving you crazy?"

"No. Yes. No! Not dead. Besides, I can't even murder a spider."

The inspector had the grace to laugh, albeit sardonically. "That's the image you present, Mr Frazer. Mr Consultant-to-the-police Frazer. Mild and inoffensive. But you're doggedly persistent. Murderously mild, maybe. Know what the guys in the fraud squad call you?"

Ted knew. He was known as 'the tortoise'. The guy who just keeps plodding along until he passes all the cheeky hares. He'd taken it as a compliment.

"I think if we had a tortoise planning a murder, he'd do it meticulously, don't you think, Mr Frazer?"

Ted straightened his back and locked his eyes on the inspector's, recognizing the posture as a response to being roasted by someone like his father or the headmaster at school. He knew he was dangerously close to losing it.

"We'll find out, Mr Frazer. We always do."

"I wasn't anywhere near that boat!" He spat it out.

"Oh, you were there all right. Must have missed a few bits when you cleaned up." The inspector leaned his chair back on its two back legs.

Ted took a long, juddering breath. But it was no use. He had no way of calming himself down. The police were accusing him of murder. "You can't know I was out in the boat when I wasn't. Hell, I was nowhere near the bay when Marcia died." This was stupid. Ludicrous.

"Oh, but we do know you were in that boat, Mr Frazer." Not a hint of a frown. Ted saw that the sergeant was watching it all, her notebook forgotten.

"You cannot, because I haven't been in that boat for over five years." He felt his voice deepen. Right was on his side, and he had to convince them.

"Please explain, then, Mr Frazer, how your fingerprints—together with those of your ex-wife—were on the boat. Moreover, fibres from your clothes were found there as well."

Ted was flummoxed. No way were his fingerprints ... he suddenly had a clear image. The beach. His sandals. "Oh," he said into the silence. "It's okay, inspector. I know now. You'll have found my fingerprints along the gunwale at the stern. I leaned on the boat when it was on the sand. The morning after Marcia had been killed. Putting my sandals on. You took the boat away after that."

The inspector stared at him, letting the silence build once more.

"Very clever, Mr Frazer. But watch your cleverness. I've known many a clever man who tripped over his own two feet, sandals or no sandals.

Stumbling out of Police Central, Ted wondered whether he should hire a lawyer. He didn't have a clue whether it was a solicitor or a barrister that was needed but he probably needed advice. At this point, he was in over his head and being innocent was not a protection. Did having all this unwelcome attention on him ease the pressure on Jonathan? Maybe.

Instead of going home, Ted drove to Jonathan's glass box. Boxes. Jonathan's car was on the drive.

"The police have been grilling me. Thought you might like to hear about it," Ted said when ushered into a pleasant, sun-filled room at the back of the house. Seated at a table cluttered with lunchtime bits were both Jonathan and Vivien.

"First, sit down. You're undoubtedly starving. This is a make-your-own-sandwich kind of lunch." Vivien gestured to a chair and grabbed a fresh plate for him.

Ted helped himself to bread, salad and some cold cuts, suddenly realising how hungry he was. "Perfect," he said as he made his sandwich. "My kind of lunch."

He filled them in on the questioning. Got laughs out of his tale about Marcia's laptop, but they sobered when he told them about the accusations. He then got to the tricky part.

"Jonathan, there's something I need to ask you. Did you know about this recent will that Marcia made?"

Jonathan shoved his empty plate into the middle of the table and leaned forward on his arms. "Nope. Nothing. My guys are working on it now. Seeing if it's legal, that sort of thing. We had prenuptial agreements, of course, and they're going over the details."

Ted stole a quick glance at Vivien. She looked curious but calm.

"I've seen her lawyer. Yesterday. She put me in the will."

"You? She left something to you?" Jonathan was clearly astounded.

"Mmm, she did. Surprised me too." Ted was unsure whether to proceed or not. Too late, he realized he was digging himself into a hole that he might not know how to get out of.

"And?" Vivien said. "Come on, Ted. You've been to the lawyer. What did she leave you?"

"Well, hold on," he prevaricated. "Maybe we should leave it till Jonathan does his investigation." He looked at Jonathan as he said it.

"Won't change anything she wrote," Jonathan said. "My guys are finding out whether it's legal, that's all. I thought we had a done deal. Haven't given wills a thought in years." He smiled. "Come on, don't be coy, Frazer. What did Marcia want to leave you?" Ted noticed the words. This was excruciating.

"The Bay House." Ted couldn't look at either of them. He could feel his heart speed up. This was not the time. Not for Jonathan and hellishly not the time after what he'd been through that morning.

Silence.

"You must be kidding," Vivien said. "She's left you the Bay House? How perfect!" Ted looked at Jonathan who was staring at him under scowling eyebrows.

"How did you do it, Frazer? Those cosy lunches? Working on her?" His voice was low. Threatening.

"Father! Ted wouldn't do that," Vivien said with some spirit.

"I didn't even know she'd made a new will," Ted said to Jonathan as calmly as he could, his heart thudding in his chest. "And it sounds as if you didn't either. This is as great a surprise to me as it is to you." Damn, damn, damn.

"And you plan on accepting it? Taking it? From me?"

Chapter Fifteen

THE UNFAIRNESS OF JONATHAN'S reaction stabbed Ted through his very being. He got up, not able to trust that he could maintain civility one more second. "From you? The Bay House is not yours. It's mine. I designed it. I paid for it. I built it, brick by bloody brick. It was taken from me and now I have it back. Nobody, and I mean NOBODY, will ever take it from me again."

Ted spun on his heel and left the room, the glass house. By the time he had backed down the drive, he could see Vivien running towards him. He stepped on the accelerator.

Damn Jonathan. How dare he? Marcia could do what she liked with the Bay House. It was obviously her part of the pre-nup, peanuts compared to Jonathan's holdings. Jonathan was.... Ted caught himself driving too quickly. His phone rang. He ignored it. He needed time and space to think before any further discussion, and going through this sort of topic while driving was dangerous. He relaxed his grip on the wheel, lessened the tension on the accelerator and swung off his usual route.

He drove along Greenlane Road to the entrance to One Tree Hill domain and wound his way to the carpark that opened to the path to the top. It was windy, but he badly needed to clear his head. He walked up to where the one tree had stood until a Maori activist had cut it down in what Ted saw as a misguided but publicity-seeking gesture of anger. Someone had planted more trees. A probably futile attempt to replace the old pine, itself a replacement for the original Totara. In his present mood, he doubted any would survive.

He could see not only over the entire city, but out to the blue horizon beyond the volcanic hump of Rangitoto Island. The day was fine with some wind-blown clouds, just enough to give contrast to the deep blue of the sky. If he had to live in a city, then Auckland was it. He turned to the north and could make out the Harbour Bridge and the highway that would take him up to the bay.

To the Bay House.

His house.

His.

There was no way he'd give it up again unless Marcia's lawyer had totally lost his competence. As his mood calmed, he felt as if he'd had an insight. The Bay House was as important to him now as he had always thought. Yes, bloody important, and now it could have the history it deserved for its projected lifespan of 300 years. He built it; he would live in it; he would pass it to Holly and then it would go to her children and so on. His original idea was to build it as a family heirloom. His dream had been dashed seven years ago, but something had made Marcia reach into her memory banks and it certainly wasn't anything about doing minor fix-ups on her laptop. He sent a silent thank you up to her soul, wherever it might be.

He stayed up there, the city at his feet, until he got thirsty. He walked back down the footpath to the car and grabbed his water bottle. His cell phone, on the dashboard, rang again.

"You okay?" Vivien asked. "Look, Ted, please forgive Father. He's under such impossible stress. Come back and we can talk it out."

Ted felt awkward and, underneath, outraged. Jonathan had been way out of line. "I'm okay, thanks. But I think I'll wait for Jonathan to invite me." There was silence.

Vivien broke it. "I'm sorry. Marcia had a mean streak in her and it was cruel not to tell Father about a new will."

"I'm feeling too grateful to her right now to think about it, Vivien." As he realized how cold this sounded, he felt his anger dissolve. "I know Jonathan loves the place, too. Maybe we can work something out."

"Yes, maybe." Her voice was detached. "Call me on my cell sometime."

Ted dropped his phone into his jacket inner pocket. He tried to be philosophical about it but he couldn't help thinking a future involving Jonathan and, by default, Vivien, was an unlikely scenario. Not if the will held up to scrutiny. He started the car and headed out of the carpark.

Over the next few days Ted concentrated on his current IT project, his time-honoured response of retreating into work when things were emotionally fraught. He put in long days, working on writing and then tidying a complex report. Friday, he pressed the 'send' button and looked at the time. Just before noon. He stood up and stretched. Earlier rain had cleared, but it had provided much needed moisture for his garden. He closed the window in his office and headed for the kitchen and some lunch. Then it hit him. The improvement in the weather, the finishing of his report, the timing and nothing to look forward to on the weekend. Perfect. He made himself a hasty sandwich and packed a bag. One phone call to Duncan and he was on his way not half an hour after deciding to go north.

Ted had always loved the drive and, with the freshness of a sunny day after rain, he felt as if he were making his way through a never ending botanical garden. He turned on the radio and sang along to classic hits all the way north.

As he crested the hill before diving down into the bay, his cell phone rang. Fortuitous timing as he was almost at the small pull-off spot for tourists with cameras. The shoreline stretched northward with bay after sandy bay separated by dark volcanic rock just begging to be photographed. The surf crashed over the shoreline, sending spumes into the air, bright white against the deep blue of the sea.

"I've brought us really good steak," Pauline's voice said into his ear. "When are you going to be home?"

He'd forgotten. Again.

"Sorry, Pauline. I'm so sorry, but something's come up and I'm out of town," he said, attempting to keep his voice firm. "I was going to ring you as soon as I got there," he lied. "I'm on the road right now. Sorry." He bit his lip. Too many 'sorries'.

"Shit, Ted. Why didn't you ring earlier?"

"The freezer? Then we can have them another time?" He really didn't want to get into a discussion about the whys-and-wherefores of it all right now. "Look, Pauline, I'm...." He swallowed hard. "Erm, can you go do some of your golf this weekend instead? You're always complaining you never have time to keep up your game."

"Shut up, Ted. Don't start telling me what to do. Especially when I was supposed to be spending the weekend with you."

"Do what you want, of course," he said with an inner sigh. "But we need to talk." As soon as it left his mouth, he regretted it. 'Needing to talk' almost always meant something negative.

"Yeah. Of course. Don't worry about me, okay?" she said. "There's always next weekend."

"Thanks, Pauline. I'll make it up to you. Promise."

Duncan met him on his drive with a wide smile. "Wonderful news, Ted. Hasn't she redeemed herself!"

"You've heard. She has, hasn't she?" He should have realised the bush telegraph would have conveyed the news to those who cared.

Duncan punched him on the shoulder and grabbed his bag. "Of course! We all think it's just great. Come on in and have a beer."

"First a dip," Ted said. "I've been anticipating the feel of that water all the way up."

"You always did that, didn't you? Always into the sea first thing."

"To wash the city off." He grinned at his old friend. "You do the same when you've been in Auckland."

They were on Duncan's deck, slurping DB Browns, Ted's hair drying in the late sunshine, and the taste of the beer sitting easily on his tongue. "How did you hear about the will? I've told almost nobody."

"Cushla, of course. She's tight with Jonathan, but you know that."

"Yes," Ted said slowly. "But I would have thought he would keep this one to himself. He wasn't best pleased, as you can imagine. Marcia didn't warn him."

"So I gather. He's pissed off, all right. Cushla just laughs. The guy's rich as Croesus. He doesn't need to have your place. Never did need to have it. That's what we think. What we've always thought."

Ted reached over and clinked his beer can with Duncan's. "To the team."

The team. Ted thought back to the team who gathered day after day to construct the adobe bricks for the Bay House. Duncan was there every day; Cushla often appeared with hot buttery scones or freshly baked biscuits. The Bennetts, the Horowhais, the Sumichs came weekend after weekend. Then the time the two farming families from closer to Russell pitched in – it had been a community effort getting that mud, rotten rock, sand and straw mixed with Ted's careful measure of a vital cupful of concrete. They poured the mixture into formers, row after row, building the thick walls in situ. He thought of that time with nostalgia.

The two men stared over the sea, an easy silence between them. The beach was empty, as usual for this time of year, the surf making soft swooshing sounds as small waves broke over damp sand. Ted felt the tensions fade away. This was what life was about.

The next morning, he was up and wandering around an empty house. Duncan had awakened early for his weekly shopping expedition into Whangarei. When Ted had come into the kitchen, he'd found a couple of eggs, bacon and tomatoes neatly laid out by the frying pan, ready for him to make a workingman's breakfast.

Cushla's house was a couple of kilometres up the road and Ted worked his breakfast off by walking up. The morning was cool, a promise of more autumnal weather in the offing. He hoped Cushla was a morning person because he did not want to disturb her if she was still in bed. But when he breasted the last hill, he could see her pegging out laundry behind her cabin. He called out to give her warning.

Her drive was steep, and he was out of breath by the time he reached the clothesline. Cushla greeted him with kisses on both cheeks and invited him in for a cuppa.

"Now you must understand what Jonathan is going through right now, Ted Frazer." Her hands were on her hips, her head tilted to one side.

Ted held up both hands. "Believe me, I do. Marcia had no right to change her will without at least hinting to Jonathan she was thinking about it. But that was Marcia."

"I know." She absentmindedly ushered him inside. "She was a difficult one, that's for sure. But she did the right thing by you and that puts her up in my estimation."

"I thought you'd think the other way, being so close to Jonathan." He watched her fill the jug and put it on. She grabbed two mugs hanging above the kitchen bench and reached for the tea cannister.

"We're long-time friends, but that doesn't mean he can tell me what to think. Never that, Ted." She waggled a finger at him, and he had to suppress a smile. She was not a tall lady, but she had a quiet dignity that went with her long wavy white hair. How did Maori women attain that self-confidence once they were older? Maybe the culture: the respect the young ones paid their elders.

"Oh, I know you're an independent thinker, Cushla. It's just that having him a close neighbour up here has been a boon, hasn't it?"

"I suppose my being here was the reason he wanted Marcia to bargain for the Bay House when you two split." She said it without modesty, just stating facts.

What? Jonathan pressured Marcia when they divorced? Is that how he lost the Bay House? "Awkward, isn't it." He wanted to appear affable. "Maybe he can use it sometimes. I haven't been able to talk to him about it."

"No, that wouldn't work. Not Jonathan. He likes to own." She laughed. "That's one of the reasons I kept my independence."

Ted noticed the intimation. Holly might have been right in that, at one time, there could have been a question of marriage between the two. They would be within five years of each other in age, he figured. He wished he could think of some way he could get Cushla to talk freely about the day of Marcia's death without him breaking his promise to Jonathan to keep away from the subject. He was no detective. "You seem to have a good life up here."

"That I do. Got another grandson since I saw you last. Lester's." She completed the tea making and pushed the milk jug towards his mug.

Ted had known Lester as a young man—a shuffling teenager who wouldn't meet his eyes. Then wasn't there some trouble? Police trouble? "How old is Lester now?"

"Coming up thirty-two. He's got three little ones now, all boys." She grabbed her own mug, added milk, and gestured to the two outside chairs on the little deck overlooking the sea.

"Ah, no more trouble, then?" Ted felt his face flush.

"All that's in the past," Cushla said firmly. "Shall we say, his horticulture business is defunct. He's got much more serious fish to fry now; quite the little businessman."

Ted then remembered. Marijuana. Lester had been growing marijuana in some quantities all over the area. Had been done for it. Lots of people had been put out that their ready supply was no longer available, including Oscar, if he remembered correctly. "Glad to hear it," he said. "What kind of business?"

Cushla tapped her nose. "Not for me to say." She laughed noisily. "Ask him. He might tell you; who knows?"

They spent the next half hour discussing her children and their families. Ted got up to go.

"Jonathan says the police have hassled you," she said. It was not a question.

"The police has hassled all of us," he said. "Jonathan especially." As he sipped his tea, Ted looked out over her view. It was 180 degrees of Narnia high hills and layers of farmland to the west and 180 degrees of sea to the east that stretched from Cushla's borders of asters and chrysanthemums to the far horizon. "They found my fingerprints on the boat."

"Yes. Jonathan told me. He got a good laugh when they realized you were just putting on your shoes. But I gather their investigation of him is more serious."

"When the police have a murdered woman, the first place they look is to the husband. And often they're right. But they also look to the ex-husband and, believe me, they're looking. Especially now I have something to gain by Marcia's death."

"And her enemies? Will they look at them?" the old lady asked, her eyes searching his.

Chapter Sixteen

TED SAT BACK DOWN and grabbed both her hands in his, the morning sun warm on his back. "What are you saying, Cushla?"

She dropped her eyes. "We didn't get along, me and Marcia. You know this."

"I know." Ted held his breath in case there was more.

"She was a beautiful young woman. She had nothing to fear from me." Cushla paused and, when he kept silent, she carried on, "But she was no dummy; she tried to stop Jonathan from seeing me. As if anyone could stop Jonathan doing exactly what he wanted." She eased her hands from under Ted's. "I think she knew somehow." Cushla sighed.

"Knew?" he prompted.

"That the two of us had picked her." She shot a glance at him. "Oh, Ted. Sorry. What am I saying? Forget it, okay? Look, have another cuppa." She got up quickly and moved towards the kitchen.

"Sit down, Cushla," Ted said. "Stop fussing. Just tell me what you meant when you said you'd picked her."

Cushla's eyes were anywhere but on his. "No. I shouldn't have said anything."

"Calm yourself, my friend. It's all a long time ago and Marcia's gone now." He should be telling himself to calm down. 'Picked' her? Jonathan and Cushla together?

Cushla nodded, but she still didn't look at him. "I'm an old lady. Nothing is very important anymore."

"Not now for Marcia, I guess. But tying up loose ends? I'd like that."

"I'm sorry, Ted. You were the victim then. But I excused myself because Marcia was so... well, so awful." She straightened her back and became regal in an instant. "My son's coming over this morning, Ted, so you'll have to get going now. But come back late this afternoon. I'll have my thoughts straight by then."

"Of course." He got up, kissed her cheek and took himself out of her crowded little cottage. After making his way to the top of the rough driveway, deeply scored from past storms that cut their own channels into the fabric of the drive, he paused to look at Cushla's home, originally designed as a garage with corrugated iron siding. Her sons had turned it into a cosy home which allowed her to retire onto family land. She had an unrivalled view that any top-notch holiday resort would covet.

But with every step he took downhill, his disquiet increased. Surely he'd misunderstood. *Picked* Marcia, forgawdsake? What was all that about? He trudged along the road, kicking the odd stone when he could. Bloody glad he had another chance to dig deeper. He would be back later and even if Cushla had thought better of telling him or decided it was all history, he deserved to know. And he would know, dammit. He stopped when the bay came into view through the trees. Blue and serene. All of this was miles away from what Cushla did on the day of Marcia's death. Not that he planned on countermanding Jonathan's directive. A promise was a promise.

The morning was still early, and few travellers used the road. He strode downhill until he came to the gate. His gate. The one he had built some years before. The gate to his property. His. All was quiet. With an agility that surprised him, he was over the gate and walking up the private road canopied with Punga, rimu and pohutukawa.

The view sprang on him, just as he had planned when he had the drive put in. Keep the bush and save the surprise. He'd known people to gasp as they rounded that last corner with the whole Pacific Ocean spread before them.

And the house. The sun was now on it, the warm terracotta walls contrasting with the richer tones of those still in the shade. He stopped and gazed at it, hardly breathing. His house. Really his house now. Again. A bubble of joy formed deep within his chest. He laughed aloud. God, he felt good.

"You hear me, Marcia? Hey, girl, you done good!" A lone tui called its musical reply in response. "I appreciate it. Thank you, Flower, from the bottom of my heart."

He made his way to the front of the house and descended part way down the path to the beach. Years before, he'd put a park bench there, shaded by one of the giant pohutukawa trees. It was getting on in years now, and he lowered himself onto it gingerly. It creaked and held, but he made a mental note to replace the slats.

He'd designed it to be a place to sit and contemplate this planet of ours. His gaze lingered on the northern coast, which alternated between beaches and rocky outcrops, ending in a forest-covered peninsula. It was a place just to be. And to think big thoughts like the death of an ex-wife. Most of his grieving had been done when they separated. Then he'd gone through missing the little things, the loss of a future together and an end to an era. Now what he felt was pure sadness, unadulterated. For the first time since he had heard that Marcia was dead, he felt tearful.

"I hope you're in a better place, Flower," he muttered. He sat for a while before getting up and making his way down to Duncan's house.

Once there, Ted kept glancing at his watch. The day dragged. Late morning, he had a swim, the water still comfortably warm, and the beach deserted. He got a start when he saw a dinghy in the usual spot on the beach. But it wasn't *the* boat—that was still in the possession of the police, of course. Just Duncan's tin dinghy.

After a cheese sandwich lunch, he grabbed the oars and took the dinghy out, wondering vaguely if Duncan would approve. The day was calm, typical of late summer. The conditions were probably similar to that fateful day. He enjoyed using his arms again as he got up a bit of speed, dropping back into a familiar rhythm, only now and then glancing over his shoulder to see where he was headed — the south-eastern gap, the one channel open at any stage of the tide. Beyond there, he was in the open Pacific Ocean and vulnerable to gusts of wind and choppy water conditions impossible to gauge when in the shelter of the bay. But today was calm with a small swell.

He stopped rowing and drifted. None of it made sense. He looked around. He could no longer see into the bay, but the next beach was close, more exposed. Landing could be tricky in even moderate seas. But today it would be easy. With little wind, the surf just lifted the rowboat onto the shingle of this beach, different from the sandy bay around the corner. Ted hopped out and pulled the dinghy up from the waterline.

Duncan seemed to think Marcia's body had drifted from here. The thought made Ted's stomach lurch. Today, the beach was deserted, not unexpected given its isolation. He walked its length, observing acutely but not knowing what he was looking for. Nothing was disturbed, nothing different, and certainly it contained nothing of Marcia. The land rose steeply above this beach. Perhaps youngsters could scramble up the bank, but not the middle-aged. Certainly not Marcia. It was a private place, this beach, accessible on foot at very low tide from the rocks of the bay, otherwise by boat only. He sat on the warm shingle, then lay back, watching wisps of clouds forming and dissolving. Marcia. Coming to this beach was uncharacteristic. What had she been up to?

Chapter Seventeen

TED RETURNED TO THE bay in plenty of time to walk up to Cushla's for his afternoon appointment.

She fussed over him, getting him a cold can of beer and offering him crisps that tasted as if they'd been stored a bit too long. They were again sitting on homemade wooden chairs on her deck, looking over a small lawn bordered by a riot of colourful annual flowers and the calm Pacific beyond. Cushla was the queen of all she surveyed.

"You've been pretty close to Jonathan for a long time, haven't you?" Ted prompted.

Cushla nodded. She had fixed herself a large mug of milky tea now resting on a wide armrest that doubled as a table. One of her sons, Ted supposed, had made the chairs.

"He was probably one of the most important people in my life," Cushla said, "and still is, in a lot of ways."

"I sort of gathered that," he said. Jonathan and Cushla? She was obviously hinting that there was more to their relationship than mere neighbourly friendship. Were they an item? He decided to take a risk. "But the two of you never married."

"Heavens no," she laughed. "Can you see Jonathan fitting in here? Or worse, can you see me fitting into his fancy-dancy lifestyle in Auckland?" She didn't bother denying the seriousness of their relationship. Almost boasting of it.

"You met him at the time of the Springbok troubles, he told me." He took a long pull at his beer. It tasted as it should, but he noticed his hand trembled. Jonathan and Cushla? Hard to accept.

"Yes. We hit it off straight away even though we were on opposite sides of that question. We connected. And we weren't silly young things, either." Ted calculated swiftly that Jonathan was 75-ish now and Cushla was probably 70 or so. That meant they met when Jonathan was much younger than Ted's present age and Cushla even younger.

"You were both married? I mean, to other people?"

Cushla nodded. "My ex was in prison, stupid git. When he got out, he didn't stay around long. Jonathan was married to ... to one of them. Terri, I think. She was stupid too, beautiful, but stupid. He was thinking of leaving her when we met. Who we were married to had nothing to do with us. Him and me."

Ted suppressed a desire to lift his eyebrows. Cushla was staring out to sea. "Lester? He wasn't...?"

Cushla's laugh rang out. "Do your arithmetic, boy! No, he was a youngster when we met. But you know Jonathan, not interested in children. Even Holly. She became friends with him once she was grown up, not when she was little." She reached over and patted Ted's arm. "Holly's a great kid. A sweet girl."

He nodded. The subject was getting away from where he wanted it to be. "So you decided not to marry."

"Never on the cards. No decision there. We just liked each other. Still do. But you know Jonathan. Make no promises and you'll not be disappointed. That was him. I've outlasted quite a few wives." She grinned at Ted.

"And you still have his heart."

"Sure do, as they say in the movies."

Ted watched Cushla's face. Bravado? Wanting it to be like a film? How realistic was all this?

He felt acutely uncomfortable. "Maybe you should have married."

"And become a statistic? Nope. We survived because we were secret lovers. I've always known that." She glanced over at him and he nodded, draining the last of his beer. There was a strange sense of pragmatism in that. Jonathan could have almost anything he wanted. But he could never have Cushla.

Ted held his breath for a second. Now was the time. "You said you picked her. Marcia."

There was a long silence, and Ted had to remind himself to breathe.

"Yes," Cushla said. "There was that."

He waited again. It had to be her decision to open up or not. And there was a part of him that wasn't sure he wanted to know.

Cushla sighed. "I didn't know you very well, Ted. No excuse, but you weren't in the picture."

"When are we talking about?"

"Oh, you know. When Jonathan met Marcia."

Ted nodded. "Through her affair with Oscar?" He wanted that out in the open; that he knew about it.

"Well, yes, there was Oscar...."

He had to ask her. How to put it? "Look, Cushla, you might have more insight into Oscar's state of mind right now. I mean, I'm being hassled by the police. So is Jonathan."

She nodded. "He told me. About you too."

"But not Oscar. As far as I know, anyway. Do you have any suspicions about him?"

"Murdering Marcia you mean?"

Ted took a deep breath. "I'm not accusing him. I just want to know if he was up here when she got murdered, that's all."

Cushla cackled. "You still haven't got over her affair with Oscar. It's time, boy. Let it go."

"It's not that. Truly, Cushla. It's just that nobody thinks about him and he was quite keen on her once-upon-a-time. You know it."

"You're absolutely right. He was. And then everything went belly-up in that regard. So, you are asking if he was exacting revenge all these years later?"

"I know it sounds illogical. But it's also illogical the police are questioning me so intently."

She nodded. "I haven't any idea whether he was up here or not. That's the truth. Jonathan didn't mention it. Lester, either. He didn't stop by here, but he doesn't, anyway. And he wouldn't be at the Bay House with both of them there."

Ted sighed. "Forget it, Cushla. Just my over-active imagination." He tipped the last drop of beer into his mouth. He'd love to ask her about Jonathan and any visit at the time, but he'd promised. "You were saying about Oscar? Way back then? Picking Marcia?"

"Yes. We were worried a bit about Oscar with our plan. Not you. Sorry."

They didn't worry that Marcia was a married woman? Ted felt his irritation building up again. "So you picked her? Chose her?" It still didn't make sense, but he would hate to be so close and still not understand what Cushla was on about.

She nodded. "Marcia was perfect, we thought. Slim and beautiful. Smart. Into the art world and knew what she was on about. She was sophisticated. Not too young. Right for Jonathan. She was the one."

She was bloody confirming it. It really happened. "So you picked her. To be Jonathan's next wife. A trophy wife." Ted found it difficult to keep his voice steady. His mounting outrage threatened to spill over.

"He needed a wife. So many functions to attend, deals to be made. He had a girlfriend, but she was an embarrassment. Not a good scene. He needed to get rid of her, that's for sure."

"Seven years ago," Ted breathed. "We're talking about seven years ago."

"Oscar brought Marcia to dinner one night. Jonathan rang me afterwards and described her, asking whether I knew her from being neighbours here, thinking she might be the one. She was married to you, of course, but she didn't come up here much at that point—you and Holly, but not her. I mean, I knew her, but only slightly. And she was seeing Oscar, so the marriage must have been over, or almost so." She glanced over at Ted. "You didn't figure. I said sorry, Ted. And I mean it."

Ted gritted his teeth. "Go on."

"I did the research. She went to some snooty private school and all that. Grew up knowing the right people. Art gallery membership. Attended openings of bright new artists. Bought and sold a few paintings, but more for other people, and took a small commission. Her own family had no money to speak of, and she didn't marry..." her voice trailed off. She cleared her throat. "Anyway, we decided she would do nicely."

"The right pedigree." This time the bitterness did show in his voice, but he was almost beyond caring. What right had these two to meddle in other people's lives? Were they beyond criticism because someone happened to fit some preconceived idea they had? He crushed the empty beer can into a small aluminium ball.

"So we decided. This time Jonathan was thinking with his head when he picked a new wife. He had a private word with Oscar and told him to butt out."

"And Oscar just went?"

Cushla's laughter echoed around the property. "It cost Jonathan the transport division. Oscar wanted it; man, did he want it. And so Jonathan could make another demand, too. That Oscar gets off drugs. Like, no deal with the transport division until he was cleaner than a Pakuranga housewife's laundry. He had to do rehab." Again that too-loud laugh.

Ted could see it. Making a deal. The two of them making a deal about Marcia. Two business people dealing. The transport division, drug rehab and the wife of that mug, Ted. "And Marcia went along with it?" The bitterness was raw.

"Well, she didn't exactly know about it. Just that Oscar faded from the scene down to rehab somewhere in the South Island and Jonathan turned his charm onto her. Hey, boy, he can do that, you know."

Ted nodded. Oh yes, Jonathan could turn the charm on. And lots of other stuff on, too. "Sorry, Cushla. You can't expect me to feel jubilant about any of this."

"No." She sipped her tea, making a face. "Cold."

"What about you? You wanted Jonathan to marry someone young and – what did you say? – slim and beautiful?"

"He'd had other wives who were younger and heaps more beautiful than me. What we have is beyond that." She spoke with cool conviction.

She got up. "Another beer? Tea?"

"Beer. Thanks." Ted wandered over to the flower bed while Cushla disappeared inside. His unexpressed rage was blotting out thinking, blotting out other emotions as well. Then a word flooded his mind. A puppet. Marcia was a puppet and, bloody hell, so was he. Damn it. He kicked at a stick on the lawn and sent it flying over the flowers and down the bank on the other side. He tossed the crumpled can from hand to hand, then heaved it with a full overhead arm swing towards the sea. That was enough. With a determined tread, he walked towards the drive. And stopped.

He needed to know more. Had to. He turned, grim-faced, back to where Cushla had brought out another can of beer, balancing it on the arm of his chair. He took a deep breath and said as lightly as he could, "So Jonathan charmed Marcia. And persuaded her to marry him." He had to know the full story.

She settled into the other chair. "Marcia was canny too, you know." Cushla turned her dark eyes to Ted. So she knew full well what he was going through. She had decided he had to know and bugger the consequences. He drank deeply, keeping the can in front of his face until he had control of himself once more.

"She got Jonathan to give her half a million dollars outright to buy artwork. Well before they married. Hers, no strings attached. That's the first bit of the money she left to Holly," Cushla said.

Ted noticed she was well informed about the content of Marcia's will. He grunted in response.

"She knew what she was doing, that one." Cushla's lips thinned.

"And my house? The Bay House going to Marcia on our divorce?"

Cushla laughed. "Not my doing. Jonathan saw it as an opportunity. My ancestral land included this bit that happened to be up the road from the Bay House. Jonathan loved the whole idea."

"Idea?"

"If he could get Marcia to keep that house as part of her divorce settlement, he could see me whenever he wanted. As long as the sea wasn't up, of course, wifey would never know." There was triumph in her voice. Ted suddenly realized how Cushla loved the game playing. And Jonathan too, it seemed. Game playing. With people's lives.

"The fishing trips." He glanced at Cushla, who nodded and smiled. "So you never did stop seeing each other when Jonathan married again." His voice was deceptively calm, either from the effects of too much beer or he was regaining some control.

"Yes, we stopped at first. We gave the marriage a flying start, and we didn't see each other for almost a year. It was supposed to be longer, but Jonathan showed up here one day looking like a randy teenager." Her laugh cut straight through him.

The callousness of it all. He couldn't take much more. He had to get out of there.

"Marcia, it seemed, wasn't all that interested in the physical side of marriage," Cushla said with that same hint of triumph in her voice. "And my Jonathan is, shall we say, very interested."

Marcia? Not interested in sex? Not the Marcia Ted had known. He was still acutely uncomfortable, but at least the anger had abated.

Cushla was still talking. "Somehow Marcia figured out something because I was suddenly on the outs with her. Eventually, I think, she actually hated me."

Ted got up so quickly, he knocked the empty can onto the deck and it rolled under the chair. He barely noticed. "I have to think this through, Cushla. I do thank you for being frank, but it's a lot to take in." He backed away from her.

"As you said, it's all ancient history now," Cushla said, her voice now soft. "And Marcia's dead."

"But some of us are being accused of her murder." He couldn't help it. Ancient history is one thing, but the present day was exerting its own pull.

"Just worry about yourself, boy. And don't worry about Jonathan. He's okay. I can attest to that."

Ted stopped and stared at her. Was she admitting she was with Jonathan that day? He still couldn't make himself break his promise. "What do you mean, Cushla?"

"Look, things are going to be all right, boy. You have your house back and good on you. Marcia has passed. Jonathan will get over losing her, just you wait and see. He didn't need her anymore. He's got bigger things to worry about, like this damn cancer. And his retirement." She looked directly into his eyes. "I'm okay. Always have been and always will be." Her laugh turned to a cackle.

Ted went down the steps onto the lawn. His last glance was of Cushla bending down to pick up the empty can, her white hair falling like a curtain around her face. He shuddered and strode off down the drive.

Chapter Eighteen

VIVIEN OPENED THE WINDOW to warm up the interior of the car. The air-conditioning in the Mercedes worked only too well and the tide of frigid air had produced goose bumps on her exposed skin. She couldn't be bothered fiddling with the unfamiliar controls when opening a window would do.

The traffic was unaccountably heavy for a Saturday. Okay, lots of people going places, but slowing to twenty kilometres an hour on the motorway? She could have been back on London's M25. Eventually cars started piling into the slow lane ready to get off at Sylvia Park, just like her, dammit.

She liked shopping at Sylvia Park; good parking, masses of shops and that meant lots of choice. She needed some winter clothes that weren't as heavy as those she wore in London. No need for lined wool slacks here. And she wanted a waterproof coat for the cooler weather that wasn't puffy with padding. She hadn't bothered to bring any of her heavy woollen coats and she had no need of the down-filled winter boots she liked to wear when out walking in the English winter. Besides, she had to admit, having an excuse to do some serious shopping was fun.

The day was glorious, with bright sunshine, blue skies reaching to the horizon and the air was balmy. She knew she should experience the day properly, going for a walk along the waterfront or climbing one of Auckland's many mini-mountains, not heading for a shopping mall. But there was something about being in this car, on her own in this half-remembered city a world away from her troubles in England. A car this size was nice to drive even if parking would be a pain. She prodded at a button which might be the radio, got static and poked it again to turn it off. Jazzy music filled the car. Oh well. The congestion suddenly eased and the powerful motor of the Mercedes kicked in. Sixty, seventy and finally almost up to eighty. Not actually overly fast as it was kilometres an hour, not miles.

Nice enough music. Marcia had obviously liked classic hits. Not Vivien's kind of classic and she was leaning forward to find some truly classical music when the steering wheel went spongy, then freewheeled in her hands. She jabbed frantically at the brake but, with no steering, the car careered onto the shoulder. For a wonderful moment, she thought she'd stay on the road as the brakes bit in, but one wheel caught on the soft soil of the verge and she headed down the bank. Nothing she could do and she knew, beyond doubt, she was going to crash. A scream strangled in her throat as she saw the fencepost a split second before impact.

Sudden silence. She didn't lose consciousness, but the world had changed and her mind had not yet caught up. She struggled to get her breath back. Moments later, a man wrenched at the car door.

"You okay?"

It was only then she felt the searing heat of something very wrong with one leg.

"My ankle," she said. A crescendo of pain caught her unawares, and she became dizzy with its intensity.

"We'll have you out of there in a jif," her rescuer said. Vivien was dimly aware of a crowd that had somehow materialized around the car. Several people held cell phones to their ears. She could hear a siren already. The sun shone into her eyes and she shut them, as if by doing so, she could magic this situation away.

The man reached over and undid her seat belt, but when he tried to ease her towards the door, the pain became unbearable.

"STOP!' she screamed. She took a long juddering breath. "Sorry, sorry," she said, knowing she'd blasted his ear with her reaction. "I'm caught down there. My foot ... it's stuck, and it hurts like hell."

"The ambulance guys are coming now," someone yelled.

Vivien's rescuer straightened, looked discomforted. "I'll leave it to them." He patted her shoulder and stood above her, his role changing from rescuer to protector against the gathering crowd.

Chapter Nineteen

TED WASN'T SURE HOW he got back to Duncan's place. But he walked into the house to find it filled with dinner smells.

"There you are," Duncan called out from the kitchen. "Hope you like pork chops in mushroom sauce."

"Sounds great. Smells great too." Ted took himself off to the loo where he stared at his image in the mirror.

He had been the invisible man. The invisible husband. He'd had intimations of that when married to Marcia. She was the vivacious one, the wild one, the out-going part of their partnership which had fascinated him when they were courting. But her intensity came at a price. He had always been aware that people liked her or loathed her and she was the same with people herself—if something had turned her off Cushla then that would have been it. However, if she'd had any inkling of the story Cushla had just told him, she would have exploded so quickly and so loudly everyone would have known about it. No, she'd had no idea. Small mercies. Marcia had disliked Cushla for more prosaic reasons.

Then it came to him. He had been so focused on Marcia hating Cushla, he hadn't given consideration to the opposite. Did Cushla hate Marcia? That younger, vibrant, intelligent and lively woman Jonathan married? The woman that he came to love, and apparently, love deeply? Ted's heart lurched. Surely, Cushla didn't hate Marcia enough to...

"Where are you, Ted?" Duncan's voice came from the dining room.

After dinner, Ted made all the right noises about the stewed pork.

"Cushla's recipe," Duncan said. "She's a superb cook, that woman. Don't know why she didn't marry again."

"Come on," Ted said with more vinegar than he'd planned.

Duncan sent him a sharp look. "You've been up there?"

Ted nodded. "She's quite something, that one," he growled.

Duncan shot a look of understanding to Ted. "Yes, never underestimate her, and take that as a warning. There's a lot of good in her, but be careful, okay?"

"I hadn't realized the extent of her relationship with Jonathan." Ted was fishing again.

"Water under the bridge now Marcia's gone," Duncan said as he piled the two plates together to take them into the kitchen. "Interesting she told you about it, though."

"Why?" Ted followed him into the kitchen.

"She's probably got an agenda, knowing Cushla. Tread lightly, my friend."

"Got the message," Ted muttered. "I guess we'll find out when she wants us to."

"That's right."

Duncan deftly washed the dishes and Ted dried them. They talked of safer things: of fishing and storms and the weather patterns *el Niño* and *la Niña* until Ted was yawning. He tucked in early, hoping sleep would help sort out his confusion about Cushla.

They spent Sunday morning in Duncan's boat fishing out in the bay. The morning was still, with a few wisps of fog still visible against the dark hills. They caught several medium-sized snapper by the time they called it a day. Ted had one last walk up to the Bay House with Duncan. They talked about the next phase. Rejuvenating the vegetable plots, maybe building a garden shed in the woods beyond the path to Marcia's studio. Friendly, future-oriented talk, both men looking forward to the good times ahead. Ted loaded up his car, ready for the trip south, promising to keep Duncan informed when the transfer of ownership would take place. They parted with loud claps on each other's backs.

After fileting the three fish—one for each of them and one for Duncan's freezer—Ted had left a bit late and by the time he was on the main highway, darkness had fallen. Driving at night, as usual, enhanced introspective thoughts. Marcia had been chosen by Cushla and Jonathan. 'Picked'. Not because Jonathan had fallen in love with her, but because Marcia came out of the right mould. Ted's mind wouldn't, couldn't, get past that point. Cushla said she was chosen with absolutely no thought nor care about the consequences.

But he was too self-aware not to acknowledge the state of his marriage back then. He had been holding in there, but only by a thread. He certainly had no thoughts of leaving her, not with her vulnerabilities, but happiness in the marriage was notable for its absence. She needed him, but when she met Jonathan, that liability was taken off his own shoulders and transferred to Jonathan's. Ted couldn't pretend it didn't relieve him. If he had wanted their marriage to continue, should he have fought for her? The sad truth was he didn't even argue for her, much less lift a little finger. He let her go and felt okay about it. He had never been angry at Jonathan, ironically prolonging his ire at Oscar. But when all was said and done, poor Marcia was just a puppet—they both were puppets—manipulated on very strong strings by expert puppeteers.

In the old days, the drive back and forth between Auckland and the bay was made quicker by listening to a 'talking book'—back then they listened to sets of cds, often borrowed from the library. Now, he supposed, he could get a talking book electronically downloaded to his phone. He smiled. Yes, he'd do that in anticipation of many trips in the future.

Or maybe, use the time for thinking. Holly was obsessing about who had killed her mother. Time for him to take up that challenge, given the police were running around in circles.

Who should he consider? The police always started with relatives. And the closer, the better. So, Jonathan (husband), Oscar (ex-lover and step-son, although that was a laughable relationship and irrelevant), Vivien (ditto step-daughter), Holly (daughter) and himself as an ex. Probably Cushla as a long-time lover/friend of Marcia's husband. Who else? He felt a million miles away from Marcia's ordinary life. She must have had friends. Although, thinking back, there were few who lasted longer than Marcia's enthusiasms. Stargazer, of course, but even she was relegated into a corner of Marcia's mind, only to be contacted when she could be useful. Who did Marcia confide in? He sighed. He'd stick with those he knew about. In the meantime, anyway.

Seriously? First, he could eliminate himself and Holly. Who else? Jonathan because of his frailty. He pulled himself up short. It didn't take muscles to entice Marcia into the rowboat, which she could pull over the sand easily. She didn't like the boat, but if Jonathan in his weakened state wanted to go out in it, she might have had a spark of kindness in her and helped him do so. And the Sangria was their special drink. Could Jonathan have deliberately poisoned it? Difficult to picture the grieving and ill Jonathan as deliberately planning to murder Marcia. But the police had not stopped hassling him. And he was definitely at the bay so Jonathan was not to be eliminated.

Oscar. Ted wanted Oscar on the list, but had to admit it was more because he couldn't stand the man than anything that pointed to him as a suspect. Oscar may have blamed Marcia for breaking up with him all those years ago, but he gained the Transport Division as a reward. And years had passed. Besides, nobody had seen him at the bay. He toyed with keeping Oscar on the list, but recognised it as his antipathy. Any new information that could put him back on the list would be noted, anyway. And then Ted would re-insert his name. With alacrity.

Vivien. Tiny tick in that she admitted to disliking Marcia, but she was not present at the bay, either. And Ted got the feeling Vivien's antipathy towards Marcia was mild, an ocean way from hatred. He compared this dislike to a weak version of his own aversion to Oscar. And knew he could never engender enough negative emotion to contemplate murdering him. Eliminate Vivien from the list.

He'd already eliminated Holly.

Cushla. Again, she disliked Marcia. Certainly more intense and with more reason than Vivien. So a tick for motive. But he couldn't imagine Cushla enticing Marcia into the rowboat. Still, Cushla was at the bay. He'd keep her on the list, although merely pencilled in.

Last was Cushla's son Lester. Not a relative and not very close to Marcia. He would obviously know her. But he was an improbable suspect. Could he have enticed Marcia into the rowboat? A total unknown. Would he have known the Sangria was a special drink? Unlikely. But he was probably at the bay. He would keep Lester on the list because Ted realised he did not know much about him. He remembered the boy Lester. A gawky teen who appeared with his grandmother every now and again. Wait, was he the kid who became flustered, bright red and stammering whenever Marcia spoke to him? Could be.

The dusk had fallen, and stars were coming out. Traffic was light, and Ted had negotiated through one set of roadworks with hardly a glance. He checked the fuel gauge and decided to top up in Wellsford to avoid Auckland prices. And buy a coffee to go.

With poor to non-existent cell coverage at The Bay House, Ted always turned his phone to 'airplane' mode, often forgetting to turn it back until he arrived home in Auckland. This time too. Once home, he saw he'd missed one call. Vivien. He put the phone back into his pocket without calling her back. The last thing he wanted at that moment was to become embroiled in another Jonathan situation, no matter what it was. He grabbed his book and headed for bed.

The next morning, he had put a good two hours into his current project and had stopped for breakfast before he again thought of that missed call. Once he had his coffee in his hand, he saw he had a voice mail message recorded on Saturday night and it was from Vivien, as expected.

"I'm in hospital," she said. "I've wrecked Father's car, would you believe, and tried hard to wreck my ankle as well." Her voice was uncertain. "They're going to operate tomorrow. Kind of a nasty break, they say. Anyway, I'm topped up with morphine and successfully floating, so thought I'd let you know. I'm in Auckland Hospital." There was a pause. "Bye," she said.

Ted screwed his face up. Damn. This was Monday morning already. He looked up the white pages on the internet to get the number for the hospital. They told him she had been discharged that morning. He rang her cell phone.

"Vivien? I just got your message," he said. "Sorry, I..."

"You were away. I know. I figured it out. And do stop saying, 'Sorry'."

"A habit. Sorry," he said with a grin he hoped she could hear. Time to switch the subject. "The op? How did it go?"

"They seem pleased and that's the main thing. It's a bit more comfortable today. I must keep it elevated. You coming over?"

Ted's heart sank. He could have visited her in the hospital if only he'd picked up the message last night. "Where are you?"

"Home. But Father is out. Aveolela's looking after me today. If you're too busy..."

Jonathan was out. His heart bounced back. "Tell her I'll be right over."

Ted swung into the broad but empty drive and parked, feeling as if his car was as exposed as a rock on a bed of sea sand. Lela led him into the sunny conservatory at the back of the house. Vivien was sitting on a settee, one leg propped up on pillows. The room was sun filled, with wide windows thrown open to get the best balance of light and fresh air.

"You look a little, erm, wan," Ted said, feeling awkward given what she'd just been through. But she indeed did look pale and unwell. He bent over to kiss her cheek. It felt cool against his lips.

"No wonder," she said. "I came off the side of the motorway and the car got stopped a tad quickly. Scared the bejesus, to put it mildly."

"For heaven's sake, Vivien, what happened?" He pulled up a steel and plastic stool to sit where she could see him easily.

"I've no idea. I was just happily driving along on my way to do some clothes shopping. Translate that to mean I was in a good mood," she said with a smile. "Then things went pear-shaped. Internal to the car, I mean. My steering. I seem to remember it went all mushy. And then the car was all over the place. It's lucky so much traffic was heading for Sylvia Park; the traffic had slowed. I wasn't going much over seventy. I remembered you're supposed to make yourself totally floppy when you know you're going to crash, but I had no time before I crunched against a fence post. My foot got jammed. Broke both bones just above my ankle. And you should see the bruising where my seat belt held me in." She gingerly touched her chest. "The airbag held my head, luckily. The major damage is the leg."

Ted winced. "What do they say now they've operated?"

"That it should heal fine. They put a couple of screws in to hold it together, so if you ever have to identify an unknown body you think is me, just tell them to x-ray my right ankle."

Ted cringed at the image. The toes on the elevated foot looked swollen and red. Fine bones. Delicate. "Thank goodness you got off so lightly. Hitting a fence post any faster and it would have been far worse."

"I did want to ask you something, Ted," she said. "Something mechanical happened to the steering, I'm pretty sure. Can you discuss it with the guys who look after the car?"

"Of course. Where is it?"

"Towed to the garage Father uses. At the top of the road. Don't know the name of the garage or I'd ring them myself."

"I'll go see them on my way home," Ted said. "The steering. I'm really glad you noticed. Most women..."

"You're not going to make a sexist remark, are you, Mr Frazer?" Vivien spoke over him.

Ted laughed. "Caught. Sorry. I was trying to give you a compliment." Hey, he felt good. Something he could contribute. "Why don't I get onto that straight away?"

"Thank you, Ted. I didn't want to ask Father. He's gone to his solicitor's this morning. Then meeting Oscar. I gather Father's going to make a donation to some charity Oscar's involved in. It's all too much for poor Father. Nobody remembers he's fighting cancer to say nothing about being newly widowed."

Ted felt uncomfortable. "Count me in on that, too. Sorry. I'm not making allowances for him." He let a long breath out. Jonathan. Ted had always been cursed with seeing both black and white of situations and people. Jonathan was a genius at business. Yet, as a man, he was cursed with arrogance and prejudices. A man easy to admire but difficult to like.

"You're fine, Ted. You've been a rock and Father was out of line last time we were here. But give it some time, okay?"

"No prob. I'll keep all he's going through closer to mind."

"One other thing," Vivien asked. "Do you think you could bring me the laptop? There are some emails I must get into. And Lela won't touch it. Techno-phobic."

"Have you told Liam and Stephanie about the accident?" Ted congratulated himself on remembering the names of Vivien's children.

"That's what I have to do. And Gerald, of course. At least it's an excuse not to rush off back to the UK."

Lela showed Ted upstairs to the guest bedroom Vivien was presently occupying. The room was pleasant enough, painted stark white with the only colour provided by the wooden furniture. Leftovers from the Epsom villa relegated to the guest room, he surmised. A small desk was placed against an inner wall, complete with a newish laptop.

"You're a little nervous about bringing the laptop to Vivien?" he asked Lela.

"Don't really want to touch it, Mr Frazer. I might do something wrong."

"Okay, Aveo... sorry, tell me your name again?" The 'sorry' had slipped out. At least he was becoming more aware of it.

She laughed her throaty laugh. "Most people call me Lela. It's just Vivien who can say it right."

"Thanks, Lela. And you must call me Ted. Look, the first thing you do is to shut the top down." He demonstrated it, then lifted the screen back up. "Now you do it." Lela cautiously shut the laptop with a satisfactory click and grinned at him. "Now we're going to pull out the power cord and turn off the mouse. Vivien won't want either where she is right now." He pulled the power cord out of the side of the laptop and plugged it in again. "Your turn." She did the two jobs neatly and quickly, and Ted realized how easily he could underestimate her.

"Is that all?" she said.

"That's it. And she needs nothing but the machine itself. It's got a battery to use in just these circumstances and a touch pad instead of a mouse."

"I can do this, Mr Ted. Anytime. And when she's finished, I bring it up here, poke the bit in at the side again but not turn on the mouse, I guess."

"That's right. As long as the power is plugged in, the battery will recharge." He smiled at her. "I'll give you a beginner's lesson one day if Vivien lets you use the laptop."

"I will ask her. She's a lovely lady."

They trouped back downstairs, Lela carrying the laptop with some élan.

Chapter Twenty

Jim, the owner of the garage at the top of the road, was also the head mechanic. The workshop was neat, not overly large, especially with Jonathan's sad-looking Mercedes taking up one side of the workshop. Ted introduced himself.

"It's just waiting for the tow wagon to take it to a lot owned by the insurance company. It belongs to them now."

Ted nodded. The car was obviously a write-off, the side front horribly mangled, the driver's door buckled and the glass on the front and side gone.

"The chassis?" Ted asked.

Jim shook his head slowly with his lips turned down. "Someone will buy it and fix it up. I wouldn't touch it in a month of Sundays, not even to flick it onto a stranger."

Ted nodded. "Hard to believe Vivien survived the crash so well."

"Very lucky. She must have spun then hit, I figure."

"She told me the steering was faulty."

Jim laughed. "They all say that," he said. "Most likely a bit of inattention – the phone or a text or something happening on the road ahead or behind. Tyre goes off the tarmac and pulls the rest of the car with it. She ended up at the bottom of a small embankment. Easy to see what happened." He raised his eyebrows. "Besides, the steering doesn't go wrong. Just doesn't. Unless you take it apart deliberately, but nobody is suggesting that."

"Could we take a look? I want to report back to Vivien we'd done that."

"Look all you want," Jim said, wiping his hands. "But better do it now because it's being picked up sometime today."

The car was disappearing today? Ted felt he was pushing Jim's boundaries, but the situation demanded it.

Jim wrenched at the bent metal injuring Ted's eardrums as he did so. He propped up the wrecked bonnet on a piece of four by two. Someone yelled for him across the workshop and he headed over there. "Coming!" he yelled back.

He turned to Ted. "Knock yourself out," he said with a grin as he headed to the waiting mechanic.

"But I..." Too late. Jim was disappearing under a car with his employee.

Ted peered at the engine. He was in foreign territory. He wouldn't know the difference between what he was seeing and what he should be seeing. The amount of mechanical knowledge he possessed could fit on the head of a very small pin. The only thing he noticed was that the engine was completely clean, not like the engine under his own bonnet.

He turned to go, waving at Jim who was head down inside the guts of another car. He'd ring the insurance people. Maybe they'd be interested in what Vivien had experienced. Funny the mechanic mentioned that nobody was suggesting anything but an accident. Now such a thought was there, it was difficult to ignore.

He stepped outside. The day was dark with lowering cloud. The first spits of rain splattered on the tarmac.

The day matched his mood.

Vivien balanced the computer awkwardly, aware how seldom anyone ever really used a laptop from a lap. Besides, she preferred using a proper mouse rather than the touch pad and her finger. Maybe she should get her emails on her phone, but she preferred to type. Okay, on with it, in spite of having to sit in one position, which made her ache after only a few minutes. But she had emails to get and send.

Stephanie's name was at the top of the list of received emails. She was a great correspondent, continuously letting her mother have a flavour of her life. This one described a tramp she had taken with her new friends up near Aberdeen for the weekend. Photo attached. There she was, grinning at the camera, dressed for winter in a jacket, scarf and gloves but with spring-green foliage behind. Vivien smiled. Why hadn't she been smart like this daughter of hers when she was the same age? She, too, had been adventurous, fun-loving and gregarious. Why had she swapped making a life for herself like Stephanie was doing for marriage with Gerald? Didn't she realise it was instant middle age?

These were rhetorical questions. She knew why, or rather, she had explored why when she was seeing the counsellor at that time. Security felt important—a left-over from her international childhood when she was uneasily balancing being either a Pom visiting New Zealand or a Kiwi transplanted to the UK. Marriage to an older, big and dominating man seemed the right way to go. Her mother thought Gerald was offering everything a girl could want. And Vivien had suppressed any doubts.

Vivien sent an enthusiastic reply to her daughter. She saved the photo.

The next email was from John, her solicitor. Things were getting tricky. He kept receiving lists of items Gerald wanted to keep, one replacing another. She scanned the latest John had attached to the email. All big stuff. Things she didn't give a hoot about. What she wanted were the personal bits and pieces that felt like hers. The silver her mother had given them for a wedding present and the antique collection of little Toby jugs her great-aunt Ruby had collected, that sort of thing. She replied, asking John a question that had been burning in her head for a few days. If something had come from her side of the family, could she rightly claim it? She told him she didn't care who got the dining room suite, the television or the microwave and if Gerald wanted any of it, so be it. She clicked 'send'. Nuisance though it was, she would have to go to London, no getting away from it. As soon as the ankle allowed her to travel, she'd be off.

She laid her head on the back of the settee and shut her eyes. All this brought to mind the time when she'd contacted the counsellor. A couple of years ago, now, another time when she'd felt she was quietly going crazy. Liam was acting the teenaged lout and Gerald was so busy putting Liam down at every opportunity, he had neither time nor inclination to notice that his wife was not her usual self. She wondered if she was depressed but dismissed it. She was merely disheartened and on the edge of not coping. Who could she go to for support? Her great friend Kate, a lawyer in the city, was in the midst of a new romance; Sally from down the road was overseas and Bridget was not the sort of person to whom she could talk about this kind of thing—Bridget would have told her to pull her socks up or made some other oh-so-helpful comment.

Vivien had found the Fulham Family Counselling Centre in the yellow pages. She'd been assigned to Willa, a lucky match. Willa was middle-aged and motherly. Vivien had found, to her surprise, that telling her life's story was amazingly easy to the right pair of ears, and Willa had turned out to be practical and useful. An earth-mother with brains. That had been the beginning of the process that returned her to New Zealand. She needed her freedom. Not from any real constrictions, just from the expectations of her sheltered and dull life. And from Gerald. Now she could admit to herself that she was colossally bored with the man and always had been. She stretched painfully, and almost knocked her computer off her lap.

Time for the loo. She closed the laptop and slid it carefully down onto the table top. With care she swung her elevated leg off the end of the couch and reached for her crutches. Her arms protested and she almost groaned aloud. That was the problem with having a massive shake-up of your entire body, not just one injured leg, then being required to use your arms for walking afterwards. Everything hurt. Especially the joints of her arms. The physiotherapist thought she had probably held the steering wheel in a death grip when the car went off the road and the impact with the fence post was transmitted through her wrists, elbows and shoulders unabated.

When she stood, she straightened her robe, covering the long purple bruise where the seat belt had held her firm. She let the arm pain settle and her balance correct itself. These little things, rather than the broken ankle, engendered a sense of feebleness and that too added to her misery.

Ted dashed back through the rain to where he had parked his car on the road and got in. He didn't start the engine; he needed to think. Vivien thought the steering was off. But what does she know? She was driving a borrowed car. Traffic was thick. She's a stranger to driving habits in New Zealand. But to think someone had purposely made certain she would go off the road or have an accident? Unlikely.

The pavement in front of the garage where he had parked was a sea of bobbing umbrellas. Several people walking past his car peered in, either curious or making sure he was all right. Ted waved and smiled. He had better get out of here. Although he had intended going back to see Vivien, he really needed to nut this out. He drove home in sunshine that came as suddenly as had the cloudburst, found himself a beer in the fridge and sat outside enjoying the smell of sun-warmed damp earth. His French marigolds made a golden-orange mat, glistening in the sun. They reminded him of the visit with Cushla. Could she be involved? He realized the extent of his mistrust. In fact, he felt she was capable of anything. But sabotaging a car? No, not her scene, although Cushla had sons.... But what had she against Vivien? Marcia, yes, but Vivien?

He reached for his phone.

"Hello, Ted," Vivien said on hearing his voice. "Did you see the mechanics?"

"Saw the head guy there; saw the car. I have a few things to run by you."

"Why don't you pop by? Father is still out."

"But he's expected any time, I bet. No, just let me know when I can come over so I don't run into him," Ted said. "But I have a question or two, if you don't mind speaking by phone for a moment. The car. Who drives it? Always you?"

"Nobody, now. Father said I could use it. This was the first time I'd needed to. Father likes his Range Rover for anything major, except when he goes into the city. Then he takes the Prius—you know, the hybrid battery driven one."

"Didn't know he had one."

"His attempt at being eco-conscious. I have to smile every time I see those two cars parked together, his gas-gobbling mean machine and the Prius. Well, that's Father, a mass of contradictions."

"And the Merc?"

"He's not driven it much. He bought it for himself, but handed it over to Marcia. Lela says Marcia had a little Smart Car she liked far better."

"I know it. That's the only one I've ever seen her drive. Little green job."

"Fluorescent green. Father hated it. I suppose that's why he bought the Merc. To tempt her into driving something a bit safer."

"And you prefer the Merc to the little car, too?"

"Not really, but Father is preserving the Smart Car as if Marcia was coming home tomorrow. Sentiment, I guess."

"So you're the only one driving the Merc."

"What are you on about?"

"Your idea that the steering was off. That's all. The mechanic was busy but I can ring the insurance mechanics tomorrow. I'll let you know if they have an explanation."

Vivien held her hand over the receiver and Ted heard her call, "In here, Father."

"I'll let you go, Vivien. Let me know when the coast is clear."

"Thanks, Ted. Hopefully, see you tomorrow?"

Vivien had the phone back in the pocket of her robe by the time Jonathan came in. He bent to kiss her cheek as usual.

"How's my daughter?" he asked.

"Sore. Grumpy. Bored. How about you?"

"Irritated. Anxious. So what's new?" They both laughed. Then Jonathan's grin faded.

"How do you feel about wearing something I gave Marcia?"

"What do you mean?"

"I gave Marcia a silk robe shortly before she died. It's a lovely thing, but she never had a chance to wear it. I keep seeing you in this old robe you brought from London, and, my dear, it is, in a word, tatty."

Vivien looked down at the robe. A pleasant pale blue. But, yes, worn but still serviceable. "It's an old friend, but I take your point." She smiled at him.

"Can I show it to you?"

"Of course." She didn't quite know what to think about it all but she had no problem if her father wanted her to have it. Unless it was ugly, of course, then she'd have a readymade excuse about why she didn't want it.

Jonathan brought in the robe. It was a softly draping silk in a brilliant Japanese print of flowers and cranes in reds and pinks on black. A kimono.

"You gave it to her as a present?" It was lovely. Wonderful, even. The sort of thing Gerald would never, ever have bought her.

"She spotted it," Jonathan said, lost in the memory, "mentioned it. I went back and bought it for her, but she never wore it. I'm sure she wouldn't want it to go to a charity shop. Try it on."

It fit perfectly, as robes tend to do. Vivien fingered the fabric. "Thank you, Father. It's perfect." And it was. Better, Marcia had never worn it. Had Gerald even once in more than twenty years of marriage got her something like this, maybe she wouldn't feel about him the way she did. But birthday and Christmas gifts were soaps, perfumes if she was lucky. Usually, he made weak excuses why he had forgotten.

Ted looked down at his narrow back garden. Late summer and it was at its seasonal prime with annuals providing pools of yellows, oranges and reds interspersed with beds of blues, purples and whites. He made a mental note to water again tonight.

The conundrum. This whole thing about the car just didn't make sense. Vivien had only been back in the country for a matter of weeks. Why would anyone want to injure her? Or, as it could so easily have been, kill her? Doubtful. Unless that ape of a husband of hers was around. But he was on the other side of the world. Ted drank deeply from his can of beer, then frowned. He needed to have a clear head. He returned to the kitchen and poured himself a big glass of water and drank it down standing at the sink. That would take care of his thirst. Stupid, he should have done that before opening the beer. He returned to his seat outside under the big market umbrella and picked up the can again and took a small swallow. It tasted good but he no longer needed to quaff it down. He laughed at himself. He was such a middle-of-the-road man. The invisible man treading the safe and narrow.

But he wanted to think this through slowly. Vivien driving a car Jonathan had bought for Marcia. Then he knew. This wasn't about Vivien, and it wasn't about Jonathan either. It was all about Marcia. Always had been. Someone had wanted Marcia dead. When the sabotaged car didn't kill her, plans had to be changed to something more direct. She didn't accidentally drown, and it wasn't a spur-of-the-moment thing either. Someone wanted Marcia very dead, one way or another.

Vivien's accident was just collateral damage.

Chapter Twenty-One

Ted woke from a disturbing dream that featured a twisted version of Cushla's face bearing down on him. It left him with a bad taste and he got up before his six a.m. alarm. He couldn't get her story out of his mind. He pictured her up in her toy-sized cottage in its fairy-tale surroundings and thought how nothing appeared to be as it seemed. Underneath that image of the wise old *kuia* was a hard woman.

Mid-morning Ted rang the insurance company. He relayed Vivien's belief the steering had become unresponsive just before she went off the motorway. The woman at the end of the telephone assured him she'd pass on his message to the appropriate person. He came off the phone with no such confidence.

Shortly thereafter, he received a telephone call from Inspector Johnston. They were on their way over yet again.

Inspector Johnston. Bloody bloodhound sniffing up all the wrong trees. Probably peeing on them too. Ted hid his breakfast things in the dishwasher and had the jug on for when the police arrived. If they weren't ready for a coffee, he certainly was. The last thing he wanted was to be submitted to more useless questions.

"Tell me, Mr Frazer, about your relationship with the Fleet family," the inspector said after refusing a coffee.

Ted stifled a sigh. Inspector Johnston always seemed to start off softy softly. "As I have said before, I'm Marcia Fleet's ex-husband." He shut his eyes as he recited the litany. "I was still in contact with her, as you know. My relations with her were ordinary. We had become like brother and sister, sort of—no, more like cousins who had lunch every now and again. I did know her husband from years before but we move in different social circles. I'm acquainted with Oscar Fleet but I'd not actually talked to him in years until after Marcia died. I met Vivien McAvoy only recently."

Johnston sighed heavily. "Tell us your relationships as they stand today." His voice was deceptively mild, bored even, but that sigh told it all.

Ted opened his eyes to meet an unblinking stare. Those brown eyes were amazingly frosty. His urge to present himself as Mr Cool-but-Cooperative took a nosedive. "Please be more precise, Inspector. You're always asking me about things you already know." Ted knew he was being pedantic, but his patience was wearing thin. He left a pause, but the inspector waited him out. He shrugged. "Today. Well, today I've no idea where Oscar is, as I haven't seen or spoken to him since we were up north. Vivien, as you no doubt know, has been in a car accident and is convalescing at her father's home. I saw her yesterday briefly. Jonathan Fleet? We haven't been in contact for some days. We had a slight misunderstanding the last time I saw him. But that was due to circumstances over which neither of us had any control."

"The will." The inspector still stared at him with those unsociable eyes.

"The will," Ted confirmed.

"Do you now have a better idea why Mrs Fleet left you this large legacy?"

"No." Ted remembered the rules about volunteering information.

The inspector shuffled some papers. "And what is your relationship with Mrs McAvoy?"

"As you know, I've only just met her, but we're friendly enough."

"In spite of having fallen out with her father?"

"I said we had a misunderstanding. That's not a falling out in my world." He squared his shoulders. "Look, Johnstone, Vivien is bedridden. As it turns out, the car's a write-off."

Johnston raised an eyebrow. "What explanation do you have for the accident?"

Ted felt backed into a corner. "It seems ... Mrs McAvoy thought the steering was off. I'm worried someone interfered with the car."

"Come on, Mr Frazer. Tell us what you've figured out." Johnston's voice was still mild.

Ted noticed the sergeant. Her eyes were fixed on him too, as if studying his reactions to the questions. Stupidly, he was itching to expand on his ideas, to have a normal discussion about it all. He bit back the thought; talking too much landed him in more trouble than too little. "I guess it all hangs on when the car was sabotaged."

"If, Mr Frazer." Inspector Johnston smiled grimly. "And if it had been damaged by someone, who would do such a thing?"

"I honestly don't know."

"When do you think it happened?"

"No idea."

"And what are the implications of the timing?"

Shit. "Who would be driving."

"Such as who would be driving at the various times you're thinking about? Come on, Mr Frazer, we know you've been speculating."

Ted deliberately relaxed his hands and his jaw. He forced himself to speak slowly. "I gather three people drove that car. Marcia before her death. Jonathan, perhaps, because the car is his. And Vivien latterly. I'm sure you've figured that out yourselves." Damn, he shouldn't have said that last sentence.

"We're just cops. We don't figure. We deal in facts." Johnston turned over a piece of paper. "Have you driven that car, Mr Frazer?"

Ted just shook his head. What was the man on about?

"Have you ever looked at the engine?"

"Not until yesterday. I have little mechanical understanding, Inspector."

"Yet Mrs McAvoy asked you to look at the car. Why?"

"She's laid up, that's all." Nothing like the prospect of being falsely accused to set the heart hammering. If he'd been connected to a lie detector, the reading would be off the scale.

"Did you sabotage the car?" The brown eyes bore into Ted's.

He held steady, but his stomach did a flip. In their sights yet again. "No, I have never sabotaged that car, nor any other car. I would have no idea how to do so. Not my field."

The inspector stood up and motioned to the sergeant who flicked shut her notebook. "Thank you for your time, sir. We'll be in touch."

Not a mention of fingerprints or boats or murder. Ted swayed on his feet. He picked up his mug of cold coffee and threw it down the sink. Every time he had to talk to that man, he felt as if he'd been sucker-punched.

Vivien rang after Ted's late lunch. "Have you finished your day yet?"

Wonder of wonders: she remembered his schedule. "Yes, all done. Is the coast clear?"

Vivien's laugh came down the wire. "Come on over. Lela will give us some of her special cheesecake when you get here."

Ted mulled over Cushla's story as he drove to visit Vivien. It seemed as if Marcia's wedding had been a sham. The beginning of her marriage was nothing if not a scam. Poor Marcia. Or was she sufficiently self-absorbed that she never figured it out? But Holly had said her mother had not liked Cushla. That fitted with what Cushla had said. For once, he hoped Marcia had been oblivious to the nuances.

Then he had a thought that made him smile. What if Marcia's motivation in leaving him the Bay House was not as pure as he had thought? By giving him the Bay House, she was effectively cutting Jonathan off from easy access to Cushla. Food for thought. But, as he knew from long experience, it was a fool's game to second guess Marcia.

Vivien had put the phone down only to notice that her hand was shaking. It was almost like... what? Danger? Surely not. Excitement? Couldn't be. It was just that Ted was kind and reliable and...; besides, she was doing nothing wrong. Nothing. She picked up her book again, but closed it after pretending to read the page. She stared out the window where she could see the tops of the bamboo jiving in the breeze.

She had little experience with male-female relationships other than a few romances when she was at university and that special casualness she affected with the husbands of her friends. She'd been the recipient of a few minor flirtations over the years, but they were always in the context of safety as a married woman.

Vivien had met Gerald soon after finishing university when she was struggling with her first job in London. He was older and going through a divorce at the time. She felt both sorry for him and attracted to his easy self-confidence, a man who knew where he was going and why. His first marriage had been unwise when she looked at it from the perspective of her 22 years. And when it was obvious he was interested in making her the next Mrs McAvoy, she was more than flattered. She concluded she must have more going for her than the ex-Mrs McAvoy. Her middle-aged self now saw she'd confused this boost to her ego with being in love.

Vivien put thoughts of Gerald to one side. Ted was no Gerald, thank goodness. And besides, he was close to becoming a friend. What she needed was a friend; she did not need the complications of a lover. She picked up the book and again tried to read.

Lela was an excellent cook. The cheesecake was heavy, moist and not overly sweet, just how Vivien liked it. Was Ted enjoying it as much as she was? She caught his eye when his mouth was full and he gave her the thumbs up sign. She nibbled at her piece and felt like a bright butterfly wrapped in pink, red and black silk. Her leg was still elevated, but she knew she was looking good.

"I've had the police over this morning," Ted said. "Asking me if it was me who'd sabotaged the car." He spoke matter-of-factly. No use bothering her with his own exasperation at the police, but otherwise he filled her in on the details.

"Us too. Father was quite agitated about it."

"You really think it was sabotage?" He stared at her as he said it

"Hard not to," she said. A simple statement. She paused. "What I can't understand is why the police are treating you so badly. After all, you work for them. They should know your character."

Ted shrugged. "I get along really well with the fraud team. They respect my opinions; ask for me whenever there's an interesting IT job, all that sort of thing. But it certainly hasn't filtered over to the homicide squad."

"They should know you have integrity. That you would never…' Vivien realized she was getting indignant on Ted's behalf and calmed herself down. He was a big boy; he could undoubtedly look after himself.

"Thanks, Vivien. For the support, I mean." He smiled briefly and cleared his throat. "Where's Jonathan?"

"Doctor's appointment. He had a scan the other day."

"Scan for what?"

"To see if the cancer has spread. Routine for the next three or four years. Poor Father. He suffers every time he's about to have one. Probably the actual explanation why he was rude to you the other day." Although as a child Vivien had learned not to decipher her father's moods, she thought this a reasonable explanation. Aspects of her father reminded her of Gerald, never giving away anything that might come back and bite him.

"Give me the nod when I should talk to him, will you, Vivien? When you think the time is right?"

"Of course. The last thing I want is my two favourite men having problems with each other." She smiled at Ted to keep things light.

After the afternoon tea things had been cleared away, Ted cleared his throat. "I'd like to change the subject drastically."

"Of course." Vivien made a moue.

"How did Marcia and Jonathan get along? Generally, I mean."

"Pretty well, amazingly enough," she said. "Given the disparity in their ages and their divergent interests."

"I always had the idea that Marcia liked her life with Jonathan or, if she didn't, she hid it well." Ted got up and stood by the back window, which looked over the compact back garden dominated by a swimming pool. Vivien guessed what he was thinking: neither Jonathan nor Marcia were interested in gardening, a problem fixed by hiring a landscape maintenance firm. Sterile, but everything in order. No annuals, little colour, just neat shrubs bordering a weed-free lawn against the backdrop of the tall bamboo hedge stretching up to the heavens. Smart, tidy, sophisticated even, but dull.

Vivien brought her mind back to Ted's comment. "Me too," she said. "I put it down to Father being besotted. Bent to her every whim."

"Did he?" Incredulity showed in his voice.

"He bought and bought and bought for her. Investments in her name, art that's stored in a vault because it's too valuable to hang anywhere, a part interest in a hotel, for heaven's sake. In Italy. It's a little gold mine, according to what Marcia told me. Boasted to me. Stuff Father had no interest in, but if Marcia crooked her little finger, soon it was theirs. No ... wrong. Hers. His excuse was that he would pre-decease her and Fleet Corp would go to Oscar and me. He wanted his precious Marcia to continue with the lifestyle she was rapidly becoming accustomed to and he wanted no argie-bargie over his will. What he spent before he died had nothing to do with either of us heirs."

"I had no idea," Ted said, gazing out the window. "This must be the portfolio mentioned by the solicitor. So Holly is now a wealthy young woman. It also explains why your father had been disturbed the mutual wills he had constructed were no longer valid." He shook his head, smiling. "Marcia looking after her daughter. It all fits."

Vivien nodded. Instead of a chunk of her father's considerable fortune reverting to him, it had passed out of his control, mostly to Holly but also to Ted himself. She thought it just fine—the Ted part in particular.

But that Marcia. True to type. Machiavellian Marcia.

Chapter Twenty-Two

Vivien sighed. "Not that I'm objecting, Ted, but everything that Marcia wanted, she got. Eventually anyway."

"That part sounds like her all right. But maybe it was just bloody-minded persistence on her part. That was part of her nature. I should know." Was he actually becoming defensive of Marcia? He told himself to settle down; he was the one who introduced the subject.

"Don't get me wrong. I saw her manipulations clearly," Vivien said. "She tried it on me and on my dear ex. Had better luck with him than with me, I can tell you. He was quite taken by her in the beginning."

"Marcia and Gerald? Hard to believe."

"She was a beauty and she could be charming. He liked to think women found him attractive. However, she quickly put him down, and it wasn't all that gentle." She found herself frowning and smiling at the same time. "Early days. Marcia didn't have to do much more than hint to Father oh-so-sweetly, and whatever she wanted magically appeared. Until lately, of course."

"Lately? What changed?" Ted turned so Vivien could see his face.

"Father got cancer. That's what changed. For a while there she had to be nursemaid. He had a pretty rough time with his chemo. And Marcia hated to be at his beck and call, hated the ugliness of his illness. But Father didn't want anyone else. That's when I really started becoming angry with her. Take, take, take. Then, when he really needed her, she wasn't there for him. Either emotionally or physically." She grimaced. "Sorry, Ted. I know you've still got feelings for her. But that is just the way it was."

Ted frowned. "You're wrong. I've no feelings left for her. I got over her years ago." He said it flatly.

"Oh, yeah?" Vivien drawled in a fake American accent.

"Does getting annoyed at her mean I still have feelings?"

"Of course. Feelings are feelings, both positive and negative, you ninny," she said. She gave him a half smile.

"Hardly the same, though." He sat back in the strange metal and plastic chair across the coffee table from where Vivien was reclining. He stretched out his legs. "If so, that means you have feelings for your ex, too."

"I do and I admit it," she said. "But they're fading every day. I'm dreading having to go back to the UK to sort things out because everything will be stirred up again. Somehow, the longer I stay here, the more detached I'm getting. I need the distance, both physically and emotionally, to do the right thing. In a way, it's the rest of my life that's at stake." She inwardly berated herself; she had not meant to talk about Gerald again. How often had she been bored silly by the newly separated who had only one topic of conversation? "Anyway, back to Marcia and Father...."

"Yes, Marcia and Jonathan. They had their travelling in common. And art."

"Both of which took masses of Father's money. Talk about lifestyle!' It was difficult keeping her own resentment at bay.

"But you say he was a willing participant."

Vivien sighed. "Ignore me. I could barely stand the woman. I was appreciative that she could buck Father up when they first married. And she gave him some excitement and maybe even happiness before he got cancer. They really did have fun on their explorations. They travelled maybe two or three times a year. And not just little get-aways, but long visits. Did you know they'd been to China, to Vietnam and they even took a river trip in Borneo?"

Ted grinned. "That's not the half of it. South Africa, Chile, Mexico, Peru. I could go on and on. Wonderful places. And I've seen every last one of their photos, I bet."

"Oh, yes. Your luncheons at Pierre's. You see? Marcia kept your involvement from fading. I bet she had a calendar, so your lunches were perfectly spaced, not too soon, not too long in between."

Ted's eyes narrowed. Vivien could sense how uncomfortable he felt when his own relationships were being examined. "Marcia had an eye for photography too. I tried to encourage her," Ted said in a heavy-handed attempt to get the topic onto safer ground. "She had talents, you know. Just never got her head straight about following through."

"Poor little Marcia."

"Come on, Vivien. The woman is dead. We should be trying to figure out how and why. Your accident, for instance. Was that an attempt on Marcia's life?"

Vivien was brought up short. "Marcia's? You out of your mind?" She fought for composure. "Does everything have to come back to Marcia?" She turned her head away. Dammit. Somehow, she can't even have a bloody car accident without Marcia taking over.

Ted said nothing, and the silence dragged. He slowly got up, looking at the door. "I said I'd teach Lela basic computer skills. Can I borrow your laptop for lesson one?"

Vivien struggled to keep her voice even. "Be my guest."

Ted couldn't get away fast enough. He shouldn't have mentioned his theory about Marcia. He'd thought it would have reassured Vivien she wasn't in danger. Stupid.

Lela was bright eyed and enthusiastic. She had quickly learned to switch on the required bits. By the end of the lesson she could get into the email account Ted had set up for her on one of the free servers, open an email, hit reply and agonizingly type out a short answer. Ted had always liked teaching and Lela was quick.

"I'm going to recommend something, Lela. Something most people don't do but should do right at the start. Take a short typing course. We'll find one close by. Community classes, that sort of thing."

"I don't have the money...," she said, lowering her eyes.

"My treat," he said firmly. "But we'll have to arrange for enough time off for you to go to the classes. We'll ask Vivien."

When Ted re-entered the sunroom, he saw Vivien had fallen asleep, a book still in her hands. He smiled at Lela without speaking, and they tiptoed out.

Ted did not dismiss what Vivien had been implying. She was a perceptive woman. Did he have feelings for Marcia? Probably, although most were of the negative sort. He didn't mind that, not really. What he did mind was that Marcia had stolen his dreams of the future. That was important. Everyone should have dreams and somehow he no longer did – not since Marcia's behaviour precipitated their divorce. A dream stealer. Yes. Even the thought of it made his blood boil.

Ted didn't drive home, but turned down to the seafront instead. He parked at St Heliers Bay and got out. He needed some wind in his hair and some far horizons to pull at his eyes. The beach was quiet for a sunny afternoon, but he put that down to lower temperatures and the feeling that autumn was coming. He walked quickly at first, as if to sweat out his toxic thoughts.

Cushla painted a picture of long-term affection between herself and Jonathan, of conspiring to find a suitable wife—a trophy wife—who could enhance his standing in business and in the art world. If it weren't so cold-blooded and it hadn't affected other people, he could understand. A time-honoured way of picking a wife, still common in many cultures and, until comparatively recent times, in European culture. He let himself get freshly angry at the whole scenario and he increased his walking speed.

On the other hand, Vivien was painting a very different scene. Jonathan, the devoted husband, who delighted in pleasing his much younger wife. Indulging her then wanting only Marcia to nurse him when he became ill.

Ted's footsteps slowed as he came to the beach at Kohimarama. He swung off the footpath and headed for a park bench looking out over Auckland's outer harbour. The volcanic Rangitoto Island loomed dark and forbidding on the horizon, but several cheerful spinnakers lightened the scene offshore.

Forget what others are saying, he told himself, and he set to examine his own impressions. All those years ago, Marcia had been his willing bride, but she became bored; she should never have married a staid nerd like himself. Years ago, he had accepted that as the truth. Her new life with Jonathan opened up the world. She loved buying and selling art; again, one of her talents. She adored their trips to outlandish places, thought out the itinerary and made all the arrangements. Another career she could have had: a travel agent. Ted knew she also loved the social side of her marriage to Jonathan: dinner parties, people over for cocktails, entertaining overseas visitors. She had told Ted how wonderful it all was, careless about how such statements affected him. And they did affect him. He went through a long period of feeling like a failure. Was Vivien right? Had he still not let go?

He was acutely aware that he really was an invisible man. Or, to put it slightly less negatively, a background person. And Marcia needed more. Then the big question—what did he feel once Marcia had left? He could honestly say that part of him was relieved and part of him aggrieved. He settled into his lonely and work-centred existence shortly after she took off. Punctuated by lunches at Pierre's, of course. He had the feeling, in retrospect, that Marcia may well have thought she was injecting a bit of needed sophistication into his lacklustre life. He let his head slump into his hands, no longer seeing the beach and the blue sea, the primeval pohutukawa trees casting their shade onto the grassy verge, no longer noticing the wind in his hair, but sinking into that self-absorbed state he had struggled with back when Marcia had first left him.

He abruptly sat up. God, how he let that woman affect him. Vivien was absolutely right. He had not been rid of her, even now she was dead. The problem was, he had absolutely no idea how to exorcise ghosts.

He got up, stretched and power-walked beyond the Kohi beach, only stopping when Mission Bay appeared around a corner. He turned on his heel and picked up the pace again back towards his car, lifting his face to the sun, convinced there were changes that would have to be made in his life. His thoughts turned to Vivien. Such an attractive woman.

Damn, he had behaved like an oaf earlier.

Chapter Twenty-Three

HOLLY RANG. "DAD," SHE said, and Ted knew immediately she was going to say something he wouldn't like. "I'm going to stay here to study this year." She was a little breathless, emphasizing Ted's misgivings.

"Why? You always say you can study better at home away from the social distractions of Dunedin." Holly's study break started at the end of May before the semester exams. These exams would be her finals.

"Yeah, you're right; the social stuff does get in the way. And, well, I do have a social thing...." Her voice petered out.

"Surely you can come up after your social thing?"

"It's awkward, Dad. It's a weekend. So too short to come up before and too short and too close to exams afterwards. I'll just give it a miss. Sorry."

Ted looked forward to Holly's visits. He was especially wanting her home this year to explore some of the Marcia questions.

"I can't say I'm not disappointed, Holly. I thought with your mother's death ... you know, we could sort of talk it through." There was a dead silence at the other end.

"I knew you'd say that," she said, a bit of her old adolescent rebelliousness coming through. "Or something like that. Dad, please."

"What about Easter? How about you skip that thing you do each Easter and come home instead?"

"That's next week, and we have all our arrangements in place." She sighed. "Bloody hell, Dad, why do you make me feel so guilty?" She paused, then Ted heard her say, "Oscar said you'd react that way," and she hung up.

Oscar? Ted sat down with a thump as if he'd been clobbered. What was Oscar to Holly? He started to punch in Holly's telephone number before he stopped himself. No, she would phone back. Her anger never lasted. But until she did, he knew he'd have trouble concentrating. He closed his computer and headed to the garden, taking the phone with him.

Sure enough, he was only halfway through weeding the bed of marigolds when the phone rang.

"Sorry, Dad. I shouldn't have spoken to you like that," his daughter said. "I was really annoyed that my routine had to be changed then took it out on you."

"What is the social thing?" Ted asked, holding his breath.

"Oscar has a convention in Queenstown that weekend at some extravagantly expensive place. He's flying to Dunedin, renting a super car, then picking me up and we're going up there for a fancy dinner and evening on the Saturday night. He's going to drive me back on Sunday."

Driving with him?

"Holly, you can't! He was your mother's.... No! He broke up our marriage, forgawdsake! I forbid it, do you hear me? You are not allowed to meet that, that despicable man!"

"Shut up! Just keep quiet," Holly was saying and maybe had been saying well before he had drawn breath. "I will not—do you hear me?—will not be told who I can or cannot see. Do you understand?"

"Holly, stop this nonsense. He destroyed me, that man. Destroyed your mother's marriage. Which meant she found someone else. And my beloved Bay House was taken from me. All to do with that vile man."

"You're not listening to me, Dad."

"And there's more, Holly. You have to know something about Oscar's history. He was into drugs once upon a time. I've just found out. Driving with him? I don't think...."

"Don't, Dad. I can tell if someone's drugged up by now. There's more drug use at uni than in half of the rest of the population."

"It's just that...."

"Dad. I'm twenty-two years old. Not sixteen. Okay?"

Ted remembered the times he had to bite down his anxiety about his daughter, the boys she dated, the times she was out too late, the defiance when he tried to punish her by imposing what she called 'house arrest', all the teenaged angst that parents have to cope with. This was just another one. And she was fully adult, he reminded himself. It was just that despicable man. Oscar, of all people on the entire earth.

He took a long breath. This was un-winnable. "Okay. My turn to apologize. I'm just surprised you're involved with Oscar, that's all." He tried to keep his voice light.

"I'm hardly involved with him, for heaven's sake. It's just a great opportunity. It's like going into another world, another planet. Compared to my life as an impoverished student, I mean. If you were my age, you'd know that."

He didn't remind her she was far from impoverished, not now and certainly not when probate for Marcia's will went through. "You're right. I would have jumped at the chance too. But be careful of that man, Holly. I mean it."

"Don't worry. I can take care of myself."

Ted laughed. "You've been saying that since you were thirteen."

Holly laughed too, and the tension lessened. "Anyway," she said. "I was ringing to say I will come back for the first study week. But I'll really have to be head down because of taking that time off during the weekend—none of our afternoon lattes this time, okay?"

"I'll collect them and you can sip while studying. That suit you?"

He came off the phone feeling better about the situation between them but was doubly disturbed at Oscar turning up in Holly's life. How could she have anything to do with a man who had caused her parent's marriage to break up? Besides, he hadn't eliminated Oscar as a suspect in her mother's murder. Not completely, anyway.

Oscar and Marcia. Yes, it still made him angry. What would have happened if they hadn't met? Would Marcia have been looking for someone else? That stopped him. Had he hit on the truth of the matter? Another uncomfortable truth: when Marcia was finished with something, it would never be re-kindled. Maybe Oscar was merely an indicator she'd moved on. Oscar, with his flashy car and suave manners, had appeared. But eventually she discarded Oscar, too. He shouldn't forget that. Marcia switched from Oscar to Jonathan. A man like Oscar never forgives that sort of thing. Yet it was years ago—the same argument Ted had used to explain why he shouldn't be an object of interest to the police.

The problem was, Ted argued to himself, Oscar was such an odious person. Big question: did he have such a yawning character deficit he was capable of murdering somebody? Put that way, he shouldn't dismiss Oscar.

He pulled himself up. Truth be told, Jonathan had many of the same characteristics.

Oh.

According to Holly, Marcia had been acting out of character. Was Marcia readying herself to finish it with Jonathan? Once Marcia had accepted she'd be on her own sooner rather than later because of Jonathan's cancer and, given Marcia never deviated from pursuing a goal, was she incapable of waiting for Jonathan's coming death? And Marcia always looked for distractions—excuses really—from unpleasantness. If sickness and death of your husband could be described as merely unpleasant.

And Jonathan? He was pathetically grateful for Marcia's slightest willingness to tend to him. Grateful, not murderous.

Holly and bloody Oscar. Maybe she just saw an older man with suave manners, good suits and an awesome car. In spite of the morality of the situation, Ted couldn't blame Oscar for trying it on. Why wouldn't a single man not want an attractive young woman almost half his age on his arm? Half his age.... Oh, oh. A thought came unbidden: Pauline.

Ouch.

Vivien stretched out on the chaise longue in the conservatory. She brushed her hand along the edge of the thin pad over its metal base. Velvety smooth. It was amazingly comfortable for such a strange-looking piece of furniture. Very Marcia, in fact. Modern to the point of ridiculousness, but supporting the bod at all the right points. An uninjured bod, of course.

Marcia. Vivien kept stumbling over her. She had been such an annoying woman in so many ways, destroying everything that had come before so she could put her own stamp on Jonathan's life. Of course, that was a natural inclination for second wives—or thirds or fourths—but intensely irritating for all that. Her father, of course, was the exception. He loved the changes because they had been made by his beloved. And, ostensibly anyway, the changes were for him. Phoenix-like, the end result had produced a lifestyle that very much suited him. Back then. What about now?

The house was silent. Not just because she and Lela were the only ones home, but because there were no creaks or cracks, no subtle shifting of wooden floors or flexing of walls or roofs when in an old house, as if it periodically had to stretch its stiffened joints. Vivien pushed thoughts of their old villa aside. This glass and concrete monolith wasn't alive. Double glazing of thick greenish glass kept sights and sounds either firmly inside or out. Mostly outside. The floors were either tiled or carpeted and there was little, unless stiletto heels were involved, that warned of another's approach. Nothing so warm as wood could be found anywhere downstairs. She knew all mementos of the pre-Marcia era were in that specially designed storeroom at the back of the garage.

Vivien desperately missed the old villa in Mount Eden, had, in fact, made inquiries to the real estate company when it was put up for sale, but it was all too late. It had been an elegant old lady, built in the latter part of Queen Victoria's reign. She suddenly had a vivid image of sitting in late afternoon sunlight with her then boyfriend. They sprawled on the curved set of steps that led up from the half acre of garden, his too-long legs in jeans that must have been sweat-inducing and she was wearing her favourite pink shorts. The garden was green and gold, overflowing with the sound of cicadas. The steps led up to a shady porch with a squeaky swing, faded chairs and wooden floors which sang at every step. Her bedroom had been at the back, looking over the vegetable plot and a bank of tall hibiscus bushes bursting with reds, pinks and oranges year round. Nothing so untidy grew around the glass boxes here. Sterility rules. Vivien sighed as Lela brought in a cup of tea.

"Didn't hear you coming," she said unnecessarily. "Thanks."

"I'm not stopping. I'm doing a meringue." Lela usually brought in a cup for herself. Vivien enjoyed these moments in her long day where she could be caught up in the doings of Lela's large family.

Stupid leg. Heal, dammit.

The bruising across her chest was no longer sore, although the multi-coloured effects were more than evident under her robe. She was still stiff, especially arms and hips, but that could be due to the necessarily awkward elevation of her leg more than the accident, *per se*. She shifted and twisted, constantly trying to get comfortable on this chaise longue day bed. She slithered down, bending her good knee and propping her head on a pillow. Crazy accident. Just when she had so much to organise. So much to handle in getting ready for her divorce. Gerald. John the lawyer. The children. Too much to figure out. Well, at least she had plenty of time to do some thinking. But in her life, thinking preceded action each step of the way. And action was now precluded. She pulled the Japanese robe around her and scowled. Life was becoming a bore.

She finished the tea and put the cup down on its matching saucer on the glass-topped table. Most of the furniture was metal, high-grade plastic or glass in this house. Softened with cushions, of course, but that was almost an afterthought. She let her head loll back. Surely she could put this time to good use. Thinking time. She had always felt she didn't have enough of it.

She pulled herself up, both physically and figuratively. Okay. Gerald. He had been so much a part of her life for so long, it was sometimes difficult thinking what life could be like without him. As an exercise, she decided to weigh up the good and the bad. First the good. He was a decent provider ... to a point. Had she been allowed to work, they'd have enjoyed a better lifestyle. Allowed. She firmly put the word to one side. This first list was about positive things. Their house in Fulham was pleasant. They had bought it with money she had been given on her twenty-first by her father. The house swallowed the lot and then some. But, without a job, she no longer had any money of her own. Stupid, stupid, stupid. Over the years, they had the house done up and Gerald had paid for the maintenance. She never had any complaints about the house. She could talk Gerald into a new dishwasher more easily than a holiday in Italy.

Stop it. Nothing negative. Yet.

What else? The kids, of course. They were undoubtedly a combination of both of them. Stephanie, a little conservative like her father and Liam, for all his wildness in his teens, was turning out to be an interesting young man now.

Going back to the UK would allow her to spend time with both. Which brought up the question of the division of the house. Surely she was more entitled to it than Gerald? But John-the-solicitor had said no. Best to sell and divide the profits. Cleaner. Could she talk to her father about buying Gerald out? But that led to the larger question of whether or not she wanted to maintain a house in London. Her father might have money, but she didn't. Life was stupidly complex. Which was why she'd been making these abortive attempts to get a job. In a finance house again? In the cold light of day, it seemed ridiculous. She was a middle-aged matron with her only work experience dating from her twenties. Dismiss the thought. Her father? Maybe she could be a receptionist or a file clerk somewhere in his empire. Or data entry? She had always enjoyed numbers.

She jerked herself back on track. Gerald's positive traits. He didn't do drugs and his drinking was fairly contained. Mostly. He wasn't too overweight; he didn't make disgusting noises or smells or have any other habits she couldn't tolerate. But definitely not sexy. Not that it seemed to bother him much. She tried to remember when they last made love. Maybe a couple of months before she came to New Zealand? Not that it mattered. The plain fact was, she no longer found him attractive. Hadn't for years. It was difficult to overlook the constant nagging, the sour faces, the criticisms, and, when suddenly groped, how impossible it was to turn on lust. No. 'Difficult to overlook' was not the phrase; it had become impossible. It made her doubt she was still a sexual being. Lots of women her age weren't. Something to be explored. She smiled to herself. The thought produced the faintest hint of a physical reaction. Did that prove anything? Maybe there was something deep inside ready to be awakened. A glimmer of something? Maybe.

Ted rang Vivien. Before she could say anything, he said, "I have three important words to say to you, Vivien. You. Were. Right. Absolutely."

"That's four," she said.

"Scrub the 'absolutely'."

"You coming over?"

Ted looked at his half-finished gardening job. "Yup. In an hour or so?"

"Good. Then you can explain to me what I was right about."

"Oh, it was just..."

"No. Save it, please. I'll enjoy the anticipation."

Chapter Twenty-Four

Holly had left a message for Ted to ring her. "I've been thinking about Mum's drowning," she said, once he'd rung back. "Specifically, who could possibly want her dead?"

"The big question." The obvious question.

"What about Cushla? You don't seem to be taking that possibility at all seriously."

"It's not that I haven't thought about it," he said cautiously.

"You've dismissed her. I can tell. And she deserves pride of place. Gramps was nearing death and she wasn't going to get a penny. With Mum gone, she'd be sitting pretty to be the caring friend. And in a good place to get him to include her in his will."

"I really don't think she's a woman motivated by money, Holly." He told her his theory about Vivien's car accident in Marcia's car. "It fits, Holly. If the car was sabotaged to cause an accident – and that's a big 'if' – then it would much more likely be for when Marcia took it out. Who would know Vivien would be driving that particular car? And, by the way, Cushla has no ability to carry out sabotaging a car."

"Sometimes you're so blinkered, Dad," Holly cried. "Remember those wooden chairs you described to me?"

"At Cushla's? What about them?"

"Who made them?"

"One of her sons. Lester, I think. Why?"

"And Lester is, what ... in his thirties?"

"About that."

"And grew up in rural New Zealand?"

"You know that, Holly. Get on with it. What are you trying to say?"

Holly sighed loudly as if to underline her reactions. "If Lester is a typical Maori male, brought up in the wops, he can turn his hand to anything. Making his beloved old mother some wooden deck chairs, fix anything with number eight fencing wire and mess about with tractor engines..."

"And cars." Ted nodded to himself. "Okay. Point taken. Lester or one of his brothers could be involved. But only if the car was the result of deliberate damage aimed at Marcia."

"Precisely. So is Cushla on your list?"

He turned his head to look out the window. Maybe they would finally get some decent rain. Heavy clouds to the west. He suppressed a sigh. "Yes, if you want. My mythical list. I have her on the list for several reasons, not the least because I've found out Jonathan had more than a friendship with her for years. Decades. I think he treated her badly, all told. And, in the same context, there are some questionable aspects of how he treated your mother too. His record with women leaves a lot to be desired. And that son of Cushla's. Involved in drugs when he was a teenager and not just smoking. He grew and supplied marijuana and went to prison for it."

"Yeah, I remember," Holly said. "Let me know when you have something new, okay?"

Ted came off the phone thinking he should find out a bit more about Cushla and her strange story so at variance with his own understanding. But Cushla committing a pre-meditated murder? That was a difficult concept. One of her sons carrying out such an act on her behalf? Stranger things had happened, but usually in families that were way beyond dysfunctional. Weighing it up? Unlikely.

Mind you, buried and long festering resentment about how Jonathan treated Cushla over the years could have influenced a young man as he grew up.

Oh.

Putting Marcia's death to one side for the moment but thinking of the steering fault, Lester could have been carrying out his own agenda, not Cushla's. Could her mechanically competent son, a young man who often made the journey back and forth between Auckland and the north, have decided he would exact revenge on someone he'd come to hate because of how his mother had been treated over the years?

After all, who owned that fancy car? Jonathan.

"I've no idea what to do about it," Ted said after explaining it all to Vivien. "For years, literally years, I'd thought I was not only over Marcia but pleased to be so. But she does come to mind often. Too often, as you pointed out." Again, he was talking with his head in his hands, hunched over while sitting on the cushioned metal seat near where Vivien was half lying. The afternoon sunlight was slanting into the room giving bright evidence that the summer was segueing into autumn.

"I wonder if talking about her would help or hinder," she mused. "When it's more than obvious a person is trying to avoid a topic, psychologists always get the person to talk it through, don't they?" She paused before continuing. "You felt relieved, you said, when Marcia left?"

"I did, yes, and ever since I always felt Marcia was using me, always asking me to do things for her, sort of paying me with lunches I didn't always enjoy." He felt the frustration welling up yet again. Manipulated. Why hadn't he refused? That was a question to ponder some time.

"Are you saying you were caught in a pattern you couldn't fight?" She shifted her position so she could look right at Ted's face.

"A spider's web." Ted immediately remembered that female spiders ate their mates. Maybe he should be pleased he hadn't been killed, metaphorically at least. But he had been exposing himself to the same danger every time he had one of the Pierre lunches. He told Vivien this idea.

She looked up at him, her eyes bright. "That's probably an insight. Maybe you should figure out what part of you she ate." Vivien giggled. "Seriously, though, maybe you should talk about her. See if you can free yourself."

"Talk about what?"

"Your last question. How about coming back to that? You asked me how Father and Marcia got along. We've talked about it before and I rabbited on about what I knew. What did you observe from your angle?"

"The reason I asked you about their relationship was that I got a totally different view on it from Cushla."

"Cushla? But you promised...."

"Oh, I was very careful not to ask whether Jonathan visited her that fateful day. I keep my promises even when I don't agree with them. And she said nothing on her own. Not really anyway."

"'Not really' is a prevarication, my friend."

"She said, and I quote, 'Jonathan will be okay. I can attest to that.'"

Vivien shifted her position yet again. "Yes, I see what you mean. She could simply mean that she knows his character and has faith that he'll be okay."

"I did get the impression it was more than that, but those were the actual words. I've played them over and over in my mind."

"You were saying that Cushla has a different take on their relationship?"

"Yes, very different. She told me that she and Jonathan together chose Marcia for his next wife. Chose her. Picked her." He could hear his voice rising and took a deep breath. "Marcia had the creds they thought a wife for Jonathan needed.

They interpreted her dalliance with Oscar as a green light that her marriage was foundering and she was open to something new."

Vivien stared at him then looked away. "Oscar? Yes, that. Embarrassing."

Ted pulled at a thread he found dangling from one button. The thread pulled straight out and the button fell to the floor. "Damn."

"Damn the button or damn mentioning Oscar?"

Ted got down on his hands and knees and felt for the button under Vivien's chaise longue. "Got it," he said as he sat back on his haunches.

She waited until he was again seated. "Something about Oscar?"

Ted sighed. "Marcia's fling with Oscar. That's how Jonathan met her, of course. Oscar brought her home to dinner for some unknown reason."

Vivien nodded. "I see. Jonathan and Marcia said they'd met at an art opening. Long story about the artist and wine being spilt and ... so that was all hogwash?"

"The partial truth, from what I know," Ted said as he got to his feet. "Oscar and Marcia went to that opening but I certainly don't know or care what happened there. The important thing is that Oscar brought Marcia back to Jonathan's place for dinner afterwards." He abruptly strode over to the windows and started to pace. "I don't feel very good talking about all this. Truly."

"I'm no shrink, Ted, but surely this is an old story for you. Can't you keep going? You're testing out whether it helps."

He turned to her, seeing her in that colourful kimono, noticing how the sunlight made her hair shine. It disconcerted him. He sighed. "I may have been fooling myself about how I haven't let go of Marcia but I've never fooled myself about your brother. I can't stand him. Sorry." He turned away again.

"Don't be sorry," she said softly. "I've had plenty of times when I couldn't tolerate him either. He knows how to push the boundaries. But, basically, underneath, he's okay."

Okay? Hardly. He wanted out of this conversation. "I could have understood it if it were the other way around. Marcia dating an older guy then meeting the young good-looking one. Younger than her by a few good years." He turned away again. Dammit, he was uncomfortable.

"Oscar and Marcia were way closer in age than Jonathan and Marcia. I imagine Father appealed to her because of his money."

Ted was unconvinced the money was important. "Oscar has money. Look at that car he drives," he said, pacing again.

"Oscar flashes it. But Father pulls the strings, have no doubt about that. The term 'control freak' was invented for him."

Ted stopped to look at Vivien once more. "So you think Jonathan could have told Oscar to butt out?"

"Butt out? What do you mean?"

"If Jonathan liked the look of Marcia, he could order Oscar to stop seeing her?"

"I really can't imagine Oscar rolling over if he didn't want to."

"What if Jonathan made it worth his while? I'm talking about the transport division."

"Heavens." Vivien swung her elevated foot down to the floor. "Pass me the stool, please, Ted." He settled the foot on the stool and Vivien draped the bright colours of her robe over her knees. "I'm just trying to remember when he took over." She frowned. "How did the association come into your mind?"

"Cushla. She said that's what happened."

Vivien looked shocked. "I recall Marcia and Father coming to our place in England on their honeymoon. I've told you about that. And Oscar was running the show back here while they were away. I remember that clearly." She tied and retied the belt to her robe. "Was he the head of the transport division by then? I'm not sure. He was definitely back in Father's favour, I do remember that."

"They didn't always see eye to eye?" Ted knew they didn't but wanted to stimulate Vivien's recall.

"Eye to eye? Usually eyeball to eyeball, those two," she said with a wry smile. "All to do with control. Father has it; Oscar wants it. Father wins. But he's getting on now. And this cancer has upset various apple carts. I really wonder what would happen if Father couldn't contain Oscar. He's a grown up kid, my brother."

"I'd guessed," Ted said, trying to keep everything he said understated. He again sat down. "You were talking about the honeymoon visit?"

"I do remember Father fussing. Calling Oscar every day, that sort of thing. Oscar wanted money to build up the transport division once more. He figured that Father had rather let it slide and he'd been sold a pup. You wouldn't believe the phone calls, day and night. Oscar kept at Father the whole time they were in England. Trying to get money out of stone, of course, and providing Father with ever more dinnertime entertainment. He enjoyed the power he had over Oscar. Marcia sat stony-faced throughout it all but that could be due to other things." She looked at Ted. "Cushla's whole explanation is weird. Are you sure she wasn't just winding you up?"

"Maybe. I couldn't believe she was so unemotional about the whole thing. Icy. Saying she and Jonathan have been an item for over twenty years. Only interrupted briefly after he married Marcia."

Vivien shook her head. "Frankly, I don't believe it. Not while Marcia was around, anyway. Maybe Cushla just wanted to impress you with what she desperately wished were true."

Ted looked out the window to the green on green garden. Could that be the explanation? He threw up his hands. "Could have been, I suppose. At the time, I didn't query it. And it fits with aspects of Jonathan's history. It's just so different from your observations." Ted looked over at her. The sparkle had gone from her eyes and her face was pale. "You're finding this distressing. Enough for today."

Vivien nodded. "I'm okay. I was just thinking about the transport division. It had always been an important part of Fleet Corp and Father's handing it over to Oscar was out of the blue now I think about it. But 'handing it over' sounds better than the actuality. Father still held the big stick." She furrowed her forehead. "The whole idea of buying Oscar off is crass. So I don't know, Ted. Hard to think my family would act that way, although, on the other hand, I think it could be possible, I suppose. Theoretically." She ran her fingers through her hair. "Yes, it could have happened. Father does sometimes go to extraordinary efforts to get his own way even now and Oscar is a crafty bastard sometimes. They're too alike." She slumped in her seat and closed her eyes. "Bloody Marcia. Sorry, gutter language," she said. "So many awful things happened that were connected to her, she deserves to be cussed, as they say in America. She moved through life surrounded by storm clouds yet she lived under perpetually blue skies."

"Let's give it a rest, Vivien. Tomorrow is another day," Ted said as he got to his feet. He had a brief thought of gathering Vivien in his arms and comforting her.

Just then, the front door slammed shut. Vivien's eyes widened.

"Your father?" Ted whispered.

It was. Jonathan walked in and collapsed into the chair Ted had vacated only seconds before. "Oh. You're here." His face was drawn and a worrying grey colour.

Ted let out the breath he was unconsciously holding.

"What did the doctor say?" Vivien asked Jonathan, leaning forward to touch his arm.

He shook his head. "As I figured. Got a couple of hot spots again."

"Hot spots?" Vivien asked.

"Where the cancer has spread. Secondaries. Back on chemo starting tomorrow." He took a shuddering breath. "Bloody chemo."

Ted froze. Cancer. It had come back. It had been easy to forget Jonathan's cancer, all of them overwhelmed by the immensity of Marcia's murder. "I'm sorry to hear that, Jonathan. What can I do?"

Jonathan ignored his question.

"One thing comes to mind, Ted," Vivien said quickly. "If you could manage it, of course. Could you run father up to the hospital for his appointments?" She turned to Jonathan. "That would be wonderful, wouldn't it, Father?"

"Well, I'd rather it was you driving than Lela." Jonathan said. Then his eyes filled. "I do miss Marcia. She would have made sure I got there and back. Even though hospitals terrify her." He wiped his tears with an impatient hand.

On his way home, Ted reflected how he had been manoeuvred into becoming a taxi driver. Vivien. Pleasing her. Now, look where it got him. Still, given the old man's cancer, he would have been churlish to refuse. All his life he'd been cursed with seeing both black and white in people. Jonathan was a good example of a mix of admirable characteristics and distinctly the opposite. Usually when having to deal with people like this, he ran as fast or far as he could.

Hot spots – it sounded like a cutesy way of avoiding saying it like it was. But there was nothing cute about the words when they came from Jonathan's mouth. Marcia, and now maybe Jonathan, not making old bones. He drove. Seeing but barely registering the first few trees showing hints of autumnal colours, the yachts bobbing at their moorings, the oversize flags asserting their nationality on the harbour. Cars and trucks surrounded him like locusts in a swarm. But he felt as if he was being swept along by larger forces than Auckland's traffic.

All the same, he drove with extra care, perhaps getting in practice for transporting Jonathan for his cancer treatments, having to put up with his moods and bad temper three times every week but maybe just that bit more aware of the fragility of life. Ted deliberately relaxed his hands at the wheel and let the tension leave his body. He'd have to rearrange his daily schedule, make changes to the rut he was in. All for Jonathan.

By the time he drove into his driveway, he'd come to consider his contribution as nothing, at least not when compared to fighting cancer.

Chapter Twenty-Five

"I MUST RETURN TO England," Vivien said to Ted some days after they had implemented their complex new routine. "I've talked to the doctor, and he thinks I'll be able to travel in a couple of weeks." She was again on the chaise longue, but she no longer had to keep her foot elevated all the time. "I have booked the tickets. It's just that I hate leaving Father like this."

Jonathan was having a tough time with his chemo. He had developed some uncomfortable side effects from the drugs being poured into his veins. He was often nauseous and off his food, his skin was peeling, especially on his hands and feet, leaving them raw and reddened. And his hair was falling out.

"You know I'll do what I can while you're away," Ted said. He wanted to reassure Vivien as much as he could, but he was feeling helpless. "And Lela's great with him."

"We're lucky to have her. So don't get her all trained up on the computer, so she then ups and leaves us for a hotshot IT job." Her voice was light, but there was a serious undercurrent there.

"What's happening in England?" Ted asked. They were sitting outside. Vivien was managing on crutches fairly well at this point and she had regained some of the vitality she had lost after the accident. The sun was shining, but it was late enough in the season to enjoy getting their Vitamin D the natural way.

"I've been talking with my solicitor in London and he's stalling things until I get back. Gerald doesn't want me in the house unless I'm back as his wife. I can understand where he's coming from. It's typical Gerald." She threw her head back to get the sun on her face. "John, that's my solicitor, says that he's going to propose that Gerald stays at his club periodically. Gerald has the house when I'm not in the UK. That's most of the time, but I have it those few times when I travel back. It's a sensible solution so Gerald will manage to kibosh it, just you wait."

Ted dutifully smiled. "You're not painting a pretty picture of your husband."

"My ex. That's how I think of him. Definitely an ex."

"What will you do if he refuses?"

"Easy. Wait till he's gone to work, then move back in and change the locks. I won't tell him I'm in the country. It's my house even more than his, as far as I'm concerned. It's a stupid thing to do, maybe, but it means I have a place to stay while we get things figured out. I'll have to arrange for its sale, of course."

Ted shook his head. "If he's as wily as you say, he'll have changed the locks himself. Put in security, that sort of thing."

"Maybe," she said. "That's what you or I would do. But he's an arrogant son of a B. I doubt he's gone to the trouble. I bet he'll depend on threatening lawyer's letters. More his style. Just pressuring me to obey by telling me what to do, like he's always done. In the same way he's always underestimated me." She looked almost pleased as she said it and Ted saw that the whole situation was a challenge to her. He felt a miasma of melancholy settle over him.

Ted's involvement with the Fleets was wreaking havoc on his own schedule. But he was treating it rather like having an icy shower. Definitely jolting him awake. Three days a week he worked from five am through till nine, scoffed a quick breakfast and set off at ten for the Remuera house to take Jonathan to his chemo appointments. After dropping Jonathan off at the hospital, Ted would drive back to Jonathan's house for his reward. He'd visit with Vivien and share a lunch, always substantial, after which Ted would give Lela her computer lesson. After picking up Jonathan again at three from the hospital, he dropped him home and arrived back at his own place something after four. That left a couple of hours to get some work done before making himself a light supper. He had to be that bit more organized and to watch the time more closely, but it was do-able.

Not that he liked it. He berated himself for being selfish and was extra solicitous with Jonathan to compensate for his inner attitude, but he never considered getting out of the commitment. Spending the middle part of the day with Vivien made it all worthwhile. He enjoyed her company. That's all. Yet he was plagued with doubts that she would ever return to New Zealand once back in the familiarity of England. She had lived a lifetime in the UK and, although Jonathan was a draw card this end, friends and family, to say nothing of a husband, were powerful forces. He tried to keep thoughts of Vivien firmly down. She was not free, he repeatedly told himself.

Then there was Pauline. He presumed she'd arrive on the Friday as had become usual. A massive dilemma. Of course, he wanted to make things better between them because he'd been treating her badly, and yet....

"Pauline?" he asked when he heard her voice. "Isn't it about time we had those steaks?"

"They're in your freezer," she said, warmth coming down the wire. "I'll be over about five, as usual."

"Fine," he said, then winced at the patently false heartiness in his voice. "I'll get them out now. Glad I phoned."

"Me, too," she said.

"See you then." He put the phone down with a sigh. What did he want? Not Vivien. She wasn't free. And Pauline? He sighed. He promised thinking about it until she came over.

Holly rang again. "Should be studying, but I become so caught up with Mum's murder, I take nothing in."

Ted felt the powerlessness of the absent parent. "Can I do anything, young lady?"

"Cushla. Did you find out anything about her? Or her sons?"

Powerless and now guilt. "Sorry, Holly. I've done nothing to speak of except go over her story in my head."

"But you will do something?"

"Of course." Ted came off the phone wanting to make good his promise even if only to provide more peace of mind for Holly. But he was bereft of ideas. Nowhere even to start; not even a glimmer of a plan. As was his wont when needing puzzle-solving time, he headed for the back garden. Automatically he donned gumboots, tucked his trousers inside and zipped himself into his old orange anorak.

Cushla? Lester? He still knew little about Lester and less about his brothers. He couldn't really square Cushla and Lester's involvement with Marcia's murder, anyway.

He grabbed his lawn-weeder, a long-handled tool he had crafted himself years in the past. Starting at the far corner of the garden, he positioned its two narrow prongs on each side of the stem of each weed at ground level and jabbed down at an angle, cutting it from its roots under the surface. The ground was hard. It took muscle power. Soon he had worked up a sweat, and he undid his jacket.

Marcia and the Waakas. Means, motive and opportunity. What means? For Cushla, none he could think of. He couldn't imagine that Marcia could be enticed into that rowboat by Cushla. Maybe Lester, a tall, good-looking and well-muscled man. Young.

He brought himself up short. Trying to justify his embarrassment at not following through on Holly's suggestion, he berated himself.

Start again.

What could Cushla have used to get Marcia into that boat? The obvious answers, money or assignation, didn't seem to apply. Information? A possible. Lester: assignation? Maybe. A remote maybe. Very remote. He was even younger than Oscar and a married man with children.

Ted bent to his task and removed a cluster of dandelions. He decided that getting into a hated rowboat to gain information was no more than a faint possibility, and he should still include it only because he knew Marcia's personality. Gaining information could get her juices running. But what type of information? He jabbed at another weed. Total speculation.

He went onto the subject of motivation. Why would Cushla want Marcia dead? Jealousy? But surely that would be a smouldering motivation, hardly the acute conflagration that resulted in murder. Had something occurred that Ted didn't know about? Jonathan had stopped by on his way from Russell ... timing. Gawd, he must be tired. Jonathan stopped by with Cushla just as the murder was happening or immediately thereafter. And Jonathan detected nothing untoward, it seemed. This scenario was getting more remote by the second.

Opportunity? Not Cushla herself; that was becoming apparent either for Marcia's drowning or the car sabotage. Lester? Even if he could figure out means and opportunity, having sufficient motivation to murder someone on your mother's behalf was far-fetched in the extreme.

Concentrate.

But Vivien's car accident? Yes, the Waaka family comes and goes between Auckland and the bay. That's a small tick. But wanting Vivien dead? No tick at all. That insidious thought he'd had about Jonathan being the intended victim welled up again. The fact was, he could imagine a son being incensed about how his mother lives in poverty while being a long term *de facto* wife for a wealthy man. Ridiculous? Not entirely.

Jonathan had been around Cushla for most of Lester's life. What expectations did Cushla have? Or, a more relevant question would be, what expectations did she convey to her son? Did Lester see Jonathan as a father-figure? A father-figure who proved to be a grave disappointment? In his opinion, Jonathan was an inadequate father to both of his children and that defect in his character would be multiplied when talking about the son of his long-time lover. This train of thought was building up to a tick.

The more Ted thought about it, the more likely it was that the intended victim of the sabotaged car was not Marcia and definitely not Vivien who had only driven that car only a couple of times. No, the most likely target was Jonathan himself.

But who would want Jonathan dead? Holly's description of Marcia's silliness before her death came to mind, the type of change she'd exhibited when she took a lover all those years ago. Did she want an end to the disgusting demands of a sick man so badly she'd orchestrate a car accident for him?

Answer: only if she knew he'd use that car sometime. With two other vehicles at his disposal, unlikely. And, due to his frailty, he wasn't driving much. The only circumstance would be if she specifically asked him to bring her that car if she needed picking up.... He shook his head. This type of thinking was driving him crazy.

He glanced up. The clouds were thickening. First came a general mistiness in the air, followed by fat drops which seemed to materialize out of nowhere. He stuck his weeder in the ground and retraced his steps, gathering up the decapitated weeds, and throwing them onto his compost pile near the back fence. The rain increased. He grabbed up the weeder and trotted back across his lawn, his gumboots clumping.

A good hour's work, he figured, as he padded in stocking feet to the kitchen to turn on the jug. He'd tidy his thinking by finding out what he could about Cushla and Lester, but he was as satisfied as he could be, given the state of the available facts: Cushla and her sons were probably not involved in Marcia's death. The tricky bit would be telling Holly. She obviously wanted someone to be held responsible for her mother's death, and who could blame her?

And that meant he had only Oscar and Jonathan left on his list of suspects. Motivation, means and opportunity. In the cold light of a rainy afternoon, neither of the Fleet men had enough motivation, even if the means was available in the form of the rowboat. And Oscar wasn't at the bay and Jonathan's medical infirmity meant he couldn't take advantage of any opportunity had he so wished. Dead end.

In a way, it was relieving.

Chapter Twenty-Six

TED WAS WELL PREPARED for Pauline. The steaks were defrosted, washed and patted dry with a paper towel; the rain had stopped and the wine uncorked. He'd cleaned the BBQ, and he'd made a green salad. He'd bought some of those almost-cooked bread rolls that take ten minutes in the oven.

He watched as her tall form freed itself from her car. She had a model's figure and a steel trap mind. He knew lots of people who first didn't take her seriously because of her looks, then were so overawed at her competence that they became almost frightened of her. They'd had a laugh about that many times. How could anyone find her anything but competent and decorative? She was a bit young for him, he knew, but he'd had lots of admiring glances when she was on his arm and that tickled his sense of humour. She came in with her usual overnight bag, which she deposited in his bedroom.

"Are things settling down at last?" she asked when she had her gin and tonic in hand and he was lighting the barbecue.

"Finally," he said. "I'm helping Jonathan Fleet as much as I can. He's not a well man."

"Don't let him suck you in," she said as she reached for an olive. They were outside at the back and she was sitting at the table under the oversized umbrella. "He's made of money, that guy. He can hire whoever he likes."

Ted caught himself wanting to correct 'whoever' to 'whomever'. Something about Pauline being more Holly's generation than his own. "Hiring someone is not exactly like having a friend do something for you."

"Friend? Don't make me laugh," she said. "That guy has no friends, just lackeys and servants."

"Hold on, he's a newly widowed man. He's going through it right now. I'm doing all I can."

She mumbled something. Ted thought it might have been, "More fool you." He chose to ignore it.

Soon the steak was done to a turn; the salad was crisp, and the butter melted on the freshly baked rolls. As he was clearing away their plates, he realised he'd forgotten dessert, but he couldn't have eaten anything more anyway with the size of the steaks Pauline had provided. He made some fresh coffee, and they adjourned back into the living room. The night was chilling off, signs of the cooler weather to come.

Ted took a deep breath. "I'm pleased you're here," he said. Her head jerked upward. Wrong thing to say. "I mean, I'm awfully sorry about our other weekends, and it's nice we're together now."

"Yeah, well, I like our weekends," she said.

"Me too."

"I think there's a 'but' coming," she said, a worry line appearing between her eyebrows.

Ted laughed. "You're so bright, my friend. Yes, there's a 'but'. I hate letting you down and my failure to be here for those two weekends ... I'm sorry. It gutted me. I hate disappointing you."

"It's okay," she said. "I'm over it."

"Not the point," he said. "I think we're in a bit of a...." He stopped himself saying 'rut'. "Erm ... into a set of expectations that are inflexible and maybe that's not good." He paused to swig his coffee. It was still too hot, and he swallowed with difficulty. "Building up anticipation in one of us and then a let-down. No good."

"What are you trying to say?"

Ted looked her in the eye. "We should make fresh arrangements for each weekend. No expectation, no disappointment. My life is chaotic right now, in case you haven't noticed." He sipped more cautiously this time.

"Oh. Yes. I can see that. Be in touch to do the planning. I can do that."

Ted let out a silent sigh of relief. "Me, too." She was a lovely sight, curled up in the corner of the couch, her long legs folded under her. "How about some whisky in that coffee?"

Sunday morning, things became a bit rough.

"Let's plan next weekend, shall we?" Pauline suggested, leaning over his body to reach some of the paper lying on the other side of the bed.

"Too early," Ted said, not looking up from the article he was reading.

"Why not?"

"I should think Vivien could tolerate a car trip by then. Probably take her over to Piha or Murawai for a day trip. I'd like to see her smile again."

"Who's Vivien?"

Bad mistake bringing up Vivien's name. "Surely I've told you. Vivien Fleet that-was, as they say. Vivien McAvoy. Jonathan's daughter. Didn't I tell you she was in a car accident?"

"No. No car accident. Nothing about a daughter of Jonathan Bloody Fleet's. Nothing." Her voice could refrigerate hot tamales.

"Hey, lighten up. Sorry, I must have forgotten to mention it. Life's a tad hectic," Ted said, picking his paper up again. He was in no mood for an argument.

"Hectic, bloody schmectic," Pauline said. "I'll ask again. Who is this Vivien, and don't give me bullshit about whose daughter she is. Who is she to you?"

The words he was reading blurred, and he felt hot acid push up towards his throat. Not another tantrum. He swallowed hard and suppressed an angry retort. "I'm having a shower," he said, pushing paper and duvet towards Pauline. He closed the door with a sigh. She could be difficult, this young woman. And he was no longer sure it was worth it.

Through the noise of the water he'd just turned on, he could hear Pauline shouting. "You fucking her? That what it's all about?"

Ted began to sing. Loudly.

When he emerged, towel firmly wrapped around his waist, Pauline was up and dressed.

"You bastard," she growled. "Life's hectic. Something's come up." She mocked his speech patterns. "I knew you'd met someone else. Can't hide it from me, you shit."

"Enough," he said through clenched teeth. "I think you'd better get your things and go. This isn't working."

Pauline slammed the bedroom door, leaving Ted standing bemused. He then heard her rev the motor on her car and screech down the driveway. All he felt was relief. He flopped back into bed and picked up the paper again.

That afternoon he took Vivien for a drive out to the west coast beaches and didn't think of Pauline once.

The following Wednesday afternoon, while Ted was teaching Lela the secrets of writing a letter, saving it, and printing it, his mobile rang. Vivien, calling from downstairs.

"They're keeping Father in overnight. He's been vomiting badly and they're worried he's getting dehydrated."

"Hold on, I'll be right down."

She was sitting in the conservatory again. Ted thought of it as Vivien's day room now. "Nothing to worry about, the nurse said. Just that he's too thin, and the nausea provoked frank vomiting today, so they're keeping an eye on him. It's too bad, because Lela is cooking a special dinner tonight."

"So no need to hang around now." Ted got up from the steel and plastic chair he often sat on. "Did they say when he'll be discharged?"

"Probably tomorrow. And they're considering giving him a day or so 'holiday' from his chemo to let his system recover."

"Let me know, please. I'll pick him up whatever the time."

Just then, the front doorbell rang. Lela answered it; Ted and Vivien kept their eyes on the door of the conservatory, waiting to find out who had called.

Lela returned. "Mr Jonathan's friend is here, Ms Vivien. Mrs Cushla. And her son."

Ted looked at Vivien who raised her eyebrows. "Show them in, Lela, please."

Lela ushered Cushla into the room followed by a tall young Maori man, clearly her son with the same big slanted eyes and wavy locks. Cushla was dressed very differently from the time Ted had seen her last, now wearing a velvet frock and makeup, her hair in an elaborate twist on the top of her head.

"I haven't seen you since you were a nipper," Cushla said to Vivien before noticing Ted. "Well, hello again," she said, turning to him and kissing his cheeks. "But no Jonathan? I haven't seen him for so long, the mountain had to come to Mohammed." She laughed loudly.

"He's reacting badly to his chemo again, Mrs Waaka," Vivien said. "He's over-nighting in hospital to get stabilized again. But we're told not to take his hospitalization too seriously."

"Call me Cushla, girl. Everyone else does," Cushla said as she sat down. "This here's my son, Lester. He drove me down." Lester duly shook hands with Vivien.

"Nice to see you again," Ted murmured.

"If you've time, you can visit Father," Vivien said. "He's feeling better already."

"And Oscar? How's he?"

"Fine," Vivien said. "He's coming over after work."

"Ah, we won't be that long. You can tell him Lester and I dropped by." She was obviously talking to Vivien, but her eyes were on Lester. She turned back to Vivien. "Just wanted to catch up with Jonathan. You tell us where he is and we'll pop in and visit."

Lela came in with tea and biscuits. "Now sit down, Ms Cushla," she said, "and have some tea and a cookie." Lela shot a glance at Vivien who nodded and smiled.

"Any chance you have a coke?" Lester asked.

"Oh, sorry, I forgot," Lela said, jumping up.

"Sit down, Lela. I'll get it myself. There's a cold one?"

"In the fridge," Lela said as she distributed tea cups.

"Tell me about your family, Lela," Cushla said once she had her cup of tea in hand.

Lela turned to Vivien. "Do you want us to go into the dining room? You're maybe not interested in hearing about my family."

"Of course I am," Vivien said stoutly. She turned to Cushla. "She'll probably tell you more than she tells me and I'd like to hear."

Lester appeared at the door. "Ted?" He beckoned with the hand holding a coke.

Ted got up. "Sorry, folks, but I'd better be getting on," he said. The last thing he wanted was to be stuck listening to an interminable tale of children and grandchildren. "Lester?" He followed the young man into the kitchen.

"Hey, man, sorry about Marcia," Lester said.

"It was a shocker all right," Ted said. He'd known Lester as a youngster, but he'd had little to do with him in the intervening years.

"Just wanted to know if the police were still hassling you." He swigged at the can of coke.

"To be expected," Ted said. "I'm the ex-husband. Jonathan is getting the same treatment."

"Me, too," Lester said.

"You? Why? Were you friends with Marcia?"

"Sort of. We knew each other. Smart lady, Marcia."

"But why you? She knew lots of people."

"Cause I was up there that weekend, I guess, and the pigs never forget nothing."

"Oh. You mean your marijuana problems."

Lester crumpled the empty coke can and dropped it onto the side. "Just wanted to know that I was not the only one, that's all. Oscar been questioned, too?"

"Oscar, Vivien, Holly—we all have. Most of the interest is on Jonathan and me now, though," Ted paused. "You heard I'll be getting the Bay House back?" he said to change the subject.

"Yeah. Good one." But he didn't smile.

"We'll be neighbours again." He smiled at the young man's scowl and walked to the door of the kitchen. "See you up at the bay, then." He left the house wondering why he was feeling as if he'd escaped.

Chapter Twenty-Seven

THE NEXT MORNING TED opened his laptop early, anticipating the phone call which would interrupt later work. But by three in the afternoon and no word, he rang Vivien. No answer. He left a message on the voice mail. By almost five and still no word, he rang again. Where was she? Out with Lela, obviously. He rang the hospital.

"Mr Fleet is resting comfortably," the person on the ward said. "He has his own telephone. Do you want the number?"

At least Jonathan was all right. Ted rang, but the phone at Jonathan's bedside just rang and rang with no voice mail facility. Where was everybody? He felt annoyed. He was treated as part of the family when taxiing was required, but not when other things came up.

His head was whirling with unanswered questions. Where was Vivien? Did something dire happen to Jonathan? Had Lela driven Vivien into the hospital to be by his bedside? Or had something happened to Vivien? Or Lela, for that matter, although by this late in the afternoon, Lela should have gone home to her family. Or Vivien had fallen, lying alone, unable to get to the phone. No, the phone had not been answered since mid-afternoon. Jonathan, it must be Jonathan.

Enough was enough. He got his keys and headed for his car. Almost out of his drive, his mobile rang.

"Len Rogers here. TopCar Insurance. You rang wanting a mechanic to look at Mr Fleet's car, the one in the accident?" a voice asked.

Ted braked the car to a stop. "Thanks for ringing back." He'd almost forgotten he'd asked. But it was important. "You found anything?"

"The nut at the end of the steering column. It was missing. Loose, I guess, then worked its way off. Fits the lady's story."

A missing nut? Something so small? "Could this missing nut have caused the crash?"

"Almost certainly caused the crash," Len Rogers said. "I'll let the police know, too."

"The police?" Ted felt stupid. "You're saying it was deliberate?"

"Someone did it, for sure. Can't loosen by itself. Then someone cleaned up the whole engine. I thought that was suspicious when I first looked at it."

"I noticed it, too," Ted said, feeling a wave of relief his suspicions had been confirmed. "Look, thanks very much. I'm on my way now to see Mr Fleet and his daughter—the woman who was driving. I'll let them know."

He sat for a moment at the implications. Someone actually did sabotage the car. He'd come to think Jim the mechanic had been right. That Vivien had been distracted, one tyre had gone off the road then she'd found headed down the dip. Almost killed her. But sabotage? Suddenly, he needed to find her right away. He rang her mobile again. And the landline at the Fleet house. Still no answer. He put the car into gear and took off around the corner onto the road. He had to get to her. Warn her. Someone actually sabotaged the car. Vivien's life was in danger.

Ted risked driving on the motorway five kilometres faster than the speed limit, switching lanes like a boy racer. But when it came to which off-ramp he should take, he opted to swing past the house first, just in case.

The house was dark. Lifeless. But Jonathan's car was still there, sitting on the gravel drive, not in the garage. Ted got out of his car and circled as much of the house as he could, peering through the fence to the little yard beyond the conservatory. All looked ordinary. He came back to the front of the house. Would Lela drive Jonathan's big car? Maybe she had driven Marcia's Smart Car for preference? By now it was dusk. He pulled his phone out and turned on the built-in torch, shining it into the dark window of the garage. Difficult to see but one of the cars was there. He couldn't remember which one was parked under the window. Useless.

He ran back to his own car and headed for the hospital. His anxiety was such that the parking building seemed as if it was miles from the hospital itself and by the time he found out where Jonathan was, and then found his ward, it had become sky high. Jonathan was still a patient, and no one suggested he not visit, so hopefully that meant Jonathan must be all right. Where, then, were Vivien and Lela?

On the ward, he stuck his head around the door of Jonathan's room. No Vivien, no Lela. Jonathan was lounging on the bed, half sitting up, watching something on the television hanging from the ceiling. Ted took a deep breath to calm himself.

"Hello, old man. You're looking better." He put on a smile for Jonathan's sake.

"Feeling better," Jonathan said.

"Do you know where Vivien is?"

"She's still in intensive care," Jonathan said.

"What?" Ted gasped.

"Lela's back in an ordinary ward now, thank God, but Vivien...' His voice broke. "Goddamit. Just worried, that's all."

Vivien? Ted found it hard to catch his breath. "What happened? Another car accident?"

"Oh." Jonathan sounded bewildered. "You haven't heard. Ill. Both of them. They think it was something they ate at lunch today. Probably the fish."

"Food poisoning?"

"Apparently. If I'd eaten it, I would have been a goner, the nurse cheerfully told me. As it is, Vivien is strong..." His voice trailed off. "She's very ill, Ted. Very. On a respirator."

Ted collapsed onto the small visitor's chair. He was too late. Someone had got to Vivien before he realised she'd been right. Someone had tried to kill her and now had tried again. But food poisoning? He asked Jonathan. "Food poisoning? In this day and age?"

Jonathan shook his head. "They had some idea which poison right away and some government official was collecting samples from the house today. Meanwhile, I've told Oscar not to go over to my place and certainly not to eat anything there."

Ted was impatient with tales about Oscar. "Is Vivien in danger?"

"Bloody hell, she is. They're doing everything to save her, but botulism is a fatal illness in almost ten percent of cases. She has severe botulism. Bad." He took a deep breath. "Lela is out of danger now. I guess she didn't eat so much fish. But Vivien ... she can't breathe. I can't imagine anything worse, gasping for air. Why I always worried I'd get COVID."

"Breathing with the help of the respirator. That must have been a relief." Ted was struggling to take it all in, struggling to cope with Vivien being at risk.

"She was slipping in and out of consciousness coming to the hospital, I'm told. God, Ted, I've only just got her back and now this."

Ted put his hand on Jonathan's shoulder.

But Jonathan shrugged him off.

"Can I see her?" Ted asked.

"They've put her into an artificial coma. To let everything heal."

Ted felt useless. Probably not as much as Jonathan, not only old but incapacitated by his illness and the chemo. "But you're looking and sounding much better, Jonathan."

"I am. They've given me some good stuff. And no chemo today. Was supposed to be discharged but can't now until they get a nurse organized. Supposedly I need someone twenty-four seven."

"Will they let me go see Vivien? Maybe talk to her, even if she's in a coma?"

"Doubt it, but you can try."

Shortly Ted was outside the Intensive Care ward but, as Jonathan expected, he was not allowed in. The nurse was helpful, though. "She's hooked up to various devices and we have things under control now. She's not conscious and no visitors, sorry. Her friend has gone back to a general ward." Ted had almost forgotten about Lela.

He found her a few floors down. He peeked around the edge of the door. "How are you, Lela?" he asked. She looked awful to his eyes, her face as pasty as her naturally brown skin would allow. Her whole extended family was around her bed but all were silent as their eyes followed Ted to her beside.

"Better now," she said, reaching out to him, and he grasped her hand firmly. "Do you know how Ms Vivien is doing?" she asked.

He told her what the nurse said. "And Jonathan is fine. I've just seen him. Very worried about Vivien, but relieved you're all right." She just nodded and Ted could see, family or no family, she needed to rest. He left, promising to visit again in the morning.

He returned to Jonathan. "Lela's fine and pleased you're doing so well," he lied to Jonathan. A little social grease.

"And Vivien?"

"Not allowed to see her, just as you predicted. But the Intensive Care nurse was cheerful."

"That's not saying anything," Jonathan grumbled.

Someone Ted presumed was the ward clerk appeared at the door. "Dr Piper is here to see you, Mr Fleet." Ted stood up, ready to leave.

"Sit down, Ted. Might as well hear this," Jonathan said. "It's Vivien's doctor."

Dr Piper was a middle-aged man, dressed in a white coat that flowed around either side of his ample stomach. Jonathan didn't introduce Ted.

"If I could have a word...,' Dr Piper said, glancing at Ted.

"Get on with it," Jonathan said.

"Mrs McAvoy is doing as well as we could possibly hope, Mr Fleet. We were successful in getting the botulism anti-toxin into her straight away and her stomach pumped so no more toxin could get into her system. That was vital and our people were onto it immediately. But she had taken in an enormous amount of the toxin before that, which has left her needing help with her breathing."

"She's still on a respirator?" Jonathan asked, his voice strained.

"And will be for some time. That's because she has some paralysis of her breathing muscles and, I must warn you, of other muscles, too. We'll keep her breathing and hope her constitution does its bit."

"Paralyzed. Like in the polio epidemics. I remember them well. Iron lungs. Deaths," Jonathan said, more to himself than the others.

"This is not polio, but the effects are similar in a way. This is a bacterial infection, not a virus, but it's not the bug doing the damage; it's the toxin that the bacterium produces. We're stopping the process; the paralysis won't get any worse than now. I must emphasize she's not out of danger, Mr Fleet. But, all going well, the paralysis should slowly clear over the next few weeks. Remember, it's not going to get any worse. Please realize she's not out of danger; don't misunderstand, she's still seriously ill. And her age is against her and we don't know whether having suffered her recent accident will have any effect on her progress. She's in the right place, that's all I can say. If I had botulinim toxin in my system, I would want to be in this Intensive Care ward in this hospital because I'm confident in the excellence of our care." Ted had the feeling this doctor had repeated similar little speeches before.

"How long will she be on the respirator?" Ted asked.

"If or when she recovers is anyone's guess; plan on something over several weeks."

"You keep saying weeks. My god," Jonathan said.

"They put her onto the respirator really quickly and she's in a safe place now." He said it with a patronizing air.

"And later? Will she be handicapped? Paralyzed?" Ted almost whispered his questions.

"She has a good chance of a complete recovery eventually, but we'll not know about any residual effects until much later." He smiled. "I've confidence that she's having the best care, gentlemen. We'll worry about other things when the time comes, shall we?"

After the doctor had left, both men let the silence last until a clattering out in the corridor broke the spell.

"She's not going to be able to get back to England, is she?" Ted asked, more to himself than Jonathan. "Even if, if...."

"Not for a while." Jonathan glanced at Ted.

"I can't get it through my head that she's fighting for her life," Ted said with a shake of his head. "Vivien."

"And there's not a damn thing we can do to help her."

Ted met Jonathan's eyes briefly. "We should let her kids know. And her husband." He realized his mistake. "I mean you, not we."

Jonathan gave Ted the combination for the front door of his house and they arranged that Ted would look up Vivien's various phone numbers in England in the telephone notebook located on the telephone stand in the front hallway. He could then ring Jonathan's phone in the hospital.

"I tried and tried the number the front desk gave me and yet you never got my calls." Ted picked up the phone. On the side of the handset was a little knob.

'Vibrate' or 'Ring'. "By the way, Jonathan, every now and again have you been hearing a buzzing sound you couldn't place?"

Ted drove out of the hospital carpark like an automaton. Vivien had been targeted all along. Not Marcia. Vivien. Two Fleet women, one dead and one seriously ill. He could hardly breathe. He shoved those thoughts to the back of his mind; he was on a necessary mission. When he arrived at Jonathan's house, he found the front door open and various people dressed in white coming and going. He waylaid one figure.

He introduced himself. "I'm here to collect a phone number or two for Mr Fleet. Do you think I could have the list by the telephone in the front hallway?"

"I'm Kim Jansen. Hold on and I'll check. It's just the kitchen that's out of bounds." The speaker was female. Ted hadn't been sure until she spoke. She walked smartly to the van and was back in a couple of minutes. "If it's all right with Mr Fleet, you can take the phone list. My boss is ringing him at the hospital right now." They both turned and watched the van. Shortly, a man came out the back door and waved.

"I'll get it for you just now," she said.

On her return, Ted asked about what they were doing.

"We're taking samples of all sorts, as much as we can—the bench tops, drains, all opened food in the fridge and freezer. And the rubbish, of course."

"I understand it's botulism," Ted said. "Is it always in food?"

"Not always, no," Kim said. "It's in the soil; well, the bacteria are in the soil. Most cleaning and cooking destroys it. And for the lady having such an acute case, it's got to be here, either in the food or the rubbish."

"Can I give you a call to find out what you've found?"

"I guess so, my boss anyway. Yes, give my boss a call in a couple of days. He'll either tell you or not tell you, I guess." She fished out a card from her pocket under the coverall.

Back home, Ted called Jonathan with the phone numbers.

"You okay to ring the UK, Jonathan?"

"Yes, fine. But they won't let me go back to my house, nurse or no nurse. Medically, I can be discharged but ... bloody medics."

"What do they expect you to do, for heaven's sake? Stay in a hotel?"

"Never thought of that one. But I put it to Oscar that he has an enormous apartment and no wife, so how about it? He actually sounded quite pleased. Underneath, he's got a good heart. He's picking me up at eight, so you can get hold of me there."

Ted suppressed a sigh. "Your chemo? Should I pick you up for your chemo tomorrow?"

"Not tomorrow. One more day of chemo-holiday. The day after." No appreciation. Always the expectation everyone was at his beck and call.

Actually, it could have been worse. Oscar lived in Takapuna, not ten minutes away from Ted's place. But his day would be shattered with the trips over the bridge with a grumpy old man and no sweetener of lunches with Vivien.

Vivien. Ted still found it difficult to accept she was so gravely ill. How could it have happened? He'd been in Lela's kitchen. She kept things tidy and clean to a fault. He was looking forward to seeing her in the morning. He had quite a few questions he wanted to ask.

Chapter Twenty-Eight

VISITORS' HOURS STARTED AT eleven. With no need to take Jonathan into the hospital, Ted could get to Lela early enough to avoid her family. He had been quite inhibited by all those intense eyes staring at him.

In the event, he was there about twenty minutes before visiting officially started but, because he knew where to go and no one stopped him, he slipped into Lela's room.

"Mr Ted. You've come like you said." Lela's voice was much stronger.

"You're feeling better? You look better."

"I am. I want to go home. I can rest there just like here. I try to tell them and maybe they'll let me go later."

"Lela, you and Vivien have botulism poisoning. Do you know what it is?"

"Yes, of course. Everybody knows. Sometimes you get it from putting up garden vegetables and that's why you use the metal lids that pop. If they've popped, you throw out the jar. But we didn't have home bottled veggies. I don't have time to do that."

"I heard it was the fish. Fish can have the botulism bacteria too, I gather." He was looking at her intently.

"But I didn't eat any fish, Mr Ted. Just Ms Vivien. She likes tinned salmon for lunch. All that Omega Three, which is supposed to be good for you. But me, I like fresh fish, not that tinned stuff."

"No fish. You're sure, Lela? Not even a little bit?"

"Not eating it. Except I tasted the spoon, you know, just before putting it in the dishwasher. Just to taste. Not to eat."

"You licked the spoon? Is that it?"

Lela smiled and put her hand over her mouth, in what Ted recognized as a characteristic gesture. "Sorry. Yes. I always lick the serving spoons. Lots of tastes. Then I put the spoon right into the dishwasher. Always. Each time."

Ted thought it through. Certainly she had a far milder case than Vivien, but she still landed in hospital. Could licking the spoon transfer enough bacteria into her system to have such an acute reaction that she would be hospitalized?

"What happened? Can you tell me everything? For instance, when did you decide what you and Vivien were having for lunch?"

"Well, you weren't coming, so we decided to have a light lunch. Ms Vivien wanted a salmon salad like she often eats, and I like to have a cheese and pickle sandwich."

Ted felt a frisson in his solar plexus that they had changed their eating habits because he wasn't there. "So you went back into the kitchen after speaking with Vivien?"

"I talked to her from the door. Then I went to make the lunch. We were going to eat it in the conservatory." Ted nodded. "So I first got out the cheese and sliced it and wrapped it up again and put it back in the fridge. This is what you want to know, Mr Ted?"

"Perfect. Yes, all the details. We have to figure it out, Lela, you and me."

"Okay. Then I put the cheese back and got out the salmon and the mayo. The fish mayo stuff that Vivien likes."

"The pink-coloured stuff?" He had seen Vivien eat that particular fish sauce at other times.

"That's it. The pinky-orange coloured mayo in the tall jar. First, I smelled the salmon. I opened it the day before but it had a cover on it and it smelled perfect. It really did, Mr Ted. I usually get the bigger tin because Ms Vivien likes it and it lasts at least two days."

She was getting agitated, so Ted reached over and patted the back of her hand. "That's the type of detail I like, Lela. You usually get a larger tin and Vivien eats it over two days with that fish sauce stuff."

"Okay, then I take out two pieces of white bread. Vivien likes the brown but I like white. So I spread margarine on the bread and put the cheese on and the pickles and press them together for a sandwich. Then I get the lettuce and celery out of the fridge and prepare it for the salad. This time, I mixed celery and the fish sauce and the salmon together. Then I've this special spoon that makes a ball out of it and I put it on the lettuce for Ms Vivien."

"Did you drink anything?"

"Water for her. Sprite Zero for me. I poured our glasses. I can tell which is which because mine has bubbles."

"Then?"

"We sat at the little table and ate our lunch. My sandwich was okay, but Vivien didn't like her salad very much. Not too hungry, I guess. Maybe worried about her father. Then I took the plates and my glass into the kitchen. Vivien was still sipping her water." She looked at Ted to see if he wanted to hear this bit. He nodded. "I dumped the remains of the salad and I put the dishes into the dishwasher. And the preparation stuff, too."

"This is when you licked the spoon?"

"I licked the special spoon that makes the ball and the wooden spoon I mixed everything up with and put everything into the dishwasher. I didn't put it on because it wasn't nearly full. I was going to put our dinner stuff in before turning it on."

"So I guess the things that could have the bacteria were the two salad vegetables—the lettuce or the celery—or the sauce. Or the salmon."

"That's right. Nothing else. Because Vivien didn't have cheese or bread or margarine, just me. And I didn't have lettuce, so we can get rid of lettuce. Just what was in the fish ball. Salmon or celery or sauce."

"That should help, shouldn't it, Lela. I'll ring the scientists and tell them what we've figured out."

"I should tell you about what happened then, shouldn't I?"

"Tell me."

"First Vivien dropped her glass. I rushed into the conservatory and she was sort of lying back against the cushions like she never does. She says, 'Sorry Lela. I'm not feeling well. Sick. Can't breathe.'"

"How long after lunch?"

"I don't know, Mr Ted. I've been trying to figure that out. I had the dishes put away, and I had wiped down the kitchen bench and I was figuring out what vegetables to have for dinner, something like that. But I wasn't feeling so good either by that time."

"So she said she was unwell. Did she look unwell?"

"Awful. She looked terrible. Nauseous, like me. She couldn't get her eyes to keep open and I could see she was getting panicky because she couldn't catch her breath. I said to her, "Should I get the doctor?" and she said, "Call 111." So I did."

"I'm very glad you did. Thank goodness for that. You saved her life, Lela." He squeezed her hand. "But you didn't feel well yourself?"

"I threw up when we were getting Vivien to the ambulance. Then I stumbled on the front step and the ambulance guy said I had to come too. They pumped my stomach and gave me all sorts, but before long they said I could come down here." She grabbed Ted's arm. "You know how Vivien is today?"

"I'll ask."

"Go to the desk and look for the little lady with the orange hair. She's good, that one."

Ted dutifully sought out the orange-haired woman and asked how they could find out about a patient in Intensive Care. Not five minutes after he got back to Lela's room and after several relatives had come in for the visiting hours, the woman with the orange hair came back to him.

"Mrs McAvoy is in a serious condition still, but stable."

"And that means?" he asked.

"It means she's very ill, but there's no change. Probably no change is a good thing with botulism." She turned to Lela. "Just ask me through the day to ring about her. I don't mind."

"If you're still here tomorrow, I'll drop Jonathan for his chemo and pop up here afterwards. Okay?"

Lela smiled. "I hope I'm home by then. If I'm not here, could you please give me a ring when there's any news?"

Ted went home and called Kim's boss to tell him which foods were suspicious.

The boss thanked him for finding out the information. "We did find the dishes in the dishwasher, but I'll tell the lab guys to concentrate on the wooden spoon and the spoon that forms the salad ball. Also, we're in the midst of testing the food from the fridge. So far, the salmon is clear and there's nothing on any of the vegetables. No dirt, no bacteria. I must tell you, it's very unlikely to be the fish sauce. It contains high acidity and the bacteria cannot survive those sorts of pH levels. So it's unlikely to be the sauce. Doesn't leave us much to go on."

Ted couldn't settle down to work. His eyes kept being drawn to his back garden, now heading into its autumnal somnambulance. It was cool outside but mostly sunny and the garden was calling. He put on a sweatshirt and his gumboots and set out to tackle the leaves and dead remains of summer flowers. Shortly he had worked up a welcome sweat, living in the here and now, smelling the sweet decay of autumn and appreciating the cool breeze. He piled the weeds and leaves onto the compost pile at the back of his section. It would all go back into the garden in the spring, by then smelling and looking like fresh new soil. But he knew what he was really out here for. Getting lost in gardening was his way of forgetting. Letting the world get on and leaving him to concentrate on something real.

The idea of Vivien lying in that hospital bed, a machine producing her very breathing, not knowing anything, the essential Vivien absent, was too much. He felt so absurdly helpless. He jumped on the compost heap, compressing it slightly, enough so that his next load would fit. Back and forth with his wheelbarrow, he transported the detritus left from a summer's abundance. Everything was going into winter mode. And he needed to figure out what to put in. Winter in Auckland was planting season. Everything survived the winter; it was the dryness of the summers that killed plants.

He started by digging over the annual beds at the back of the section. He had left it a little late, and the soil was cloggy. This was a job for late April, not the middle of May. Soon Holly would be returning for her week of study for her exams that were looming. Thinking of her visit lifted his spirits enough that he didn't mind heading for shelter when a passing shower wet his back enough to be uncomfortable.

He climbed onto the deck for protection under the sun umbrella, reluctant to go back inside.

Interesting that the fish was clear of botulism. But the improbability the fish sauce was the culprit was odd. Could the bacteria have been lurking in the wooden spoon somehow?

The shower turned into rain and he ducked inside for his waterproof; he needed to get his tools put away into the garage. The phone rang.

"Hi, Dad," Holly said when she heard her father's voice. "I bet you want to know which plane to meet."

"Got it in one, young lady," he said. "And I've a few things to tell you quickly. I'll fill you in when you get here." He wanted to warn her about Vivien. He didn't want her to be confronted with a severe illness nobody had told her about or, even, god forbid, a death she knew nothing about either. Vivien was her step-sister, after all. "And I don't want you to be disappointed if Oscar can't make your date. He now has Jonathan staying with him because the authorities don't want him in the house before they give it the all clear."

It wasn't until he'd put the phone down that he revisited the horrific thoughts that had come to him in the car. Vivien had been poisoned. Not Marcia. Nothing to do with Marcia. Vivien. First Marcia and now Vivien. Two Fleet women. Who could be next? Holly? His knees weakened at the thought. He sat heavily on the nearest kitchen chair. Why would anyone be after Holly? For that matter, why Marcia? Why Vivien? So far, he had not been successful in coming up with any sort of motive behind Marcia's murder. And nothing came to mind as a motive behind the attempt on Vivien, either. Unknown territory. Unknown perp. But the logical consequence was ... the women in the Fleet family.

"Holly," he said into the phone when he'd rung back. "I have a favour to ask."

"Sure, Dad," she said when she heard his voice. "Shoot."

"I want you to take extra precautions right now." He took a deep breath. His daughter wasn't noted for obeying danger signals, especially those espoused by her father. "First your mother, now your step-sister. You could be in danger, too."

"Step-sister? Oh, I guess she is. I always think of her just as Vivien. Her car accident looks suspicious?"

"Erm, yes, it does. I'll tell you all about it when I see you, okay?"

"Sure thing, Dad," she said casually.

"Listen to me, please. I'm trying to make a point." He could hear his voice become strained. He deliberately calmed it down. "We don't know why your mother was killed or by whom. Someone has just tried to kill Vivien and we don't know who did that, either. Or why. Ergo, I need you to be cautious. Vigilant. Guarded even. Would you do that for your old dad?"

She laughed. "You still worry over me, but you do forget that I'm a grown-up."

"Both your mother and Vivien are grownups, young lady. It's nothing to do with age."

There was a short silence. "Yeah, I see what you mean. Okay, I'll take care. Check the windows and locks, that sort of thing. My study group's coming tomorrow and I've flat mates here in the evenings and nights. On Saturday, I'll get to the airport early, maybe. A friend's taking me to the airport. I'll get her to stay until boarding time. That suit you?"

Ted felt as if he'd stepped out of a shadowy tunnel. "Thanks. I appreciate it."

"For now, Dad. Because this thing with Vivien has been such a shock to you. But I'm not going to be kept in cotton wool when I get home. I'm giving you fair warning right now."

"Okay. We'll talk it through when you get here. I'll be at the airport to pick you up."

Chapter Twenty-Nine

The next day Ted made his way to Oscar's apartment block on the north side of the city of Takapuna. He parked and took the lift up. As expected, the flat had stupendous views out over the channel and Rangitoto Island, Takapuna at its feet. Ted had expected nothing less. He had no problem collecting Jonathan as Oscar was long gone to work.

"How are you feeling, Jonathan?" Ted asked as he ushered Jonathan into the lift.

"Physically, quite good, for the moment. But I know what's in store. And then there's Vivien. Couldn't sleep."

"I rang this morning. Serious but stable still."

"Ditto."

They drove in silence along the motorway that led to the Auckland Harbour Bridge. The day would be like the day before. Sunny with odd showers that passed through. Ted hardly noticed.

"I'm having the kitchen replaced," Jonathan said, breaking the silence.

"The whole thing?"

"Yup. Fridge, cooker and oven. And new flooring, paint, the lot."

"Is that necessary?"

"That damn bacteria came from somewhere and so far they can't find where."

Ted told him his idea about the wooden spoon.

"Even that wooden spoon has been knocking against who knows what. No, this is clean and neat and will certainly do the job."

"How about commercial cleaners? We can get a list of who specializes in this sort of thing from the lab that's doing the testing."

"Butt out, Ted. I have it arranged."

Ted clamped his mouth shut. Then he said, "How long?"

"They say they'll be done in a couple of weeks. Maybe sooner. I offered a bonus."

"Do you want me to ask Lela what she'd like in the new kitchen?"

There was a long and somehow uncomfortable silence. Finally, Jonathan said, "I don't want to see that woman ever again."

"Jonathan! You can't think that Lela had anything to do with what happened, surely?"

"Don't know. Don't care. But we don't have to have her around so we won't." Ted glanced at him. His mouth was set in a thin line.

"Can I ask you something of you, Jonathan? Can I ask that you make no decisions until Vivien is able to speak to us again? Please, for her sake?"

Another long silence lasted until Ted was turning into the drop-off lane at the hospital. He had to remind himself to breathe and his hands were sticky against the steering wheel. Jonathan could be a hard man. Ted didn't want to break the silence because, until Jonathan made up his mind, anything could tip the balance. Finally Jonathan spoke. "Okay. For Vivien. But only until she's sensible again." His voice was gruff.

After dropping Jonathan off, Ted used his mobile to call the hospital. He imagined just behind that glass window he could see, someone was answering his call. Lela had been discharged home. He was relieved. One less to worry about. He decided to go back to his computer to do some work and give her a ring later. Work was suffering.

When he got home, he rang the lab boss again to hear the latest.

"Yes, there have been developments," the lab man said. "We did find traces of toxin on the spoons, as your lady friend told you we might. And on Mrs McAvoy's plate, the napkin she used and in the rubbish where the remains of her meal was scraped. The fish salad was loaded with toxin. Loaded. Enough to kill several people. Mrs McAvoy hadn't eaten much of her lunch or she'd be a goner by now."

"Did you test the fish sauce?"

"We did and there was a massive lot of toxin there too."

"So it was the sauce."

"Doesn't make sense. An acid environment kills the bacteria. So the toxin wasn't due to a growth of bacteria."

Ted waited for more.

"Look, up till now we, you and I, were trying to find out how the bacteria got into the food. Now it's a police matter. Can't say more than that, sorry, but you can work it out."

Ted came off the phone with his mind awhirl. Vivien's food was full of toxin that is produced by bacteria. But bacteria can't survive the pH of the sauce. Ergo, it wasn't bacteria producing the toxin. So a load of toxin had been deliberately put into the sauce, any remaining bacteria had been killed off, leaving the toxin to do its damage. Confirmation of his fears. Ted groaned.

Would this never end? First Marcia and now Vivien. The car accident could logically be aimed at either of them but this was undoubtedly intended for Vivien and no one else, bar Lela. And maybe someone knew that Lela didn't like tinned fish. He couldn't wait till Holly was safely home.

When Ted picked up Jonathan after his chemo treatment, he brought him up to date with what the scientist told him and went on with his own conclusions. They rode in silence yet again.

When they were nearing the apartment block, Jonathan turned to Ted. "You asked that I delay doing something about Lela and I said yes, for Vivien's sake. Now I'd like you to do something for me. I'll pay whatever it takes. That tight-assed husband of hers. Could you find out if he's been in London the whole time?"

Chapter Thirty

Vivien swam up towards a light. A light? Something made her pause. It was a light. She had to think. It reminded her of something. Something about death. Had she died? Heaven? But the light was reddish. Red. Things sort of moving. Who was she? Why was she going up?

She couldn't think. Why did she need to think? Maybe because she could hear voices. She knew those sounds were voices. People. Spirits? Did people talk with voices in heaven?

She relaxed. Maybe it was all right. She felt herself sinking. Going down again. And she ceased to care.

Chapter Thirty-One

TED HAD AGREED TO do as Jonathan wanted, inwardly groaning even as he said he'd contact Vivien's solicitor. Nevertheless, he got onto it straight away; after all, he had the telephone notebook from the house. As he thumbed through it, he noticed most of the entries were in Jonathan's cramped hand, but Ted found it easy to identify Vivien's more cursive writing. She had added numbers for the two children and the husband, plus four more entries. He racked his brains for the solicitor's name, knowing that Vivien had used it in his presence. Three of the four numbers were for male names, one female. The solicitor was a man, he remembered. He could eliminate another, Sanji. He thought he would have remembered if the solicitor was Asian. So either John or Trevor. Neither caused a ripple in his brain.

He looked at the time. London was near enough halfway around the world, therefore halfway around the clock, give or take an hour for summertime. Then he remembered he could look up the time difference online. He would ring during the evening.

At nine, he rang the number for 'John'. Something was going well, as it did connect to a solicitor's office. It was at the beginning of their working day.

"Could I please speak with John?" he asked the receptionist. "I'm ringing from New Zealand."

The rather desultory voice became instantly more interested. "Hold on, I'll put you straight through."

"I'm Ted Frazer, a friend of Vivien McAvoy's," he said as quickly as he could when the phone was answered with a curt, 'Robertson'. "Am I right in assuming that you're her solicitor?" Ted asked.

"Yes, I am. Her friend? Has something happened?" The voice was concerned.

"Yes, I'm afraid Vivien is very ill in hospital with food poisoning. Her father wished me to ring you," he said, covering himself with the white lie.

"Thank you for telling me. You're correct. I am acting on her behalf. She was due to come home, and I'd been expecting her to call with her arrival times. Will she be all right?"

"Honestly, we don't know. She's in a serious but stable condition. But she's very ill and on a respirator."

"My heavens. Vivien. That's terrible," John said. "I'll start postponing some actions I had initiated. Thank you again for telling me."

"John, there's something Vivien's father would like to know. Is there any way you can find out if Vivien's ex-husband has been in the UK continuously over the past few weeks, and especially the past few days?"

A dead silence lasted several long seconds. "I can find out," he said slowly. "Am I correct in surmising that ... that foul play is suspected?"

"The police are involved, as they have been since she had her car accident."

"And before that was Mrs Fleet's death. Murder, I mean. I am sorry that Vivien didn't catch that plane home. Have the children been informed about her condition?"

"Yes, thanks. Their grandfather talked to both of them. Of course you know he's ill too."

"Yes, yes, I do. I understand her father's health was the main reason for going out to New Zealand." They exchanged telephone numbers, including mobiles, and Ted came off the phone thinking that John was not only Vivien's solicitor but most likely her friend too.

Still, the more Ted thought about it, the less likely he figured that John Robertson could help. He fully expected to be told that Gerald had never left the UK.

He felt lethargic. Nothing made sense. Vivien had only been in the country for such a short time. If this had all happened in the UK, the husband would be centre stage, but this was New Zealand and Vivien's history here was decades old. What could have happened at that end? He could take the Gerald situation a step or two further if Robertson confirmed his suspicions he had never left home.

Not now, but the next time Ted had to travel to the UK for business.

The police, Auckland cops this time, arrived in the morning not long after Ted had settled into reducing his backlog of work. He sighed when he realized who was at the door.

"Come in, gentlemen, and, er, lady," he said with an attempt at hiding his feelings.

"We're here about the latest incident to affect the Fleet family," Inspector Johnston said. "Mrs Vivien McAvoy is in hospital, as you know. Seriously ill."

Ted nodded. "They're keeping her on a respirator while the toxin clears from her system."

"Tell me what you know about this, Mr Frazer."

"All my knowledge is secondhand, I'm afraid. The person to talk to is Lela. I'm sorry I don't have her last name."

"We have spoken to her. Tell me your movements on that day before Mrs McAvoy became ill, the Tuesday, and who you spoke to, saw, etc."

Ted stifled a sigh. "I saw the family, that is, Vivien and Lela, and Jonathan too, that day. I went home earlier than usual because Jonathan was staying overnight in hospital. The next day both Vivien and Lela were also in hospital after the food poisoning episode. I had gone over to their house and found it locked up."

"When you were there, did you go inside?"

"No, of course not. I had a good middle class upbringing and you don't go into other people's homes without an invitation." If he thought the inspector would smile, he was disappointed. The inspector just gazed at him in his unblinking way.

"Did you try the doors?"

Ted tried to remember. "I may have."

"But, of course, you would never go in," the inspector said, lifting an eyebrow.

"No." Ted was getting irritated yet again. "If a door had been open, I would have called through the open door, not gone in."

The inspector's mouth smiled briefly at that one. "And you're always a good little lad, aren't you, Mr Frazer?"

"Always, Inspector. Being good is well ingrained, I can assure you."

"I understand you have a contract with a pharmacology company."

Ted was surprised and annoyed that they could have found that out. "Is this relevant?"

"We're trying to trace the toxin."

"My work is in software development. Even when I go on site, which is very rare, I can assure you, I'm only in the IT department. In fact, I've had no contact with any employee other than IT professionals. No pharmacists. I wouldn't know a toxin from ordinary flour."

"So the toxin is a white powder, is it?"

"Wouldn't have a clue," Ted said. "From memory of chemistry classes, most pharmaceuticals are in powder form and most are white; correct me if I'm wrong."

"I suggest, Mr Frazer, that you know very well what form the toxin comes in; you bought it in the UK and smuggled it past the airport authorities knowing its toxicity. Ready to use on your ex-wife. Or your current lover. Or on anyone else your sick mind decides needs dispatching."

"What? You're off your rocker," Ted exploded. "I've never handled botulism toxin in my life. I've never spoken to a pharmacologist about botulism toxin or any other toxin in the UK or anywhere else. And I have no reason—none—to kill anybody. To be more precise. I did not kill my ex-wife. I did not poison Vivien McAvoy."

The inspector stood and the sergeant snapped her notebook shut. Apparently the interview was over.

"We'll be back," the inspector said.

Ted was left a quivering mess. He headed for the kitchen and poured himself a hefty glass of whisky. After downing it in several minutes, he held out a still shaking hand to see if it had settled him. It hadn't. Whisky was overrated. He went back into the living room and collapsed onto the couch. How could they accuse him like that? Surely they had better targets? Gradually, the alcohol permeated his system and, in spite of his continuing anger, his eyes closed. He woke in a sweat. Crazy dream images of white powder and grinning death masks. He went into the bathroom to splash cold water on his face. Work. Turn his mind to work and forget this mad situation.

Ted honestly tried to lose himself in work, but he was still too annoyed and agitated. He pushed back his chair and stared out the window. Racing clouds, patches of blue, a whining wind. He tried to turn his agitation into some positive action he could take. But he felt hamstrung about anything useful he could contribute. He headed outside to do more weeding in the garden. One side-effect about aborted anger: it made doing manual work a breeze.

Chapter Thirty-Two

THE NEXT DAY TED met Holly at the airport. As always, his heart sang when he saw her rushing towards him.

"I'm glad you bullied me into coming home, Dad. Truly. I am counting the days, as always. Just sad there's no Mum here too."

Ted reached over and held her hand for a moment. They were surging along the motorway along with every other car in Auckland, it seemed. "Are you missing her?"

"It comes in waves," Holly said, her voice low. "I hadn't spent much time with her these past few years, what with me being in Dunedin and everything she did with Jonathan, and dividing my time between you both when I was up here. Now I regret it, of course. But it's probably helped me through this time. Sometimes I feel guilty I'm not suffering more weepy spells." She smiled at Ted. "Mostly, I remember the neat things we did when I was little. The climbing up the so-called mountains of Auckland. Remember that?" They had a project of climbing each dormant Auckland volcano. Ted had found many he didn't know existed. It made him realize what a volcanic lake the city is sitting on.

"I remember. That's one of the good ones, isn't it, young lady?"

Once home, Ted pulled Holly's case out of the boot and bumped it up the steps and into the house. She always packed way too many clothes, given she still had a closet full here in Auckland.

"What on earth have you done to the autumn marigolds?" Holly sang out from the back of the house.

"Weeded them so they'd look good for you. They're at their best right now, don't you think?" he called as he heaved the heavy suitcase onto her bed.

"You'd better come look," she said.

What he saw was a mass of beheaded flowers, their petals strewn widely on the lawn, the stems denuded in the flower bed.

"Who would have done this?" Holly asked. "It's just wanton destruction. Purposeless."

"Vandalism," Ted said, his anger rising so fast, he thought he'd choke. "Bloody senseless vandalism. Pointlessly ruining something beautiful." He bent down and picked up a more-or-less undamaged flower head. He crushed it in his hand and tossed it to join its ruined fellows scattered over the lawn.

"Lovely bright colour," Holly said, picking up another, taking a quick glance at her father's face. "This one, I'll put it in a glass. Maybe we can find a couple more and we can enjoy a little bouquet on the table for a few days."

Ted sighed and did as Holly asked. There were a few, only a few. He got out the rake and tidied the mess, picking up several more flowers that had a bit of stem on them as he went. Such stupid damage. Who would bother? It hurt nobody but him. Him. Only him.

Food for thought.

Marcia, Vivien and now this. Trivial in comparison, but it gave him pause.

Over dinner, Holly asked how the vandal could have done so much damage.

"I think he must have used a hoe," Ted said as he helped himself to more spaghetti. "Something he could swing, anyway."

"You haven't fallen out with Pauline, have you?"

Ted looked up, surprised. "Pauline? Why?"

"She's the only one I know with golf clubs." Holly pantomimed a golf swing. "Hole in one with each marigold."

True to her promise, Holly did some revision that evening. They met in the kitchen, late, Holly making herself a cup of hot chocolate and Ted a cup of tea. Such a cosy thing to do, domestic, a ritual which had started when Holly was much younger—a time to discuss things without the intrusions of daily life and without interruptions.

"Mum was almost beautiful, wasn't she, Dad?" Holly wrapped her hands around the mug as if she needed the warmth.

"She was beautiful as a young woman and, when I noticed recently, she was beautiful again in middle age, yes."

"Course, it probably had a lot to do with her plastic surgery, I guess. But she never got that stretched look so many women get."

"Surgery? Marcia?" This was news to Ted. "When?"

"You can't pretend you didn't know. Dad, for heaven's sake."

"She didn't need plastic surgery, surely."

"But you know she got more beautiful as she aged. You said it yourself. That just gives credit to the surgeon. And the Botox, of course."

Ted just shook his head. "Why on earth would she want to mess with her face? She was lovely looking anyway. And she was married to a man old enough to be her father. Looking younger would just emphasize their age difference."

"I actually told her that once. She just laughed and said I would know one day. Oh, and, cryptic as she often was, she said not to write her off just yet."

After Holly went off to bed, Ted savoured his tea, looking out over the dark garden at the back of the house. Not that he could see it, but he was feeling satisfied with the tidy-up of the marigold bed. He'd decided to pull the ruined plants, even though a few buds might still have sprouted. Now, all his annual beds were dug over and covered in a layer of compost. His winter vegetables were growing well in the sunniest spot. Luckily, Pauline hadn't spotted them.

Pauline. Who else could it have been?

She also hadn't noticed the first few green spears poking up through the grass, the harbinger of his favourite winter flower, the highly scented paper-white narcissi which would be blooming in July.

If, of course, the vandalism had been Pauline's. Somehow, once her name had been mentioned, he didn't doubt it was her. How could she do such a thing? What on earth should he do about it? They were friends, or he thought they were. Maybe friends who shared a bed, but friends and colleagues before anything else. He wouldn't hurt her, no matter the circumstances. Maybe she didn't feel the same way. Obviously didn't. After this, he didn't care if he never saw her again. The woman must be nuts.

His thoughts drifted. Plastic surgery? Why would Marcia want to be any different than she was? She was vain, yes, but putting yourself under the knife just to tweak an already attractive face? Probably her figure, too. He had noticed that she was back to wearing jeans and looking damn good in them. At the time, he had thought she had shed a few kilos. Not that he ever considered that she was overweight, but he knew she was conscious of her generous thighs.

Before heading to bed himself, he checked and doubled checked all the windows and doors were locked firmly. He hated shutting the house up so tightly, but whenever he thought of Holly being part of the Fleet family, his gut clenched. He'd sworn he'd keep her safe.

As he was turning out the lights, his thoughts turned again to Marcia. Was she trying to recapture her youth because of another man? After all, she had been unfaithful when she was married to him and a leopard and spots and all that. But as he turned off the electric blanket and snuggled into his pre-warmed bed, he thought the most likely explanation was just plain, old-fashioned vanity. She had always been a woman who liked to look at herself in the mirror.

The next day passed quietly with Holly head-down over her books and, other than taking Jonathan to hospital as usual, Ted was able to work on the various tasks that actually provided his income. He had lunch with Holly—hot soup and toasted rolls—outside in the autumnal sunshine, both dressed in fleece tops for warmth and sunhats to shield their eyes from the low sun. Later in the afternoon, after cautioning Holly once again about locks and windows and not answering any knock on the door, Ted picked up Jonathan after the chemo and ferried him to Oscar's apartment block. Jonathan looked drained.

"Still nauseous?" Ted asked.

Jonathan nodded. "And can't sleep and look at my stupid hands." He held them up for inspection, the palms again raw and peeling. "All to do with side-effects of this damn poison they're filling me up with. I keep telling myself that if it's poisoning me like this, it must be hell on the cancer cells."

Ted helped him out of the car and accompanied him up to the apartment. He didn't want Jonathan collapsing in the lift. Ted could hear voices when Jonathan opened the door of the apartment.

"Hi, Dad," Holly said. "I left you a note at home to say I've been invited to see Oscar's latest project. Now we're going out to grab a bite." She was dressed in a diaphanous top over slim black trousers. Hardly the scruffy jeans and fleece top he saw at lunch. "We've been at the City Mission where Oscar volunteers."

Ted was dismayed Holly was spending more time with Oscar. Nevertheless, he forced a smile. "City Mission?"

"Oscar's organizing a funding drive to buy a new oven."

"Very commendable, I'm sure," Ted said. Why didn't this guy just disappear? Standing there, Holly looked about eighteen and Oscar looked ... what? Maybe a good looking forty, but twice her age none the less.

"Their present oven is too small for all the meals they have to prepare there. In this economic climate, they're getting whole families in for meals. You should see the size of the roasts they cook. Oscar's already got six businesses to sponsor the new oven, haven't you, Oscar?"

"Drink?" Oscar asked the two men, his voice smooth.

Both made excuses and Jonathan disappeared into his bedroom as Ted said his goodbyes. He congratulated himself on not saying something sarcastic to Holly about studying, but it didn't improve his temper. What was she playing at? Oscar's good deeds or no good deeds at all, this was her mother's ex-lover and her step-brother, for heaven's sake, and she was going out to dinner with him. By the time he reached home, he regretted finishing the digging in the garden.

That would have been a suitable activity, feeling the way he was. Instead, he got out his water blaster and attacked his concrete driveway, a task he had been putting off because it was a cold wet job in winter temperatures. Not a chore he liked, ever, but his anger carried him through. He ended up with an antiseptically clean driveway, followed by a long and luxurious hot shower. Now to go back to the hospital and see if he was allowed to visit Vivien.

Ted entered the room quietly and with some trepidation, feeling big and clumsy, an intruder in this white and antiseptic world. Adding to his discomfort, he imagined bringing clouds of germs from the outside.

The very regularity of the noise from the machine that provided air into Vivien's lungs was disconcerting. They had her breathing from something attached to her neck now, so her face was clear. She looked younger than normal, and it wasn't until he sat down beside her that he realized how peaceful she looked. Peaceful now probably meant she must have been under considerable strain before.

Ted bent forward and talked into her ear. Not loudly because of the other people in the room and not with any expectation she could hear, but just in case. He told her about the toxin, how she just needed time for her own body to get rid of its effects, how he expected her to make a full recovery in a matter of weeks and then it would be in time for the first of the so-called spring flowers. He promised her a bouquet of paper-whites once she was home. He told her Jonathan was sticking to his chemo and he was ferrying her father to and fro as always. He also told her about contacting John Robertson in England and how everything was just on hold and, last, about Holly going out to dinner with her step-brother.

Did he feel a twitch? He had been holding her hand. It was smooth and warm. For the first time, Ted had not felt self-conscious about touching Vivien. He wanted to hold her hand as he wanted to transfer energy, his own energy, to repair the damage caused by the toxin. Her hand, passive in his larger one, seemed small and delicate. He sighed. The twitch was only his imagination and his desire to see her well again. He covered her hand with his other hand.

"Get well, Vivien. I need to bounce ideas off you." He stopped talking because his voice might break and just sat silently for another few minutes. "I miss you."

He left her bedside considerably calmer than when he had arrived.

Chapter Thirty-Three

THAT VOICE ... SHE listened again. Still the red light. Black to red to black to ... but she was also hearing now. To no avail. It was all confusing, baffling. So difficult to clear her mind, as if a fog permeated every nook and cranny. Couldn't move. Not even a tremble. Try as she might. But she could listen. Pleasant voice. Whose? She knew. She must know, but whose? Something soothing about that voice. She thought of things that gave her pleasure. Flowers? Fields of spring flowers. Why was she thinking of these things?

Who? A name came out of nowhere. Ted. Yes, of course, Ted. She relaxed. That's why the voice brought lovely thoughts. Safety and comfort. She wanted to let him know she recognized him. She concentrated on her leg. Move, dammit. Just a little bit. Move. MOVE.

But whatever they were giving her kicked in once more and she sank back down. Ted. She tried to capture his voice. To keep it with her. But she kept losing it until she went beyond caring once more.

Chapter Thirty-Four

TED HEARD HOLLY ARRIVE home. It was just before midnight, according to his bedside clock. Time enough to talk to her in the morning, not that he had a clue what to say to her. The whole scenario wrenched his guts. What kind of man dates a mother, then her daughter, after her death? He punched his pillow into shape and pulled the duvet high. He turned over and had to punch the pillow again. Finally, he got up to check the doors were fully locked and to make himself a hot drink. Hopefully, that would settle him down enough to get off to sleep.

Holly didn't want to talk about it. "Just butt out, Dad. There's nothing between me and Oscar, so stop fussing. I was interested in his volunteer work and so should you be. He's doing some real good, for heaven's sake. And then we went out to dinner. Big deal. He wanted to take me out in style in that magnificent car of his. He won't have it next weekend because he's flying down and renting something, so he said we could go out to dinner in it while I was in Auckland." She sighed loudly and turned away to get on with her studying. Ted's jaw ached from being clenched so tight. What did he need to do to get Holly to see reason?

"I have some of Mum's things," Holly said, changing the subject abruptly. She brought in a cardboard box. "The police dropped this stuff off for Gramps and he's said there's nothing of interest in here either for the police or for him and I can throw it all out once I've gone through it."

"Have you had a look?" Ted asked.

Holly nodded. "Nothing much here. Some books she was reading, a notepad, all stuff from her desk." She paused. "Except maybe her calendars."

"Oh? Why?"

Holly put the box on the floor and sat down beside it. She pulled up two beautiful art calendars, one for last year and a current one. Each month was illustrated with a different painting.

"See, she's written on it. When did you meet for lunch? I can see if you're here."

He grabbed his phone. There it was, a 'Pierre's' lunch on a date some two weeks before Marcia died. He pointed it out to Holly. "Anything for this date?"

"A 'T', look. 'T' for Ted, obviously." Holly sat back on her heels. "I'm finding this slightly spooky, Dad. Look, she's got 'rb' written on that last day."

"Leave it then, young lady. I don't want you upset." He would have a look at it later.

"No. It might give us some information. You game to keep looking?"

"Up to you."

"I want to." Her voice was resolute.

Ted took the proffered calendar. "Okay, but I have to work this morning. I'll get onto it as soon as I can."

An hour or so later, when Ted made coffee-making noises in the kitchen, Holly appeared. "What's this?" she pointed to some minute doodles on the date of Marcia's death.

Ted adjusted his glasses. The marks were in pencil and almost indecipherable. "Could be nothing. Could stand for something. Don't know." He handed the calendar back to Holly.

"I found similar squiggles in other places, too."

"Oh, did you now." Ted took the calendar back again and held it up to the light. "I'll make a guess and say the top one is a sigma. A little sigma. Greek letter. And the others, maybe a tau—another Greek letter—and three capital Is. Roman numeral three? Perhaps."

"Greek letters. Okay. What about this one? It's a pi, isn't it?" Holly pointed to a date several days earlier.

"A third Greek letter. Got to be some sort of personal code." Typical Marcia. A calendar open to anyone who looked, so things in cipher.

"You're right," Holly said slowly. "Greek symbols and Roman numerals. Bound to be for her eyes only."

They looked at the date square of Marcia's last day again. The more Ted looked at it, the clearer it was: 'σ', a small sigma, in the middle of a circle, then a small tau, followed by three capital 'I's. 'τ III'—presumably 'tau three'—and finally, 'rb'. In the week before her death was 'Lπ'. He looked at Holly. "Show me where else you found them."

"I was thinking, Jonathan," Ted said in the car on the way to hospital, "about who could be responsible for hurting Vivien."

"I told you. Nobody but her damn husband."

"I'm onto him. I've talked to Vivien's solicitor and I'll call him back tomorrow to see if he has any info."

"Everybody loves Vivien," Jonathan said into the scarf he was holding up around his neck and mouth. He felt the cold nowadays and even with the car heater turned up full, he shivered. "Her bloody husband's the only one with motivation."

Ted nodded. "Our number one suspect, except for the uncomfortable notion that he was most likely on the other side of the world."

"Don't give up on it."

"I said I'm onto it." He hated it when Jonathan queried him. He could be an irritating man. They were crawling in traffic around a construction site on the motorway. It was set to be a slow trip in. "You knew him, Jonathan. Tell me what you remember."

"Big bastard. One of those overgrown schoolboy types like Boris Johnson. Never can keep his shirt tucked in. Paunch even when he was much younger. Bit older than you, I guess, but much younger than me. Dark hair, always needs a haircut, beetling eyebrows, wet sloppy lips. Ugly bugger. Never could figure out what Vivien saw in him."

"I get the picture." The tide was low and the greywacke rocks were exposed towards Bayswater. The sun was hazy, but the city across the harbour shone golden in the morning light.

"Runs a marketing outfit. Never been sure how successful it is. They have a pleasant house but I bought that; kids went to excellent schools, though, and he's never touched me for money. Successful enough, I'd say, without really making a mark."

Ted grunted. That would about sum up his own life, too. Successful enough, but....

"Bosses everyone about. Kids, Vivien. And I've heard him on the telephone over the years. Bet he has staff retention problems."

Takes one to know one. "Out and about a lot? Social? Homebody?"

"Golfs. He's got golf mates. He can toss back a few when he's with them. I've been there when he's called Vivien to come collect him. She takes a taxi to the golf club and then drives the car home. At least he doesn't drive drunk."

"And the marriage?" He kept his voice steady.

"As I said, never could see what Vivien saw in him. Of course, I've never understood why Vivien and Marcia didn't get along. After all, they had New Zealand in common and were not that different in age."

"That may have been part of the problem, Jonathan."

"The age thing? I'm not the only man to marry a younger woman. I mean, look at Oscar. He's interested in your Holly. And there's a sizeable gap there, too."

Ted had to loosen his hands from the death grip he had on the steering wheel. He told himself to relax. Jonathan was talking about his son.

"I don't get the idea that Holly is much interested," Ted said as calmly as he could.

"You never know, Ted. Oscar needs a steady wife. Someone with brains and beauty and our Holly certainly meets those criteria."

Ted concentrated on manoeuvring into the left-hand lane for the Gillies Avenue off ramp. "Vivien's marriage. You were saying?"

"Seemed all right. Lasted long enough. No other women or that sort of thing. I don't think he was ever violent except with his tongue. But he could go on and on sometimes, that's for sure."

"About what sort of things?"

"Usual stuff. Dinner was not what he expected. What Vivien was wearing. And the kids' behaviour. He was a bore about the kids. No, come to think of it, he was a bore, full stop."

Driving home, Ted reflected on this new knowledge. Gerald sounded like a petty dictator, overly concerned with trivia and willing to embarrass his wife and children in front of his father-in-law. Yet Vivien was apparently willing to go the extra mile, like rescuing him from his drinking episodes. He wondered how she had stood it for so long.

Father and daughter sat at the outside table. Dinner was cooking. Holly had gone through the calendars carefully looking for repetitions. Each she had marked with a sticky. "I've found 'τ II' and before that, 'Test I'. Could 'τ' stand for 'test' the second time? See, she'd already used 'T' for 'Ted' so she substituted the Greek letter after that?"

"Always paired with a sigma?"

"Always. But there are lots of circled sigma signs without the tau and the number."

They stared at each other. Ted's mind was racing. Sigma. Tau. The 'I's had to be Roman numerals; that was clear. So the sigma and the tau stood for something, too.

"Rb?" Ted queried. "Anything else on the dates with 'Tau two' and 'Test one'?"

"Nope." Holly paged back to where 'Tau II' was scribbled on the date.

"Anything unusual before or after?"

He looked over her shoulder. "What's that? 'Avo jumps 24th 4pm'?"

"Her stupid parachute jump."

"God, yes. Forgot about that one. She did it into some inaccessible island. Something like that. I couldn't believe it." In fact, he hadn't believed it. Thought she was winding him up when she bragged she'd done it. Marcia had more than a few phobias and a fear of heights was definitely on the list. No way would she have jumped from an airplane even if it had been stationary on the tarmac.

"She told me she was on a dare and damned if she wasn't going to do it. Told me where her will was kept." Holly shook her head. "Doing things on a dare? I got over that when I was twelve."

"Well, good on her for tackling her fears, I guess," Ted said. Then it hit him. "The 24th. That's the date of the second tau."

"If tau is 'Test'...," Holly said, "this is her second test. Jumping out of an airplane." She grinned at him. "Got to be!"

"Oh, boy," Ted said. "And the third test was going out in that boat she hated. Rowboat: 'rb'." A wave of sadness enveloped him. She had tested herself in the rowboat. And lost.

He brought the dinner outside and they ate in silence. Too much Marcia. Too much worry about Holly. He put his fork down. He couldn't swallow another bite.

In spite of good intentions, he decided to open up the subject again. "You said about Oscar, Holly, that you weren't interested in him."

"Dad! Just leave him out of it, okay? You're treating me like a fifteen-year-old."

"Sorry, Holly, but I just don't like him. Don't trust him."

"As if that wasn't patently obvious." She swivelled her chair so she was looking down the garden. "I'm not going to talk to you about him. This is ridiculous. So don't mention him. Ever again."

"Holly, this is the man who dated your mother when she was married to me." He had quickly substituted 'dated' for what he really meant. "She was a married woman. You can't be seriously considering becoming involved with him. You just can't!' He knew he had blown it by the look on her face.

"This conversation is finishing right now. Don't bother asking me about anything concerning Oscar because this is a verboten topic." She took a long drink from her mug of tea and bumped it down on the wooden tabletop with an unnecessary thud.

"I'm sorry, young lady. It's just that..."

"Nothing, Dad. Not a word." She lifted her forefinger to forestall any more conversation. "If you can't change the subject, I'm going in."

Ted sighed and bit back the retort he wanted to make. "Okay, subject change. Jonathan is not doing very well. He's having awful reactions to the chemo.

"Like last time." It wasn't a question.

"I suppose so. Did you see him during that time?"

"Yeah. He was really sick. I mean sick like sick to his stomach, kind of without warning. So he always had this bowl beside him. Yuck. Mum hated it." Ted was trying hard to concentrate on the conversation and push down the subject of Oscar. Why couldn't Holly see things like he did?

He wrenched his thoughts back. "I can imagine. She was never the nursing type."

"It was pathetic. Here's this old guy, so sick and, well, sort of disgusting, and then there was Mum, dressed to the nines and going out to lunch or whatever. Waving goodbye and blowing kisses at us, then floating out the door."

"Leaving you to look after him?" He was genuinely interested in what Holly was saying at this point.

"Mostly Lela. You know Lela?"

"Yes, of course. So Lela did a lot of the work?"

"She was very good with Gramps, but he sort of didn't see her, if you know what I mean. Like when she did things for him—cleaning him up after he was sick, that sort of thing—it was as if he got cleaned magically. Whereas when Mum helped clean him up, and that was not very often, he was all over her, saying how much he appreciated her helping him, how much he loved her. Tons of gooey stuff."

Ted shook his head. Holly's description fitted the image of their relationship as explained by Vivien rather than the one Cushla described. Jonathan was a complex character. Pathetic one moment and driving him nuts the next. Still, it would be wretched to be at other people's mercy. It sounded as if he was desperately wanting attention from Marcia. And some of that time, she was swanning around doing 'tests' of her fears. His mind clicked back onto the significance of the sigma sign. Sigma in statistics meant 'mean', didn't it? As in 'average'?

Mean? The only mean one here was Oscar. The thought made him grin for the first time in ages.

Chapter Thirty-Five

MARCIA AND JONATHAN: IF he was desperately seeking her attention, did that mean she had lessened the attention she had given him before? Poor, pathetic Jonathan. Now, of course, she was permanently out of his life. Would she have stuck around through this latest bout of chemo? Maybe, but somehow Ted thought not. But it brought him to thinking about Lela again. He decided to give her a ring. See how she was.

She was fine, she assured him. Fighting fit and back at work.

"At Jonathan's house? The police let you in?"

"Oh, yes, Mr Ted. I'm watching how they put in the new kitchen."

"Of course. I'd forgotten. How is it shaping up?"

"It will be beautiful. Lots of stainless steel like Gordon Ramsay's restaurants."

"That's good?" Ted said dubiously. His ideal kitchen was a farm kitchen with wooden butcher block bench tops, chintz curtains, a big family table, and an aura of cosiness. But, he had to admit, hardly suitable for that house. "How about your next computer lesson? When will that be?"

"As soon as possible, Mr Ted. I'm missing my lessons, but I'm practicing what you told me on Ms Vivien's laptop."

"Tomorrow morning after I take Jonathan to the hospital?"

Ted was relieved to see that Lela did look good. Back to normal. She greeted him with her wide smile and ushered him to the conservatory that Ted thought of as Vivien's day room.

"Did you know that Mr Jonathan is coming home for the weekend?"

"No, he didn't tell me," Ted said as he settled himself in front of the laptop. "Because Oscar will be away?" Whenever he thought of Oscar, he got a spasm in his lower abdomen.

"I suppose so. My husband, he didn't like that I'm staying over for three nights, but there's no one to look after Mr Jonathan in the night now that Ms

Marcia has ... passed. I can look after him. I know what to do. And he's not so sick this time. Not like last time."

"Holly was just saying how well you looked after him during his last course of chemo."

"She's a good girl, your Holly."

They reviewed the previous lessons and Lela told him how she was now doing a typing course. Ted grinned at her. "Thanks for listening to me, Lela. You will never regret learning to type properly." He reminded her he was going to pay for them.

"No need, Mr Ted, but thank you for the thought. I got a volunteer to teach me—in our community, like you said. She used to teach in high schools and she's good. A nice lady, too."

He smiled at her, loving how she'd taken on a problem and found a way forward.

Lela looked up at the wall clock. "Your Holly's about to come over. Any time now."

"Is she? Why?"

"She wants to try on her mother's frocks; luckily she's little, like her mother. She needs one to wear when she goes to Queenstown with Mr Oscar. The big dinner-dance she's going to. Silly buying one when Ms Marcia's wardrobe is still here."

Ted felt as if he'd been hit. Holly really meant it when she said she was not going to talk about her plans with Oscar. He certainly did not want to be there when Holly came over. He made hasty goodbyes to Lela and got safely away before Holly arrived. How he hated the whole charade.

Later that evening the telephone rang: the English pharmacology company wanting him back for another stint of work on site.

"You're off on Friday, as planned?" he asked Holly.

Her face darkened. Looking momentarily eerily like Marcia. "I told you...."

"Hold it right there, young lady. I have to get to London again and you're my first priority. I need to know when you're away so I can get you to the airport. Then plan my trip after that."

"Oh, Dad, sorry. Jumping to conclusions. You're being very good about keeping off the subject," she said, giving him a hug. "I'm away on Friday night. Flying directly to Queenstown instead of you-know-who coming to pick me up in Dunedin. He'll be taking me home on Sunday, but this is neater." Ted felt his body become more and more rigid. Yet he smiled at his daughter.

"Going to the airport with anybody?"

Holly laughed. "Yes, thanks. You and I can say our goodbyes after dinner on Friday night. I have a late flight down."

He had already guessed. "Okay," he said. "I'll try to get a Saturday flight to England. The timing is going to be fine." He gave her a bear hug. "Just you be careful, young lady. You're my most precious daughter."

"Your only daughter." It was a game they had played for almost twenty years. He said nothing more, even though he was dying to ask about the evening dress. He would tough it out. No matter how hard it was.

After Holly left, Ted dragged out his well-worn suitcase. He counted out underwear and socks, shirts and his suit and several ties. In England to fit in, he always wore a suit and tie. He put travelling clothes on the chair, including a pair of chinos, a short-sleeved shirt and lightweight jumper.

The doorbell rang.

"Pauline?" In front of him was a bedraggled Pauline, her head bent, and her cheeks wet, and not only by the rain that was coming down. "Whatever's the matter? Come in."

He helped her out of her raincoat and wiped her face with his fingers. "What's wrong?"

She leaned against him, sobbing. "I've been so awful to you," she said, almost wailing. "Your beautiful garden. How could I? I don't know what possessed me. I don't. I don't. I'm so sorry."

"There, there," he said. "It's all forgotten now. I have it cleaned up to its winter state. Had to be done sooner rather than later. So, stop crying." He hated women crying. Hated anybody crying, even on television. "Look, you just lean back here, put your feet up, and I'll put the kettle on for a cup of tea."

She nodded, her eyes downcast, still hiccoughing from the crying jag. "I'm shivering. Cold, so cold."

He got out a blanket and draped it over her long form. "Won't be a moment."

By the time he came back with tea and biscuits, Pauline was asleep. He set the tray down and grabbed a mug. He had a plane to catch in the morning. And he had packing to complete, so he left Pauline sleeping on the couch and went back to the bedroom. He gathered his travelling kit, packed everything in the suitcase and checked on Pauline. Still asleep. He shrugged his shoulders and left her there.

The next morning he slipped out of bed trying not to awaken Pauline curled up beside him. He groaned silently, knowing he had made a terrible mistake. Sometime during the night, he'd awakened to very pleasant sensations indeed. He'd opened his eyes to see Pauline's grin in the semi-darkness. Should have stopped right there, but he didn't.

He grabbed the clothes he'd set out and crept out to Holly's bathroom to shower there. Pauline was still sleeping when he left the house. Better that than confronting her. He berated himself for being a coward, but he had a plane to catch.

Ted settled himself into the window seat of the big plane. As usual, he was at the very back of the plane where there were only two instead of three seats across. He paid for his own travel, so felt no need to upgrade himself unless he was exceptionally tired. Partly this was because he was a Frequent Traveller and the special concessions to which he was entitled. The airport lounges for Frequent Travellers had showers, food, booze and places to lie down. He had the travelling down pat. Needed to, with his schedule.

The rest of Holly's visit had been uneventful, and they'd indulged in a special treat of Indian take-aways that last night. The only problem had been Pauline, but the less he thought about that episode, the better. Oh, and Jonathan. He'd told him he was to be away for a week, so unable to transport him back and forth from the hospital. He gave Jonathan a choice: Lela, taxis or Uber. Jonathan, with ill grace, chose Lela. Ted decided the old guy was not only a snob but a skinflint at heart.

Once on the plane, he dismissed the Pauline problem. The only set of thoughts pressing on his mind was what was happening in Queenstown. He couldn't help it; he was bloody angry and sitting next to an overweight snoring man didn't help. Every time he tried to snooze, the image of Holly in a long evening dress slowly merged into Marcia in the same dress, both or either watched by Oscar who looked like a cat with cream. Holly. His Holly. Somehow, he had accepted what had happened between Marcia and Oscar better than the prospect of Oscar and Holly becoming an item.

He switched his mind back to Pauline. She was trouble and maybe the problem was bigger than he was acknowledging. He had met Pauline when they had both been working on a glitch in the databases of a huge supermarket chain. He was called in as the Oracle expert and her expertise was in Linux. They did most of the work off-site, but periodically Ted had to fly down to Wellington to work with the on-site engineers. The office set aside for the visiting IT consultants had only one desk to be shared by whoever needed it. In this case, he shared with Pauline. Most of the time, she was busy elsewhere; they communicated by telephone and email and it didn't matter who was where. Then one time, they were competing with each other for that desk, both under huge pressure to fix problems during time-constricted windows of when the database could be shut down and that meant working in the middle of the night. But they got along well, jostling each other for desk space and doing lots of laughing in the process.

After that, Pauline seemed to be turning up every time Ted was in Wellington. Not that he put any significance to it at the time, but, in retrospect, things had changed. Ted couldn't help admiring Pauline; who wouldn't? Young and bright and capable, not to mention her long legs and wonderful eyes. They didn't discover their compatibility in bed until the project was almost finished. And it seemed as if it was spontaneous. Back in Auckland, he ran into her frequently, mostly over coffee.

Did he ever invite her out? Not that he could recall. Somehow, she was often there when he popped into the café close to the city office and being waved over. Lots of bright conversation over coffees. And how did the weekends start? He honestly couldn't remember.

The plane was dark now, most people either watching movies or curled up under blankets trying to sleep. The drone of the engines blanked out most little sounds, but somehow the noise was the opposite of soporific. Ted shifted into yet another position, trying to get comfortable. Damn Holly. Her ignorance of men was annoying. More than annoying. Dangerous. Why did the young think they knew it all?

He wrenched his mind away from Holly and back to Pauline. Did she organize that first weekend at his place? Then he remembered. He had a barbecue for all the various IT personnel from Auckland who were working on that wretched supermarket problem. Five of them, including Pauline, of course. They were celebrating the successful completion of the job at the pub and he'd spontaneously invited them back ... no, not like that. Pauline had suggested they buy some big steaks and tubs of potato salad to soak up the alcohol. Who had a garden where they could barbecue? He did. And when the others left, Pauline helped clean up. And stayed.

Ted had a fleeting thought about Holly and men. Damn. He's been the ignorant one. He had been a Bambi-in-the-headlights. Certainly, he had no excuse about being young and inexperienced but maybe it had all come down to being overly trusting. Then meeting up with expert manipulation.

He opened his eyes. A steward was coming down the darkened aisle with a bottle of wine. He grabbed his water glass and waved it. The steward gave him a good half glass of wine with a smile and Ted finally fell into a fitful alcohol-assisted doze. The shower and break in Singapore did little to revive him.

When in London, Ted always stayed at the Barbican where he could get a room in a modern hotel within walking distance of the IT division of the pharmacology company for which he was developing the software. By arriving on the British Saturday night, he had a full day for recuperation from his jet-lag and time to let the distance from Queenstown finally calm his over-stimulated consciousness. Sunday afternoon, he felt like taking a long walk. London was warm and sunny and, except for the tourist buses, almost sleepy. Stretching his legs after a twenty-seven hour plane trip felt good. He ended up walking down to St Paul's and along the embankment, then back up to the Templar Church. He had recently reread Dan Brown's book and thought he would take the opportunity to see the crusader effigies. As it happened, few people were there and he could gape as long as he wanted. The custodian was helpful. The extensive damage done to the effigies was comparatively recent, due to World War II bombing damage. Ted bent down and gingerly touched the jagged edge of where a stone nose should have jutted out. Yes, the break was fresh even though it was more than seventy years in the past. A mere seventy, not seven hundred. But little things like the broken nose helped keep his mind away from what was happening in Queenstown.

Ted worked long days on both Monday and Tuesday, finding and sorting through the technical problems with the people at the company. Wednesday, he finally found time to ring John Robertson, Vivien's solicitor. He was put straight through, maybe because the telephonist thought he was again calling from New Zealand.

"I can't guarantee it, but it's unlikely McAvoy would have had time to get to New Zealand and back," John reported after asking about Vivien's condition. "His kids come down to London some weekends and a friend of mine golfs with him mid-week. I asked him if McAvoy had been away at all over the past month, and he said he wished he had. All he can talk about is his wife deserting him. Everyone runs for cover when he comes into their clubrooms."

"How do you think he would react if I rang him?" Ted asked.

"He's a salesman type. You'd have no problem. How much he'd tell you, I couldn't hazard a guess. He's a businessman through and through. I have trouble sorting useful information out of the rubbish he dumps on me, but he might be different with you. Do you want his number?"

"Marcia's ex?" McAvoy asked when Ted identified himself.

"Yes. And I've recently met Vivien. I've been trying to help the Fleet family through all this mess. As I was in London on business, I thought I should let you know I was here in case you wanted to have some first-hand information." Ted had thought out what he would say to Gerald carefully. He wanted to sound solicitous and that Gerald could gain by communicating with him.

"Hang on and I'll check the diary," McAvoy said. "How long are you here?"

"I'll be finished work Friday sometime. My flight out is Saturday, early afternoon from Heathrow."

"Friday evening? How about we meet at my golf club and have a drink?"

Chapter Thirty-Six

HER CHEST HURT. REALLY hurt. And she couldn't hold her breath. Couldn't get her breath. Bloody pain. Surely it was getting worse with every breath. And she couldn't move. She couldn't cough. Try as she might, nothing worked. The painful breaths just kept filling her tender lungs, over and over, stretching them, torturing them, on and on, relentlessly. And it was getting worse.

Then she heard his voice. And the raw edge of fear vanquished everything else. She needed help! It was him! Him. His voice, frightening, terrifying. She couldn't move; she couldn't get away! She hadn't been able to tell.... She wanted to scream: No. No. NO NO NO....

Chapter Thirty-Seven

THE CLUBROOMS WERE HOUSED in an old-fashioned building that smelled of beer intermingled with wafts of fresh air whenever the door opened. The atmosphere was that of a country pub. When Ted told the barman he was meeting Gerald McAvoy, he nodded at a man in a corner booth by a window, a man easily recognizable from Jonathan's description.

"Nice to meet you, Ted. And please call me Gerald." His voice was hearty as he stood to shake Ted's hand. He gestured to the outstanding view from the window which was overlooking an oval-shaped pond reflecting clumps of tall shrubs and distant glimpses of tree ringed greens. People were still golfing in the evening light. The scene was picture perfect and Ted didn't want to guess what a membership must cost. "How do you like it?"

Ted made appropriate noises, and Gerald headed back to the bar to buy drinks. Ted noticed that Gerald had almost finished his whisky.

"Tell me how she is," Gerald said, looking straight at Ted who informed him in some detail about the induced coma, the respirator, the paralysis and the guarded optimism for her future. "How does she look?" Gerald asked.

"Vivien had this enormous tube in her mouth, Gerald, but now they've inserted the tube surgically in her neck. She looked awful, that went with the territory, but she appears a bit more normal now. She's getting fed by tube too, of course, but so far she's infection-free and every day she survives, the prognosis gets better."

"Thank god, for that," Gerald said, his eyes moistening. "Maybe some good will come of all this. Maybe it will make her see reason."

Ted thought he knew what Gerald was on about, but played dumb. "Reason?"

"She had decided to leave me. I don't know if you knew that. She told people she was going on holiday—me too, I might add—then decided to stay away. I think it was all due to Marcia's death. She could go back to her precious daddy's house and play Lady Muck. He's most likely persuaded her to stay. Slippery bloke, that Jonathan. You know him, too?"

"Yes, I've known him for decades, well before Marcia left me for him."

"Well, you know what it feels like, then." Gerald reached over and clapped Ted on the shoulder. "Another?" he asked, as he swept up his own empty glass. Ted held up his glass, showing that it was still more than half full. As he watched Gerald wend his way to the bar, he realized the man must have been tossing them back well before he got there and was half cut already.

"It's not easy, your wife leaving. We know that, don't we Ted? We know what it's like. None of these other ignoramuses do, the bastards." He gulped at this fresh drink. Ted glanced around and saw several eyes slide off his. Gerald's voice was obviously carrying well beyond their corner booth.

"Course, with bloody Marcia, not so hard, I bet."

Ted was taken aback at his vehemence, but decided to continue to play dumb. "You knew Marcia?"

"How could I not? She was my bloody mother-in-law." He guffawed. "Officially. Like she was my..." He spluttered into his glass. "She was something, I can tell you." He stopped and leaned forward. "But I don't need to tell you. You lived it, man. Don't know how, eh?" He winked. "Bloody bossy women. When did it all go to shit, Ted? You tell me. Bloody Marcia. Bloody Vivien." Gerald was obviously feeling the alcohol he'd imbibed.

Ted needed to get him away from his ranting. "Another?" he asked, standing.

On his return, Gerald carried on as if there'd been no pause. "Bloody hard. This whole thing. 'Life, the Universe and Everything'." He snorted at the quote.

Ted smiled dutifully.

"First the bloody kids carrying on, then Vivien taking it into her head that she wants to be independent. Family values. That's what it's all about. The destruction of family values."

Ted was getting desperate to get Gerald back on track before he got too drunk to communicate. He waited until Gerald took a long pull at his refreshed glass of whisky. "I quite like getting out of the country," Ted said. "Gives some perspective on life as one usually lives it. You have been out of England in the past little while?"

"How could I?" Gerald said, tears threatening once more. "I'm bloody hovering over the telephone in case she rings. That's what I'm doing. If she thinks I'm going to ring her, she's got another think coming."

"She's not in any shape to ring anyone right now, Gerald. She's in a medical coma. And paralyzed. I hate to emphasise it, but she's very ill."

"So you say. But maybe this is all hogwash. Maybe you're just a spy. Maybe right this minute she's sitting in her precious father's mansion laughing at me."

"Right this minute, she's battling for her life. Rest assured about that. Last I saw her, she couldn't move a muscle, not even to breathe. That's how serious it is." Ted's voice rose to meet his. This was getting a little out of hand. Unless the man was a consummate actor, he was also getting more assured that Gerald had nothing to do with poisoning Vivien.

"Have you any idea who could have done this to her, Gerald?" He looked deep into Gerald's eyes in hopes of triggering some lurking intelligence.

"To Vivien? God, I don't know. Someone who hates her. Maybe she's got a bloody boyfriend. Hell, I don't know. Maybe her old boyfriends in New Zealand. Someone wanted to kill her. Probably sex at the bottom of it." He heard his own terrible pun and started to giggle. Ted wanted to shake him.

"What boyfriends? Did she have boyfriends while you were married?"

"No, course not; she wouldn't dare." His head slumped onto his chest and he struggled to get it upright. Ted knew the questioning was almost at an end.

"What boyfriends, Gerald? And why would an old boyfriend want to kill her?"

"Cuz she's a bitch at heart, that's why." His words were slurred. "One of 'em pestered her after we were married. Came to London. A bloody photographer with a paparazzo long lens. She had a hard time."

"Who? Tell me his name, Gerald. Who was it?"

"Can't remember. Oh, yes. Hiram. That's it. Hiram Somebody or other."

"Come on. Hiram Who?"

"Dunno. Really. Long time ago." His head slumped again.

Ted paused. Time to wrap up. "Maybe we should get on our way now, Gerald. It's a long way back to town." He had taken a train, then a taxi to the golf club.

"Z'no Vivien to come get me," he said, tears now flowing. "She's not here. Left me. Shit, what'm I going to do?"

"We'll both get a taxi. I can get home from your place, but we'll share that far."

"M'car. Gotta get m'car."

"No, that's out, Gerald. It's taxi time." He arranged with the barman to tell them when the taxi arrived. On the signal, he helped Gerald to his feet, and they lumbered out of the clubhouse.

The taxi took them to a large town house that seemed to soar above them when they climbed the steps that led to the shiny blue front door. Gerald fumbled with his keys, but before he could figure out how to use them, the door opened.

A tall young man said, "Dad!"

Ted introduced himself and said, "We've come by taxi. He wasn't driving."

The boy asked him to wait in the sitting room while he got his father upstairs. "If you wouldn't mind."

Ted said he had a taxi waiting.

"Please. I'd love to talk to you. Let the taxi go. I'll run you back to your hotel in Mum's car."

Ted paid off the taxi and returned to the sitting room as requested, intrigued in spite of the long day. He heard loud voices from up the stairs and felt relieved he wasn't involved.

The sitting room was quietly elegant in shades of grey-green. Several family photos were on a table near the front window. Ted recognized Gerald and Vivien and this young man who had reminded him his name was Liam. And the daughter. Stephanie, he remembered that. Then two little girls. It was coming back to him. Gerald had a daughter by a previous wife whose daughters had been partially brought up by Vivien. Two little angels, quite literally, as the photo caught them with angel wings in what was possibly a Christmas play.

Liam returned. "He's out for the count. Sorry about all that. He gets into the booze a bit more regularly now that Mum's left him. How about a coffee before I take you back?"

They sat in the kitchen over mugs of instant. It was hot and wet and therefore not to be spurned. Ted went over the technicalities of Vivien's health.

"I really appreciate your telling me all this, Ted," Liam said. "I've been terribly worried and Gramps is not all that good at giving many details. I'll give Stephanie a ring in the morning. She's worried too and she can let the girls know. Dad seems to forget that it's my mother we're talking about."

"Your dad, he's been telling me he has been hovering over the telephone waiting for a call from Vivien."

"I think that's about right. Stephanie and I take turns in calling and sometimes he berates us because it's tying up the line." Liam sighed. "It's hard to do the right thing sometimes. I did what he asked—sent a couple of emails to Mum saying how much he missed her, that sort of thing—but it's all a bit much."

"Your mother is very proud of you, young man. She has talked of you both, often, and the two little girls too."

"I'm glad, you know, that she got away. I just hope it works out."

Ted noticed Liam's moist eyes.

Liam cleared his throat as he regained control. "If she needs me to come, just tell me and I'll be there. Or Steph. We're here for her, no matter what."

Ted put down the receiver after yet another abortive call to Holly. He had managed to talk to her once, and she assured him she had her own safety in mind all the time and he was not to worry. Not worry? Impossible. But worry was a commitment he made when he and Marcia decided to have a child.

He did one other small thing while overseas. He Googled 'sigma' and 'statistics' and got Wikipedia. Found out that sigma meant a standard deviation.

Within one standard deviation meant kind of normal. Did that give him any clue? Nope.

He arrived at Heathrow in plenty of time and sat over a beer, listening to his phone. He had a good selection of audible books on it, a digital library carried with him. Bored with one book? Switch to another. He'd bought bluetooth ear buds, which allowed him to listen to the talking books without disturbing anyone else. And it made the hours fly.

He'd managed to get a window seat at the back again, where the plane narrowed to two seats instead of three. He liked the window seat so he could drape himself along the bulkhead and catch a few hours' sleep. Besides, crawling over one body was annoying, but far superior to two.

His routine was to listen, eyes closed but not falling asleep, until dinner was served. He always organised a 'special' meal, usually Indian or Thai, so they served him before everyone else. After his delicious Thai meal was cleared away, he snuggled down with his talking book until he felt himself drifting. After that, he snatched a couple of hours' sleep. When the plane landed at Singapore, his 'frequent flyer' status allowed him to have a shower and a wait in the private lounge with food and drink until called for the next flight. All well and good, except the closer he came to New Zealand, the more his internal anger grew as if the distance between London and Queenstown had acted as a barrier that was now being breached. Yet he could not see that he could do anything about the situation. He felt totally powerless in changing his daughter's seemingly naïve attitude towards this despicable man. His tortured thinking came up with a couple of agonized questions. Was she in competition with her own mother? Was it something she couldn't express somehow when Marcia was alive? Going over and over it was tearing him apart.

Thus, Ted was more tired than usual by the time he got back to Auckland airport. And grumpy. And definitely in no mood to be singled out by customs. First, the dog dragged his handler towards him. They had his gear in the centre of a room on the floor. The dog went all over it, sniffing and looking up at his handler. After the suitcases were opened, the dog had another good sniff. They then put the cases onto a bench and two people in plastic gloves took everything out. They then felt around the insides and jumbled the clothes back in. Ted was allowed to neaten the case and shut it again. Meanwhile, the customs officers were going through his toiletries. They were particularly interested in his foot powder and took samples. He was directed to a metal folding chair at the side of the room and told to wait, too tired to care. He closed his eyes and could feel sleep creeping up when a woman spoke to him.

"Mr Frazer? You're free to go. We're keeping the foot powder for further analysis, but it will be sent back to you when it's got the all-clear." The woman was friendly enough. Ted thanked her and got out of there as quickly as he could. Just bad luck, he presumed, unless the interest in the powder had something to do with the police. That thought jolted him awake, and he was able to hail a taxi and get home before sleep threatened again. He would ring Holly later in the morning to see how her studying was going. And how the weekend went. Although how he could introduce that subject without breaking his ban, he had no idea. Luckily, his fatigue ushered in sleep.

Ted woke to a pounding on the front door.

Chapter Thirty-Eight

DISORIENTED, TED GLANCED AT the clock. Nine. Nine on his own clock beside his own bed. He rubbed his eyes, and the pounding came again. Nine. Very late for him. He got up, shrugging on a bathrobe which he needed for the cold as much as decency. One week of summer and he was no longer acclimatized.

"Mr Frazer," the inspector said. "We need to have a little talk."

"Sorry. Just back into the country at five this morning."

"So it appears. That's what we're here to talk about, Mr Frazer."

"Can I get us coffee? I'll need the caffeine if I'm to make any sense."

The inspector sighed but followed Ted into the kitchen, the sergeant trailing behind. "What made you think you could leave the country without informing us?"

Ted turned to face him. "Inform you? Sorry, it never crossed my mind."

"You were told not to leave the country by my colleague up north."

Ted remembered. "Yes, he did say that. But that was months ago."

"This is a murder enquiry, Mr Frazer. Never forget that. Murder of your ex-wife."

Ted realized he had been so caught up with this latest crisis that Marcia's murder had slipped into the background. He handed black coffees to the two police officers and sipped his own. "Sorry, no milk. As far as going over to London, I can only apologise. It was straight-forward business."

"Yes. The pharmacology company. Tell us about it, Mr Frazer."

Ted herded them back to the lounge. He turned on the heater to take some of the chill off the neglected little house. "I'm doing some development work for them. Periodically I go over there. Always at their instigation." He filled them in, emphasising the boring aspects of the job. Served them right.

The inspector interrupted the flow. "Did you ask anyone about the botulism toxin?"

Ted closed his eyes. He had asked his colleagues about it, of course. "Did you want me to do some detecting for you, Inspector?"

"What did they say?"

"That the toxin is available on prescription. But I assume you know that."

The inspector grunted. He flipped a page on the notebook he held. "And what did Mr McAvoy have to say for himself?"

Ted became suddenly alert. "Your colleagues in the UK have been in touch?"

"The world is a village, Mr Frazer, as you know more than most of us."

Ted was unsure how to handle this bizarre conversation. "I can't imagine you're remotely interested in my opinions."

"Try not to second-guess us, please. Just answer the question."

"Jonathan ... that is, Mr Fleet, wondered whether Vivien's husband had anything to do with these attacks on Vivien. I had a drink with the man and became convinced he had no opportunity to get to New Zealand. He's clear."

"How would you know?"

Ted shrivelled inside. Good question: how would he know? "It seems his kids are there at least every fortnight and he plays golf mid-week. Nobody's missed him."

"But nothing certain." The inspector flipped to another page. "Now, to something a little closer to home, be assured you will get that foot powder back, eventually. It's gone for testing."

Ted nodded. Yes. Clear as clear—telling him his movements were under the microscope, probably quite literally.

"When was the last time you had sex with your ex-wife?"

Ted was thrown. "Sex? With Marcia?" He remembered very well. "Why on earth do you want to up drag that?"

The inspector sighed. "Please, Mr Frazer, we never ask trivial questions."

"It was a long time ago. Maybe six years. Does that satisfy you?"

"Please answer the question."

"Sex, for god's sake." He took a deep breath. "Okay, it was after she left me, but before she decided to marry Jonathan. I can't be more precise than that."

"She was carrying on with three men: yourself, Jonathan Fleet and Jonathan's son Oscar?"

"In retrospect, yes. Maybe. She was hardly carrying on with me, though. It was a once-er. A last hurrah."

Two notebooks were snapped shut and Ted realized it had been planned that they would ask this question at the end of the interview. He was now thoroughly awake and uncomfortably aware of their interest in every detail about his relationship with Marcia. Yes, he was on their list, all right, and they were doing their bulldog thing.

After seeing them out, Ted wandered into the kitchen to fix himself some breakfast. Could McAvoy have travelled out to New Zealand—at the very least a twenty-four-hour journey each way—to poison his wife here with no one the wiser? Impossible. And totally far-fetched. But stranger things had happened and McAvoy had, or at least could have, the motivation. Means? Who knows, but the toxin, Ted had found out, was identical to Botox and thus commercially available. Opportunity? Stretching it, but a qualified yes. Vivien, a modified okay, but Marcia? Still, logic dictated that the two attacks on the Fleet women were connected.

The only good thing to come out of the police visit would be that it woke him up thoroughly and that would help get him over the jetlag, always worse coming home than getting into London. He found some frozen bread and made a stack of toast.

Sex. Yes, often at the bottom of things, as McAvoy so succinctly said. Sex had been important when he was married to Marcia, no question. She was an active and enthusiastic participant, often initiating their love-making and pooh-poohing his reluctance at making love anywhere but in the marital bed. She used to tease him about liking his creature comforts. Then, she was a vital woman, always interested in the next thing, the newest gadget, the latest trends. Her movements were swift and precise, her eyes darting from one thing to another whenever they went somewhere new. But the downside was she needed constant stimulation. He thought about her marriage to Jonathan. They had a good life from the outside. She had planned their travels, to the last detail. But what happened when Jonathan could no longer travel? The cancer might have had far-reaching consequences. Prostate cancer. It sometimes did things to a man's ability to have an erection.

Sex. Marcia liked sex. Wasn't there something Cushla said about sex? Something to think about.

He crunched into the toast. It tasted good. One thing people never mention about jetlag after you'd been halfway around the globe. You're always more hungry in the mornings than in the evenings for a while. He demolished the stack and hunted for something else to eat. Beans. He toasted some more of the frozen bread and heated the beans. A childhood treat.

Hiram. An unusual name. Maybe Jonathan would remember. He would follow it up for the sake of completeness, but somehow thinking that someone would harbour a murderous grudge for more than twenty years was far-fetched in the extreme.

He cleaned up the kitchen and reached for his phone, but stopped when he remembered. It was Holly's first exam this morning.

Ted forced himself to ring Pauline. While in the UK, he'd decided to put a stop to anything that would reinforce this crazy idea they had a future together. He felt a certain relief at having taken that decision. But he wanted to let her down gently. He hadn't thought about her much with all that was going on but, while in the kitchen, he caught sight of his neat flower beds at the back of the house. That reminded him forcefully.

"I think we need to talk again," Ted said once Pauline had answered her cell phone. "How about meeting for coffee?"

"Lovely," Pauline said. "Today?"

"If you can make it," Ted said. The sooner the better.

He had a shower and wandered out into his winter-ready garden. It had rained earlier and the grass was wet, making him glad he had put on his gumboots. The paper-whites were fattening and more green spears had popped up through the grass. Maybe they would have a good show this year. He thought of the bouquet he had promised Vivien. He would visit her after his coffee date with Pauline. Coffee and a quick chat shouldn't take long, which meant he could be at the hospital well before noon.

He met Pauline at a place familiar from the days they were working together, a pub with private booths at the back. It held happy memories untainted by the complications that had developed since. She was already there when Ted arrived.

She talked about work. Ted realized that most of their conversation involved their shared interest in complex IT problems. They had nothing else in common. Other than the bed thing.

"You didn't ring," she said.

"Sorry, Pauline. I was overseas. I told you that."

"There are telephones in London."

Ted closed his eyes; she knew all the right buttons to push. "No, Pauline. No phones in London." He took a deep breath. "Of course there are telephones in bloody London, but I was not thinking of you, okay?"

"You hate me for what I did to your flowers," she said, the tears rising.

"No." He felt out of his depth yet again.

She mumbled something into a paper napkin with which she was dabbing her eyes.

"What did you say?"

"You don't love me, do you?"

Ted looked away. This was out of control already. "I'm too old for you, Pauline. Always have been and always will be. My pleasures are those of a middle-aged man. You're young and beautiful and you belong in the spotlight."

"Don't you dare tell me where I belong," she said, her voice low.

Ted lifted both hands in a classic I-give-up gesture. "Whoa there, young lady. I'm trying to be civilized."

Pauline burst into tears. "You don't see me as a person, much less a woman," she cried.

"I thought we were friends," Ted said, thoughts of his marigolds flooding his mind and his remembered anger caused his stomach to clench. "Friends don't do horrible things to each other."

"We are friends," Pauline said, grabbing his hand and kissing it. "We are." She dropped his hand and blew her nose into the tissue. "Start again?"

He sighed, his anger dissipating. "Friends," he said. "Meet for coffee? That sort of thing?"

Pauline nodded and smiled. "And see where it goes from there."

As they came out into the sunshine, Pauline said, "How about inviting me over this weekend?"

His heart did a flip-flop. Fergawdsake, this problem had been solved; at the very least, it was on hold. The thought allowed him to feel relieved. He turned his thoughts to getting to the hospital. And Vivien. Pauline, in spite of walking out of the pub with him, had ceased to exist.

Pauline cleared her throat. "Ted?"

He became aware of her again with a start. "Sorry, I'm committed. Besides, I like us having coffee without complications. Like old times. Don't you think?" He swore to himself. Shouldn't have asked that question.

Pauline glared at him. "You're a bastard, you know that?" She spun on her heel and strode off down the road. Ted watched her long-legged flight until she was out of sight. Why were there no manuals on how to handle irate women?

But he had things to do. He rang the hospital.

"Mrs McAvoy's in a serious but stable condition," said the ward clerk or whoever answered queries like this.

"Still on a respirator?"

"Yes, I think so ... hang on," the woman said and covered the receiver while she conversed with someone her end. "Yes, still on the respirator."

Ted came off the phone, his anxiety mitigated somewhat. First, no deterioration. Second, no change, and that had to be good. And third, why would the woman have to check with someone else except that they were considering taking her off the respirator in the foreseeable?

As it happened, his visit was cut short. He was telling Vivien about the paper-whites coming up through his lawn and how he wanted to give her a bouquet once she could smell them properly when a senior nurse threw him out. Told him he had no right to be there. He went outside and peered through the windowed door. Several nurses, all doing things, checking things, adding another bag of something that was dripping into Vivien's arm. His anxiety went up. What was happening? He tried to persuade himself that this was just not a good time of day to visit. He even tried asking at the nursing station if anything was wrong; he was told Mrs McAvoy was in a serious but stable condition. Now it was his turn to spin on his heel and stride away before his anger bubbled over.

Ted put in a couple of hours' work before he figured Holly would be back at her flat.

"How was the exam?" He had planned to ask this question first. After all, it would be top of her interest right now.

"Not too bad. I came out of it on a high, but since then I've remembered stuff I should have written about. You know how it is." He did.

"Onto the next one?"

"Yup. I have our study group here now. I am doing something about it, you see. Gotta go. And so you don't have to ask, I survived the weekend. Don't worry, I'm perfectly fine. Totally on top of it, so you can stop being concerned."

"That's fine, Holly. I'll ring you later. But one last thing. Has there been a change in Vivien's condition?"

There was a brief silence. "Sorry, Dad, should have told you right away. She's got pneumonia. One of the things they worry about when someone's on a respirator. She's being filled with antibiotics and everybody's praying for her."

Ted rocked on his feet. Vivien, pneumonia? "I went to see her, but they kicked me out."

"No visitors right now except immediate family; Jonathan and Oscar, I guess. Sorry, Dad. I deliberately didn't ring you when you were away. Sorry."

He wanted to yell at her to stop saying sorry. Instead, he said, "I'll call Jonathan. You get back to your group. I'll find out more this end. Talk later?"

"Yeah, Dad. Hey, I'm really sorry."

He put the phone down, his heart heavy. There had been something wrong. He needed to talk to Jonathan right away. Fingers crossed Oscar wouldn't answer the phone. Only one semi-good thing out of all this: Holly didn't say the weekend went well, just that she came out of it well. After all was said and done, that could be important.

Chapter Thirty-Nine

THEY LET HIM SEE her. On special request from her father. Ten minutes only.

To Ted's eyes, Vivien looked the same. He sat close to her bed and held her hand once more. The respirator wheezed in and out and her skin was dry and warm. He talked: the flying over with the fat man who snored, the meals he ate, arriving at Heathrow and all that followed. He included details he knew he would never presume she would be interested in, just because he felt that a human voice was better than silence. Finally, he told her about Gerald and everything that Liam had said. Nobody kicked him out, so he stayed. And talked.

She moved. Just a bit, but Ted was sure. Her leg had shifted under the covers. He kept his eyes on the spot for the rest of his visit, but there was nothing more. On his way out, he asked the young nurse behind the desk whether Vivien would be coming off the respirator on time in spite of the pneumonia.

"They need to do tests and they can't start them now, of course. This has been a setback. But everyone is hopeful." Oh, yes, hopeful. Nursing keep-everyone-happy talk.

"Is she still in a medical coma?"

"Heavens no. Not since a while before this episode. Just strong sedation. She needs it. The paralysis is deeply disturbing—having something mechanical breathing for you is awful, Mr.... Mr McAvoy. She's far better sedated."

"Frazer. Ted Frazer. Close friend."

The nurse looked confused. "Sorry, thought you must be the husband."

Ted went on, "So I did notice movement. I was afraid I was imagining things."

"I'm sorry, Mr Frazer. I shouldn't be talking to you at all. Please excuse me."

Ted was left knowing he'd been lucky the nurse had him mixed up with McAvoy. He'd got far more information than he'd ever get from Jonathan. And forget Oscar.

He got into his car and headed towards the motorway, then slowed. The last thing he wanted was to return home to his cold and empty house. Lela?

Why not drop into the Remuera house? Lela would know where Jonathan was, which could mean he wouldn't have to ring Oscar's apartment.

Lela answered the door and ushered him in. He explained he was just back into the country that morning.

"Ms Vivien got pneumonia," Lela said. "She's really ill."

"I've heard. I've just been to see her," Ted said. "I talked to her as if she could hear me. That's what I usually do." He followed Lela down the corridor.

"She might die, Mr Ted. I'm worried sick." She looked up at Ted, her eyes brimming.

"She's being pumped full of antibiotics. We've just got to have faith that they work." Faith. A concept somewhat foreign to Ted's thinking. But, by gawd, the medication had better work. "Jonathan? How's he?"

"It's very worrying for Mr Jonathan. But it's making him mad and sometimes that's good," Lela said. "Wants to come home here. Mr Oscar doesn't want him to, though. He says he can take better care of Mr Jonathan than me. That's not true; I know what Mr Jonathan needs better'n him. We were fine when Mr Oscar went away that weekend. No trouble and Mr Jonathan stayed over the last night just as we planned even though Mr Oscar came back early."

"Did he now?" Ted said, and hastily changed the subject. "Heavens, Lela, when will things settle down? What we need is a period where nothing happens and Vivien can recover to her normal self and Jonathan...." He couldn't go on.

"And I can still be learning the computer." Lela shot him a glance and Ted thought again of how rewarding teaching a willing pupil was. They had wandered down to the sunlit conservatory again. Lela offered him a cup of tea and Ted relaxed into the oddly comfortable metal and plastic armchair he'd so often sat in when Vivien was recuperating from her broken ankle. As always, the room was quiet and a pleasant temperature. Jonathan probably had a heat pump or central heating with computer control for the temperature.

He thought about his own house, originally bought to be a rental. Maybe it was time to do something about it. Exchange it for a pied-à-terre. Plenty of apartments were available. Could he see himself in a bachelor's apartment? There was no reason to stay living in the little house once he had the Bay House again, but having a bolt hole in Auckland would be a luxury he would appreciate. Holly would too. The sun was beaming in through the windows of the conservatory and he pulled off his jacket. His house was cold and small. The garden? He loved his garden, but getting the gardens going at the Bay House would be slaking his gardening thirst big time. Another alternative came to mind. Could he keep the house and turn it into a rental just as planned so many years ago? He could put the annual beds into perennials and get a gardener to keep things in trim. It would be an instant money earner. Then he could take his time to decide about an apartment. Somehow, the future was still too hazy to be making decisions.

Lela came in with his mug of tea and one for herself. She was relaxing around him more and more. A pleasant woman, friendly, intelligent and willing to learn. Maybe there was something in Vivien's fear that Lela would get a better job and be off. Would it be stretching their friendship too much if he encouraged Lela to get more office instruction? Even now, she could probably handle data entry and with some training behind her and a certificate to wave under the noses of potential bosses, she could be earning much more than she could get as a domestic.

After the lesson, Ted got back in the car and turned the key. The engine turned over but didn't catch. His old reliable four-wheel drive. He tried again. Nothing. He took a deep and shuddering breath. Not now. Not something else going wrong. Finally, it caught, ran roughly, but kept going. He got only halfway up the road before it coughed one last time and stopped. He almost ran the battery down trying to get it to fire again but it was no use. In despair, he slumped over the steering wheel. Vivien. Holly. To say nothing of Marcia. His energy had finally run out.

Wearily, he climbed out of the driver's seat and lifted the bonnet. Who was he fooling? His engine looked fine, but it would look perfect to his ignorant eyes, even if it had totally blown up. He lowered the bonnet again and sat in the car with no inclination to do anything. Idea-man that he was, now he was bereft. He turned the key once more. His fuel was low, he noticed. Maybe the tilt on the road was enough to cause it to run out of petrol? That's what it felt like, a fuel problem. He released the brake so he could coast closer to the curb. With heavy steps, he started the walk up the hill to the garage at the top of the road.

The mechanic lent him a petrol can, filled to the brim, and Ted trudged back down to his car. He emptied the little can into the tank. Sure enough, the engine started enabling him to drive back up to the garage to fill the tank and return the petrol can. He'd not realized the tank was so sensitive. One problem solved, but his weariness stayed. He headed the car towards home.

Not far along the road, his cell phone rang. He pulled off and read that the missed call was from Jonathan's house. Probably Lela.

"I was just talking to my neighbour, Mr Ted. He said he saw someone fiddling with your car. Putting something into your petrol tank, he said. Have you had any trouble?"

"I have, Lela, yes. Who was fiddling with my car? Did your neighbour see who it was?"

"He didn't know her. But she was tall and skinny. Maybe someone else trying to do Ms Vivien some harm," she said, her voice as dark as her words.

"Not this time," he said, with no doubts at all who it was. "I think I've made an enemy, and she's angry with me. I'll deal with it. You can forget it, okay?" He'd never thought of Pauline as skinny, slim maybe, but she was certainly skinny in comparison to the ample Lela. Maybe even compared to all the other women in his life: Holly and Vivien and even Marcia after she lost the weight.

"Okay," Lela said slowly. "But you take care."

Ted put the phone away. This was too much; he would have to accept it. Pauline was a dangerous enemy.

Holly rang not long after he returned, as promised. She provided him with all sorts of details about what exam was next, where she was studying and plans for coming back to Auckland the weekend after her last exam. Her final final. But not a word about any weekend away, about Oscar, or about why he came back to Auckland early.

"By the way, you were right about the golf clubs and the marigolds," Ted said, as much to distract his own thoughts about what Holly had been up to than anything else.

"Pauline? Why do you think so now?"

"She admitted it. Apologized. But I've had another row with her and now someone's put water in my petrol tank, or so the mechanic thinks," Ted said. "And it was a woman described as tall and skinny. Over at Jonathan's place."

"Pauline. She followed you over there?"

So Holly thought of Pauline as skinny, too. "It's all very weird," Ted said. "But what else can I think?"

"You be careful, Dad. I don't trust her one little bit and if she thinks she's a woman scorned..."

"We never really had a romance, Holly. We were just good friends." His voice sounded hollow to his own ears.

"Oh, sure. You're so naïve, Dad. You had her over every weekend for weeks and weeks, for heaven's sake. She was your girlfriend. And she probably thought there was a future with you."

"Don't be ridiculous, Holly. Never a girlfriend; not even a relationship. I wouldn't have discussed anything about the future with her because I've never raised the thought in my own mind. She's far too young for me. Not wife material, for god's sake." His voice became tinny.

"Calm down, Dad. That's what you thought, but she may have believed things were much more serious. I think you should be wary; she could be in a very dodgy state of mind. This petrol tank stupidity is the second nasty she's done to you and this one was potentially dangerous."

"You're remembering about locked doors and windows?" he said as much to get her onto less emotive ground than anything else.

"You're the one who has to take care, Dad. You make sure everything's locked up, okay?"

He laughed, conceding the point. As he put the phone down, he had to admit he couldn't hide from it any longer. Pauline was dangerous. He then had an alarming thought. He'd have to check the dates. But could it have been Pauline who sabotaged the car Vivien was driving? Did women really behave like Glenn Close in Fatal Attraction? He'd always thought the character totally overdrawn. Now he was not so sure.

His next call was to Oscar's apartment, again hoping that Jonathan would pick up the phone. No one answered, so he left a message that he would be outside the apartment block at the usual time in the morning and to call if there were changes to the routine. After dinner, Jonathan returned the call.

"You've heard how Vivien is?" Jonathan asked with no preamble.

"No, tell me, please," Ted said.

"Still serious, they say. The damn medication takes ages to work. They won't know for a while. You did see her? I arranged it."

"Thanks, Jonathan. I did see her. Talked to her, as always. God, I hate that machine that breathes for her. Drives me nuts."

"I know," Jonathan said. "They tell you about her getting off it?"

Getting off the respirator? His heart leapt. "They don't tell me much, Jonathan. I'm not family. Tell me, please, if you know. It's very frustrating." Ted noticed that Jonathan's voice was stronger than before his visit to England.

Jonathan told him the various experts agreed to start physiotherapy just before Vivien developed pneumonia and how pleased they were about her progress up until that point. Vivien couldn't talk with the respirator, but he thought she had smiled at one point. So old news. Ted thought the smile most likely had been wishful thinking on Jonathan's part.

"That's when the sedation was wearing off a bit. Then they pumped it into her again. It lets her rest," Jonathan said.

"But back to square one with the pneumonia."

"They keep saying to me that underneath, she's slowly losing her paralysis; the recovery process continues whether she's got pneumonia or not. If she lives...." Jonathan's voice broke. He coughed as if to get rid of his emotional display. "When she gets through the pneumonia, they might lessen the sedation and think about the physiotherapy again."

"This is very good news." Very good as long as the 'if' was right. An awfully big 'if'.

"It is. And when the doctors give the okay, she'll come here to Oscar's for recuperation. Oscar's idea is that we'll both be here and physically cared for by some nursing group he's organizing. Two patients, Vivien and me."

Ted hated the thought of Vivien going to Oscar's place, nursing or no nursing, Jonathan or no Jonathan. "I thought you wanted to go home."

"I do. I'll have to decide."

Ted thought how typical that was of Jonathan. He was the decision-maker. Others made suggestions; Jonathan thought about it and what he decided, went.

They agreed that Ted would pick up Jonathan the next morning as usual.

"Before you go, can you tell me anything about someone called Hiram? An old boyfriend of Vivien's?" He had to take his mind off what was happening at the hospital. Hiram served the purpose.

"Him. Oh, yes. A weirdo, that one. Why do you ask? That was years ago, before Vivien went away to university."

"I met up with Gerald. He put me onto Hiram."

"Wouldn't trust that. Did you find out about Gerald?" Jonathan's voice was fading.

"He could be in the clear, Jonathan. It would have been difficult for him to come here without anyone noticing."

Silence at the other end of the phone. "Bloody hell."

"Yes. It would have been easy...." Jonathan didn't bother to finish his sentence.

Easy emotionally, maybe, the disliked son-in-law. Time to change the subject. "Hiram who? Do you have a last name?"

"Not a clue. It'll be out in the garage, though, I bet."

"Your garage in Remuera?"

"When we moved from Epson, I cleared the attic into a storeroom at the back of the garage. I know Vivien's dolls are still there, so probably other stuff of hers too. Do you want to have a peek?"

Ted now thought this was a total waste of time and energy, but it would be silly not to check. "Might as well. I'll have a look after dropping you at the hospital."

"The police keep coming over right in the middle of my working hours," Ted commented to Jonathan on the way to his chemo. "They're still interested in you, too?"

"Bloody nuisance," Jonathan said. "Can't turn around without them asking the same questions over and over. 'Did Marcia do anything different that day? Tell me the exact words she said when she listened to the radio.' On and on. Ignorant bastards."

"Why the radio?" There was a queue to get into the hospital that morning. Ted liked to drop Jonathan off right by the door. Like everybody else going in for chemo.

"Because she wanted the weather forecast. Sometimes she liked to know. Not often, as I keep telling the buggers. But she did that day. Had to listen right through the stupid sports broadcast. Bloody radio, the sports takes as long as proper news. Then the forecast, all two bloody seconds of it, at the end."

Ted stopped finally at the doors and Jonathan got out without a by-your-leave. As usual. As Ted drove away, he thought about why Marcia wanted that forecast: 'τIII rb' translated into 'Test 3, rowboat'. Maybe. Even Marcia on a dare wouldn't go out in a rowboat if it weren't dead calm. Dead calm. He winced.

The storeroom was just that, a windowless concrete room lined with wide industrial shelving. The dolls were prominent on the top shelf and sports gear took up almost half the space. Ted wearily started at one corner and pulled down a large cardboard box. Oscar's stuff from school. The box was returned and the next examined. Costumes. Fancy dress or Halloween. The next was more interesting. Cards kept by Vivien. Masses of them, bound with elastic bands, probably one batch per year. Why keep old Christmas cards? He rifled through them. At the bottom of the box were some smaller bundles. Valentines. Mostly from Hiram. 'Love, Hiram.' 'All my love, Hiram.' 'Your Hiram.' 'Your devoted, Hiram' and so on. But Hiram Who? Ted replaced the box and grabbed another. And another. He found a notebook for telephone numbers in a childish version of Vivien's handwriting and there was Hiram again. No last name. He straightened his aching back and decided enough was enough.

After Lela's computer lesson, they shared cheese and pickle sandwiches. He was neglecting his own work, which meant he left to do an hour's head-down before needing to pick up Jonathan. He was halfway over the bridge when he berated himself for not copying Hiram's phone number. Or taken a quick photo on his phone. There was an outside chance it was still operational, perhaps his parents' number. And the old people may not have moved. He'd have to pop into the storage room again later. A long shot.

When he accompanied a weak and nauseous Jonathan up to Oscar's apartment, he found Oscar already home. Ted averted his eyes, trying not to see him, realising he'd not seen him since before Holly had been to Queenstown. Ted said goodbye to Jonathan and turned to go.

"Hold on, Ted," Oscar said. "You were asking Father about Hiram? That wimp of a boyfriend of Viv's?"

"Yes. Her husband mentioned something. I thought I'd follow it up." He tried to relax his gritted teeth. No matter what the man said, it always grated.

"His last name is Brownstone. Like the houses in Boston."

"Brownstone. Thanks. I'll get onto it." So Oscar could be useful.

"And thanks for all you're doing for Father. I really appreciate it."

Ted nodded. Oscar waited at his apartment door until Ted's lift door closed.

All the way home Ted berated himself that he hadn't stayed to grill Oscar a bit more about the Hiram character. And he didn't remember until he was caught in traffic on the North Shore that he'd meant to look up Hiram's old telephone number again. He cursed himself and had to admit he was not functioning at his usual levels. Once back home, he stomped into his home office. First, he tried the online White Pages. No Brownstones, but not everyone had a landline any more. Then he Googled 'Hiram Brownstone'. There was one, a teenager. He had bought a first copy of a Harry Potter book somewhere in the USA and got his name in lights. Ted sighed.

After a re-heated dish of left-overs, Ted decided to make the trip back over the bridge to get the telephone number after all. Maybe parents, maybe the phone could be the landline of a flat. It was so long ago, he had little hope, but the itch was there and the trip for the telephone number would scratch it.

When he got to the Remuera house, it was dark. Of course, Lela would be away by now, and even the workmen in the new kitchen had long gone. Ted stood outside his car to stretch his back and sighed aloud. He was just not thinking well. Probably due to jetlag. He slowly drove home and collapsed into bed, praying he would be his usual self in the morning.

Chapter Forty

HER CHEST HURT; HER head hurt; her whole body ached; she was hot. Burning from within.

Voices. The voices had words. Silly words like 'meds', 'respirator' and 'paralysis' that had nothing to do with anything. Or did they? Paralysis? She had felt a creeping paralysis. Of course, she had. That day. Lela and ... my god. She still hadn't told anyone. She tried to open her mouth. Nothing came out. Her breathing. Something odd, something frightening.... She tried to scream. Air was being pumped into her lungs. What if it just kept pumping? She'd rupture her lungs! She tried to scream again. Tried to move. Couldn't!

Then everything calmed down as she sank once more. What was it that she needed to say? She had to tell them something. Something vital.

Oh, well.

Whatever.

Chapter Forty-One

BACK IN HIS OLD routine, Ted got through several hours of work by the time he set out to pick up Jonathan. As usual, the old man was waiting just inside the glass doors of the apartment block. However, this time he had a suitcase-on-wheels in tow. Ted helped heave it into the back.

"I'm going home," Jonathan said when he settled himself in the front seat. "After my chemo today, you can drop me there. Lela's going to look after me."

"But what about when she leaves in the afternoon?" Ted noticed that Jonathan looked grey and wizened. Not at all well.

"She says she'll stay over tonight and get a night nurse in as soon as possible. If she can, that is. Time for me to be back in my own bed. Don't like it at Oscar's. He fusses. Getting me to drink yogurt, eat fresh green veggies, that sort of thing. Lela doesn't fuss."

"What about this idea of the nursing firm? To look after both you and Vivien when she gets discharged?"

"She can stay with Oscar. I'm going home."

"Does Oscar know you're going?" Ted asked with sudden insight.

"Nope. Not yet. Too bad." Jonathan sounded like his old self for a moment. Ted got a flash of childish satisfaction. Good, something that Oscar doesn't like.

Ted quizzed Jonathan about Hiram Brownstone for the rest of the journey. The boy had been studying Fine Art at university when Vivien knew him, specializing in photography. He had been flatting, as Ted had surmised, and he had fallen in love with her even though apparently things were more casual on Vivien's part. Going back to the UK had been a way for her to extricate herself from a relationship for which she was not yet ready.

"But I gather he kept on trying? Contacting her, etc.?"

"Made a nuisance of himself. He had it bad, poor kid," Jonathan said. "Then it took a more sinister turn. Even though he'd been writing to Vivien for a couple of years, even when she was adamant she was not interested, he turned up in England. She'd just got married, fergodsake."

"Trying to stop the wedding?"

"I guess so. He was too late. Gerald and Vivien had already returned from their honeymoon. Brownstone was a total misfit. One time, Vivien and Gerald took him out to dinner, feeling sorry for the blighter. And he proceeded to talk to Vivien as if Gerald wasn't even there." Jonathan's voice strengthened momentarily. He was enjoying telling the story. "That was a once-er. But it did no good, of course. Vivien refused to talk to him whenever he rang after that."

"He came back to Auckland?"

"Think so." His voice was barely a whisper; his head slumped onto his chest. To Ted's eyes, every day the man looked more ill.

Ted collected the old phone number and tried it from his mobile. A woman with a screaming child answered. Nothing to do with Brownstone. Ted shrugged. What did he expect?

After starting the car, Ted had time to mull over this new intelligence about Hiram Brownstone as he drove home. Carrying a torch for three or four years was definitely more than merely being a social misfit. This sounded like an obsession. Maybe it could be classified as stalking. Probably Vivien was lucky to have escaped. But it was too long ago now. Even stalkers get over things in twenty or more years.

What do people with Fine Arts degrees do? Paint or sculpt or practice whatever they learned in university. Usually. Or go into commercial art. Often teaching. In schools or privately. Art restoration. The more he thought about it, the more possibilities crossed his mind.

Instead of settling down to work, he rang the university but got nowhere. Privacy laws. It meant he would have to use unofficial sources of information or word of mouth. He thought about contacts he had with anything artistic. Nobody unless he counted Holly's art teacher from her high school days.

Why not? Another long shot, but his IT profession was always sensitive to oddities, discrepancies and little things that only the aware noticed. His brain popped Holly's teacher out of long unused memory banks. Good. Now he could find out if the teacher had any further ideas.

"Hiram Brownstone?" the teacher asked. "It sort of rings a bell, but I'll have to let my subconscious work on that one. How is Holly and what is she doing now?" Ted spent a happy ten minutes boasting about his daughter. The teacher promised to ring in a day or so, regardless of whether he remembered anything. Just the faintest glow of an iron in the fire, Ted thought. Better than nothing.

Later, Ted dropped Jonathan off at his Remuera house as promised. Another car was in the driveway, a Land Cruiser, an impressive machine.

"You have visitors," Ted commented.

"Cushla," Jonathan said. "Can't get north to see her so Lester's brought her here. Bring my bag, will you."

More out of curiosity than anything, and mindful of his promise to find out more about Lester, Ted picked up Jonathan's case and followed him inside.

"Look who's here," Lela said to him. "Ms Cushla and her son. And now Mr Ted as well." She had already brought out an impressive afternoon tea and the two Waakas were in the midst of it. Lela ushered Jonathan to his favourite leather chair and sat Ted beside him. His chair afforded a good vantage for watching Lester Waaka.

The young man was driving serious wheels and now Ted could see his clothes were no longer from The Warehouse. He was quietly sipping his tea and helping himself to the freshly baked miniature muffins produced by Lela. His eyes were down. It wasn't until there was a natural break in the conversation that he spoke.

"Seen much of Oscar?" he asked Jonathan out of the blue. Interrupting a serious conversation about Maori settlements on the Waitangi issues. Jonathan was looking as animated as Ted had seen in a long time. He and Cushla certainly had rapport.

Jonathan looked up in surprise, as if he'd forgotten Lester was in the room. "Of course." He turned back to Cushla and Ted was almost embarrassed for Lester, he'd been so rude.

Ted got up. "Thanks for the tea and those delicious lemon cakes," he said to Lela. He waved at Jonathan and Cushla and turned to go. Lester also rose.

"Pick you up in an hour, Ma. And you," he said, turning to Jonathan, "make sure you tell Oscar I was here. And that I was asking after him."

That night, Ted had another thought, one which disturbed him greatly. He was in the kitchen, cleaning up after making one of his favourite curry dinners. The perfume of the meal still hung around, something he enjoyed. He had learned to cook curries when married to Marcia. She insisted he took his turn as cook on weekend evenings. Fair enough, but it was a steep learning curve. His first cookbook was 'Simple Indian Meals for Bachelors'. He fell in love at his first bite. His curries were more imaginative now, and he tended to use spices he blended himself and his enthusiasm remained.

He thought back over the visit to the Remuera glass box. What was Lester on about? It was almost as if he were making a threat to Oscar via Jonathan. Some sort of complexity there to be figured out. Yet another complication in spite of his confidence in his own deductive abilities.

Ted had enjoyed the evening until that thought. All along, he had assumed it was too coincidental for two members of the Fleet family to be involved in murder attempts, albeit one successful and one, no, two, not. A sole perpetrator was a much more likely explanation. How had he lost sight of that? Even if Hiram Brownstone turned out to be a nut-case, he had no connection whatsoever with Marcia.

He went to bed that night thinking his iron was in a fire that had gone out.

Holly's old teacher rang on the Saturday morning, as promised. "First, I searched my memory banks and came up with zilch. But it niggled. So I deliberately put it out of mind until this morning. The only thing that came to mind freshly today was that I vaguely recall that someone mentioned Brownstone a year or so back. Can't remember who or why, but I guess maybe he could still be in Auckland."

"Nothing comes to mind about that conversation? Any detail?" Ted wasn't sure why he was prolonging the questioning when he had decided Hiram Brownstone could not be involved, but the teacher was trying to be helpful.

"Let me think. Maybe it was a conversation in a café? That's awfully weak, sorry. But I'm not a coffee drinker, so why would I be in a café?" Ted realized the teacher was thinking aloud and let him ramble on. "Wait a mo. We went to lunch after my wife got capped a year ago May. For lunch. She was still in her academic gown, I remember. That was a café downtown. Who else was there? Look, Mr Frazer, I'll ask her, then ring you back."

Ted forgot about the conversation as soon as he put the phone down. He was cleaning the house in preparation for Holly's return. The least he could do was to air her room and put her electric blanket onto low to make sure her bed was warm and dry. He ran the vacuum cleaner around the house then got out the duster. Guilt hovered at the edges of his consciousness. When had he last vacuumed? Probably when Holly was coming home after Marcia's death. Lucky Jonathan to have a Lela. The thought sobered him. Jonathan, lucky? His wife killed, fighting cancer, having a rotten son and someone trying to do in his daughter? No, he'd choose his own life any day.

As Ted was finishing wiping off oven cleaner, the phone rang again.

"My wife knows Brownstone, Mr Frazer. Says he designs book covers. He works for some publishers on the shore. That would be him, wouldn't it?"

"Sounds likely. Thanks. Any idea which publishers?"

"Sorry, no idea. But they all know each other. Publishers live in a village, after all."

"You're right. I'll get onto it right away."

"Erm..., Mr Frazer," the teacher said with some hesitation, "my wife says Brownstone had some troubles a few years back. She wanted you to know."

"Troubles? What kind?"

"She's a bit hesitant about letting you know. He wasn't charged or anything."

"Thanks for warning me," Ted said with some care. "But I would like at least a hint about what it was all about." Ted knew he was pushing, but he had more than mild curiosity. This was about Vivien, after all.

"Hang on, please." Ted could hear conversation in the background.

"Mr Frazer?" a pleasant female voice said. "I'm afraid this is terribly gossipy and I'm still wrestling with passing it on. Do you really need to know anything about this man if you're going to contact him yourself?"

"Forewarned, I suppose," Ted said. "And I'm calling in regards to a serious incident involving a friend. Brownstone's involvement is all a bit nebulous."

A silence came down the line. He could hear the woman sigh.

"How about you tell me what happened to your friend," she asked, "and I'll decide whether to pass on this bit of ... bit of gossip."

Ted briefly talked about the car accident without mentioning Vivien's name. "I'm just trying to contact anyone who knew her. My friend has lived in the UK for years so all contacts are from the distant past."

"Okay," she said, slowly. "This was a while ago, too. Brownstone was an art teacher at the time. Not a very good one, from all accounts. I don't think he could relate to the kids, that sort of thing."

There was a pause, so Ted said, "And then the incident?"

"One of the teachers at the school said he'd been following her. Offering her rides to school early in the morning, ringing her at odd times. She had a boyfriend and he was the one who was bothered about it more than she was, I think. She asked Brownstone to stop, and it seemed he did. Then she started getting heavy breathing calls late at night."

"She went to the police?"

"No. It stopped before that. But Brownstone's contract wasn't renewed and he never did get another teaching job. I think the boyfriend had words with him." She made a sound that Ted realized must be a sardonic laugh. "Or it was more than words. Anyway, problem solved."

"Thanks for being so open with me. It is food for thought."

"I probably shouldn't...."

"No, it was the right thing to do. Thanks." Ted got off the phone quickly before the woman agonized about whether she should have told him. His own comment echoed around his brain: food for thought. More than that because this incident fitted with Brownstone's earlier trip to London when Vivien was getting married. He made a decision to follow up on it, whether or not there was any Marcia involvement.

Ted rang one of the larger publishing houses immediately. The telephonist didn't know a Hiram Brownstone, but he left his name and number in case she found someone who did. Not ten minutes later, Hiram Brownstone rang. Ted said he was a friend of Vivien Fleet McAvoy's and she had been trying to reach him.

"Vivien? She's in the country?"

"She's after some photographs." His story sounded a little thin to his own ears.

"Which ones?"

"Erm..., photos from years ago. She said you took some marvellous shots of the old house. And you'd taken heaps of her when she was young." Ted figured all this must surely be true. The fellow was in art school at the time. Of course he would have taken photos of his girlfriend.

"Why? She's got those." Hiram's voice was flat.

"They're long gone," Ted said, thinking fast. "Unfortunately. Probably when her father moved to that modern house he now owns. Or when he remarried."

There was a silence. "Why didn't she ring me herself?"

"She couldn't find your number." That surely would have been true. "I got it finally through someone in the art world. Knew you were now working in publishing."

"What's your involvement?" His voice was distinctly suspicious now.

"Just a friend. When I got the return phone call about your work, I followed up because Vivien would have wanted me to. No big deal, Mr Brownstone. Do you still have copies?"

"Of course. It was good work. I don't throw away my portfolio."

"Can I give you my number? If you have time, maybe you could get some copies for her. Then I could pick them up."

To Ted's surprise, Brownstone rang the next day.

"Got a whole boxful here for her to look through," he said. "Too many to post. You can pick them up if you want."

"Can I treat you to coffee somewhere?"

The café was near where Brownstone worked and Ted found it so easily, within ten minutes of his home, that he arrived early. He ordered a cappuccino and took a seat where he could see people coming and going. A potential Brownstone crossed the road, head and shoulders hunched, clutching a cardboard box labelled 'Cabernet Sauvignon'. Yes, must be him. He was a slight man, the wispy remains of his hair floating above his balding pate. Life did not appear to have been kind to him. Once in the café, he headed straight for Ted, who realized he must be equally recognizable.

"Mr Frazer? I'm Hiram Brownstone."

Ted rose to his feet, shaking the proffered hand. He stared at Brownstone. He knew him from somewhere. "Let me get you a cup. What do you prefer? Long black? Cappuccino?"

"Chai tea, please," Brownstone said, sitting himself down with a fleeting smile. "With milk."

Once their drinks were in front of them, Brownstone asked what connection Ted had with Vivien.

"I'm a friend of hers."

Brownstone frowned. "Friend? She's married, mate."

"Friend of the family. Besides, she lives in the UK." Ted was wary too. Where did he know him from? "She was over here visiting her father for a bit."

It came to him. Damn.

Marcia.

He'd have to address it. "Her step-mother died. Marcia." He watched the man's face, but his head was down and his eyes veiled. Not a flicker. Yet, wasn't he the man at Marcia's funeral?

The man in the raincoat?

Chapter Forty-Two

TED PUT THOUGHTS ABOUT Marcia and Brownstone to one side for the moment. "Vivien is doing a family history and raved on about your amazing photographs from when she was a teenager. That's why she was trying to contact you."

"Okay," Brownstone said, his eyebrows furrowed. "Yes, I did some good work back then."

"So she seemed to think." There was an awkward pause. Then Brownstone leaned back in his chair and started talking. He described his successes at university, then, as if forgetting he was talking to a stranger, his first exhibitions and their reviews and always how Vivien supported and encouraged him. Then Vivien lost interest, as seventeen-year-olds are prone to do. Hiram had taken it hard.

"That was it, man. Downhill ever since. All because she decided she wanted her freedom. To 'find herself', she said. Bollocks."

"You loved her?"

The man nodded slowly. "Oh, yes, I loved her. She was the love of my life, my soul mate. I had a pure, almost a sacred, love for her and she didn't see it. She spurned me."

"Yes, it can be tough." Ted felt his awkwardness must be showing. "Erm..., you eventually married?"

"Tried it once. Didn't work out. My wife said that Vivien was in our bed. Little did she know." He let out a bark that Ted supposed was meant to be a laugh.

Ted kept his voice low. He didn't want to disrupt the reminiscences by the present intruding. "You've been true to her, all these years?"

"True to her in my heart, yes. There's no one on earth like her."

"But you're angry with her also?" Ted said, holding his breath.

"Wouldn't you be? She was my inspiration, my muse, my motivation, my...." His voice caught. "It all turned to custard after she left."

"Later, you went to the UK, I gather."

"Who told you that?"

"Her husband," Ted said truthfully. "I gather it wasn't the most successful of meetings."

"He's a Neanderthal."

"But a sophisticated Neanderthal." He wasn't going to point out recent anthropological theories about real Neanderthal sophistication during the ice age, and how both he and Hiram most likely had some Neanderthal genes.

Hiram nodded and grimaced. "She'll like these." He patted the box. "When she comes next time, would you please tell her to ring? I can come and collect the shots she doesn't want." Ted could hear the yearning in his voice. "I've left my contact numbers with the photos."

Ted got up. "Thanks, Mr Brownstone. I will tell her. I know she'll appreciate the photos."

"No worries," he said. "And it's Hiram."

After picking up Jonathan that afternoon, Ted went over Brownstone's reactions and his conversation.

"If he had had any contact with Marcia, he would be on my suspect list," Ted said. "But I couldn't see any reaction when Marcia's death was mentioned. And I'm not one hundred percent sure he was the man in the raincoat."

"I do remember the name," Jonathan said. "Can't put a face to it, though." As was usual these days, his voice was weak. Half the time, his eyes were closed.

Ted helped Jonathan out of the passenger seat and into the house. Jonathan wanted to sit in his leather chair in the library and Ted saw to it that he was comfortable. Lela scurried out to get him a cup of tea. Ted turned to leave, freshly aware of Jonathan's frailty.

"Bloody enormous books," the old man said. "All Marcia's." He gestured to a large shelf groaning under what appeared to be coffee-table art books. "I seem to remember somebody published a book of photos. Could be over there with the rest of the arty stuff." He leaned back in the chair and closed his eyes. "Might be that Brownstone chap."

Ted squatted down and dutifully started at the left-hand side, his head on an angle to read the names. He worked his way methodically along the bookshelf. Marcia had collected an extraordinary set of books on the impressionists, maybe half of her collection, but her tastes were eclectic. Books on Byzantine art, South African art, Russian icons and even collections of Chinese artefacts made up the other half. Marcia had a busy mind and formidable knowledge of the art world.

The bottom shelf held books on New Zealand art from Goldie to McMahon, and one by Hiram Brownstone.

"My god, you're right," Ted said, not hiding his astonishment. "It's a book on the Auckland shoreline." He hefted it over to the desk and opened it at random.

He quickly turned several pages. Close-up shots of lichen on rocks, sea spray white against the clear blue of an Auckland summer sky, a tiny hermit crab poking his front pincers out from an abandoned crustacean shell; page after page of nature at its best.

"The photos are spectacular. This is a book to savour."

Jonathan grunted in reply. He was holding the mug with both hands and still the tea was in danger of slopping. Ted turned to the front of the book. It was inscribed, 'For Marcia, and this is just the beginning, Hiram."

"Where did Marcia get this?"

"How would I know? Maybe this is the fellow she thought was an undiscovered genius. Some photographer fellow. Must be him. If I remember it correctly, she was of the opinion that someone should take him in hand and market his work the way it deserved. Something like that." His voice faded away.

Ted stared at the inscription. Marcia, Hiram—first names only. Did it mean anything? 'Just the beginning?' Beginning of what? Could this possibly be the missing Marcia connection? Ted returned home thinking he'd probably have a closer look at his new mate Hiram Brownstone.

Holly gave her father a bear hug at the airport, as usual. She was full of the last exam. "It was a doddle, Dad. I had nightmares of freezing, not being able to remember stuff that I know perfectly well, that sort of thing, just because it was my last exam. I honestly don't think I slept more than an hour or two the night before."

"But you aced it?"

"If not an A, damn close!"

Ted carried the two enormous suitcases from the car to Holly's room. "You sure you have everything here?"

"I gave away heaps. I know it doesn't look like it, but I did. Really," she said. "It's so unbelievable that my university days are done; that I'm not going back."

"Except for your graduation."

"Yes!"

After lunch, Holly asked if she could rake up the leaves that again littered the lawn. "Get some air in my lungs. Use my atrophied muscles."

"You rake and I'll pile them into the wheelbarrow and feed the compost heap." Ted loved doing jobs with this daughter of his. They had always worked easily together, even when she was a rebellious teen. Often, it was the only time they really talked, bent over some task they were attacking together.

Holly started in the soggy back corner of the garden under the birch trees. At first they worked silently, stirring up the smell of wet leaves and fresh compost. The day was mild for June and they both soon shed their outer layers until they were working in their shirtsleeves.

"That Oscar is something else," Holly said, still bent to her task.

"What do you mean?" he asked. Ted could hardly believe it. Holly had just brought Oscar into a conversation. Throwing caution to the winds, he continued, "Other than he's one of the most selfish individuals I have ever had the dubious pleasure to know."

"You really don't mince words, do you?" She pulled the soggy leaves onto the pile in the wheelbarrow and straightened her back. "But my teasing went too far last month. Sorry."

"Just worrying about you, that's all. The usual." But his heart was singing.

She bent down to scoop up another bolus of damp leaves.

As Ted manoeuvred the overloaded wheelbarrow to his compost pile, Holly walked beside. "I thought you were going to build proper bins this year."

"I was. But with everything, Marcia and all that was happening, some things didn't get done." He heaved the whole wheelbarrow up to the top of the pile before tipping it to the back. "Leap about on it, will you?"

Holly grinned, then obediently went to the top and jumped. "Whoopee! This was always the best part!"

"You're still just a big kid, you know that?"

"But I'm good at pretending I'm all growed up, aren't I?"

After dinner, Ted and Holly sat over coffee and hot chocolate in their small lounge.

"I have had a lovely thought'; we'll get the Bay House back before long. This time next year, we'll be in front of a roaring fire up north."

"Total heaven," Holly said. "Gramps didn't like an open fire; he thought it was messy, which meant we never used it. Did you see what's in the fireplace? He's got grey stones in the bottom of it with three candles stuck in artistically. Mum did, I mean. She put the stones and candles in. But it was because Gramps didn't want open fires. Not that we went up to the Bay House much, in the off season anyway."

"But Marcia used to love an open fire."

"She was changing, Dad. She hardly ever wore old clothes, even up at the bay. She was into designer togs and jeans that cost over two hundred bucks, that sort of thing. The only old things she ever wore were her painting smocks and even they got washed every time she'd been in her studio."

"I'm glad my time with her was when she could relax into the real world." This was the unvarnished truth. Marcia had obviously slipped into superficiality since their divorce, to say nothing about wasting money on inconsequentials. Not his scene.

"I've thought of it, too. You knew her when her feet were solidly on the ground well before she got so obsessed with her appearance." They shared a comfortable silence.

"I haven't stopped trying to find out what happened to her, you know."

"I've had a thought," Holly said, as if picking her words carefully.

"Go on, young lady. I like your thoughts."

"We said the *tau* was the 't' for test, right?"

Ted nodded.

"So the *sigma*..."

"I found out what it's used for mathematically," Ted said. "Sigma, in statistics, stands for a standard deviation. And one standard deviation is a statistical way of saying 'normal'. Does that give us a clue?"

Holly frowned. "That's more complicated than my reasoning. I thought that if *tau* was just a 't' that stood for 'test' then *sigma* was just an 's' that stands for...' She looked up at her father. "Well, I thought it might stand for 'sex'." She blushed.

Ted was flummoxed. "Ah, sex. I had figured that poor old Jonathan was beyond that since his prostate cancer...." Oh. He cleared his throat. "Yes, of course. The extra-marital kind."

"I sort of thought that with the surgery, the Botox, the fashionable clothes ... you know. It adds up."

"*Sigma* is for sex and she sees it as normal. It does make sense. Your mother liked ... what a thing to be discussing with your daughter." He stopped.

"She liked sex. I know. She told me." Holly giggled. "But that was years ago."

Ted laughed. "Some things don't change, young lady. Even when people get impossibly old and decrepit. Like me."

"I know that *pi* is twenty-two over seven. From school."

"*Pi*. The letter 'p'?"

"The only 'P' I know is the drug. Methamphetamine or whatever it's properly called. You know, meth, crank, crack, speed, ice, pure... What else is it called? Base, rock, shabu—most people around here call it P." Holly shrugged.

"You know a lot about it."

"Bad stuff."

"Your mother wasn't into drugs." He paused. "Was she?"

"I certainly never suspected it, and I can recognize the signs from a mile away. Not her. Unlike too many people I know." Holly finished her hot chocolate. "There's an 'L' with the *pi*. Lela? Liam? Lester? The only connection with drugs is Lester. He was into drugs, marijuana anyway. Growing wacky-baccy – we all knew about it at the time."

"I wonder if Lester is still being hassled."

"Lester? What's he being hassled about?"

"Sorry, Holly. With all that's been going on, I forgot to tell you that the police had interviewed Lester about Marcia's death. More than one interview, I gather."

"Have they something on him?"

"He thought it was two things. First, he was at the bay that weekend and second, once a crim, always a crim."

"The drug bust?"

"That's what kindled their interest, according to him."

"How are we going to find out more?" Holly asked. "Jonathan? Is he in touch with Cushla?"

"I can ask him."

"Or the police when you tell them about the Greek symbols?"

"Dunno if I should. I hate having to talk to them. They keep their beady little eyes on me. But I never have anything new to tell them. They keep running over and over the same ground and it's unbelievably boring. Unbelievably scary too, I might add. I'm still in the frame. As is Jonathan. They're easier on him than me. Because of his cancer, I suppose."

"I talked to him this week. His voice sounds awful."

"He's weakening." They both let the silence lengthen.

"Oh, I got my foot powder back, by the way," Ted said.

"Good. That was one stupid episode."

"To give them their due, they were just being thorough." He paused. "Okay, I'll talk to the police. They'll be along sooner rather than later." He glanced at his watch. "I thought I'd go sit with Vivien for a bit. Do you want to come?"

"No, you go." She glanced at her father. "You don't just sit, do you, Dad? You do talk to her, don't you? Even though she doesn't answer? You're saying positive things?"

"Of course."

"Then tell her I'm sending healing energy through the ethers."

Vivien was still totally sedated. Her appearance was unchanged except for the extra bag of something or other which was dripping into the tube in her arm. Ted felt shy about holding her hand now he knew she could know he was doing so. But she needed any strength she could get from him. He picked up her hand gently and cupped it in both of his.

"Come on, Vivien. Get that immune system of yours working. Use the antibiotics and fight those damned bacteria. You can do it; I know you can. You're strong." He sat close to her head and spoke softly into her ear, thinking of Holly's instructions. "You're doing extremely well and I want you to know that I'm your chief cheerleader. It'll be no time before we get you back into that conservatory of your father's and you can sit in the sunshine bossing us around once more." He thought of the plan for her recuperation at Oscar's apartment and had a renewed sense of disquiet. Maybe Jonathan could hire the nursing firm and have her at his place. He decided not to mention it now, instead switching to Holly coming home, her exams and even the tale about Hiram Brownstone. He told her that Holly was sending healing thoughts to her.

Ted glanced at his watch and carefully put her hand back on the counterpane. "I'm horribly impatient for the day when we can converse again, Vivien. But since you can't tell me, I'm going to wander down to the nursing station and see if I can prize from someone what the latest status report is. I'll be right back and tell you if I find out anything. Either you'll be awfully bored being told things you already know or you'll be brought up to date. Better be safe than." He reached over and touched her hand. Did it move, ever so slightly? Jonathan wasn't the only one who indulged in wishful thinking.

He walked along the corridor, glancing into rooms as he passed. The hospital was quiet in the evenings, and many people had visitors gathered around the beds. He was getting used to the hospital with its strange antiseptic smells, its clinks and clanks and the predominance of white and stainless steel.

At the nursing station, he gazed at the tops of heads bent over notes, searching for a familiar face. Maybe he'd be lucky enough to get an ignorant young nurse again. It was no use asking any of the experienced ones for any information. He was not family, therefore he'd get nothing but the 'serious but stable' bit of non-information. Ted searched in vain for a student's uniform. Through the open door of the inner office, he could see a nurse talking to a man in an overcoat; an older woman who was often in charge. He felt in no rush; he would wait. After another five minutes when Ted was starting to feel the first tendrils of impatience, the man stood up and shook hands with the smiling nurse. Ted moved to the side so as not to call attention to himself when the man turned.

"Well, if it isn't Ted Frazer. Hello. I hoped to catch up with you while I'm over here," he said with a broad smile.

"For heaven's sake. McAvoy," Ted said, unable to keep the surprise from his voice. "You've come to see Vivien."

"Not just to see her. I'm making arrangements to take Vivien home."

"Home? What do you mean?" Ted gulped. "Which home, Gerald?"

Chapter Forty-Three

That voice. How? Why? Couldn't be. Shouldn't be.

She listened, struggling to concentrate, trying to ignore the air being pushed into her tender lungs and the feverish heat and sweating; aware she was ill; trying to decide whether she was still hallucinating. But she knew this voice. Gerald. Yes, for sure. Gerald. His voice had snapped her into an awareness not experienced before. And she felt crude, unchecked anger flood her being. Her hand was taken up, rubbed against a bristly face; she tried to snatch it back but she still had no muscle movement. No control. None. Tears of frustration spilled from her red-seeing eyes and despair flooded her being.

Usually she tried hard to move when she surfaced. Not this time. She lay, passive, unresponsive. Willing him to go away.

Chapter Forty-Four

"I'M BRINGING HER HOME. To our home, of course, where she belongs. She has only one home." They had paused outside Vivien's room.

"But, Gerald, she's come here, to New Zealand. To be with her father. He's ill." He didn't dare mention that as far as Vivien was concerned, Gerald was her ex. He wanted to say the best thing to do was to wait until Vivien was compos mentis and ask her but that would be inflammatory.

"And now she's the one who's ill. Very ill. She's certainly no use to her father now and needs looking after herself. As soon as I get the green light from these good people here, I'm taking her home. Jonathan will just have to do without her." Gerald's voice was hearty. The nurses all stopped talking and were intent on watching the tableau.

"But will she want that, Gerald?" Ted felt a surge of anxiety when he spoke, but in for a penny.

"Sometimes she doesn't always know what's good for her, I'll give you that. But she'll see that it's best. The last thing she'd want is to be a burden on her old sick father."

Ted didn't trust himself to speak again, so turned away, muttering that he'd best be on his way. He strode through the hospital corridors as if with purpose, but it was a ruse. He needed to think.

Gerald. Here. Taking Vivien home. The man was her husband. Fully married husband with more legal rights in determining her fate than a mere father. And he possessed all the power in this restricted medical world in comparison to a mere friend. A sense of utter frustration hit like a tsunami as he headed out. But by the time he negotiated his way through corridors, lifts and tunnels, he had seesawed from frustration to reluctant acceptance and back again. At first, he was burdened by knowing he could do nothing about it. If Gerald wanted her back, he had the right to take her. Unless Vivien was allowed to wake up.

Ted opened the door of his car. But what about her kids? Liam and his sister. He had to contact them. Surely they were not part of this hare-brained scheme.

And what did John Robertson, Vivien's lawyer, think about it? The sense of powerlessness dissipated; there were things he could do.

If she lived. The stark reality of the danger Vivien was in hit him afresh.

Life was shitty sometimes.

He drove his car into the artificial brightness of a street-lit Auckland night and manoeuvred his way into the stream of traffic heading over the Harbour Bridge and home. Then he remembered. He had returned the Fleet telephone notebook to Jonathan, and he had not had the foresight to copy out the UK numbers he needed. Damn.

Once over the bridge, he took the Onewa off ramp and circled back over the motorway to re-join the bridge approach, retracing his route towards Remuera. Traffic was heavy going into town, and Ted's frustration level was rising every time he glanced at his speedometer. A long two kilometres later, due to road works closing half the lanes, and finally he was at the turnoff towards Fanshawe Street. He knew he could do better off the motorway and taking the route through the bottom of the city, along the waterfront to Stanley Street, past the tennis venue and into the leafy Auckland Domain. On the other side of the park, he could take Ayr Street down from Parnell to Remuera. Complex, but anything was better than sitting impotently in a traffic jam.

He was slowing to turn into Jonathan's drive when he noticed the new rental parked in front of the garage. So Gerald had come here. Damn again. He drove a little past the house and used someone's spacious drive to turn around and park on the street.

If he rang Lela from his cell phone, would she answer the landline telephone? He thought back. Yes, he realized, she always answered. Certainly Gerald wouldn't unless he was alone in the house and the likelihood was both Jonathan and Lela would be there. He rang the number.

"The Fleet residence," Lela said into his ear.

"Hi Lela. It's me," he said, realizing he wanted to whisper, but there was no need. "I'd like to contact Stephanie and Liam, but I would rather Gerald didn't know I was doing so. Can you get the telephone notebook to me somehow?"

"Hello, erm, Terri. I'm a bit busy. We have guests." Lela paused.

Ted was nonplussed for a moment, then quickly realized that Gerald was within hearing range and Lela was instinctively keeping this call private. Terri, indeed. But he said, "Yes, got it, Lela, a guest."

"If you want to pick up the doll collection later," Lela said cheerfully, "just come into the garage. You know where it is. I'm so glad those dolls are going to a good home. I'll just go unlock it now and I can lock up later after we finish dinner."

"You'll leave it there?"

"Surely will, Terri. I'm just serving our sweet dish now, but I'll unlock the doors before. That okay?"

"So I can come in, say, ten minutes?"

"Perfect. Talk to you tomorrow?"

"You're a star, Lela. Yes, I'll ring tomorrow. And I'll take the dolls to my place."

"That's good. Those dolls are precious."

Ted closed his phone and laughed aloud. Yes, definitely Lela was capable of so much more than people expected, and he loved it.

Ten minutes later, he was skulking along the fence line to the garage's side door. As promised, it opened at his touch. Because Lela had set it up that someone was calling, he dared turn on the light in the little storeroom. The doll collection was as he had last seen it and he hauled down the box, ready to take it away. Rather than the little notebook of telephone numbers, he found Lela had left Vivien's computer for him. Emails. Yes. The notebook must not have been returned to its place by the telephone and Lela had substituted the computer. The only problem, if he remembered correctly, was that it was password protected.

By that time of night, traffic had calmed and fifteen minutes later he had crossed the bridge and arrived at his own house. He hurried in with the laptop and set it up next to his own computer in his office. Yes, he'd been right. He needed the password. He glanced at the time. After ten. He decided to risk it. He rang the house, almost sure that with Gerald in residence, Lela would spend the night there.

She answered on the second ring. "I am pleased you found them, Terri," she said. "I've locked up now and saw you have been and gone."

"Sorry for ringing so late, but can you hint about the password or should I wait till tomorrow?" Ted noticed that Holly, clad in her pyjamas, was listening from the door to his office. He motioned her in, pointing to his visitor's chair. She mimed drinking motions and when he nodded, she left.

"Yes, they all belonged to the kids. Mostly Stephanie's, but some were Liam's. As a little girl, Stephanie liked numbers of dolls. Numbers of them."

"The kids' names?"

"Yes!"

"Something about numbers?"

Lela's laugh tinkled down the line. "I knew I could count on you, Terri. You're a smart cookie."

"I'll have a go, Lela. Thanks very much. And, by the way, it's you who's the smart cookie around here."

Ted was in his element. Hacking into a computer with clues to help? He loved it. Now, how long would take him? He first tried Stephanie1Liam2 then

Steph1Liam2. He put in and took out caps and an ampersand. The winning combination was to put in the look-alike number for the vowels in each name, 'st3phl14m'.

"Gotcha!" he said as he glanced at his watch. Two minutes and two seconds. He could hear Holly stirring a mug in the kitchen.

He found the email addresses for both young people easily in Vivien's 'Contacts' file and composed an email, not on Vivien's computer but on his own. By the time Holly brought in his mug of tea, the emails were on their way, simple emails just saying he wanted to contact one or both because their father was in the country. He had only time for a single sip when the telephone rang.

"Ted? Liam here. Just got your email."

"Thanks, Liam. I would have rung but couldn't get hold of your number."

"You wouldn't have got me if you rang the house. I'm up in the Lake District with a couple of mates. Just thought I'd check my emails before going out for a sail."

"Lucky you." Ted said. "Did you know your father was coming to New Zealand?"

"He never said a word. What's he playing at?"

"He wants to ship Vivien home to the UK as soon as the medics give the all-clear."

"What? You have to be joking! Bringing Mum back when she's finally away from him? The bastard."

"He has the right. He's her closest relative. In the law, closer than her father. But I'm convinced that if your mother could voice her wishes, it would be to stay put." He didn't voice his continuing concern that Gerald was still a suspect.

"She would. I know it," Liam said with some emphasis. "She finally found the formula to get away." He swore softly.

"I'm going to see her in the morning. Sometimes I think she's trying to communicate with me. Just a little movement every now and again."

"I'm coming," Liam said. "I'll get the first flight out."

"You don't have to, Liam. I can keep you fully informed."

"Bugger that, Ted. Sorry. Don't need to swear. I've been toying with coming anyway with this damn pneumonia. And maybe I can get through where you may not be able to."

"You can stay with Holly and me. Your father is at your grandfather's," Ted said. "We'd love to have you. I think your input could be vital."

"I'll tell Steph." The call ended with Liam promising to email his travel schedule.

One last thing before hitting the sack. Marcia's calendar. Looking at the frequency of the *sigmas*. It felt almost prurient now they'd had a possible translation, but he had to see for himself. He found lots of *sigma*s early last year. Then they spread out a bit. Not so many this year. The *tau*/tests were all during this past summer. Tests for what? Proving how crazy she was? Or maybe crazy about some lover?

Chapter Forty-Five

A BUBBLE OF FRUSTRATION formed deep within her. Something she had to tell them. As she slowly made her way towards the light, she had to keep that in mind. She cursed the fog that permeated her mind. It was something important. It would come to her, just as soon as the fog lifted a bit more. She had to tell them. Had to. Important.

Voices. Female. Male. Talking about her. Paralysis. Sedation. She struggled to let them know she was there. It had been such a relief when she remembered her own name. She was Vivien. Not a thing. Not an object. She was herself. Vivien. She stopped struggling for a moment and listened.

Then she remembered. Gerald. Here. Double bloody hell.

When the familiar lassitude caused her to drift down once more, she welcomed it for the very first time. She didn't want to have to deal with with Gerald. And that other thing, whatever it was.

Chapter Forty-Six

THE NEXT MORNING, A haggard Ted woke early enough to get into the ward before Gerald would think of getting there. He ran up the stairs instead of waiting for the lift, which required him to catch his breath as he walked down the corridor leading to Vivien. This whole thing felt sneaky.

As always, she was looking peaceful, beautiful even, in the morning light slanting through the window. His breath caught. He was very fond of this woman. He picked up her hand and leaned towards her ear.

"Vivien. It's me, Ted. First, I want to reassure you that I remember what you said about making a new life for yourself away from Gerald. Second, I'm on your side, totally. Remember that." Did he feel a slight movement? He placed one hand above and one below hers. "Third, everything I've seen about you says you have a fighting spirit and I know you'll come through this brilliantly. And fourth, I've talked to Liam. He's coming out here. He'll arrive in a day or so. Staying at my place." He stared at her face. Did her eyelids flutter just a little? Frustration welled up within. She had to live, had to.

"You're having a wonderful antibiotic that's specifically aimed at helping your lungs. Can you feel its healing properties, Vivien? It's there to help you fight off that infection. Maybe you can see it as a hidden weapon, ready to search and destroy the invaders. A weapon you can use to regain your health. Remember how strong you are. Use that strength." He stopped because his imagination was working overtime. Why were they keeping her so sedated? He had to find out.

The kindly nurse who had always treated him well was on duty. "I can't talk about Mrs McAvoy specifically, you understand. But people who are paralyzed get very agitated, Mr Frazer. That's not uncommon with botulism poisoning. The paralysis is frightening, as is having a machine breathing for you. And then you couple that with feeling ill with an infection ... you do understand, I'm sure."

Ted thanked her and went back to Vivien's bedside. Of course, she hadn't moved. The sunlight backlit her hair, turning it golden. He longed to see her eyes once more, her lovely blue eyes. He tore his gaze away. Her husband was in town and it was no time to be mooning over someone who was clearly still married. There was a pile of get-well cards on the cabinet beside her bed and he idly picked them up. He had sent one early on, but he couldn't remember what he'd said. He thought he had better remove it if it contained any hint of something that could be taken the wrong way.

The first two were from Stephanie and Liam. Then one from the friend she had stayed with before Marcia's death. Plus one from Gerald. He froze.

The handwriting inside an innocuous card picturing a bowl of roses said, "Coming to get you. Gerald." Coming to get her? He searched in vain for a date. When had he written it? It must not have been before she became ill, surely. But, 'get' her? That could be read more than one way. Certainly, there was nothing tender or even friendly about the message. On the other hand, maybe it was a threat—even if it had been only a note to state his intentions, it have hugely distressed Vivien when receiving it.

Ted leaned over to her ear once more. "I've seen the card from Gerald. Has that been bothering you?" For an instant, Ted thought he glimpsed those blue eyes. He held her hand.

"I'll take that as a 'yes'. I'll do my damnedest to keep you safe, Vivien. You can rely on that." He felt a faint movement of her hand. Maybe. It was extremely difficult to tell.

Ted found the friendly nurse once more. "I understand Mr McAvoy wants to take Vivien back to the UK. Could you please tell the powers-that-be that her son Liam is on his way here? This is not a simple exercise."

"You forget how ill she is, Mr Frazer. She's in a serious condition. Nothing can happen in the short term."

"Yes, I do understand. In a way, a delay is good, because I'm not convinced Vivien wants to go back to the UK. If it's possible, could you lighten the sedative enough to ask her?"

The good nurse shook her head. "I've explained about the agitation."

Ted nodded. He knew he'd been pushing his luck. "Yes, and thank you for that. But it has occurred to me that possibly she's agitated precisely because she knows she's about to be shipped back and she's trying to communicate her distress at the idea."

The nurse flushed red. "Oh," she said. "I'll pass on your ideas. But I know the staff is pleased that her husband has turned up. In her circumstances, she needs as much support as she can get."

"Okay." He knew a brick wall when he hit one. "Please don't make any decisions until her son gets here. Please." But the nurse had turned away and was fussing with some papers. Ted walked back to Vivien's room but Gerald was there, holding the same hand that Ted had cupped between his own only minutes before.

Time to make himself scarce.

With so much going on, Ted wondered what he should do next. He'd tried sitting at the computer, but work was out of the question; he was too restless. Liam was on his way. Gerald was doing Gerald-things and Ted had to leave him to it. Something was niggling at him just outside of consciousness, something he had meant to do.

He wandered out into the garden. It was neat and tidy and nothing demanded his attention. He looked at the narcissi. More had poked up through the winter grass. No sign of flowers yet. Waiting for Vivien, maybe?

And he hadn't given Marcia's killer a thought in too long. Who was it? Hiram Brownstone, whom he'd spotted at her funeral? They say killers often attended funerals of their victims. That thought sparked something. He had meant to dig around some more to find out if anyone else knew Hiram Brownstone. He went inside to ring the art teacher's wife once more.

"I went to see him," he said to her. "He's a bit of a weirdo, isn't he?"

"Plus, plus," she said. "The last time I saw him, he had long scraggly hair and a beard—he looked like a latter day Jesus. Is he like that now?"

Ted caught his breath. "No, no, not now. But you have seen him?"

"Not for a while. A year or more back."

"Where?" Oh dear, too intrusive. "Sorry, I'm curious to know more about the man, that's all."

"I was giving some overseas visitors a tour of the beauties of Auckland. We went up into the hills, the Waitakeres, that big observation area with the little museum or whatever it is. He was with a group of trampers, I guess. Or volunteers? Something like that. Does that help, Mr Frazer?"

"Ted," he said automatically.

She laughed. "Marjorie. But is that useful?"

"Yes, thanks, Marjorie. I'll follow it up. I'll call you when or if I find anything new. How's that?"

"You have piqued my curiosity," she said. "I would appreciate it."

"Thanks, Marjorie."

Ted came off the telephone in a thoughtful frame of mind. A tramping group or a set of nature-loving volunteers. From his brief encounter with the man, he would expect it to be the latter. Ted got onto Google yet again. Waitakere Ranges. Department of Conservation. Aha, a Protection Society.

He rang the number. The first person he spoke to said there were no official meetings, but working bees happened every now and again. He suggested Ted ring someone else who would know. That person thought the name of the group that did the working bees was something like 'Friends of the Forest'.

After several unsuccessful attempts at variants of 'Friends of the Forest' he Googled 'Waitakere', 'forest' and 'volunteer' and got 'Forest'n'Flora'. It was a well-constructed website. Ted guessed a professional web designer had volunteered his efforts to construct a website. The group helped to replant native trees in various places around New Zealand, with one of the main places sited in the Waitakere Ranges. They had a training scheme and regular meetings. He searched the photo section for pictures containing Brownstone to no avail until he twigged. Of course. Photography. And there his name was: 'Photographs by H. Brownstone'. His professional contribution. And the photos were exceptional, both those of people and especially those of the local flora. The man had talent.

Now what? Ted sat back, pleased he had got as far as he had, but stymied at where it led him. He flicked through the pages of the website. A meeting was to take place later that night, but there was no way he could attend without being obvious. Maybe wearing a disguise? Ted laughed at himself. He would have to sleep on how he could use this new information.

He could hear crashes and bangs from the kitchen. Time for a break.

"Sandwich? I bought some fresh hummus," Holly said.

"That'll do me," he said, settling himself opposite her. She had picked up some crusty brown bread and leafy greenery as well. A bit of a feast, compared to his usual lunchtime snacking.

"I've been trying to track down any new information about Hiram Brownstone," he began. He told her about his morning's activities.

"I'll go," she said. "I'm the right age group to be interested in outdoor stuff."

"No way. Hey, he's a weirdo. Your mother is dead and Vivien's a victim of an attempted murder, for heaven's sake. And we haven't cleared him. Not totally anyway."

Holly sighed. "I warned you that I would not be wrapped in cotton wool when I came home. And that's as true today as it was when I said it. I'm going to live life normally. Okay, maybe having that added awareness, parking under lights, that sort of thing. But essentially normal." Her voice was firm. Adult. Her eyes steady. "I'm going to a meeting. Nothing extraordinary about it."

"I don't really want you to have any contact with him, young lady. He has a history." He filled her in about Brownstone's following Vivien to the UK and the fresh gossip about his stalking of a colleague. "And you're young and pretty. I don't want you to be in any danger. This is only a long-shot after all."

"I don't have to talk to him, Dad. I can just observe how he's treated in the group. And stop harping about my supposed beauty. That's nothing to do with anything."

After dinner, Holly left in Ted's car. He tried to watch some television; he got out a pot-boiler novel he was keeping until another long plane trip; he paced and he twitched the curtains a dozen times or more but Holly didn't come back until an uncomfortable three hours later. When he heard the car turn in, he put her chocolate drink into the microwave.

"How did it go?" He was damned if he would tell her how he'd spent the evening.

"Interesting," Holly said, as she collapsed onto the couch. "Oh good. You got my message through the ethers. Hot chocolate. Num."

"Start at the beginning. You found the place all right?"

"No prob. Snagged a park near the door too. Then I followed two people into the hall. About a dozen of us were there, I suppose. One other younger woman, but mostly couples in their thirties and forties, I would say. After the meeting, the woman my age sought me out."

"And?"

"And warned me about Hiram Brownstone."

"Oh, Holly."

"Don't you 'Oh, Holly' me, Dad. This is what we needed. Someone who had experienced him first hand. Forewarned is forearmed, for heaven's sake. Janine, that's the woman I was talking to, she said he had a reputation of fixating on someone...."

"Someone female," Ted interrupted.

"Yes, someone female, fixating on someone and then ringing them up. Always to talk about some flower or plant he spotted, that sort of thing. So not so awful, I guess. But he's really unattractive and old. It would creep me out for sure."

"Yes, old like me. But I get your meaning."

"We were sitting having a cuppa after the meeting at the side of the little hall and we could see him across the room. Not talking to anyone, just drinking his tea. But he had scary eyes, Dad. He sort of kept glancing at us while half turned away. Gave me the willies."

"And gave Janine the willies too?"

"She was more dismissive. Called him harmless. She was really telling me to ignore him and not encourage him, that's all."

"But she did warn you. It sounds as if she's handling it fine. And wants you to do so as well. Coping with an oddball."

"You didn't think he was a weirdo when you met him?"

"Slightly odd, yes, but nothing abnormal."

"You're probably of the wrong gender."

Ted laughed. "Undoubtedly. But all in all, I'm pleased you don't have to have anything more to do with him."

"Me, too." Holly picked up her empty cup. "Just a thought. He really is a contender, isn't he? An oddball; and he has a bad history with Vivien. I think we need to delve a little deeper to see if there's any way he could have known Mum."

"He did." Ted's stomach wrenched. How did he miss telling Holly? "Sorry I didn't ring you when I found out. He did know Marcia. Quite innocuously, I believe." As he said it, he realized how easily he had dismissed the man from serious consideration.

"I can't believe you didn't tell me," Holly cried. She plopped back onto the chair she'd just vacated.

"I said I'm sorry."

"Dad, this is it. We have to consider him. How did he know Mum?"

"She bought his book. He dedicated it to her. Wrote something slightly strange, 'This is only the beginning'."

"Beginning of a love affair?"

"Holly, can you see your mother giving Hiram Brownstone a second glance?"

She laughed. "You're right. So this 'beginning' was something else. Mum couldn't have been less interested in anything green, so it must be the photography. Was he one of her enthusiasms?"

"An enthusiasm that died a natural death when she got distracted? He's a very good photographer, believe me. That book of his is stunning."

"And he took it personally? We know he goes off the deep end emotionally. Maybe he went into despair. She was his white hope. When she lost interest, he became murderously angry." Holly was leaning forward, her words spilling out.

Ted held both hands in the air. "Whoa. Just hold on. He has no reason to harm Vivien and less to kill your mother. His history with both of them is ancient."

Holly's face flushed. "How can you sit there and say that! I've always said you had an open mind, but this makes me sadly mistaken!"

"Holly, please. It's late and I'm tired and so are you."

"You can't just let it go at that."

"I will think it through again, promise, but not until I'm more awake."

"Okay." Her voice was that of the aggrieved teen she used to be. "Sorry I yelled. We can talk it through tomorrow." She left the room and called goodnight. Ted got up and turned off the light, then sat back in the chair again.

Could that weirdo possibly be responsible for the carnage in the Fleet family?

Suppose Hiram had found out Vivien was now in New Zealand. Maybe from the friend. Was it Gretchen? Maybe their friendship dated from the time Hiram was in the picture. So maybe he contacts Vivien and she spurns him. He gets enraged. Plans to do her in and somehow gets the poison into Lela's kitchen.

Far-fetched.

But that would have been after killing Marcia. Back to how unlikely there were two violent offenders attacking the Fleet women. But, a big 'but', Marcia knew him. On a first name basis with him. He had to find out what kind of story existed, because, for sure, there was a story.

Holly's theory? Could anyone get so incensed by being dropped by a potential sponsor that they would commit murder? Ted wanted to examine it all slowly and see if there was even a remote possibility that Hiram could have been involved. He knew Brownstone had fallen for Vivien. Had he also fallen for the attractive but wily Marcia?

Chapter Forty-Seven

HOLLY CAME BACK INTO the room. "You're not in bed yet?"

"Nuttin' through the Brownstone possibilities."

"Tell me," she said. "He's actually near the top of my list."

"Only near?"

"Pauline is top."

"Come on, Holly," Ted said. "I know you don't like her, but she's peripheral to this whole thing. For one thing, she's a woman and most murderers are men."

"I'm going to pretend you didn't make that remark," Holly said with some acid. She curled up at the end of the couch, in unconscious imitation of where Pauline had sat when last in this room. Ted was forcibly reminded yet again how Pauline was more Holly's generation than his.

"I've been thinking it through," Holly said. "First, we have one pissed off lady." Ted started to reply but Holly rushed on. "Listen to me, Dad. Just listen for once."

"Okay, okay. Go on. I really am interested." He sat back in his chair. He reminded himself that his daughter was a fully adult woman finishing a good university degree. Plus, he knew her verbal and analytical skills. She could have been an IT trouble-shooter like him, had she been interested enough.

"She's pissed off. For sure. And willing to do things most people wouldn't even contemplate. She hacked your marigolds to bits, for one thing, and added water or whatever to your petrol tank and that could have caused a nasty accident. And she knows where Vivien lives. Motivation for doing something drastic to Vivien is easy to imagine. I figure she thinks Vivien caused your breakup."

Ted rolled his eyes. "I keep telling you, Pauline was never my girlfriend, much less Vivien. How can you break up something that didn't exist?"

"You're the only one who would ever say that. Pauline was your girlfriend in everyone's eyes, including hers. You broke up. Full stop."

"Okay, okay. Go on." He sighed loudly.

"So she's got motivation if she thinks Vivien is your new love interest. Displaced by an older woman who hasn't half the youth or beauty she has? That's motivation."

"Vivien is lovely looking."

"Attractive, yes, for someone twenty years older than Pauline," Holly said. "You have to see it through her eyes."

"Okay. In this scenario, she could possibly be angry at being dropped, jealous of Vivien." Ted didn't like it, but the logic was as firm as anything they'd surmised about Hiram Brownstone. And he knew how Pauline could become fixated on getting her own way.

"Now Mum."

"Go on. I'd like to see how you construct that one."

"It's the same thing, Dad. Jealousy. You hadn't let Mum go."

"Of course I'd let her go." Not another one making this suggestion. He hated to admit it, but she—and Vivien—had a point. He hadn't let Marcia go. Not completely. He'd done some deep introspection after Vivien had pointed it out. "Okay, it's not quite as strong as that. I still saw her every couple of weeks, helped her out from time to time and she treated me to lunches. You know all this."

"I know it and undoubtedly Pauline knew it."

"I trust you know there was nothing romantic between Marcia and me, for heaven's sake. It wasn't even me wanting to keep in contact—she didn't want to let me go. I was like her favourite cousin. We were friends, of a sort, on her terms."

"I know, Dad. But I bet Pauline didn't. She may have thought all Mum had to do was crook her little finger."

Ted thought about it. Did he mention Marcia to Pauline? Probably, because not much happened in his life and going out to lunch and talking through the many subjects he and Marcia covered was a reasonably important part. It never occurred to him that Pauline could be jealous of Marcia. Did he mention Marcia to her? Undoubtedly. Just as he told Marcia all about Pauline. Marcia had been mildly interested and thereafter always asked about her.

"You may be right. For this scenario, we can say that maybe Pauline was jealous of an ex-wife still in the picture. For this exercise, yes, it's a maybe."

Holly smiled. "See? She fits."

"But the boat? Can you imagine Marcia getting into a small boat with Pauline, whom she's never met?"

"We don't know that, Dad. Maybe Pauline did contact her. Maybe there was some elaborate ruse. I don't have many answers, but I think it would be silly in the extreme to dismiss any of this."

"No," Ted said slowly. "I'm not going to dismiss anything right now. But I'm also not going to tell tales to the police."

Holly nodded. "You said you'd tell them about the sigma thing."

Ted was getting irritated. "Okay, okay. But not the Pauline speculation. Besides, I've been thinking the Hiram thing through."

"Go on. He's next on my list."

Ted went through his thinking. "Maybe Hiram knew Vivien's friend Gretchen; maybe he did contact Vivien; maybe he felt spurned afresh and took it out on her. But your theory about Marcia and Hiram is too speculative."

"We do know other things about this man," Holly said. "We know he's unsuccessful with women because he's such a nerd."

"I'm a nerd," Ted said with a smile. "And I haven't done too badly."

"You're a loveable nerd," Holly said with a grin. "Different category."

"Thanks, young lady," Ted said. Funny how a compliment from a daughter was worth a dozen from anyone else.

"So, we have this guy who is on his own, meets my glamorous mother who thinks he's Talent Personified. And he's not used to this, right? He's now suddenly in the spotlight of my extremely focused mother. She's going to 'discover' him, make him a star. And what does his heart do? He falls madly in obsession with her!' Her voice rose in triumph.

Ted smiled. "It fits as a creative series of thoughts. In this scenario, anyway. But we have the same old problem with the boat and the bay."

"Yeah, I know. I can't imagine Mum getting into that little rowboat with anybody but Gramps or me, and that hardly ever happened. And I can't imagine who could dare her to do so. But we know she was into dares."

"I keep forgetting about the tau-tests. So unlike the Marcia I knew." Ted yawned. "Good session. You have quite an imagination. So keep on it. See what else your creativity comes up with. But tell me in the morning."

"G'night, Dad. Thanks for listening." She dropped a kiss on his temple as she passed by his chair. "With the two of us on the case, we're bound to nut something out."

As Ted put the mug into the dishwasher, he thought of what Holly had said. Marcia wouldn't have been anywhere near the rowboat with anybody but Jonathan or Holly herself.

Jonathan had just nudged himself back into the picture.

Before turning out his light, Ted received a text from Liam with an arrival time into Auckland Airport of 6am. Ted was there to meet him.

"Have you told your father you were on your way?" Ted asked as they walked out of the airport into the Auckland dawn.

"No. I'm going to be a delightful surprise." He grinned at Ted and then, as the grin faded, he shook his head. "I'll do what I can, Ted, but my father has never taken much notice of my likes or dislikes. All in all, I probably won't be able to have much effect on him. I'm pinning my hopes on the other people involved. Perhaps I can have some influence on them."

"Mind if I ask you something? Did your mother tell you what she was intending when she let the UK for New Zealand?"

"She did tell me. Not until she was safely out of the UK, though. She pretended this was a holiday at first, but we had a decent conversation on the phone after Marcia was killed. She intended to stay here permanently; that came over loud and clear."

"Have you discussed it with your father?"

"With Stephanie but not with Dad. I would ever bring up that sort of thing with him. I'd just be told to take my sticky beak out of what was none of my business."

Ted smiled at him. Just as he expected. "You have some plans?"

"Other than taking up your offer to stay at your place? Yes, I do. Or rather, I'd like to run something past you, if I may."

Ted noted how Liam was at that threshold of adulthood independence with the remains of boyish deference clinging still. "Should we wait till we get home? I'd like you to meet Holly. We can discuss it together."

Liam's eyes widened when he saw Holly, and Ted was made freshly aware of his daughter's attractiveness. No wonder Oscar was panting after her. Holly had prepared a substantial English breakfast for the two men.

"You would never know I had breakfast about four this morning. Thank you, Holly, that was delicious," Liam said as he pushed away his empty plate.

"More toast?" Holly asked.

"Couldn't," Liam said and Ted smiled. Two young people who had obviously taken to one another.

Liam became serious. "I'd like to go in to see Mum, if you don't mind. Now, if pos."

"Of course," Ted said. "But I think you'll run into your father there if we go now."

"That's a bugger," Liam said. "I think I'd rather meet him on more neutral territory than by Mum's bed."

"She's comatose, Liam," Holly said, one hand brushing his shoulder. "I hate to remind you, but she won't know you're there." She bent over to take his empty plate away. "Have you figured out the best way to meet up with your father?"

"My idea was to have a family conference. As soon as possible. Get everything out in the open. I know how my father works—everything covert, keeping people in the dark. The need-to-know fallacy that he's convinced works in business. He thinks anything that functions to earn money must, therefore, work in the family."

"Who should be involved?" Holly asked.

"Us three. Then Gramps, Dad. Oscar, I guess."

"And Lela," Ted added. "She knows your mother's mind as well as anyone."

"I'll call Gramps."

Ted showed Liam into his office and left him to it as he helped Holly clean up the kitchen. Liam joined them again more than half an hour later.

"It's arranged, I hope, as long as everyone can come. Coffee and cake at seven-thirty at Gramps' house. He wants it tonight, if possible. He's just told Dad about the meeting, but did not spill the beans about me being here. I really need others around me when my father spots me."

"Tonight? I'm free; what about you, Holly?" Ted said.

"No prob."

"Gramps is calling Oscar. He's the only one left who doesn't know so far," Liam said. "And I had a bit of a time convincing him that Lela should be part of it. But he saw reason eventually. Or maybe I just wore him down. He really sounds unwell."

"He is unwell, Liam," Holly said gently. "The cancer has come back, you know, and the chemo is as bad as the cancer. Worse."

"He sounded awful. His voice kept falling away so I could hardly hear him."

"Like when?" She handed Liam a dishtowel, and he took it absentmindedly, totally comfortable helping in the kitchen.

"Actually, the conversation was bizarre, now I think about it. He said he was about to call Ted. I told him we three had been talking and wanted to get everyone together and he said something about ... about that was why he was ringing. But it was me who rang him."

"He's elderly," Holly said. "And who knows what that poisonous chemo does to an old man's brain."

"Yes, maybe. At the end, when I said how important it was to be together on what should happen with Mum, he said, 'Yes, that, too'. Sort of out of it."

Ted hung up the dishcloth he was using to wipe down the bench-top. "I have a deadline, sorry, Liam, but I need to work. Can I leave you in the capable care of my daughter for a few hours? When I'm finished, I'll hand over my office to you so you can turn it into your bedroom. The couch in there pulls out into a bed and we can make it up in a jiffy."

Ted heard the two young people come in, chattering happily. He didn't intend to listen, but their voices carried.

"He was a friend of my mother's. He came onto me," Holly was saying. "Asked me out."

"That's sick. One of your mother's friends?"

"Don't you start, please. I get that sort of comment from my dad all the time. Of course, he can't see anything good in Oscar but they have a history so he's prejudiced. Look, Oscar drives a Lotus. Full stop. And I can take care of myself. Especially with an old fart like that."

"He came on strong?"

"At first. Then I got him, but good. He saw me in one of Mum's dresses and that really freaked him out. You should have seen his face! He accused me of having him on. I found it screamingly funny but he didn't. No sense of humour. He invites me to this fancy dinner where there's no way I have the appropriate clothes and when I come dressed in this glittery blue dress, all sequins—the sort of over-the-top dress my mother used to buy—he goes all paranoid. Then he gives me the silent treatment. Totally ignored me at the dinner table in front of other people. Needed more of his stupid uppers, probably, but it was bloody rude. So I politely excuse myself to the others and go straight up to my room. I wriggle out of that dress as fast as I can and stuff it into my bag, change into jeans and head for the coach terminal to get back to Dunedin. I was outa there," she said with a flourish.

"You got back home without him?"

"He's a rich bastard. I knew he'd only think of planes and rental cars. I was fine on that coach; I slept all the way. Then didn't answer my phone when he called. I told you he was weird."

"That was it? He didn't contact you again?"

"I took his call a few days later. He was all apologetic. Said he had drunk too much. But he hadn't. He was stone cold sober."

"Well, I think it's off. He's a kind of brother, for god's sake."

Ted smiled to himself. So that's what happened in Queenstown. An 'old fart'. He loved it.

Chapter Forty-Eight

THE THREE MET UP for drinks before dinner. Holly and Liam had hovered across the road from Jonathan's house keeping an eye out for the return of Gerald's rental car. Once he was safely back inside, they sped to the hospital to see Vivien.

Liam was still obviously shaken. "I ... I couldn't ... it was a bit of a shock seeing her like that," he said, "even though I thought I was mentally prepared."

"I think she responded a little to Liam," Holly said to her father in a soft voice. "I'm sure her face flushed a little, and she was trying to open her eyes."

"That breathing machine. It's terrifying," Liam said, and to Ted's eyes, he looked quite shaken and very young. "Have they told you her chances?"

Ted sighed. He knew so little. Jonathan was the only one the hospital authorities talked to, and he was not overly communicative. "You'll have to ask your grandfather." The boy's eyes widened and Ted realized that sounded as if he didn't want to tell him how bad it was.

"The doctors don't talk to me, only to him," he said quickly. "I don't know, honestly. They keep saying she's in a serious condition but stable. All we can interpret from that is that if she's stable, she's not deteriorating."

"I do understand," Liam said, his head down. Ted could see he was close to breaking down.

"She's kept sedated because the paralysis is frightening for her—for anyone in that condition. I suppose it's the sense of helplessness." They were sitting in the lounge sipping drinks. Ted had put together a simple curry meal that was still cooking. "However, I've my own ideas about that."

"Come on, tell us," Holly jumped in. "It's about that card Gerald sent, isn't it?"

Ted glanced sharply at his daughter. She must trust Liam implicitly to be mentioning it in front of him. "She told you about the card?" he said to Liam.

Liam nodded. "Quote, 'I'm coming to get you.' Unquote. Jesus wept."

"So you had the same reaction as I had."

"That can't have been innocent. I know my father. Those words were carefully composed. Chosen to frighten her."

"By the way, Dad," Holly said. "Cushla and Lester were at Gramps' house when we arrived to wait for Gerald to turn up. Stayed almost until he returned. Gramps and Cushla get along really well, don't they? But I don't know about Lester; he spun his wheels on that beautiful driveway when he took his mother away. Git."

They arrived at Jonathan's glass box house precisely at seven-thirty as arranged. All were present, including Oscar, except Gerald who was still at the hospital. Ted felt an irrational wave of annoyance. He took a deep breath and told himself to keep a lid on his personal feelings if they were going to make any progress tonight.

Liam couldn't take his eyes off his grandfather's appearance at first, but covered his distress well until he could make a fuss of the old man.

Oscar interrupted the reunion between grandson and grandfather. "It's probably been at least five years," Oscar said to Liam, extending his hand with a smile. "You've become a young man since."

Liam shook it. "Nice to see you again, Uncle Oscar. I think I was fourteen when you last came to stay with us in London. That's almost six years. You were on your honeymoon, weren't you?"

"A subject best dropped," Oscar said, raising his distinctive winged eyebrows at Holly. It reminded Ted of the portrait Marcia painted of him. Bastard.

"My son was a bit surprised you were to be involved in this meeting I've called, Ted," Jonathan said in Oscar's hearing. "But I explained that you were a neutral person who knows the situation. You've been involved."

The meeting that *he* called? Ted inwardly shook his head. Jonathan and his need to be in control. He composed his features. "If there's any problem...." Ted was aware of Oscar turning slightly to include Holly.

"Heavens no," Oscar said. "You can chair it; yes, that's a good idea."

Even though Ted had been slightly taken aback that Jonathan was pretending that he had called the meeting, he certainly didn't want to step on any toes.

Jonathan was nodding. "Good idea, Oscar. Ted is more neutral than any of us can be."

Ted thought how untrue that was, but he nodded and smiled at Jonathan, anyway. He was aware of the undercurrents building in this gathering even before Gerald had made his appearance.

"Dad does know we're meeting tonight?" Liam asked Jonathan.

"Absolutely. He thought he had enough time to get in a quick visit. He wanted to tell Vivien he had found another expert who is going to examine her tomorrow and assess her current treatment. A second opinion."

"She just needs peace and quiet," Oscar said. "Let her body recuperate. There's no way she should be taking a trip to the other side of the world."

"You can tell that to my father," Liam said.

The doorbell rang, and the gathering went quiet as they all listened to Lela greet Gerald. He swept into the lounge, bringing cool air with him. "She's doing great, Jonathan. I think we'll be able to transport her sooner than we thought. She tried to open her eyes tonight and her heart beat went way up when she recognized my voice." He suddenly stopped stock still when he noticed Liam. "What are you doing here?" His voice was sharp.

"Hi, Dad. Nice to see you, too."

"I asked you a question, young man."

"I'm here because my mother is very ill. Fighting for her life." He took a deep breath. "My mother left you to live in New Zealand. Transporting her back to the UK is out of the question. She'll tell you that herself as soon as she's able." Two bright spots of colour stained his cheeks but his eyes were clear.

"That's enough out of you, young man. This is neither the time nor the place."

"I beg to differ," Jonathan said before dissolving in a fit of coughing.

Ted stood. "Please sit down, Gerald. Jonathan has asked me to chair this meeting and Liam here has just articulated one view. It sounds as if you're proposing a second view?"

Gerald's face became a blotchy red, but he sat as requested. "As Vivien's husband," he started to say.

"...you've a definite say in what happens," Ted finished his thought. "Now, let's make sure we all know each other and get Lela in. Liam, will you introduce Holly to your father? I'll get Lela."

Once settled, everyone turned to Ted. He looked around this modern and exquisitely furnished lounge. Holly and Liam were at each end of a three-seater couch, their faces young and eager; Jonathan was a diminutive figure swallowed by his large leather armchair; Lela was sitting on an upright chair that normally faced a small writing desk, situating herself a bit out of the family circle; Oscar sat beside Gerald on a two-seater couch and Ted had pulled up another leather chair to sit by Jonathan.

"We have a dilemma," he said over Jonathan who was coughing deeply. He decided to carry on to divert attention from it. "Gerald here has arrived to get his wife and take her home." Ted deliberately used the phraseology of the card, but Gerald just smiled and nodded. "Can you please articulate your view, Gerald?"

Ted was amused to see Gerald's chest puff out. He started to rise, but Ted motioned him to stay seated.

"My dear wife is gravely ill, as you all know. Worse than ill. She has been deliberately poisoned. And with this pneumonia, she's in serious danger. She's still on a type of life support because of terrible paralysis. Is that not so, Jonathan?" But Jonathan was struggling to catch his breath after coughing. He waved his hands to indicate to carry on.

"Jesus H. Christ. This is ridiculously formal. Can't we lighten up?" Oscar asked, half standing.

Jonathan frowned at his son as if to settle him down. He turned to Gerald. "Yes, you're absolutely right." His voice was not much above a whisper.

"My job is to arrange for her return to England where she can receive the best of British medicine to effect her recovery."

"Dad, that's silly reasoning," Liam said. "Half the doctors here are British-trained for one thing, and the rest have been to medical schools that are equal if not better than ours."

Gerald looked at Ted, as chair, for control of this son of his.

"Liam, let's get your father's views out in the open first."

The young man looked abashed then nodded. "Okay. You're right."

"Go on, Gerald," Ted said.

"I must apologize for my son. He's not known for his ability to function in polite society."

Ted glanced at Liam. He had flushed again and Holly moved closer to him so she could put her hand on his forearm; but he said nothing.

Gerald went on. "As I said, British medicine is the best in the world. Others imitate our superiority."

Ted noticed Holly's hand once more. She leaned towards Liam and whispered something into his ear.

"So—correct me if I'm wrong—you want to get Vivien to British medicine? That's your argument?" Ted asked. "After she recovers from the infection? After she's off the machines?"

"Yes, of course. And I am her husband."

Ted snorted. "Come on, McAvoy. This is the 21st century, not the 19th."

"I am her legal husband. Her next of kin." His voice was icy.

Ted shrugged. "And as her husband, you want to take her to your home."

"My home and hers."

"Okay. Liam, do you want to make your points next or, perhaps, your grandfather?"

"Why so bloody formal, Ted?" Oscar asked. "Surely we can just contribute when we feel like it?"

"Gramps, you take it first," the young man said with some firmness.

Jonathan cleared his throat. His jaw was shaking. "Vivien wanted to live with me. That's all I have to say."

"Good point, Jonathan. Vivien conveyed her view clearly to you. So, your contribution is that Vivien indicated she wanted to stay in Auckland. Not go home to London."

"Yes. She wanted to make her home with me." Ted could see that Jonathan was fading fast.

"Liam?"

"My mother told me she had left my father. He must have no influence on where she goes. None." He sat back against the chair with arms folded.

"Typical dogmatism of the very young," Oscar said. "There are lots of permutations we can discuss. For one thing—it seems I'm the only one she told—but Vivien said she was going back to the UK to settle her affairs there. So she was not averse to going back." He sat back with a Cheshire grin.

Ted knew that someone was bound to bring up Vivien's decision to go back to the UK. "Thank you, Oscar. Yes, you're right—we do need to go over all the permutations. So far, where are we? Gerald, Vivien's husband, wants her back in London and second, in the marital home. Liam, as the most vociferous opponent of this view, can you see a way that this is possible?"

Liam closed his eyes for a moment. "I did discuss this with John Robertson, Mum's lawyer. He said that Mum was coming back to do the negotiating about the divorce."

"Nobody is talking about a divorce," Gerald expostulated, half rising from his seat.

"I said that John said this, Dad. I'm being precise," Liam said. "He said that Mum could take over half the house. The only way it would work is if she had the upstairs sitting room and the master bedroom could become a kitchen-diner. That allows Stephanie and me to keep our old rooms on the second floor. She would turn the guest room into her own bedroom. Dad could be quite separate. He'd have the existing sitting room; his study would become his bedroom and the dining room his study. Then downstairs he's got the kitchen and breakfast room. It's an idea. But not in the foreseeable, in my opinion."

"Did John discuss this with you?" Ted asked Gerald.

"Not with me, with my lawyer," he mumbled. "Impractical. She's too ill to be on her own."

"She's too ill to be moved," Liam said.

"I happen to agree with Liam," Oscar said. "We have to face reality here. My sister is in intensive care and on a respirator. Talking about taking her to England is premature."

"That's an important point which we'll discuss soon. Thank you, Oscar," Ted said. "First, I'd like to get Lela to tell us what she knows."

"Excuse me," she began, one hand hovering over her chin. "I can only say what Ms Vivien and I talked about. She said she had to go back to England, but she wasn't looking forward to it. Her lawyer said she must, so she was getting ready to go back because she had to—she didn't want to, that's for sure. She told me she wanted a divorce from Mr Gerald as soon as she could."

Ted could see the colour rising in Gerald's face once more.

"Where did she intend to settle—the UK or here?" Gerald asked with such sarcasm in his voice, Ted winced. "Did she happen to mention it to you?"

"Here," Lela answered, as if it had been a real question. "She wanted to look after Mr Jonathan."

"They don't know what they're talking about. They're colluding!" Gerald shouted.

"Don't be stupid, Dad. You're always going off the deep end when you've only got half the facts. I've never met Lela before tonight and I haven't talked to Uncle Oscar in years. No collusion. Just common sense, something you seem to lack," Liam said, standing up.

"That's enough. No one speaks to me like that," Gerald said, also rising. "Especially my own son." He turned on his heel and strode out, slamming the door behind him. Ted started after him, but realized how futile it would be. Liam was over-breathing and looked like he wanted a fight.

"Sorry, Liam. I blew it." Ted figured he'd calm Liam down faster if he spread the blame.

Jonathan waved his hand. Such a slight gesture, but everyone turned to him.

"I'm ill," he said. "Need to get to bed. But wanted to say a few words first. Need to. Why you're all here."

"We can put it off until tomorrow, Gramps," Holly said, moving to squat in front of him, her hands on his knee.

"I don't have to leave you anything," he said to her, his voice so low, Ted had a hard time hearing. "Marcia has made sure you are well provided for."

"We don't have to...," Holly tried to say.

"Vivien and Oscar, ditto. But you, Liam. And Stephanie as well. Must say you're not forgotten. Liam, I was going to give you the cars. Fleet's Fleet. I know you'd love them, but not practical. You'd have to sell them all. So instead, you get some shares. You and Stephanie. For when you two will want to get onto the property ladder. After uni, maybe?"

"I ... I don't know what to say," Liam said. "Except I hope I don't have to inherit any time soon."

Jonathan waved his hand again, dismissing it as sentiment, Ted thought.

"So Cushla gets my cars." He made a fleeting smile. "She laughed. Probably sell them except for one. Maybe two, because she'll want to give one to Lester. He can have the little green bug."

Jonathan started to cough again. Hugely and wetly. He took a deep breath and said to Lela, "The bowl, please. Quickly."

Lela jumped up and was back in an instant with a large stainless steel bowl. "Okay, Mr Jonathan. It's all okay." She looked up at Holly. "Grab a towel, Holly, please. We'll need it."

Jonathan's coughing ended in a retch. Holly dashed back with the towel from the front cloakroom. Jonathan emptied his stomach contents into the bowl held by Lela. Ted held his breath, looked away, and cautiously swallowed. Vomiting was hard for him to take; somehow he always wanted to retch too. He glanced around, wanting to be anywhere but there. Oscar stared at the carpet, his mouth turned down; Liam looked worried, his eyes fixed on the scene in front of him and both Lela and Holly seemed matter-of-fact. Eventually, Jonathan sat back in his chair.

"Sorry, folks. But now you know what it's like," Jonathan said in such a soft voice, Ted had to strain to hear. Jonathan took a shuddering breath. "I've something to tell you. It's the real reason I got you all together. I can't take it anymore. And it's not working, anyway. I'm quitting. Going into Palliative Care."

Chapter Forty-Nine

THE GROUP STARED AT Jonathan. His breathing was laboured and his eyes were closed.

"What's Palliative Care?" Holly asked, looking around wildly.

Ted took a deep breath. "As your Gramps has said. He's quitting the chemo. He says it's not working, and it's making him very ill. The aim of Palliative Care is to make a person comfortable but not treat the illness." Ted's voice sounded hollow to his own ears.

"No," Holly said, her hand to her mouth. "No, you can't quit now, Gramps." She rushed over to him, kneeling beside him.

He placed a hand on her head. "It's no use, little one. It's not working this time. Not the chemo that worked last time, not some new stuff they're giving me. Looks like my time is coming. In a few months, anyway."

"You have to keep trying, Gramps," Liam said, his face now pale. "I agree with Holly. You can't quit. There's too much going on right now. Think of the effect on Mum."

"Give it a rest, Liam," Oscar said. "Father is overwrought with everything that's happening. There are other things he can do if the chemo is too much."

"Oscar," Jonathan said with surprising strength. "They're allowed. They're dismayed and letting me know. Fat chance you'd be dismayed. Your eyes are too firmly fixed on taking over the company. And, if you're wondering, that's why Vivien is getting the majority. To keep you under control. And I'll be damned if I go before she's up and about, capable of being her usual competent self."

Ted barely glanced at Oscar. He had been hit hard by this turn of events. But now why Jonathan told everyone it was he who had called this meeting was clear; why it could be arranged at such short notice. Liam's desire for a family conference fitted in with Jonathan's own need to tell everyone this devastating news.

"I can never do anything right, can I, Father? Even when I'm supporting something you've just said."

Ted felt a fleeting sense of sympathy for this son of Jonathan's. Suddenly, he could hardly breathe, fighting for internal control. He looked around at the others. The mood was tense. With considerable effort, he tuned in to what Jonathan was saying.

"I expect to be feeling much better in a couple of days. My skin should clear up, my stomach settle and I should have at least some of my old energy back. Who knows how long I'll be like that, but hopefully until Vivien is recovered."

"Besides, it's all arranged that I'll take Vivien," Oscar said. "She'll be coming back to my flat when she's discharged to outpatient care. I have nursing help organized. I'll take care of her."

"That's very generous of you, Oscar," Holly said while keeping her eyes on her father.

Ted had a moment of panic. He cleared his throat. "Sorry, everyone, but Gerald's not here and we can't carry on without him." They all looked at him. "No decisions tonight. Thank you all for coming." He turned to Jonathan. "And I think we have plenty to think about until we can get together again." He knew it was precipitous, but with Jonathan's devastating news, he thought everyone had had enough, anyway.

Ted stared at Holly and when he had her eye, he gave his head the tiniest of shakes, trying to communicate to her that this was important. She looked startled for a moment, then bent to whisper something in Liam's ear.

Jonathan seemed to be following the conversation, although not contributing. "It had better be soon," he said. "I don't have all that long." No one spoke, no one moved.

"Everything we do has to be in relation to your health, Gramps. That's right, isn't it?" Holly looked around at the others.

Ted picked up on it. "Liam?"

"Of course. Everything."

"Lela?"

"I will be here for Mr Jonathan until Ms Vivien gets back on her feet."

"Oscar?"

"Father's health is my concern also, of course."

"And I'll also do my best to keep things on an even keel," Ted said. "To summarise: Gerald's expert will see Vivien tomorrow and make an assessment. We will reassess if he throws a wild card. We'll take it from there with Gerald, of course. Agreed?"

"Yes." A chorus of voices.

"It's not so easy," Oscar said sharply.

There was a silence as everyone looked at Ted. "Sorry, Oscar, you're out-voted. Depending upon the medical status, a decision will be made, but not tonight. And it will involve everyone."

Ted rose to his feet. "Shall we meet again as soon as we know the medical report?"

As soon as she shut the car door, Holly exploded. "What in heaven's name were you doing, Dad? Are you seriously considering that Vivien could be going back? That's precisely what she was afraid of—getting in Gerald's clutches once more."

"I know. But I suddenly had some dark thoughts and I couldn't think of anything else. Can't. Thanks, you two, for supporting me, trusting me, not making a fuss in there." Ted gave them both a fleeting smile. "Do up your seat belts, everyone. I want to get to the hospital as soon as pos."

"Dark thoughts?" Holly asked as she buckled up. "Go on."

"I was sitting there with all that argy-bargy going on and it suddenly became clear to me. First Marcia being killed up north, then the murderer seeing the advantage of Vivien being dead or badly injured too. And now Jonathan has decided to quit his treatment, bringing everything into focus."

"We saw your face, Dad. We knew something was going on, didn't we, Liam?"

"You pointed it out." Liam leaned forward from his seat in the middle of the backseat of the car so his head was between Holly's and Ted's. "What happened, Ted? What were you thinking?"

"Tell me, Liam, before I shoot with my mouth, is this your father's first visit to New Zealand?"

"Yes, I think so."

"Only think so?"

"Unless he came here some years ago, this will be his first visit." Liam's voice was confident.

"There's absolutely no way he could have come here since your mother's been away?"

Liam went silent. "You're not thinking that Dad ... would he hurt Mum? Hell." He took a deep breath. "Steph and I try to talk to him every week or two. And I've spent loads of weekends at home. Shit, Ted, you're not really thinking that Dad hurt Mum, are you?"

"We have to consider it."

Liam nodded. "He hates not being in charge. He hates Mum saying she's leaving him. He hates me being here. Damn, damn, damn—it does add up. Shit."

"Look, I'm trying to make sense out of all the bits and pieces. He's one of the few people I know who had anything against your mother."

"And he hated Marcia," Liam said.

Ted glanced at him in the mirror. Holly turned to him. "Hated Mum? Why?" she asked.

"My mother told me the story not long before she left for here. She laughed about it. Gerald was so taken by Marcia when he met her all those years ago, he made a total arse of himself. He was liquored up, I guess. Flirting with her, anyway. Telling dirty jokes. Then trying to put his arm around her. Pawing her, I guess. Marcia stood up and turned to Mum. She said, 'Time to take the boy home, don't you think?' They never met socially ever again. Not at our place, anyway."

Holly smiled. "So typical of Mum."

"Unfortunately, typical of my father when he gets into the booze. Embarrassing," Liam said.

Ted made himself smile. But his mind was whirling.

"Don't forget dear Pauline," Holly said. She launched into a detailed set of arguments for the case against Pauline. Jealousy of, first Marcia and second Vivien, her two attacks on Ted. Woman scorned.

Ted finally broke in. "Later, Holly, please."

Holly sighed loudly.

"Who is she?" Liam asked from the backseat.

"Dad's girlfriend," Holly said over the top of Ted trying to say she was a former friend.

"You aren't panicking about her, I guess," Liam said to Ted. "But you've someone else in mind, haven't you?"

"It was triggered by something Jonathan said while talking about his will. Cushla will inherit all his cars," Ted said. "The tense he used: not 'She'll laugh' but 'She laughed'."

"Oh," Holly said. "She already knows about it."

"Precisely," Ted said as they headed towards the hospital campus. "And you talked of hatred, Liam. Gerald hated Marcia because she'd made a fool of him in public. And I wonder if anyone else hated Marcia. Then it came to me. Not hating Marcia. Hating Jonathan. And making him as miserable as is humanly possible."

"People don't kill because they want to make someone unhappy, Dad."

"If you're a psychopath, you wouldn't care," Ted said. "Sorry, should have explained better." Ted pulled up in a parking spot outside of the hospital. "I'm being incoherent trying to drive and explain at the same time." He turned to the backseat. "How's the jetlag, Liam?"

"Okay, I guess. Right now I'm not tired."

Ted looked at his watch. Nine thirty-six. "Any chance you'd be good for another six hours?"

"In London, it's about 8:30 in the morning. I'm not sleepy. Why?"

"Vivien is now in grave danger, more so than ever before. One of us needs to be by her bedside at all times from now on."

"Danger from whom?" Holly asked.

Ted stared at his daughter. "Still not clear to you?" He stifled his impatience. "Remember, this is speculative in the extreme." He felt a huge push to get to Vivien. "Can we talk about this in the hospital? I want to see that Vivien is safe." As they were waiting for the lift, Ted's cell phone rang.

"Damn, meant to turn it off," he muttered. The name on the small screen said 'Pauline'. He clicked it on. "Sorry, Pauline, I'm in a hospital. Got to turn the phone off. I'll call you later."

"Hospital? Not going to hold hands with that corpse, are you? I know you...." Her voice was rising.

Ted turned the phone off. "We have to get up there. Now." He spotted the stairs. "Faster this way."

"No, Dad, don't be silly. It's on the eighth floor," Holly said, pulling his arm.

He halted abruptly. "Sorry. Not thinking. That was Pauline. She called Vivien a...." He caught sight of Liam's face as the lift opened its doors and swallowed the word. They got in.

With an effort to control himself, Ted continued. "If it's okay with you, the first shift till four am is yours, Liam. I'll relieve you then and you can drive back to our place to hit the sack—I'll programme the GPS with the route and you can just follow the voice. It's relatively straightforward, especially at night. Holly, you can then bring the car back here about noon and relieve me. We'll each take an eight-hour shift, using my car. Liam, tomorrow you can relieve Holly at eight in the evening. And so on. Never, ever leaving Vivien alone." They got into the lift and headed up to Vivien's ward.

"Okay, Dad. Spill. Who are we protecting Vivien from?"

"I hope I'm wrong. I'd been hoping that Marcia's death was an accident after all, as was Vivien's going off the road." They entered the large room. Ted swayed on his feet. Vivien was there, softly breathing with the respirator, her skin pink. She looked as she always did in the dim light of the night-time ward, like a softly breathing statue, beautiful and still, but alive. Ted motioned the two young people back into the corridor.

"We can see anyone approaching from here." He kept his voice low and the two moved closer. "As I said, it was talk about Jonathan's will. I'll give you the what-ifs and see if you come to the same conclusion I did."

"Shoot," Liam said.

"What if Marcia was having an affair?"

Holly nodded. "Her comments to me, her plastic surgery, the losing weight and her oh-so-trendy clothes, not to forget those *sigma*s on her calendar."

Ted didn't answer because a nurse was approaching along the corridor, peeking into each door as she did so. She smiled briefly at the little group and continued with what she was doing. They waited until she was well past them before Ted carried on. "Okay, what if we have someone who is willing to do anything and I mean ANYTHING to destroy everything that Jonathan holds dear?"

"You said something about his will." Holly frowned. "How does that come into it?"

"What if someone was told his beloved mother, who had given her all to Jonathan for over thirty years, was in her multi-millionaire lover's will? But what would she get? Not money. Not property. Only some second-hand cars."

"Lester?" Holly asked. "My god. Lester."

"What if he hates Jonathan? What if he feels Jonathan has made a fool of his mother all these years? What could he do about it? How about making Jonathan's life miserable?" He paused and looked up and down the corridor yet again. "How about that for a working theory?"

"Seducing Marcia? Is that what you're thinking?" Liam asked.

Ted shrugged. "Sort of seems unlikely given their age difference. But Marcia was worried about growing old."

"The face lift. The Botox," Holly whispered.

"A good-looking dude like Lester flirting with her would have been a massage to her ego."

He turned to Liam. "She was used to being in total control of her life. If Marcia wanted something, Marcia got it. If some young man was into her ... was having an affair with her, she would have been in control. That just might have been a bit too much for a macho dude like Lester. Became sick of her. But wanting to hurt Jonathan as much as he could. The secret affair with his enemy's wife wasn't enough anymore. But killing Marcia? That would hurt Jonathan where it really hurt. Poisoning Vivien, ditto. I'm saying this whole sorry mess centres on Jonathan."

Chapter Fifty

Liam stared at Ted then nodded. "I agree we have to take the Lester theory into consideration. Maybe," Liam said. "But I fancy my bloody father first, though. He hated Marcia for years and years. And revenge is best served cold. His mantra. Repeated to me tons of times. His anger at Mum displaced onto the symbol of hated female superiority: Marcia."

"And Vivien was doing the worst thing he could imagine. Dragging him publicly through the dirt," Holly said with some enthusiasm. "But Lester is a piece of work, truly, Liam. He was into drugs and went to prison for it. I wouldn't be surprised he's still into drugs."

"Hey, keep your voices down," Ted said. "I've been trying to get the authorities at the hospital to let Vivien come out of her sedated sleep to ask her about all this. Look, I'd be happy to get her to the UK to remove her from danger if I could be that bit more sure of Gerald." He hadn't been able to get away from it. Gerald did have the biggest motivation to kill or maim his wife. He paused. "Just had an idea. What if someone else was responsible for Marcia's death? Did Gerald become inspired by Marcia's death to do in Vivien?" That would make two perpetrators, something he had always argued against.

Holly had wandered away then came back again. She stared at the wall above her father's head. "Remember that silliness in Mum?" she asked. "I suppose you think it was because Mum was trying to start up with Oscar again."

"Again?" Liam asked.

"Marcia had an affair with him before she married Jonathan," Ted said to the young man. He rubbed the sides of his face. "This is the trouble with being active in an uncertain situation. We really don't know what's going on or what went on prior to Marcia's drowning. We'll have to be doubly aware of not stepping on any toes unnecessarily. Okay?"

Holly slumped against the wall. A trio of silent nurses pushed a trolley upon which an old lady was lying, her skin mottled in shades of yellow and grey.

"Don't dismiss Pauline. I know you're unconcerned about my suspicions about her, but she's a dangerous woman, Dad. She's intruded where she has no right to be and she's done so twice. And with sick minds, things escalate. She's still number one on my list."

"Not Hiram Brownstone?"

"Of course, Hiram Brownstone's on my list. And what about Cushla Waaka herself? What about them? I still think that Pauline is a woman scorned and she's truly dangerous. Hiram's totally weird and not just eccentric. And they knew both Mum and Vivien. So did Cushla. And Lester is into drugs, a bloody waste of space."

Liam turned to Holly. "Are you serious? All these suspects for Marcia's death? And for hurting my mother as well?"

"Not really," said Ted.

Holly spoke over her father. "Yes. Pauline is a jealous bitch."

"Holly," Ted said, warning in his voice.

She ignored him. "And Hiram stalked Vivien years ago, and he's still doing it."

"Stalked Mum?"

"Other women too. He's creepy."

"Now, Holly. We were speculating that night when we talked through the various scenarios. Everything we came up with was plausible, but unlikely. Nebulous and tenuous."

Holly glared. She turned away.

Ted wiped his arm over the sweat that was gathering on his forehead. Doubts crowded in, triggered by Holly, but really awakening those he had harboured for some time.

"But we're here because of our meeting, right?" Liam asked. "You think it's dangerous right now because Mum's still sedated and Lester probably thinks now is the time to finish her off. If the murderer is my father, he also might try something now. We didn't roll over and beg. We used logic and knowledge. Nothing would infuriate him more. He's losing control over the situation."

"I agree. If it's Gerald, the danger is right now, especially if he thinks he'll not get her back," Holly said, turning towards Liam. "I think I agree with you, Liam. I'm not totally convinced he's out of the loop. Maybe he could have flown over here without anyone being the wiser, or maybe he could have hired some low-life to do those things to your mother. He's got the best motive of all."

"But that means we still have the problem of having two nasties, one for Marcia and another for Vivien," Liam said. He looked at Ted, then Holly.

"I could argue..."

"Stop!" Ted said it in a semi-whisper, but the effect was immediate. "We're going round and round."

"I'm going to side with Ted, here," Liam said to Holly. "We just need to get onto it."

Ted nodded.

Holly frowned. "But I can build a case for it being Pauline or Hiram Brownstone, and so can you, Dad. And you know the Waakas could have put the poison in the fish sauce. You were there."

"Who is this Brownstone, anyway?" Liam asked with a sigh.

Holly filled him in with all they knew. "He freaked me out, Liam. And I've done a bit of research since." Ted looked sharply at his daughter. "It turns out that some well-known murderers have been stalkers and not just a few, either. Stalking is treated really seriously by the police, and the medical profession as well. You should see this guy. Weirdsville."

"Okay, let's leave it there. Enough speculating." Ted said. Hearing his theory watered down against the brick wall of Holly's list of suspects was wearying.

"Think what you want," Holly said. "For me, I'm going to be hugely aware of everything Hiram does, the same goes for Pauline and, should Lester turn up, him too. But you both have to promise you'll take Pauline and Hiram as seriously as Lester from now on. Ditto for Gerald." She looked at each of the men. "The only reason I'm going along with it is the timing. We have to protect Vivien. Now. So, okay, let's get on with it. Dad, you need to get to bed early if you're relieving Liam at four. Are you sure you're awake enough for this, Liam?"

Ted glanced at the determined face of his daughter. He felt a surge of pride in her. But she was growing up very fast and his influence seemed to be diminishing with every conversation they had.

At four precisely, Ted relieved Liam. "How did it go?" he whispered. The ward was as quiet as it could be with all the machines ticking or wheezing in the semi-dark.

"Just totally boring, that's all. Mum slept the whole time. I must bring a couple of good books for my next shift. All I've had to read are *Women's Weeklys* from the waiting room." Liam wasn't yawning and, to Ted's eyes, looked remarkably fresh.

"Sleepy?"

"Not really. This schedule will be okay. The nurses were a little surprised to see me here for so long, but they were okay about it. Son from England, jetlag, that sort of thing."

Ted told Liam where he'd parked and handed over the keys. As soon as Liam left, he opened up his laptop on the bedside table, somewhat awkward all in all, but doable. He felt fresh from his sleep and he settled down to work immediately. It was close enough to his normal six am start not to bother him overly much. And he could work anywhere; the lack of voices was conducive to concentration. Other than routine nursing care, Ted was undisturbed until shortly before nine in the morning. Gerald walked in.

"Frazer! What are you doing here?"

"Visiting," Ted said, standing and stretching. "Hoping she'd make a turn for the better and they would allow the sedation to lighten. We need to tell Vivien about what's going on."

"Not for you to do." Gerald swung over a chair from the next bed and sat down, looking at Vivien's face and within reach of her hand. Ted thought he looked remarkably calm. "Don't hang about. The consultant is coming any time now and I want some time with my wife." He stared at Ted, rubbed his forehead, smiled with his mouth not his eyes. "In other words, bugger off." He turned to Vivien.

"Yes, well, fingers crossed the consultant thinks she's getting good treatment," Ted said as he got up. "Most times, things work out." He was aware of the banality, but what else could he say? Either this was a murderous bastard who was a consummate actor or an innocent man who'd come halfway around the world because his wife was deathly ill. He started closing down his computer. Slowly. Trying to prolong the moment when he'd have to leave.

Vivien moved a leg. Ted saw it out of the corner of his eye. So did Gerald.

"She moved," Gerald said.

Ted nodded. He was standing closer to her head than Gerald and he leaned towards Vivien's ear.

"You're doing really well, Vivien. We're here, Gerald and I, hoping you'll be able to communicate with us." They watched while she struggled as if trying to open her eyes for a moment, then she became still again, the machine rhythmically breathing for her all the while.

"Off you go now, Frazer. I want this time alone," Gerald said, his voice low. He brushed Vivien's hair from her forehead. Tenderly. Could a man with malice in his heart do that?

A nurse came to the doorway. "Mr McAvoy? Come with me, please. Dr Christiansen is here to see you."

Gerald got up. "My new consultant. He'll probably want to examine Vivien."

"I'll make myself scarce," Ted said and bent over his papers, tidying them. But as soon as Gerald left the room, Ted leaned close to Vivien's ear once more. She moved her eyelids slightly as Ted filled her in about the sentry team of himself, Liam and Holly and their plan to watch over her at all times. She tried to open her eyes and Ted hoped that at least some of this complex message was getting through.

"We're going to keep you safe, Vivien," he said as McAvoy, the consultant and the nurse came back into the room. "And you'll never be alone."

"Thank you, Frazer, I'll fill you in later," Gerald said, his old arrogance back in full force. Ted shoved his last papers into his business bag and left, satisfied Vivien was safe with so many people paying attention to her.

He took the opportunity to dash to the hospital cafeteria to grab a coffee and an egg-filled roll to go. He ate in the waiting room, hoping that McAvoy would assume he had gone home.

Well after he'd finished his makeshift breakfast, Ted saw the little group trail behind the consultant towards the nursing station. He moved to the door so he could see both ways. Eventually the consultant and McAvoy walked towards the lifts, allowing him to slip across the corridor to re-join Vivien. A nurse, too, was there.

"She's a bit more awake than you've ever seen her," she said with a smile. "But not for long." She bent to Vivien. "That was the best yet, wasn't it, Mrs McAvoy?" Ted saw a slight smile. He wanted to push the nurse to one side so he could take advantage of this window in her sedated state.

"Is she's showing signs of improvement?" Ted asked.

"Yes, she's doing better," the nurse said. After another agonising minute, the nurse finished. "Don't over-excite her, will you?"

"Of course not," Ted said stoutly. He waited till she had left.

"Vivien? You know it's me, Ted?" He took her hand in his. She squeezed it very lightly. Her eyelids fluttered. "Should I go over what we talked about again?" Another squeeze. He summarized the watch they were taking over her, but her hand became limp and her eyelids quiet. He felt he had done what he could.

He sat contentedly holding her hand, curious about what the consultant had said. Her response right now had been more than he'd yet seen. Surely that was a good sign. He glanced at his watch, half past ten. Only an hour and a half until noon, when he'd be relieved by Holly. He worried about her shift. He was troubled she was not yet fully convinced Vivien was in any real danger. And that meant Holly herself could be in danger. He fervently hoped her presence in this hubbub of hospital activity would deter any further attempts. Broad daylight and coinciding with visiting hours. Surely the safest shift. He got out his laptop again and, in spite of his stomach telling him his breakfast was insufficient, he finished a good piece of work before Holly arrived.

"You've given me the easy stretch," Holly said. "Daytime when there are tons of people and no disruption to my sleep."

"Someone has to do it," Ted said. "What about Liam? Is he sleeping?"

"He's trying to maintain his UK schedule. We had a meal then he went to bed about ten and wants to be wakened at six so he can eat again with you."

"I forgot to warn you. Have you brought yourself something to eat?"

"Liam suggested a packed lunch. I had a big brunch with him which should last me I should think. And I have some sammies here, just in case I get peckish." She opened her carry-all and took out several novels, a pack of sandwiches and a thermos. "Looks like I'm set for a picnic." She grinned at her father.

Ted told her about trying to get the message through to Vivien about their meeting. "Nothing specific about Gerald, though," he said quietly. "Promise me?"

"Don't worry, Dad. I think nothing is going to happen, anyway. And I'm not going to blow your cover."

Chapter Fifty-One

ONCE HOME, TED'S FIRST call was to Gerald. "Your expert. What did he have to say?"

"He says she's doing as well as can be expected. Agrees with the local boys. It does seem she's getting excellent care and some of the equipment available here puts Addenbrookes—the hospital where he's from—to shame. He's talked to the head man here and they're to start the programme to get her off the respirator as soon as they can, given this damned infection she's fighting. They're going to do a rethink tomorrow and my man has invited himself to be there. Anyway, once she's off the respirator and stable, she'll be able to travel."

"One day at a time, McAvoy. Vivien herself will be telling us what she wants." Gerald didn't seem to realize how precarious her hold on life was.

"Yes, well, we'll see. Apparently to wean her off the respirator, they need a fortnight minimum—that's a bit disappointing—and a month max. I must be back in the UK by the end of the week. I'll have a word with Liam, if you don't mind, and see if he can stay to escort her home."

The man had a one-track mind. "Liam's sleeping the sleep of the just," Ted said. "He sat up with Vivien into the wee small hours, using his UK jetlag to advantage." He didn't want to say too much. Gerald was on the short-list.

"Have him give me a call at his grandfather's," Gerald said. "Speaking of Jonathan, he's as perky as I've seen him this trip."

"That's one good thing," Ted said.

"Oh, almost forgot," Gerald said. "He wants to talk to you. Hang on."

Jonathan's voice filled the receiver. "I'm going in to see Vivien later. That is, if I keep my dinner down again."

Was he asking for a lift? "Who are you going in with, Jonathan?"

"Gerald, of course."

"Sounds as if you're feeling better."

"Unbelievably so. That damn stuff they were giving me was pure poison. And it wasn't doing one scrap of damage to the big C, that's what really gets me."

"You made the right decision."

"Bloody right I did."

That afternoon Ted rang Inspector Johnston. "I'd like to fill you in on what's happening," Ted said. "Should I drop in?" There was a slight pause and Ted imagined the good inspector with a mouth dropped open in astonishment. Frazer volunteering something?

Ted was shown into the inspector's office. It was small and utilitarian but with a grand view of downtown Auckland. As Ted sat down, the sergeant was summoned.

"Now, what do you have to tell us?"

"More an update than anything drastic," Ted began. "We had a family meet ing...."

"Hold it right there," Johnston interrupted. "Family? Whose family?"

Ted kept his temper. Something about this man pushed all his buttons. "Jonathan Fleet's family plus. My daughter Holly—she's his step-daughter—his son Oscar, his grandson Liam, his housekeeper Lela, his son-in-law Gerald and me."

"Gerald McAvoy is here? With his son? Why didn't you tell me?"

Ted didn't deign to answer and, after a pause, he went on. "The meeting was last night. Liam had just arrived and Gerald has been here a couple of days."

"They didn't come together."

"No. And Liam is staying with me; Gerald with Jonathan."

"Got it. Now, you were saying about this meeting?"

"Gerald wants to take his wife home. If he has his way, he'll effect her transfer as soon as she's medically cleared to travel."

"'If he has his way? Others opposed this plan?"

"Others did. She's much too ill to move at present, and that's a given. Everyone agrees. Once she's clear of the infection—she has pneumonia—there will be a fortnight minimum before she'd be cleared to travel to the UK. More likely a month. Of course, there's a big 'if' here: *if* Vivien is willing to leave New Zealand. The young McAvoy talked about her living independently in part of their London house but, frankly, no one knows what she'll decide."

"And you, Mr Frazer? Do you agree?" Ted didn't like the insinuation. It was as if he had made a lewd suggestion.

"I just want Vivien safe. After all, we have not only a murderer of one Fleet woman out there, but also a person who has attempted to murder another. I presume it is one and the same person." He paused. Johnston stared at him.

Ted continued. "Whoever it is, one person or two, Vivien continues to be in danger."

"Could well be, Mr Frazer, could well be." The inspector sat back in his chair which squealed in protest. He leaned forward again. "You'd consider her being in the care of Mr McAvoy? Living in the same house as him? You're personally convinced that Mrs McAvoy is safer there than with anyone here in New Zealand?" His eyes bored into Ted's.

Ted resolutely kept his own eyes on Johnston's. "His son, Liam McAvoy, who definitely did not want his mother back in the UK to start with, thinks it was impossible for his father to have been out of the country at any of the operative times."

"And you believe him?"

"I don't know. No proof." He didn't mention the possibility that Gerald had hired thugs. Better to just point them in the right direction.

"Okay. I'll see both of them." The big man stood up. "Thank you, Mr Frazer. You're an upright citizen."

Ted heard the sarcasm but chose to ignore it. "One more thing," he said. "The hospital is talking about reducing Vivien's sedatives sooner rather than later, and that may place her in greater danger now than ever before. Could I please ask that a guard be placed in her hospital room?" It was worth a try.

The inspector laughed. "If I had the manpower to provide guards for everyone who asked, I would have three times the number on the force. Sorry, Mr Frazer, until we have some fresh information, it's status quo."

Ted nodded. At least he'd asked. But as he descended the outside steps, he realized he'd forgotten to pass on the message about the Greek letters on the calendar. Damn Johnston. He was a difficult man.

Over dinner, Ted warned Liam that the inspector wanted to talk to him. "If you don't make an appointment to suit your hours, you can guarantee he'll want to see you when you're asleep."

Liam looked at his watch. "Too late now. I'll ring after my shift."

Like Holly, Liam had packed a survival kit. "I raided your bookshelves, Ted. Hope you don't mind. I have your books, more books and loads of music on my phone, my earbuds, a midnight snack and some Sudoku to keep my brain working."

"See you at four. Once Holly gets back, I'm off to bed early."

"Not exactly the big fat nothing I was expecting," Holly said as soon as she came through the door.

"Lucky you," Ted said with a slight frown. "Come on, have something to eat. We'll debrief afterwards." Holly ate the microwaved left-overs with gusto, finally pushing back from the table.

"Now can I talk? I'm about to burst—both with good food and with what happened."

"Shoot," Ted said, piling her dirty dishes into the dishwasher. Filling the jug.

"Hiram came to see Vivien. With flowers."

"Hiram came to the hospital? Shit," Ted said. "Bloody h..., I must rethink this. How did he behave?"

"Very shy, could hardly look at me. Hardly looked at Vivien, either. Gave me the bouquet and shambled out."

"Did he say anything?"

"Introduced himself and me to him. He said, 'Marcia's daughter?' And I said, 'Yes.' And he said he was sorry to hear about her passing."

"Any emotion?" Ted poured boiling water over their tea bags and handed Holly her steaming mug.

"He just looked sad the whole time he was there. He glanced a couple of times over at Vivien; hardly looked at me. Cheerless and sort of uncomfortable."

"You sound as if you handled it, Holly. Well done."

"I haven't finished yet. Then Oscar came."

Ted stopped and sat down. "Did he now." An exclamation, not a question.

"It was fine, Dad. He was a bit surprised I didn't leave with him, though. He invited me out for dinner and I told him 'no'. That was, well, awkward."

Ted hid his relief. "How long was he there?"

"Ages. I think he was trying to outlast me. But don't get the wrong idea. He was fine. Charming, funny, Oscar at his best. Then Liam came and finally he gave up."

"Still pressuring you to go out?"

"Yup. But I kept thinking about something Liam said to me. He told me I was pretty but the reason I was so attractive to men was because I didn't believe it. Sort of echoed around my brain box. Kind of empowering. I just said 'no' to Oscar and he had to accept it." She giggled. "First time I've ever felt like that."

"Oh no. The end of innocence. Pandora's box," Ted said with a smile, but inwardly he groaned. His little girl.

He got up and piled their dishes together. As he did so, he again reminded himself they were dealing with a murderer. "I'm not sure you should be involved at all, Holly."

"Don't be over-protective, please. I won't accept food or drink from anyone, promise. And you've allotted me the prize shift where anyone would have a difficult time doing anything without being seen, anyway. It's the wee small hours that are the dangerous times, so *you* be careful," Holly said.

"But this Hiram thing. It's thrown me. I was so sure he wasn't involved." Ted shook his head. "Why turn up now?"

"An innocent fluke?" Holly asked, as she took their mugs to the bench. "He just turned up because he's found out she's here and she's ill? People do it all the time, you know, visit people in hospital." She popped the mugs into the dishwasher and turned it on.

"So now he's not near the top of your list anymore?"

"Pauline is top, no question. Her emotions are too unstable. She's crazy...." Holly stopped. "Okay, Hiram's slipped a little. You should have seen his face. Long. Droopy. Haggard. I didn't see anything else. He certainly wasn't giving me the eye. Nor Vivien."

"What if he was down because you were there? You thwarted his dastardly plans?"

Holly laughed. "Now it's you trying to convince me!"

"All joking aside, it's shocked me, Holly. I thought Hiram was a byplay."

Ted slept fitfully. If the time was coming when Vivien would be allowed to fully awaken, it was likely that the danger was peaking, to say nothing about Jonathan's health. He finally gave up on more sleep and dressed. By two am he was in the hospital carpark.

"You're early," Liam said. "And Oscar's been in."

"Yes, Holly told me he'd been here."

"Not just when she was here. He came in about an hour ago again. Pretending to be drunk. Got two coffees, one for me."

"Did you...?"

"Became all clumsy, didn't I. Sloshed it all down my front," Liam said with a grin, holding out his stained shirt. "I had to make it good and spilled lovely smelling, very hot coffee over my very thin shirt. You should see my skin—it's as if I have a sunburn. He then told me to go get myself cleaned up. I did, at the basin by the door. He watched me like a hawk the whole time. I've a strong suspicion that he was as drunk as I was. And the only thing I've had to drink is bottled water."

"Thank goodness you had your wits about you," Ted said. Part of his sleeplessness was his concern that he hadn't warned Liam about accepting food or drink from anybody. His first emotion was relief. "Hiram? Did he come during the night?"

"Nobody else, Ted. Except nurses and an early morning cleaner. I was totally awake and nobody did anything unexpected."

"You know Hiram Brownstone came on Holly's shift?"

Liam nodded. "But innocuous. Didn't even put the flowers near Mum. Just gave them to Holly."

"I don't like it, though," Ted said. "Don't relax your vigilance."

"Course not. If Holly had been organizing us, we would be focused on that old girlfriend of yours. And if me? Well, probably concentrating on Dad. Doesn't say we wouldn't be vigilant about anyone else, though."

Ted realized Liam was trying desperately to get the suspicions about his father out of his consciousness. "Good. I'm just twitchy," he said. "And feeling as if I'm abusing the privilege of having you here."

Liam got up and stretched. "Well, I'm awfully glad you've come early. I can use a pee break," he said.

Ted settled on the chair by Vivien's head. He picked up her hand. Still warmer than it should be, surely. He concentrated on pulling energy out of his own system and transmitting it to her. Come on, Vivien. Fight it. Kill those little bastards taking up residence in your lungs. Destroy them. He wanted her back.

Someone came in the door, and he dropped her hand. A nurse, saying there was a telephone message for Liam McAvoy.

"I'll take the message, thanks," Ted said, all his alert buttons flashing.

"Your sister Stephanie would like you to call this number in Scotland and reverse the charges. She wants you to call at three am our time."

Ted didn't bother to tell her that he wasn't Liam.

"You know you can't use cell phones here in the hospital?" she asked.

"I've been told," he said. "What about a pay phone? Is there one close?"

"Go up to the next floor. It's just around the corner from the lifts." She gave him the slip of paper with the number in Scotland and left.

Ted looked at the number without seeing it as he thought it through. First, it couldn't be Stephanie for one vital reason: she wouldn't know that Liam was on shift duty at the hospital. His second thought was that he had better make himself scarce immediately. This was an elusive but very dangerous person. And that person might just show his hand. Or her hand.

His heartbeat thundered in his ears. If this was a setup, the person was most likely calling from within or very near the hospital, and a casual walk past Vivien's room would find him there. The last thing Ted wanted was to prolong this agony, so he had to hide. But where?

Chapter Fifty-Two

TED LOOKED AROUND WILDLY. At first glance, nowhere to hide. The waiting room? Surely anyone would check there, just in case. It had to be here in this room. Somewhere.

Crouching under the high hospital beds would be too exposed. He thought briefly of pretending to be a visitor for one of the other occupied beds, but he didn't know how recognizable he would be. Besides, it was hardly visiting time.

The door. At the moment, the door was jammed open against a privacy curtain, creating an obvious hiding place, although often the door was closed. The voluminous drapery was bunched up, providing long folds of fabric that could hide an elephant in the available light. He dashed over and put his back against the wall, arranging the folds of the curtain in front of him as naturally as possible. He toed the door shut. As long as no one noticed shoes at the bottom of the curtain, the hiding place worked. He bunched more of the fabric in front of him. It would have to do.

He waited a few minutes. All was quiet. Then the doubts started. Maybe it was Stephanie, after all. She could have rung Holly to find Liam and be told to ring the ward number. Damn. He reached for his mobile. He glanced at the time. A quarter to three. What the hell. If it happened that way, it could have no different outcome once he'd become aware of the possibility. No use waking Holly.

Liam came back in and Ted hissed at him from his hiding place. "I think it's on, Liam. You've just had a message to call Stephanie at three. I figure whoever it is knows you're still here and he or she's probably somewhere in the hospital. You have this message to call Stephanie; you're concerned and you decide to return the call the only way you can."

"Leaving my post. They must know I wouldn't call my sister on my mobile—not inside the hospital—I'd have to dash down to call from outside." He looked agitated.

"The nurse suggested going upstairs to the pay phone near the stairs," Ted said. "Either choice clears the way long enough for someone to get to Vivien."

"The number is genuine," Liam said, looking at the scrap of paper Ted handed him. "It's where she works, her direct line. I imagine it'd generate a fuss about the reverse charges before I could talk to her and only when all that is straightened out, would I find out she had never called me in the first place. Clever."

Ted glanced at his mobile again. "We haven't much time. How about you go up to the phone about five minutes to three? I'll stay hidden in the curtains."

Liam nodded. "That will do." He peered at Ted's hiding place. "Can you see well enough?"

"I can, just." Ted had pulled the curtain slightly so he could peer over to Vivien's bed through the window in the door.

"What will you do?" Liam asked.

"Make a fuss. Yell for help. Stop him anyway I can. Or her."

Liam glanced at his watch. "Okay, I'll go now. I'll come down again right at three."

"To be on the safe side, give it until two minutes past." He looked at the strain showing on Liam's face. "I'll watch over your mother, Liam. Two minutes past three and then come running." Liam gazed at Vivien's peaceful face for a long moment. He turned on his heel and headed out, pushing the door wide open so that Ted's hiding place was more secure.

Three long minutes later, a tall figure came through the door an arm's length from where Ted was hidden. His heartbeat shot upwards and he was aware of his body shaking. He deliberately slowed his breathing. The figure was dressed in sloppy surgical greens complete with skullcap and mask. They wore trainers. Didn't operating room personnel wear those light plastic clogs?

The figure was tall. But all the suspects were tall—probably Pauline the tallest of the three of them, followed by Hiram at close to six feet and Lester a bit shorter. In this light, it could be any of them. Ted's fingers tightened on the rubberized fabric of the curtaining. He was grateful the illumination was faint.

The figure didn't go to Vivien's bed but to the bed opposite, taking up the chart attached to the foot of the bed and flipping over a couple of pages, reading something then closing the notes and replacing them. Maybe it was genuine. Ted watched how the person moved. He was aware that an individual's gait is highly personalised and betrays someone more accurately than any other characteristic, but he'd not seen the figure take more than three steps. The figure again moved, taking another two steps and a shuffle to the foot of the bed next to Vivien's. Same routine. Ted's heartbeat was settling again. Just someone doing their rounds. No connection.

Then to Vivien's bed. Same checking. The figure moved to the far side of the bed and glanced at the door. Ted couldn't check the time without the light of his phone's screen betraying his hiding place, but he figured only a minute or so had passed.

The figure flicked the tube coming down from the bag of saline that was slowly draining into Vivien's left arm. Her breathing machine maintained its steady rhythm. Otherwise, it was quiet.

The figure reached into a pocket and withdrew a large hypodermic.

No!

"STOP!" Ted yelled. As the silence shattered, he sprang from behind his curtain, the door swinging shut. The figure startled and dropped the hypodermic with a clatter. But before Ted was halfway to Vivien's bed, the figure had turned and run for the door, straight-arming Ted in a classic rugby play. Even though Ted went down, he was up immediately and following the green-garbed figure at full tilt, bursting through the swing doors moments after the figure had passed through.

At the end of the corridor, Liam suddenly bounded from the stairwell door. Assessing the situation in an instant, he screeched to a halt and turned to a large lady who was standing waiting for the lifts, carefully cradling a take-out container of coffee. Liam lunged for the woman, grabbed her coffee and hurled it at the surgical facemask of the running figure.

An instant's hesitation caused by the scalding liquid, hands instinctively lifted to the face mask and Ted tackled, taking the figure down in a rugby move he hadn't practiced in over thirty years. The two slid in an untidy heap over the polished floor to the wall where they crashed and broke apart. The green-clad figure was onto its knees before Ted could swing his leg to tip it over. The figure grabbed Ted's leg and Ted found himself on his back facing the wall again. He rolled free to head butt the figure from a kneeling position.

Liam pounced on the two of them. In turn, Liam was kneed in the groin and he dropped with a grunt. Ted grabbed an arm and twisted it up and behind, forcing the figure face down. Liam grabbed the other hand and sat on the green-clad head. He looked around wildly, spotting the shocked owner of the coffee. "Call somebody!" he bellowed.

The woman just stared, her mouth agape.

Still holding one hand in an armlock, Ted stretched to get access to his cell phone from his trousers pocket. Awkwardly, he punched in 111 and told the operator to send someone up to the lift lobby on the 8th floor of the hospital immediately.

Then the reaction set in. "Liam. Can you see? Who is it?"

Liam shifted slightly. "Bloody hell. I'd recognize those eyebrows anywhere." He reached over and pulled the coffee-sodden face mask down.

Oscar.

Chapter Fifty-Three

"WHAT'S GOING ON HERE?" asked a gruff voice from the stairwell as two large security personnel burst onto the scene.

"He tried to murder my mother," Liam said, his voice still close to hysterical.

"Just secure him, please. Then we can talk it all through," Ted said from his seat on Oscar's back. He may be middle-aged and unfit, but he felt like his teenaged self when he'd just come off the rugby field having scored a touchdown, all muscles to the ready.

The three of them, Ted, Liam and Oscar, were escorted into a windowless room by the two security men.

"I called the police," Ted said. "Are they coming?"

"He's lying. It was me who called the police," Oscar said. He gestured to the pile of effects retrieved from their pockets. "I thought this bastard was going to hurt my sister again. We strongly suspect that he was the one who poisoned her in the first place."

"What?" Ted retorted, his anger suffusing his whole being. "What a load of crap!"

Oscar talked over him. "First, he killed his ex-wife who was happily married to my father, then he got murderously jealous when my sister didn't return his affections. He's a dangerous man." Oscar spoke in a controlled manner, a confident smile on his lips.

Ted was so nonplussed, he started to deny it. "No, he's the one..." He realized how pathetic it sounded and collapsed into a frustrated silence.

"You're crazy," Liam said, starting to rise.

"Sit," the larger of the two security men said. "And shut up, the lot of you."

They ended up at the police station. Ted was separated from the other two and put into a cell to await the morning. As soon as the word 'murder' had been raised, the night staff had decided everything could wait an hour or two until the day shift arrived. The last Ted heard from the others was Oscar protesting his arrest for disorderly conduct. Ted had made no such protest. He knew there was nothing to be done at this stage and all of them safely locked up meant as good a security for Vivien as anything could be.

Around about eight and after a breakfast of runny porridge with no salt but heaped with white sugar, Ted was escorted to one of the bleak interview rooms.

"So you decided to do something on your own," Inspector Johnston said when he came into the room. "Couldn't keep your hands off, could you?"

"I asked you to protect Vivien and you refused," Ted said, keeping his voice as calm as he could. "No manpower, if I remember correctly. But I figured our murderer would try to finish the job sooner rather than later."

"I gather one of you was with Mrs McAvoy at all times?" Ted nodded. "You, Liam McAvoy and who else?"

"My daughter Holly—she had the daytime shift."

"Ah, yes, I've already talked to her. She's at the bedside right now." Ted was surprised. Then he figured it out. She would have awakened to find an empty house, no Liam. Her first thought would have been to call her father, but his mobile was in the possession of the police. Her second thought, when she got no answer, would be to go to the hospital.

A knock at the door and a woman put her head in. "Inspector?"

"I thought I told you...."

"Super says to interrupt. Send Frazer back downstairs."

Johnston left the room and Ted was unceremoniously escorted back to the cell wondering what that was all about. He didn't trust Oscar, not then and not now.

Chapter Fifty-Four

SHE WAS SURFACING AGAIN. This time, for sure, she'd get the message out. She clung to it, repeating it over and over to keep it in mind as things slowly became clearer. So hard to think, so difficult to keep it in her head. Mustn't get distracted. Must get through.

"Ah, there you are. Open your eyes, Mrs McAvoy. Come on, you can do it." It was the doctor's voice.

Red, that pinky, awful red she hated.

Black again. Then back to red.

"Now. Try again. Open your eyes, Vivien." The doctor's voice, more insistent now. She kept the message in her head. Not to be distracted. Thankfully, she struggled to open her eyes and, yes, she could see again. Bright lights. She shut them again to the red. Opened them; squinted. The doctor's face. Where was her father? Where was Ted? She had to tell them.

"There. That's better." The doctor sounded as if he'd done it himself.

She mouthed the words. Horrible with no air going through her throat. No sound. But her lips moved, she felt them.

No one reacted.

She cautiously clenched her hand. It made a fist. She raised it up and her arm swam into view. She clenched her fist around the fabric of the doctor's white coat and pulled to get his attention.

"Hey, there! No need for that, my dear. You're coming back to us." He turned to a little audience of nurses and while his back was turned, she punched him in the arm.

He glanced at her and swung back to his audience. "Maybe we're a bit too hasty today. She's obviously still agitated," he said. His smile had faded. "Nurse?" Vivien could see a hypodermic on a little tray.

"NO!' she tried to scream although no sound was made.

"Excuse me," a nurse in a student's uniform said. "She's trying to say something. I can read her lips. She said 'No' just now. And before that, I think she tried to say, 'It was... Something... Oscar'?"

Vivien's eyes filled up. She pointed to the young woman. She mouthed the words once more. Pointed to herself. Looked at the nurse.

"She's saying, 'Oscar did it. Poison—poisoned—me.'"

Vivien nodded. Made eating motions with her hand and mouth.

"That's one of the men who was arrested, isn't it? Her brother Oscar?" the nurse asked.

The doctor leaned over Vivien, blocking her view of the nurse. "Are you saying something about your brother Oscar?" His breath smelled of cigarettes. She pushed him to one side so she could see the nurse. She beckoned her over. The doctor had the grace to move.

Vivien mouthed, "Tell him to bugger off."

The nurse's mouth twitched. "She says she'd like to speak with me." She turned to Vivien. "Slowly now. I'm not all that great without sound."

Vivien noticed the girl had hearing aids in her ears. Discreet ones. Just a tiny clear tube running from behind each ear disappearing inside. "I know who poisoned me; Lela and me. It was Oscar. My brother." she mouthed each word slowly.

The student repeated this message clearly.

The doctor said, "Nurse, ring the police, would you please. Meanwhile, we have a test to do. Is that all right with you, Mrs McAvoy? We want to see if you can breathe on your own. Then we'll get you talking again."

Vivien smiled, relaxed back onto the pillow. Thank goodness. Message delivered and received.

Chapter Fifty-Five

THE SCENE WAS DUPLICATED. Ted in the uncomfortable metal chair, warnings given, tapes running and Johnston across the table.

"Just a few questions, if you don't mind, Mr Frazer. For my own curiosity. Then you're free to go. For now."

"Go? Ah, great." Ted sat up straighter. What had happened? Had the slimy bastard hung himself with his own lying mouth? "Fire away. I'm actually grateful for the extra time I've had to think through Oscar's involvement." He smiled.

Johnston glared at him. "Why did you suspect Oscar Fleet?"

"I didn't. Well, yes, I did, but that was much earlier. Latterly, I could find no viable motivation, so dismissed it." He was furious at himself, but he wasn't going to let Johnston know that.

"Why should I not think that you're an insanely jealous man, willing to kill when your needs are thwarted?"

"I recognize Oscar's arguments, Inspector. He's already accused me of that. His motivation is far simpler."

"And it is...?"

"Money. His father's money, to be precise." He kept quiet about Marcia's need to have the upper hand, her penchant for teasing when she found out some titbit of information, large or small, her undoubted passion for the man. That could come later if need be.

"So motivated for money that he's willing to kill his sister and his step-mother?"

"You mean his sister and his lover."

"Just words, Mr Frazer."

"Important words, Mr Johnston. Marcia would have inherited it all and been in control of too much of Oscar's life had Jonathan Fleet died of his cancer before her. But, of course, she was comparatively young and totally healthy. So, you see, it was important she died before Jonathan."

Johnston nodded. "Go on."

"After Marcia died, Jonathan changed his will so that his daughter, Vivien McAvoy, would have the controlling shares of his business, not Oscar. Jonathan, in effect, signed his daughter's death warrant when he told Oscar that unwelcome detail. But, with Vivien dead as well, Oscar would be a fabulously wealthy man in full control and able to do whatever he wanted as soon as cancer claimed the life of his father."

The inspector stared at him, and the sergeant continued to scribble notes. "Now, the means of Mrs McAvoy's poisoning, the botulism toxin?" Johnston asked. "That was aimed at both his sister and the woman who worked at the house."

"Not Lela, no," Ted said. "Oscar knew salmon was a lunchtime favourite of Vivien's. Lela's usual sandwich was cheese and pickle, never tinned fish. Vivien was to eat the tainted food which Lela had prepared and he presumed you would accuse Lela of her murder. The obvious person to have given her the poison. Oscar didn't know that Lela often tasted the serving spoons before putting them into the dishwasher."

"Why would we think the maid murdered her employer?"

"Proximity. He probably thought you wouldn't need a motive if fingerprints and everything else pointed to Lela."

The inspector just shook his head. "More evidence we're mere plods, Mr Frazer?"

"I'm trying to think like Oscar. Probably impossible."

"And where would he get the toxin?"

"I think he must have had a supply. It's available on the internet. You can check it out." The inspector shuffled his papers. Glanced at the sergeant. "I think I should tell you, Mr Frazer, that the hypodermic syringe found under Mrs McAvoy's bed was empty."

"Empty?" Ted blinked at yet another swift change of subject. Empty?

"No poison, no medication, nothing. Unused."

"I thought...."

"Yes, you thought. You're an amateur, Mr Frazer. Every time we turn around, you're there to be tripped over. I hear you're a fine computer consultant for the fraud squad, but you're not a policeman. Your expertise lies elsewhere."

"I'm good at problem solving. That's what I do every day." It sounded defensive, even to his own ears. His voice petered out. "Look, I'm sorry. I thought that you were...."

"You thought we were only the fuzz, didn't you, Mr Frazer. Unable to figure it all out."

"No. Not that. It's just that my brain could be of some use to you. That's all." He wanted out of there, but the inspector would decide when that would be. "Do you think I'm an insanely jealous man?"

"No, Mr Frazer, I do not. And I do respect your ability to put things together. Somehow, you've not put together the significance of the big empty syringe."

Ted stared at him. "It did belong to Oscar, though?"

"Oh, yes. And it was not the sort used at the hospital either."

Ted kept his eyes on Johnston's. "You're right. I've not figured out the significance of the big empty ... oh." He sat a bit straighter. "But it wasn't empty, was it, Inspector?"

He laughed. "I had a little bet with my colleague here. I said you'd figure it out. What was in it, Mr Frazer. Please tell the sergeant."

Ted glanced at the stoical woman sitting in the corner with her notebook on her lap, as usual. "Air," he said. "He was going to inject an air embolism into the tube going into the vein in her arm. Stop her heart or brain or whatever."

She smiled at the inspector. "I owe you an ice-cream, boss."

Chapter Fifty-Six

THE DAY HAD FINALLY come. The process had taken long enough that his narcissi had come into bloom. Ted pulled his vehicle onto the drive outside Jonathan's house. He reached back to get the bouquet of paper-whites, their scent almost too powerful inside his four-wheel-drive vehicle. The others would be in the house already. Holly and Liam had earlier collected Vivien from the hospital in Jonathan's car.

"I can smell them from here," said Vivien when Ted entered the sunny conservatory. She was again on her metallic chaise longue in her Japanese robe. "I dreamed of these." She lifted her face for a kiss from Ted.

"You're looking great," he said. "How's the strength?"

"I'm walking with my trusty Zimmer Frame fairly well now," she said. "And the oxygen is only for when I overdo it." She gestured to a large bottle on a trolley with a mask dangling from it. "Lela fusses over me."

"When are you going back to the UK?"

Vivien made a moue. "When are our tickets, Liam?"

"A week Friday. I still think you should take another week."

"You have things to do before the university year starts, young man. We've been over this before. Medically, I'm cleared to travel with some oxygen and, wonder of wonders, Gerald is in the process of having the kitchen put in upstairs, so I'm all set."

"The conversion of the house."

"It's a good idea. It leaves the kids with their own bedrooms upstairs for whenever they want to come home. Besides, if we can get away with not selling the house, Liam and Stephanie have a place to come home to and so do I when visiting the UK. It works out because the times I'm over there are probably the times I want to be with the kids. Gerald gets the downstairs. He can have the library for a bedroom. It smells of cigar smoke. He's welcome to it."

Ted yawned. "Sorry. Up to all hours helping the Crown Prosecutor understand the details of a comprehensive report of mine about a clever crim."

"For the police? That report?" Vivien's face was full of animation, so different from the weeks and weeks of passivity.

Ted nodded. "A complex case and the crown prosecutor has to present it right. Words of one syllable so the jury understands. It's going to be a long and painful case."

"Will you win?"

Ted laughed. "Not up to me, thank heavens. But, yes, I think my bit could hang him. Or at least catch him where he's least expecting it." He looked around the room. "Here together again." He turned to Jonathan. "Are you up to discussing what happened?"

"I'm feeling stronger every day, Ted. But I really cannot understand what turned my son into a monster. And I deserve to know."

"You do," Ted said. He took a deep breath. "Holly, Liam and I have had quite a few conversations about it. Holly, how about you tell us all about the Botox?"

She was quiet for a moment. "We were talking about what Mum had done to enhance her beauty."

"Crazy woman. She didn't need to." Jonathan frowned. "What about it?"

"Oscar had Botox, too."

Jonathan raised his eyebrows, then let out what only could be a guffaw.

"I laughed, also, when I heard it," Ted said.

"Part of it was silly, part quite smart, actually," Holly said. "He had some worry lines smoothed out. That's the silly bit. But the smart part was Botoxing his underarms, of all things. He sweats so much he said he was tempted to wear his wetsuit underneath his business clothes. He used to sweat right through both shirt and suit jacket, would you believe. And then Mum's beauty therapist suggested he have Botox to stop it."

"Really? Didn't know it worked on that," Jonathan said. His voice was almost back to normal.

"Me, neither." Holly looked at Ted.

"Seriously, it's resulted in his having access to the toxin," Ted said. "Botox wears off, you see. He'd have to have repeated injections. It's much cheaper on the internet. Why keep ordering it each time when you can buy a decent amount all at once?"

"Which meant he had the means to kill Mum," Liam said, with a glance at her.

"I've since gone off that pink fish sauce," Vivien said with a smile.

"No wonder," Ted said. "But it also brings up the topic of a wetsuit. A significant topic, all in all."

Holly turned towards Jonathan again. "It's a sick scenario, Gramps. You sure you want to hear some bad stuff about Mum?"

"Better now. Get it all out, Holly. Go ahead. It can't be worse than my imaginings, believe me."

"Well, we figured Mum agreed to meet Oscar along the coast for a romantic interlude—south of the bay, boat access only. You see, we found some cryptic scribblings she made on her calendar and it fits. We think Oscar challenged Mum to confront her fears. Sounds good, therapeutic even, but really, it was a setup for her death. This one was the third test." Holly's voice was strained. "We think Oscar swam to meet her there. In a wetsuit."

"Probably SCUBA," Ted said. "Bringing a specially prepared bottle of Sangria with him as a silly romantic offering which he knew Marcia would love. Doped Sangria, of course. He'd have swum just under the surface. It's virtually a secret method of getting somewhere unless the pattern of bubbles is noticed as he breathed out."

"He had to have started somewhere, though. And he surely would have been noticed," Liam said, glancing at Holly's troubled face.

"He probably used the carpark at the surf beach," she said. "Lots of people in wetsuits there. If we were closer to the time, we could ask if someone like Oscar was diving off the beach, but I imagine it's a bit late now."

"The police are onto it. I bet that's the scenario, though," Ted said.

"You liked Oscar, didn't you?" Jonathan asked Holly.

She nodded. "He was fun. He had a great car." She paused. "He was urbane. The only time he was nonplussed was when I appeared in Mum's blue evening dress at the top of the stairs in this fancy hotel down in Queenstown. I wanted to make an entrance, but...." Her voice faded. "I made an entrance, all right. I had pulled my hair up like this." She grasped her long hair and twisted it behind her head. "Like Mum used to," she explained to Jonathan. "He gasped. Literally. At first, I thought in admiration, but later I realised I was just a bit too Marcia."

Jonathan shook his head in distress.

"Do you take after your mother?" Liam asked. Holly nodded slowly, glancing at her father.

"She does look like her mother. And with her hair like that..," Ted said, "you shocked him. He was seeing a ghost."

"It was all in fun, then it suddenly wasn't funny anymore. I got out. It's not as if I was interested in him as a boyfriend or anything."

"Thank goodness," Ted breathed.

Lela came into the room. "Who's for cheesecake? Freshly made. Mr Ted, I know you'll have some. And Holly and Ms Vivien. And a small slice for Mr Jonathan. What about you, Liam?"

"Sounds good, thanks."

While coffees and cheesecake portions were being distributed, the doorbell rang.

"You expecting someone else, Mr Jonathan?" Lela asked.

"Nobody," he said grimly.

Lela left and returned smartly. "It's a Mr Brownstone. About some photographs?"

"Oh, damn," Ted said. He quickly explained why he'd contacted Hiram Brownstone. "I sussed him out using you, Vivien. I said you're collecting old pictures to do a family history. I met up with him and he gave me a whole boxful for you to look at. They're still in the back of the car. Sorry; this is embarrassing."

"Just tell him we haven't gone over them yet. Bring them in now and he can have a cup of coffee while we look them over. I'd love to see them again. Truly. And him too," Vivien said with a smile.

Ted went to the door. "Hi there, Brownstone. Vivien hasn't had a chance to see the photos since she got out of the hospital. I'll just get them, shall I? And we can all look at them?"

Brownstone looked worried. "I rang the hospital. They said she'd gone home."

"She's well on the mend now. Come with me to get your box and we'll go in together."

Ted ushered Hiram into the room clutching the cardboard box. "I'm sorry to hear of your problems, Vivien. And Mr Fleet." Hiram's face flushed a mottled red. "I did take some beauties of you and of the old house back then." He turned to Jonathan. "I was sorry when you sold it," he said.

"So nice to see you again," Vivien said.

He noticed Holly sitting to one side. "Oh, hello again."

"Hi, Mr Brownstone," she said.

"Hiram. No one calls me Mr Brownstone."

Hiram put his box down and scrabbled inside. "Here." He handed a pile of photos to Vivien. She took each photo, exclaimed over it and passed it over to Ted, who instantly revised his attitude. The man could take pictures. He had an accurate eye. A wonderful talent that somehow had never made him a commercial success.

"They're good," Liam said. "More than good. I'd love a copy of this one blown up." It showed a young Vivien in a summer frock, balanced on the porch railing of a large wooden villa. "This is classic."

Hiram nodded. "Thanks." He then dug down deeper into the box. "Thought I should return this too." He lifted an A4 set of papers bound with a pink ribbon.

"What's this?" Vivien asked when he put it into her hands.

"Work by your brother. His book of underwater photos. Marcia did it up like this. She was sure it would be a photographic sensation. But, as you can see..."

They crowded round. The book had been mocked up with a title page, "The Wonders of the Underwater World' by Oscar W Fleet, followed by the acknowledgement page containing a flowery thank you that extolled the virtues of Marcia Culloden.

"Marcia Culloden?" Liam asked.

"Mum's maiden name," Holly breathed. "Interesting."

Vivien turned to the first page of photographs. Each had a description that appeared to be a line or two of poetry.

"Nice idea," Hiram said. "Too bad the execution wasn't up to it."

Ted agreed. The photos were ordinary. Sometimes taken in murky water, often framed carelessly and the light values varied from too dark to too light with rarely enough contrast.

"Amateurville," Hiram said.

"How did you get this?" Ted asked.

"Marcia was one of my fans." He coloured again. "I met her at a book signing years ago when my shoreline book came out. She kept in touch, wanting me to put together enough photos for another. Then one day a year or so back, she turned up with this lot. She thought I had an inside influence with the publisher where I work, but one glance was enough. This is not up to publishable standards. Sorry."

"You didn't mention you knew Marcia." Ted said it softly, more for Hiram's ears alone.

"A bit awkward, wasn't it." It was not a question.

Vivien flipped through the pages and closed the book. "I'll return it to Oscar. Or you can, Father, when you decide you can face him." She turned the book over in her hands and exposed the back cover. "My god. Did she paint this?" It was an earlier version of the portrait discovered by Ted in Marcia's studio at the Bay House.

"I've seen the original. It's a bit better likeness now," Holly said, "but not by much."

"As I said, amateurville," Hiram said. He got to his feet from where he had been kneeling by Vivien. "I'd better go."

"Stay for coffee," Vivien said.

"And have some of my world-famous-in-New-Zealand homemade cheese-cake," Lela said.

As the conversation flowed around him, Ted wondered whether everything could have been different if Hiram had mentioned the underwater photography at their first meeting. He would have known about Oscar's SCUBA diving earlier, but Oscar's involvement would still have had to be proved.

Hiram was now chatting about his latest project, one he had been working on for years. Weather. Ted shook his head. The man was just not thinking commercially.

"Have you brought some of the weather photos?" Holly asked politely. She had finished her cheesecake but Hiram had done so much talking, he had barely touched his.

He carefully wiped his fingers. "Here," he said, handing Holly a pile. "Your mother was encouraging me with this lot. I kept saying I needed more photos, better photos. She was on and on at me to publish what I had. Maybe she was right. Don't know. See what you think."

With each new photo, Holly exclaimed freshly, as did the others. Ted, this time, was at the end of the queue. He finally got the first photo. It was of a towering thunderhead etched against a pure blue sky, Auckland's distinctive One Tree Hill backlit beneath. It took his breath away. Another revision of attitude needed. Maybe the weather could be commercial with photos like this one.

"Look here, Dad," Holly said, holding up a photo of the Harbour Bridge glowing in the sunshine of a new day and totally suspended in the mist that formed the base of the picture.

"You are going to go ahead, aren't you?" Vivien said. "If you don't, you'll have to answer to me."

Hiram looked at her in surprise. "You used to say things like that to me, Vivien." He blushed.

"Who agrees with me?" Vivien asked and Hiram looked at a sea of enthusiasm.

Chapter Fifty-Seven

AFTER HIRAM HAD LEFT, walking taller on his exit than on his entrance, Jonathan asked Ted for a word. They got up. Jonathan's gait was slow.

"How's it going, Jonathan?" he asked once he got the old man settled in the large chair in his study.

"I feel much better, of course, but my meds have had to be increased."

"Meds? I thought..."

"Pain. Not the bloody chemo. Not having any more of that stuff. But the quacks are suggesting I have radiation. Not that they haven't suggested that before, but I don't much like the idea of radioactive rays being aimed at me. You don't get cured of cancer with radioactivity; it causes it. Look at Hiroshima."

"They've been using radiation to treat cancer for a hundred years, Jonathan. A lot of people walking around wouldn't be here today without radiation therapy."

"Maybe. I said I'd think about it. Lucky I have Lela."

Ted glanced at him. Appreciating Lela? Was Jonathan mellowing?

"She's a whiz at email. Did you know she's taken a typing course?" Jonathan said. "I just dictate and she types it all up on the computer. Letters too. Got myself a home office now. Lets me keep my finger on the pulse until Vivien takes over."

"That Lela. More than meets the eye," Ted said. "I hope you're paying her appropriately."

Jonathan grunted. "I said I'd think about that too." He turned his eyes away. "All this worry about Oscar has kind of put me off. And what Marcia was really like. Uncomfortable with it all." He lifted a shaky hand to his forehead.

"It might be easier if you just keep your own memories," Ted said. "Ignore all this other twaddle. Marcia made you happy. You probably had the best of her."

Jonathan gazed at Ted over his glasses. "Maybe. Oscar had me almost convinced you were just out for yourself, you know. Lusting after Vivien."

"I can't say I haven't noticed her, Jonathan. She's an attractive lady, but there's that little problem of her being already married."

"Not for long, if we can believe her." He stared at Ted as if checking out whether he was totally trustworthy on this subject.

"We'll see what happens after she gets back from England." Ted had been reminding himself of that ever since Vivien had been allowed off the respirator. They'd had many long talks since. She told Ted that she had not understood the specifics of his comments through the fog of the sedation yet found his voice comforting. When she did surface enough, she had been desperately concerned about the danger not only to herself but to her father in particular. She had spent countless hours thinking about who could have put the poison into the food eaten by herself and Lela and had eliminated everyone but Oscar. She had never considered Pauline, Cushla or Hiram and only briefly Cushla's son Lester before eliminating him for lack of motive.

The day of the poisoning was etched in her memory. The meal Lela had prepared had been organized around a visit by Oscar, even though he'd already eaten by the time he arrived. He had ample opportunity to go into the fridge while the others were eating, which he did to help himself to milk for his coffee. No one else did, and Vivien thought nothing of it at the time. He left, saying a meeting had been called. Sorry.

She had gone on to say when Gerald had turned up to arrange her return to the UK under his care, her frustration was immense. Hence the agitation, as Ted had surmised.

Jonathan droned on and on and Ted lost track of what he was talking about.

"After saying all that, I really was willing to believe you were some sort of monster. My precious Marcia. And now trying to take Vivien away from me as well. I went a little crazy, Ted."

"I didn't know, Jonathan. I was so concentrated on protecting Vivien, I almost forgot about what you must have been going through. Going onto palliative care—that was an immense decision. Sorry, it was remiss of me." They sat in silence for a moment or two.

"I got you here for a purpose and not just to apologize, Ted. Some things I just can't understand. For instance, how Oscar could be so cruel to my darling Marcia and to his sister, yet so respected by the City Mission. You know he volunteered there?"

"Yes, Holly told me. I've thought about it, tried to figure that one out too. There's good and bad in all of us. Maybe it's as simple as that." It could be true, but his private explanation was that it was Oscar's idea for the project, raising money for the new oven; he was in charge and he had an excuse to schmoose with all those high flying CEOs with a great sob story. Ted knew that plenty of people find that charity is better than golf for covert motives.

Jonathan nodded. "Good in all of us. I hope so. But I can't imagine him being an unsung worker somewhere. No, the only way he would have been involved was that he got something out of it. Control, perhaps."

Ted smiled. The wily old bugger. Knew his son very well indeed.

Jonathan shook his head. "Thanks for saying that, anyway. But I need more. Can you please take me through what happened? I mean when Marcia died."

"You sure? It will be bringing back some unpleasant facts about Marcia and I really think you'll be more comfortable focusing on the good stuff."

"I'm good at remembering the good stuff. Let's get this over with." He sat bolt upright in his chair. In spite of his frailty, his skin was a healthier colour than Ted had seen in a long time.

Ted sat down, facing Jonathan. "Some of this is speculative."

"Tell me when," Jonathan said with some resolve, "and the opposite, when it's fact you're talking about. I want to know as much as you do. I deserve to know as much."

"Yes, you do," Ted said, truly feeling empathetic. "No matter whether it destroys some illusions. That would be my attitude as well." He looked over at Jonathan and took a deep breath. "You know that Marcia and Oscar had an affair while she was married to me. I found out and that killed something in me. My illusions, if nothing else. It certainly killed the marriage. We both agreed to divorce," Ted said. "It truly was mutual even though she initiated it."

Jonathan nodded. "That's what I understood too. But she didn't start divorce proceedings until she and I were an item. Oscar was history by that time."

"That's what I'm not sure about. Maybe he never was history. What if he saw advantages in having Marcia as your wife while keeping up some clandestine contact with her? I don't for a minute think Marcia took up with you because you were wealthy. She was curiously unworldly about money. She liked having it, as you no doubt know, but it was never a personal motivating force." He kept quiet about Marcia's undoubted motivation to make sure Holly was well provided for.

"Unlike Oscar. Money was everything to him."

"Unlike Oscar." Ted closed his eyes. "I've been wondering if Marcia fell for Oscar badly. After all, he's a damned good looking man, younger than her by quite a few years, a ladies' man, as they used to say, driving a fancy car and all the other trappings of a man-about-town."

"You don't have to remind me," Jonathan said. "Okay, as a speculation—and I'm not saying I accept this—let's say Marcia fell for him. This is early on, right?"

"Right."

"Then what?"

"He brings her to your house and manipulates the situation so that you're mightily attracted. Maybe there was a bit of the old father-son rivalry, too?"

"Get on with it."

"So for a while there, she dances a merry tune with two fine men after her. Heady stuff after a lifetime with dull old me. And clever Oscar sees an advantage in having a relationship with the woman his father married. Did you discuss with him how suitable Marcia was?"

"Maybe," Jonathan said, not looking at Ted.

"Not that it matters. You made a deal and off he went to rehab and came back to run the transport division." Ted spoke coolly. Enough had happened since finding this out to calm his temper. "Marcia was just the icing on the cake. The actual business was about money and power."

Jonathan grunted. Ted decided not to go further on that tack.

"Which brings me to your will at the time," he went on. "Oscar would have known the business was divided between Vivien and him on your death, but everything else? You put Marcia in your will for your houses, the art collection, your other investments and all that added up to a considerable fortune. So maybe Oscar wanted to keep Marcia interested in him, in the palm of his grubby paw; think of it as insurance. Maybe he had thoughts of marrying her himself once you passed on." Tricky talking to a man with a limited lifespan.

"The business is in a trust and Oscar and Vivien were the two beneficiaries," Jonathan said. "Bloody lawyer made me do that years ago. But I also set it up that Marcia would get an inflation-proofed annuity for the rest of her life. The other parts of the estate had nothing to do with him or anybody else. I can do what I want with my own money." His face flushed. "Fleet Corp. I did get the lawyer to give Vivien a slight edge, 51 to 49. She had financial experience, you know. Before she wasted herself marrying the dumb-cluck." Jonathan stopped talking. Ted waited him out. "If only I could have loved Oscar like I did Vivien. But she was—and is—lovable and he never has been. My fault, I'm sure. I didn't have the patience with him."

Ted thought he should get Jonathan off this topic as fast as possible. The man was frail and he knew that guilt is a heavy burden. "Marcia undoubtedly had a good time while married to you, Jonathan. She loved the travel, loved her fancy glass house in Remuera and she loved you too. Maybe, though, she loved her fancy man as well."

Jonathan gave him a sardonic grin. "More fool me," he said.

"Then things changed. You were diagnosed with cancer and Oscar found out his inheritance was limited by what you were doing to protect Marcia. And just maybe, he wasn't quite so sure of her anymore." Ted stopped talking for a moment. "Marcia was aging, maybe even getting somewhat wiser, for instance, making that new will to ensure Holly's future. Things may have cooled by then." He said nothing about the combined effects age and a prostate operation could have had on Jonathan's sexual capabilities.

"If I can add to this speculation," Jonathan said slowly, "when Oscar first learned we had mutual wills leaving each other everything, he would first have tried to rekindle their romance, but maybe Marcia wasn't having it like before. That's probably why she needed to protect Holly by making that new will." He nodded to himself.

Ted thought more likely she had become aware of Oscar's need to control, and she was becoming wary. Marcia was nobody's fool. He left Jonathan to his own interpretation. "With the worsening of your health, Oscar decided that your pre-Marcia will was vastly preferable to the one that left so much to the fickle Marcia. She had to go."

"And eventually, Vivien," Jonathan said, his shoulders slumping. "My wife and my daughter."

"His lover and his sister," Ted added. "He had to plan some 'accidents'. Marcia first."

"That damned rowboat."

"This romantic interlude with Marcia may have been planned well in advance. His own dolly-bird wife got in the way so he ditched her and when the coast was clear, he started coming onto Marcia again." Ted took a deep breath. "Maybe for Marcia things were not so great at home," he said as delicately as he could. "You and your cancer plus the awful reaction you always have to chemo, the loss of the travelling and the fun times. She had become vulnerable to our snake charmer's charisma yet again."

"I was grumpy. Depressed, even. A cancer diagnosis hits you like that. And then, yes, the chemo."

"No, Jonathan, don't blame yourself. She was probably susceptible to the renewed attentions of this lover who had broken off with her. Ego could have been involved," Ted said, privately convinced Marcia had been lonely as well. And her life had become constricted. "We do know that she'd been having minor plastic surgeries, Botox treatments and she had managed to lose weight. I think there's no doubt that Oscar had been rekindling their affair." Ted sighed. "He was as much a manipulator as she was. Somehow, they were into daring each other, testing each other's resolve. She hated small airplanes; she hated little boats. Hated that one in particular. Somehow he got her to challenge her fears and, I suppose, he had the rowboat in mind if she didn't kill herself first accidentally."

Jonathan shook his head.

"Something like, 'If you really care, you'll row over to meet me at that secluded little beach and I'll have a lovely surprise for you'."

Ted kept quiet about his further speculations. Oscar could have seen the situation as becoming more and more urgent because of the danger that Jonathan could die suddenly and Marcia would inherit what he considered to be his birth-right.

"The Sangria." Jonathan's eyes filled. "It was our special summer drink with wonderful little pieces of alcohol-soaked fruit. We discovered it the first time we were in Spain.... The police said she had both booze and sedative in her bloodstream. She never took stuff for sleeping. Never took any unnecessary medications. He must have...."

"My best guess is that he knew that Sangria was special and romantic. Brought it for her as a 'surprise'. And he mixed the sedative in it." Ted could easily imagine the scene. Marcia dressed to show off her new svelte figure, doing everything she could to keep this man interested for the sake of her own ego and undoubtedly enjoying the intrigue. A good-looking young man bringing a bottle of Sangria underwater to their secret tryst? She would have loved such a gesture. A heady combination. "Somehow, he prevented himself from either getting drunk or stoned on the sedative. Drink, drugs and diving don't mix and he would know that."

"He's a risk taker." Jonathan's lips thinned. "Risk taking is fine in business as long as it's combined with good reasoning ability. No judgment; that was Oscar's downfall. It's why I could never allow him to become CEO of Fleet Corp. I've seen that particular pattern in him since he was less than two years of age." He sighed loudly. "That boy was a devil to bring up. He exhausted me. That's probably where I went wrong. I could only take about fifteen minutes with him before he would do something that irritated the hell out of me. Especially after his mother died. I got the idea her death was Oscar's fault, that she was out floating on the water in order to escape the little devil the day she drowned. Imagine thinking that of a two-year-old."

"Be that as it may, Oscar got alcohol and sedatives into Marcia to make it easier for her to drown."

"But he didn't endanger himself."

"He likely swam in his SCUBA gear only deep enough to hide from any casual observers. Possibly he combated the effects of the sedative in his own system by taking 'P'; it's a massive stimulant, and he's sometimes a user, I gather."

Jonathan's eyes glittered. "I hate drugs; I hate everything about them. He would have been out on his ear if I had known about his using drugs again." Jonathan's voice was strong. "Being disinherited would have been the least of it; I'd have made damn sure he'd have nothing to do with Fleet Corp ever again.

Not one penny of my hard earned money would ever go to him." The words echoed around the room.

"If he knew your attitude...,' Ted said.

"He did. He absolutely did. I told you. I said he was a risk taker. With no bloody judgment."

"And so he drowned her," Ted said quietly. "You and I both know there's no way Marcia would go swimming with him voluntarily, but she was undoubtedly woozy from the alcohol and the drugs. I figure he just maneuvered her near the water's edge, tripped her up and held her under when she fell. Held her until she stopped struggling. We know she had the life-jacket with her. The cord was deliberately tangled around her neck after her death. After, Jonathan; that's important. When she was pushed into deeper water, she didn't sink. He most likely thought her death would be put down to an unfortunate boating accident," Ted said, more to himself than to Jonathan. "Then he packed away the bottle of doctored Sangria and geared up again with his SCUBA equipment. He must have towed the boat out and let it go, setting up the scene. Then he quietly swam underwater back to the carpark." He privately thought the cord around her neck was to make doubly sure Marcia was well and truly dead.

"Drowning." Jonathan slumped in the chair. "That gets me where it really hurts and I guess that was part of it, wasn't it? To punish me."

"Punish you?" Ted looked sharply at him.

"Death by drowning; that's significant. Marcia was to die like his own mother died. And it did successfully point the finger at me."

It fitted. Final retribution for a two-year-old's anger.

They sat in silence. The sky was dark outside and Jonathan's face was hard to distinguish in the dim light filtering through the window.

Chapter Fifty-Eight

VIVIEN PARKED THE CAR behind Ted's. She looked at the massive pohutukawa trees down the slope towards the beach, silhouetted against the bright blue of the sea. The odd spiky red flower already out was surrounded by grey-green buds ready to burst. Almost Christmas and this year the trees were going to be right on time for the holidays. This was truly New Zealand's Christmas tree. She took a deep breath of sea air and heaved her suitcase from the back. She'd dreamt of this moment while in England.

"I'll get that," Ted said from the studio's brick path before greeting her with a hug. "You get Jonathan."

Vivien helped her father out of the front passenger seat. He leaned heavily on her.

"I thought maybe you could have Holly's room," Ted said to him. "On the ground floor next to the loo. It'll be easier for you, Jonathan—easier than having to negotiate the stairs to your bedroom." Ted. Always the caregiver. Her heart warmed just being in his presence.

Jonathan cleared his throat. "This is the big hand-over, Ted. No longer my bedroom. Yours again."

"Not yet," Ted smiled. "This is your weekend." He took Jonathan's bag and followed the two of them through the front door. The sun had already made the atrium quite warm in spite of the doors open to the terrace in front. Vivien made a mental note to let the blinds down in the morning. The atrium provided sheltered warmth for three seasons, but it was frequently too hot in the summer without the sunshades. Jonathan's steps faltered. This trip was a bit long for him, she knew, but he insisted that he was capable of it, so she had acquiesced.

"I'll just have a little lie-down, if you don't mind," Jonathan said. "Yes, Holly's room would be fine."

Vivien and Ted settled with coffees on the terrace, looking out over the blue waters sparkling in the afternoon sunshine.

"Did you go to court?" he asked her.

"Of course. It was all over in a minute or so. Oscar was charged with Marcia's murder and attempted murder of me. Almost anti-climactic."

"And he's still going to fight it?"

"Stupid boy. Father's had a go; the police have been hammering him; even Cushla went to see him and asked him to admit it; save everyone from a trial."

"Cushla? She must be suffering right now," Ted said. "Jonathan said the paper had something about Lester's arrest on the weekend."

Vivien nodded. "I brought you a copy in case you hadn't read it. It doesn't say his name, but we figured it had to be him." She reached down to her handbag and pulled out the clipping. "Listen to this: 'Operation CleanNorth discovered a clandestine methamphetamine laboratory in deep bush yesterday. Police found ten 20-litre drums of chemical waste products, four cooking kits and a firearm. A local man has been arrested'."

"That Cushla. She knows it will create huge publicity if Lester's drug operation is tied into a murder trial," Ted said. "This wonderful new business that the lovely Lester went into—she bragged about it to me not long after Marcia died. I didn't twig."

Vivien adjusted her chair to get the maximum comfort level. "I talked to Duncan. He came down for the court appearance and we had coffee after. Evidently, Lester's drug operation was an open secret. According to Duncan, half the district knew he made P down in that valley."

"I can imagine," Ted said. "Lester's customers would have known and most likely his mates helped him out from time to time in the lab."

"All in the milieu of a drug-tolerant Northland," Vivien said. Not that she imagined it was any different in the more remote valleys of England or Wales. Hidden things happen where things can be hidden. Worldwide. "We shouldn't blame Northland." She stretched her arms above her head. "Duncan told me Lester is cooperating with the police now. Saying he took the rap the last time and this time there's no way he's doing it again. Implicating Oscar with every sentence."

"Oscar was involved back then? When Lester went to prison for his marijuana business?" Ted's voice betrayed his surprise. "And now? Oscar was involved with the methamphetamine scheme, too?"

"Duncan says so." Vivien took a long sip of her coffee. Getting cool. She drained her mug.

"I hadn't guessed that one," Ted said, putting his own mug down and standing up to stare out to sea. "I knew there was something fishy about the way Lester always accompanied his mother when she visited Jonathan. And the way he'd ask about Oscar. I should have known something was going on." He turned back to Vivien. "Oscar involved with P production. Hard to believe, given how much risk he was taking. Jonathan is so anti-drug, he's fanatical."

"It doesn't stop there," Vivien said. "My darling brother was using the trucks of the transport division to distribute the P up and down the country. Perfect for the purpose. Highly lucrative, but playing with fire."

Ted started to pace. "Hold on," he said. "Holly and I suspected that Marcia met up with Lester not long before her death. And we guessed it was about P. If she knew...."

"Marcia was no dummy," Vivien said. "If she knew about the P production, it was only one step more to figure out the significance of the trucks. Once there, she would have tied it into Oscar's newfound wealth. The car. The clothes. The apartment. She could have used it as a power play over him, threatening to tell Father, that sort of thing."

Ted shook his head. "Nothing so obvious. More likely she teased him about it, *taunted* him. Using a bit of information that put her back in the driver's seat. That would be very Marcia. To hypersensitive Oscar, the shift in power would have been covert but obvious. And intolerable. He was in real jeopardy then. From that moment, she was a dead woman." Maybe she was that bit more aware of his personality by then, a tad more streetwise than she'd been before. But she misjudged. She was not nearly streetwise enough.

Vivien nodded. "Power plays and Marcia. Yes. And manipulation. She was a past-master." She looked at Ted.

He stared out to where sea met sky. "Oscar had what he considered to be very good reasons for getting rid of the two of you. But then timing became important due to Jonathan's health, because both of you had to die before Jonathan did. And Marcia's teasing brought the schedule forward. She had to go before she said anything to Jonathan." He glanced over at Vivien. "Sorry, Viv. Let's leave this subject. He is your brother, after all."

She shook her head. "Then there's Cushla. She must have known about Oscar's involvement in Lester's drug business. Why didn't she tell Father?"

"Squeal on her own son? Never," he said. "The culture up here tolerates drugs, always has done. She would most likely think Jonathan's anti-drug attitudes were over the top. She's a wily old bird and loyal to a fault, but she has her priorities. And son Lester would be uppermost."

"I've just had a wicked thought," Vivien said, putting her hand on Ted's arm. "That story she told you? That she and Jonathan planned how to make Marcia available so he could court her?"

Ted shrugged. "Buying off Oscar with the transport division then sending him away to rehab for several months. More wicked than that?"

"The transport division. It was perfect."

"Absolutely. Oh. Damn," he said. "You mean the idea came from Cushla? She suggested to Jonathan that he trade that particular part of Fleet Corp for Marcia."

Vivien finished the thought. "Because of the trucks. The transport division was vital to the success of Lester's new P lab."

They watched a pair of noisy tuis chase each other in and out of the top of a large pohutukawa tree, their iridescent wings glinting in the sunshine, both Vivien and Ted lost in thought.

"I spent an awful lot of time when I was sedated trying to let someone know—anyone—about Oscar. That he was the one who poisoned me."

Ted reached over and took her hand in his. "How I wish I could have protected you from all that. It took us too damn long to figure it out."

"I shouldn't have needed protection," she said with some spirit, grabbing her hand back. "Ignorant doctors. I don't mean to sound ungrateful, but it took them too damn long to decrease my sedatives. Bloody patronizing medics shielding me from a bit of discomfort. If I'd been allowed to surface sufficiently, I could have...." She sighed. "Talking about power? That experience, my friend, was the ultimate in powerlessness." She glanced over at Ted. He was staring at her. "You try it sometime. No, I don't mean that. I wouldn't wish it on my worst enemy."

He obviously had had no idea. "Whew," he said, "and it almost cost you your life."

"At least I spoke up in time to get you out of jail."

"For which I thank you." He made a formal bow straight out of the eighteenth century. "Madam."

"Kiss my hand," she said, then, with a grin, snatched it away again before he could do so.

"When is Holly arriving?" Vivien asked, in an obvious change of subject.

"She's coming with the new boyfriend. I thought I'd put them up in the caravans. They can have one or both." He glanced at Vivien and grinned. "And no one need disturb them."

"Poor old Liam was devastated when he heard about Holly's new love. I think he had hopes."

"Holly likes him a lot. But she says she's had too much trouble with brothers—and he feels like a brother to her. I'm afraid he's out of the running," Ted said. "I know because I asked her." He smiled at Vivien. "Then she met this new fellow through the job she's just started. I don't know how serious it is, but she's enjoying the relationship. No hidden swamps, she says, just plain sailing."

"Holly's got her head screwed on just right," Vivien said. "And so, for that matter, has Liam. They're both enjoying this stage in their lives." And not making the mistake she did in looking for security.

"I'll drink to that," Ted said, catching her eye. She looked away quickly, then cursed herself. Acting like a schoolgirl, but that was how it always seemed to turn out: Ted saying something mildly flirtatious and her not handling it well. She pulled herself together and re-entered the conversation. What had he just said? Was it, 'How are the divorce legalities going?'

"Mostly there," Vivien said, with an attempt at keeping her mind on the here-and-now. "It's a matter of time." She looked up at him again. "I did tell you about the appearance of Cecily?"

"Gerald's secretary? Barely. Fill in the details."

"About Steph's age, to her utter embarrassment. Cecily is one of those young women who likes to squeal whenever something pleases her and apparently it doesn't take much. Not massively pretty, but a feminine, dependent young woman. Maybe like I used to be. Hopefully, she never grows up and they live happily ever after."

Ted laughed. "And you, Vivien? Any suitors coming out of the woodwork? I thought your lawyer had an eye on you."

"John? Nope, I'm the wrong gender. And no one else either. Mind you, whenever I'm in the London flat, it seems I have either Liam or Stephanie or both there, too. Not exactly conducive to having a life of passion myself." She glanced at Ted's profile. Strong. Probably one who had matured into that long face of his. He caught her looking and she looked away in confusion yet again. She changed the subject. "Did Father tell you about the radiation?"

"Only that you've persuaded him to have a course after all. I'm hoping it wasn't too late."

"It's left him terribly tired again, but no vomiting or skin problems. The good news is that the main tumour has shrunk. It's not a cure, but it may prolong his life. They're now saying he's probably got another year at least. Maybe more."

"Good news. And you being here is probably doing him as much good as the radiation."

"He was quite lively most of the way up here today," Vivien said. Indeed, he had talked a great deal about the business. She was to take over as soon as her father felt he could hand over control. She knew that was a difficult decision for him to make and, unless the disease's inescapable progress suddenly accelerated, a hand-over that could not be rushed. But there was really no choice now, not with Oscar out of the picture; she was going to be running things sooner rather than later. And now Jonathan had his home office, complete with a computer-literate Lela, he could direct things for as long as he was able. She realized her father wanted to stay alive long enough to give her the apprenticeship she needed. Privately, she thought that was the selling point of the radiation treatment. What amazed her was that she was becoming very interested in Fleet Corp. And in her ability to manage the money side of it. Some years before, Jonathan had recruited a team of good senior people in each of the various divisions. She didn't need to know the whole nitty gritty of the business. Jonathan was concentrating her training on the money management—which was awakening an old interest dating from her first job in the City where she dealt in shares and bonds. That interest compounded, she mused, given that the money she would eventually manage was for the family business. And even better, Liam had expressed some interest, too. She would take that one softly.

"Have you seen Oscar since he's been in the remand prison?" Ted asked.

Vivien nodded. "I went out to the prison the same week I got back. He's getting harder, Ted. His true nature is coming out from under that civilized veneer."

"I've been thinking about Marcia's will. What do you think Marcia meant by leaving her spectacles to Oscar?"

"Not a clue. Were they made from solid gold?" Vivien noticed the sun turning everything a mellow yellow as it headed towards the western horizon.

Ted shook his head. "No, although I did ask. According to Jonathan, just ordinary specs. Marcia had a curly mind. It was probably more abstruse than that."

"Spectacles... glasses. Something about glasses, the drinking kind?"

"Nothing comes to mind." Ted got up and looked out to a cerulean sea. "Maybe something about looking? Seeing?"

"Perhaps 'None so blind as those who will not see?'"

Ted whipped his head around. "Well, what do you know, I think you may have it. Thanks, Vivien. It fits. Yet again, Marcia was playing with him. They had a symbiotic relationship with both of them vying to be in control. Believe me, being in control is where she always wanted to be. She found out about the drug running and that shifted the power. Too bad she didn't realize how dangerous he was in those circumstances."

Chapter Fifty-Nine

A CAR CRUNCHED DOWN the gravel drive. Suddenly there was the hubbub of Holly and her young man arriving and Jonathan joining them, and their quiet moment was gone. Vivien inwardly shrugged her shoulders. Somehow, fate always intervened to prevent any sort of intimate time with Ted. Or maybe she sabotaged what opportunities there were. She mentally kicked herself and set to getting things organized. People into where they were staying the night, food preparation, setting the table. Eating, clearing away and putting things in the dishwasher.

Then Cushla arrived, much to Ted's surprise, driving Lester's fancy four-wheel-drive vehicle.

"I'm here for the ceremony," she said after sliding off the high seat down to the ground. She sat herself next to Jonathan and they talked quietly together as Vivien and Holly handed champagne glasses around. Ted noticed Jonathan's arm was draped over the back of Cushla's chair. They were close friends, that much was obvious. Was she the long-term love of his she thought she was? Probably on one level, yes, and his relationship with Marcia was on another level entirely. But Cushla was still here, out-surviving all the wives. Cushla, full of contradictions but with that underlying core of connection to Jonathan. Her man.

The atrium was pleasantly warm away from the cool airs of the early summer evening as their glasses were filled in turn. First one, then another pointed out the sea, the trees, or the quiet. The sky, first a translucent blue as if looking through crystal, then deepening into that unique colour of mauve edged with pink so typical of the bay. The conversation naturally quietened.

Jonathan stood, one hand on the chair back for support but standing tall and with some of his old grandeur. "We're here, dear friends and family, for the official hand-over of the Bay House to Mr Ted Frazer. This house is now back to its rightful owner." He held his champagne glass high. "To Ted!"

They all raised their glasses. "To Ted!'

"And to commemorate it, I've had prepared a little something to become part of this house." He reached under his chair where he had hidden a parcel wrapped in plain white paper. It was about 300 millimetres by 200 and was quite obviously heavy in his hands.

"Ted, for you. Thank you for my sojourn here. Marcia and I had many a happy time in this house. I'm only sorry that it was because of my son ... because...." his voice faltered. Vivien started to go to him but he gathered himself together. "I did have many happy days here. Full stop." He handed the parcel to Ted.

"Thank you, Jonathan. I'll just open it now?" At Jonathan's nod, he tore away the paper. It was a brass plaque. "'The Bay House'", he read aloud. "'Designed and built by Mr Edward Frazer' and the date when I built it." He coughed to clear the emotion from his voice.

"Marcia once told me," Jonathan said, "that an adobe building like this was good for 300 years. If so, no one should ever have to wonder who built it and when."

"Perfect," Ted said. "I cannot think of a better or more fitting present. It's wonderful."

The plaque was passed around; people talked; people drank; Jonathan tired. It was getting late.

The young couple saw Cushla safely on the road back to her place and closed the gate after her, saying their goodnights on their return before wandering up the path by torchlight.

"Come on, Father," Vivien said. "Time you retired gracefully to Holly's pink room."

Jonathan laughed. "It is pink, isn't it? We had such fun getting that room ready for her. Then by the time she got up here to see it, she wanted us to repaint it black! Marcia had a fit. It stayed pink and secretly, I know that Holly loved it."

After all was quiet, Ted re-joined Vivien. They sat in the wicker chairs looking through the pohutukawa trees which were silhouetted against a moonlit sea. The air was clear and the moon made a path of dancing light across the bay. Somewhere a morepork owl was sending out its mournful call into the night.

"You see?" Ted said quietly. "You understand why I built this place?"

"A place of renewal. A place made for contemplation. A place just to be."

Ted nodded. "I knew you'd understand. Marcia never did. She raved on about the beauty of the view, the way it was good to 'get away from it all', but she really saw it as a temporary retreat. A place to regroup. For a long while I thought she and I were talking the same language. But no." He glanced at her. "She never understood."

Vivien felt a quickening within her breast. "You're speaking of Marcia in a different way." She paused. "Or your voice is different. Has something changed?"

Ted rubbed his hands over his face, his eyes closed. "It's not been sudden. But while you were so ill, I missed you terribly. I missed our conversations most of all. I found myself saying things to you, keeping our channels of communication open, even if you couldn't respond."

"I loved hearing your voice, knowing you were there."

"I talked to you whenever I could." Ted let the silence gather once more, the only sound the swish of the surf over the sand below them. "Perhaps the details were not important. But the process was. I was feeling my way towards something. Progress of sorts."

"Tell me again," Vivien said. "Please."

"It's a general thing. Maybe I've finally realized Marcia has gone. I've said goodbye. And it's nothing to do with her death. It's the goodbye I should have said years ago within myself. I don't know why I let her continue to inhabit space inside me. I was forever irritated by her antics."

"Holly?"

"Maybe because of Holly. Mother of my child, that sort of thing. Or maybe that vow I made to look after her. And in spite of all Marcia's independence, her capabilities, her lovers, she projected that neediness to me. You can't believe how relieving it is to be finally free."

Free. The word echoed around the glass roofed atrium, finally enveloping the bay, the world, the universe.

"Free to...?" Vivien asked.

But Ted had risen. He stretched. "A small whisky before bed? You must be exhausted. I know I am."

"That would be perfect," Vivien said. She followed him to the kitchen where he got down the two Edwardian whisky glasses they had last used all those months ago up at the caravans, feeling as if the conversation had been abruptly interrupted.

"Recognize these?" Ted asked, holding up the glasses.

"Of course. I was being a bit of a prig being assigned to a caravan."

"You were curled up in one of the chairs up by the caravans with those long legs of yours highly visible." He shot her a glance, raising his eyebrows.

As usual, Vivien was nonplussed. Serious conversations she could handle. Flirtation was a foreign language. "Uh, thanks for noticing," she said and then kicked herself. Why didn't she have some witty saying ready to pop out? In annoyance, she picked up the whisky and walked quickly to the door of the atrium which was two steps up from the kitchen level. She caught her foot on the stair. Although she kept hold of the old glass, the whisky shot out and over the steps and she fell. Ted, following her closely, somehow shot out one arm and prevented her from falling.

"Whoa there," he said as he lifted her straight. "You still have weakness?"

Vivien nodded and closed her eyes. She was back to being an awkward and clumsy teenager. She struggled to regain her footing, turning towards him. He was right there when she opened her eyes; his lips were within inches. She didn't speak, she just leaned very slightly so her lips touched the corner of his mouth. "Thanks, Ted," she whispered. But she had no idea what she was saying. She breathed in the smell of him, the feel of his arms around her and the strange feeling of rightness about what was happening.

There was a frozen moment in time, and Vivien didn't dare take a breath. His arms tightened around her waist and he bent to kiss her properly, a deep and transporting kiss that went on forever. At last, she thought, as she lost herself in it all. He stroked her face, his eyes darting from one eye to the other.

"Vivien..."

She thought of all the times she had felt her hand being held in his when she couldn't respond. She leaned forward again for another kiss. And again. Then back to look at him. "I didn't misinterpret," she breathed.

"I've been waiting for this." He gathered her tighter into his arms. "But you need to sleep. You're weak and I can see you're exhausted. I'm taking you upstairs. You're having the main bedroom tonight." He shifted her weight and lifted her effortlessly, carrying her upstairs. The bedroom door was open and Vivien was aware of large windows looking out over the moonlit sea. He laid her gently on the covers and stood, ready to go.

"Ted," she said. "Come here." She patted the bed beside her. "One more kiss. Please." She reached up to him. He settled down beside her and bent over to kiss her again. Lying on the bed, fully supported, Vivien was acutely aware of touching shoulders, hips, thighs and feet. She closed her eyes. If only.... "I would love to invite you to stay but I...."

"I know. You're utterly exhausted. This is enough. More than enough," he said. He reached for her once more, angling his head to fit hers. He supported himself on one arm and bent to kiss her yet again. She knew that she was very close to taking this to its natural conclusion. But she stopped him, holding him from her so she could see him in the moonlight.

"It's not just that. This is ridiculous, but ... my father is in the bedroom right below," she blurted.

Ted laughed from the depths of his being. "And it's inhibiting?"

Vivien nodded. "Awful, isn't it? A middle-aged woman...."

"I do understand, my dear Vivien, only too well. My little house in Auckland, my daughter.... Instinctive barriers."

Vivien reached for his hand and stroked it tenderly. "In the hospital. You don't know how much your touch meant to me."

Ted bent over and kissed her hand. "I was so frightened for you."

"Will you come to see me in England?"

"You have to go back?"

"Christmas. I've promised to have Christmas in England with Stephanie and Liam and there's a pile of things to do for the divorce. I imagine Christmas with Holly is important this year for you two, too. But I have to be back here for February. Father wants me to...."

"February? Not till then?"

Vivien looked at his craggy face. His meaning clear. "No chance you can do some business over there early in the New Year? Or just come, no excuse needed? Stephanie and Liam will be back at work or university and I do have a very nice and very private flat in London."

Ted kissed her again, lightly this time. "I'll arrange it, business or pure pleasure. Count on it. I'll be there." He became serious. "I'm very aware we have our whole lives ahead of us." He slowly pushed a lock of hair off her forehead. Then he stood up and moved swiftly to the door. "I'll see you in the morning. Sleep well."

"And you," she said sleepily. She wasn't sure, but she thought she heard him say something as he walked down the stairs. Something about how she was giving him back his dreams.

Yes.

His dreams and hers, too. As it should be.

The End

Printed in Great Britain
by Amazon

25450828R00189